The Whiskerly Sisters

by
BB Occleshaw

Grosvenor House
Publishing Limited

This book is published by
Grosvenor House Publishing Ltd
28-30 High Street, Guildford, Surrey, GU1 3EL.
www.grosvenorhousepublishing.co.uk

A CIP record for this book
is available from the British Library

ISBN 978-1-78148-894-2

For Irene

With grateful thanks to:

Sheila, Vicky, Helen and Annie for their support
and friendship

The characters in this book are entirely fictitious.

PART ONE

Cat's Cradle

I

Fresna was running late – again! She'd had all day to get ready yet still she knew she would not make class on time. Chances were that Charley would put the weight against the door and refuse her entry, but she did that most weeks and yet she somehow always managed to charm her way in and she knew she always would. Fresna found that punctual people irritated her. "Why waste your time running up against the ticking of the clock," she reasoned to herself, smiling inwardly with pleasure, "when it's far more fun to waste it rubbing up against the throbbing of the cock?" which was why she again found that she was running late.

Throwing back the rumpled quilt, she leapt out of bed and threw on her sweats, lithely bending to lace up her Nikes. Straightening up, she smiled at the man sprawled naked on the queen sized bed. Fifteen years her junior (not that you would ever guess), he was tall, athletic, sexy as hell. She moved towards him and he sat up in the bed to receive her swift, farewell kiss, his toned mahogany flesh contrasting perfectly against her pale ivory skin. "Great abs" she thought, not for the first time, as she released him. She had a penchant for dark-skinned, muscular men, especially if they leaned towards sexual submission. Leaning forward, her lover tried to catch hold of her, begging her to stay a while longer.

"Not a chance," she responded, backing up and heading for the door. Grabbing her rucksack, she threw a saucy wink towards the forlorn man and left the room. "Catch you later," she called over her shoulder, offering him a reprieve. "Much later," she mused. Fresna wasted no time on the past and spent scant time planning for the future. Life was for living right here, right now. And right here was where she had been and where she wouldn't be again until she felt the urge. Whilst right now, she was late for the gym. In a parallel universe, Fresna might have been a dog trainer, but, in this phase of her life at least, it was the men in her life that she chose to keep on a leash – down boy for her pleasure, at heel, when required; sit and stay in the meantime. She hadn't always behaved with such casual arrogance.

Flooring it all the way to Fit Heaven and neatly beating an anonymous 'also-ran' to the last space in the car park, Fresna inevitably schmoozed her way into her third gym class of the week and commandeered her usual position front and centre of the room where she could fully admire her flexible form in the wall wide mirrors. You didn't leave a piece of ass in the bed she'd just left by stuffing yourself full of crunchies, she reminded herself. No, the crunchies she needed were one up four down, push, push, pulse – several times a week flat on the mat followed by the rhythmic lift, kick, step ball change of the aerobics class or the relentless swing of the kettle bell.

To Fresna's left, her best friend, Jax gritted her teeth, trying desperately not to look as miserable as she felt whilst panting and gasping her way through what she sarcastically referred to as her second Fit Hell session of the week. Recently out of a disastrous, long term relationship, Jax was a woman on a mission. Getting in shape and losing weight were her primary goals; remembering the rules of the dating game ran a close second. And then there were doors to close on too much time spent on a waster before she could open the windows and welcome in the early morning breezes of what she hoped would be a new and better life.

Immediately behind Jax was her youngest daughter, Izza, easily moving her graceful little body in time to the music. Young, fresh limbs powered seamlessly through triceps curls and hamstring stretches. That tight little butt certainly did not need its glutes working out, but Izza needed the exercise to offset her increasingly frequent bouts of depression. Gratefully stuck in an over dependent relationship with a manipulative user, Izza lived her life on a rollercoaster of highs and lows; a circle of conflict, compromise and confusion in which the over-arching rule of thumb was heads I lose, tails he wins!

At the very right hand edge of the front row, stood the outrageous, tangerine clad Celia. Neither tall nor short, neither slim nor fat, Celia was no oil painting, but she did have the most beautiful hazel eyes and the most fantastic pair of legs. Still, if her looks weren't outstanding, her personality most certainly was. Straight as the Great North Road and with a definite point of view on just about everything, here was a woman who believed in living life to the max, professional and sober during the day; hard living and even harder drinking come the evening. There wasn't a man on the planet that could drink Celia under the table and, having been divorced

3

for many years, she felt there was no longer any room for romance in her life. She was simply not interested. Besides, there was always somewhere to go – a theme party, a book signing, a girls' supper, a gallery opening, a premiere – whatever it was, Celia would be on it, larger than life, stunningly flamboyant and definitely upsetting someone with her loud voice and strong opinions.

At least she would be there if she wasn't on holiday because travel was Celia's first love and she was never without the next vacation in view. It was an established fact that Celia lived for the sun, gloried in it, delighted in it, observing it bake all but the merest strip of her flesh to a crisp as often as work and solvency would allow. She was not one to worry about the detrimental effects of ultra violet light or gamma rays, which she considered to be complete hogwash spouted by scaremongering public health wallahs with nothing better to do than rob folk of their pleasures. Sod that! Give Celia a sandy beach under the midday sun and there she would be topless, thonged and splayed, slowly roasting herself towards leather paradise. Bliss!

Directly behind Celia, beautiful, blonde, petite Tiffany moved perfunctorily with all the programming of a Pentium. There in body and spirit, if not in mind, Tiffany was in love again. Choosing to ignore the fact that he had left her at the club last night to come home alone while he had a last drink or two with his ex, she concentrated on his insistence on phoning for her taxi and then paying for it to take her home, reasoning that this meant he must be serious. Mustn't he? This time, she knew, it really would be the final first kiss. Better yet, she'd been driven home by an incredibly dishy cab driver, who didn't seem to be able to keep his eyes on the road, glued as they were to his mirror and from there onto her face. Parking neatly on the kerb outside her home, he had leapt gallantly out of the car to open the door for her, deftly offering her his card with the suggestion that she might like to call him sometime. Winking broadly, he let the lady know that he would take her anywhere she wanted to go. Tiffany had frowned slightly as she tried to think how best to respond to this double-edged offer. Two timing Jay would be unthinkable but, on the other hand, the brief time she had spent with her 'chevalier d'autos' had been enough for her to see how future suited they might be. He had seemed so interested in everything she had to say, so personable, so eager to please. It had nothing whatsoever to do with the way his Levis had fitted so snugly across those toned buns or the reflexive movement of his biceps as he pulled open the taxi door. Tiffany's pupils dilated at the memory. What would those arms feel like wrapped around her? Mortified, she hastily pulled herself from the brink and tried to concentrate on the rhythm of the class. *Where was her head at? She was in love with Jay, dammit!* she scolded herself. *But, then again*, she reflected, smiling at her perfect reflection in the mirror opposite her, *a little flirting never did any harm. Did it?*

Exercising quietly in the corner was Rebecca, a slight, elegant lady in her mid-fifties. Keen on fitness, Rebecca, or Bex to her friends, came across as shy, reticent, passive; a woman who rarely spoke unless spoken to. Ever punctual and a good listener, she gave little away so no one really knew much about her. She moved through Charley's routine with all the grace of a gazelle, in time, in step and with a pleasant smile on her face. Whatever was happening in her life, Bex knew how to rise above it. She had learned the secret of serenity.

The only man regularly present at the Tuesday night class was Sly. Tall and muscular with the face of an angel and overly long auburn hair, he was adored by every woman present, not just for his looks, but also, unusually for himself. He was their 'why can't' man. "Why can't my husband, boyfriend, lover, partner be like him?" the girls would lament, staring unashamedly at the sight of his sculptured back leaving the room. Well dressed, well mannered, well groomed and gorgeously fragrant, he was, on the surface at least, every woman's dream. He moved like a dancer, his smile could light up a room and his love for the female of the species was obvious. Although quiet by nature and sometimes a little aloof, he had an easy charm and a real respect for women, which instinctively put them at their ease. He had the uncanny knack of being able to be both their ultimate fantasy guy and simply one of the girls. Best of all, he was single! But, no matter how they tried – and some of them really, really tried – he never properly flirted with any of them and, to the best of their knowledge, he had never asked any of them out. Jeez, what did a girl have to do?

Twenty minutes into the routine and Jax was cursing the clock, willing it to move faster. Surely to God, there couldn't be forty more minutes of this purgatory? Still, it was better than last week when she hadn't been able to keep up at all. Three gym sessions a week were making inroads into her fitness, but it was tough going. What made it worse was the knowledge that behind her Izza would have barely broken into a sweat.

"Stay low and pump it," commanded Charley, all teeth and hair.

Did anyone in their right minds really own that many crop tops and matching sweat bands? wondered Jax, who had yet to see the same outfit twice.

"Come on, lower. Now squeeze – that's it – hold those glutes," ordered Charley. "If you don't squeeze them, no-one else will. Now pulse, come on, lower. Pulse it."

"Give me a break," grumbled Jax, whose backside simply refused to graze the deck no matter how hard she tried. Gritting her teeth, she tried to inch down a little lower. Christ that hurt! Sometimes life was just not fair.

Had she been able to read her mind, Celia would have agreed. Life definitely wasn't fair for Celia right now and most especially when it came to her job. She worked 45 hours a week for a toy manufacturer as PA to a megalomaniac. The pay wasn't bad, but brother did she earn it. Impossible deadlines, unrealistic expectations and far too frequent savings of the day were common themes in Celia's working world. Her boss, Patrick, was utterly disorganised, maddeningly mercurial and, some days, he could make the Victorian workhouse seem like an easy life. There were times when she even believed that he set her up to fail deliberately so that he could take his frustrations out on her. On the other hand, he had promised her the role of Office Manager with two staff to support her when they moved to the new warehouse in the autumn, so it was worth putting up with all the crap. Wasn't it?

Izza was wondering if anyone would notice if she took a sneaky peak at her mobile under the pretext of needing a sip of water. Her boyfriend, Tony, hadn't texted her all day and she was getting anxious. Why oh why did he do this? One minute, he was all loving and giving, talking about moving in together and undying devotion; the next he was pushing her away, telling her she was too clingy and that he needed some room. One day, he was texting her every five minutes declaring undying love and fidelity then, out of nowhere, the winds would change and in would pour the sidewinders – accusations of infidelity, disloyalty, putting everyone else above him, not loving him enough. On and on he would storm. Worse, she might be faced with a wall of absolute, angst-ridden silence. Eventually, when she had bitten her nails to her elbows, he would call. He had been working he'd explain. Or mending the car or down the pub or playing football or eating chop suey or watching TV – whatever, stop fussing, back off, give me some space and sometimes, terrifyingly, IT'S OVER.

Izza's heart soared. Tony had sent her a text. All smiles now, she swiftly returned her mobile to the pocket of her hoodie and resumed her place. Out of the corner of her eye, she could see that her mother was looking at her with that frown on her face again. Izza ignored her. What could she possibly know about love at her age?

Charley glowered at the class in front of her, barking instructions at them and expecting immediate compliance. A fitness instructor for many years and an attractive woman in her early forties, Charley was a perfectionist. She set herself high standards, always looked the part and furthermore expected anyone attending her class to behave in a similar manner. Failing to turn up to class was almost a hanging offence as far as she was concerned. Furthermore, she loathed newcomers and could barely tolerate the sight of the out of condition Jax sweating and heaving in front of her. In a rare moment of pity, she had graciously condescended to let her to come to her classes, but only because she was close friends with Fresna and Celia, both of whom were long standing members of the group. True, Fresna was often late, but Charley had decided long ago to overlook that because of the woman's dedication and stamina. Besides which, she could always be counted on to attend every Celebrity Gym Club Workshop or Fitness Break, plus persuade a bunch of friends to come with her, which in turn, gave Charley considerable kudos with the Women's Health and Fitness Association, but those sweet thoughts were not at the front of Charley's mind this evening.

No, this evening, Charley was in a foul mood; she felt savage and she was taking it out on her class. The Club Manager would have spoken to her severely had he known about it. However, as an experienced professional of many years' standing, Charley had gained the unswerving loyalty of the group. She knew nothing would be said. And, in any case, several members of the group delighted in this aspect of her sessions, believing they were getting exceptional workouts. So what the hell, it was win-win.

However, it was far from win-win in her personal life where she was fighting a losing battle, which for Charley was untenable. Her problem centred on the Neanderthals next door. Three months ago, her life had been pleasant, peaceful and perfectly under her control but then, in the space of one short weekend, a seemingly ordinary married couple had moved into the house next to hers. That is to say a seemingly ordinary married couple along with their two extraordinarily unattractive toddlers, their four baying hounds, their three shitty cats, their psychotic parrot and their thundering black and decker drill had moved in next door; as a consequence of which Charley's life had undergone a sudden, dramatic, downhill shift. Nothing she had done or said so far had alleviated the situation, which was beginning to alarmingly spiral increasingly out of control. The constant noise, the lack of privacy and the deep frustration she felt at being disempowered were beginning to take their toll.

Forcing herself to concentrate on the group in front of her, Charley nailed the smile back onto her face and stepped on the gas. Celia and Fresna glanced at each other and smiled knowingly. No prisoners would be taken tonight. It was going to be an outstanding workout.

II

It was the habit of a few select members of the group to meet in the upstairs bar of the Lord Nelson pub, known as the Whiskerly Room, which was opposite the gym. It was not the three line whip regimen that was the hallmark of the Tuesday class, more of a drop by if you are available kind of thing. By the time, Charley arrived, freshly made up and looking more like she had stepped out of Vogue rather than out of the shower, there were several people there already. Unfortunately, on this occasion Sly was not among of them, which slightly irritated Charley, who was determined to get her claws into the handsome man and made the most of every opportunity to do so. Tonight was not going to be one of them. Damn!

Jax was sipping on a diet coke. *Bless her,* thought Charley uncharacteristically, *she really was trying and did seem to have lost a little weight.* Izza, drinking Archer's, was consumed with texting. Celia, deep into her third glass of merlot, was giving it large about Patrick to Bex, Fresna and everyone else in the room regardless of whether or not they wanted to listen.

"The man is insane." roared Celia. "Does he think the fairies do it? Why can't he organise himself just once? Twenty marketing folders to put together, a presentation to format – all urgent – must be out the door by twelve and then he bloody well leaves the building and forgets to sign it off and then has a go at me because it arrives late. Well thank you very much. Has me running up and down those effing stairs from dawn till dusk, never a thank you and for what? For what?" she grumbled.

"Why do you do it?" asked Fresna, already knowing the answer, having heard the story before, but ever eager for further chapters from Celia's tales from the toyshop.

"You bloody well know why, Fres," said Celia passionately. "The promotion. This is it, I can feel it. Management at last! Sodding overdue, of course."

"Of course it is," soothed Bex. "With your skills, you should have been promoted years ago."

"Instead of which, he walks all over you for peanuts every single day," contributed Jax.

"Ooh very pot-kettle. Get over yourself sister! Right now, you're just anti-men," fired back Celia, who resented what she saw as an attempt to rain on her victim parade. "You'll get past him. You know what they say. Time is a great healer and all the jazz," she added, without a trace of sympathy for her friend's situation.

"Yes, look at me," sighed Tiffany. "Who'd have thought this time last month that I would have found… HIM?" she asked of no one in particular as she gazed adoringly at her blond reflection in the mirror over the bar.

"Again!" replied Celia sarcastically and who decidedly did not want the attention turning from her tales of daring don't at work to the snakes and ladders that constituted Tiffany's love life.

"Give it up Tiff," she advised. "It's doomed. You're fated to spend your entire love life seesawing between being picked up and then dumped by some charmless prick in some seedy bar somewhere in the vicinity of nowhere and couldn't care less."

"She's right," counselled Fresna, whom no man would dare to either pick up or dump. If there was any picking up to do, she'd be the one doing it and when it came to dumping, she preferred to do it at the height of the relationship when everything was at its best and most definitely before it waned as it inevitably would given enough time and attention.

"Don't be so mean," said Bex, ever the peacemaker. "She's an adult. She can make up her own mind. I'm delighted for you, Tiff. I really am."

"Thanks Bex, you're a real friend," replied Tiffany, pointedly turning her back on the offending Celia.

There was a breath or two of silence. It was at this point and with perfect timing that Charley breezed into the room.

"Let me guess," she said, sizing up the situation at once and pointing at each one in turn. "You're in love, you're still at war with your boss, you've just had a shag, you're dying for some chocolate, you're saying nothing about anything, she's texting and I'm buying."

In one single, succinct sentence, Charley had both summed up the situation and deftly stolen the limelight.

"Grab us a corner someone," she ordered, approaching the bar where Alex was waiting to serve her anything her heart might desire and a whole shedload more should she ever give him the merest flicker of interest, which she never would because, in her eyes, Alex was a nobody and quite simply beneath her.

Bringing their drinks across to the table at which the finger flicking Izza already sat hunched over her mobile, the ladies sat themselves down and watched as Charley brushed off the love struck bartender, collected her slim line tonic and joined them.

"You look tired, Charley. Everything alright?" For once, Bex was opening up the conversation.

"Fine," Charley assured them shortly, straightening her shoulders and lifting her chin, agitated that she might be betraying her anxiety.

"Rubbish," countered the belligerent Celia. "Something's up, Charley. You've been like a bear with a sore head for weeks now and, no offence, but you've got dark circles under your eyes and you're losing weight. Come on 'fess up. What's up?"

Charley knew that she would not be able to brush off a determined Celia. Drawing herself up and taking a deep breath, she gave back as good as she got.

"Well, if you must know, you nosey cow – in one sentence – noisy neighbours. Christ, it's like living next door to the Designer Gooneys. Kids, dogs, cats, even a parrot for God's sake – and he's into late night DIY."

"Oh dear, poor you. Have you spoken to them?" asked Bex with genuine concern.

"What do you think?" replied Charley tartly.

"Why don't you dob them into the Environmental Health?" asked Celia, who had little time for anyone else's problems.

"I tried threatening them with that, but it's not that straightforward. All I got from the Council was a bunch of useless advice. Besides which, I could spend a fortune on a solicitor to get nowhere," replied Charley tonelessly.

"Get up a petition – get all your neighbours involved," suggested Jax, ever eager to find a solution.

"Been there, done that. No joy," countered Charley, strangling the notion as it was born.

"You could try capturing the sound of the dogs on tape and playing it back to them.

Maybe they don't realise how noisy they are being," said Fresna ever practical.

"I've done that as well. It didn't work." Charley was beginning to sound depressed.

"Soundproofing?" tried Celia.

"Any idea what that costs?" replied Charley scornfully.

"Why don't you just move?" muttered Izza, pressing send on her mobile.

"I would if I could. Not being funny but, with your head stuck in your phone, you may not have noticed that there's a recession on and nothing is selling."

"Well, there must be something you can do," replied Izza, finally flipping the top over her Nokia and looking up at her.

"Such as?" challenged Charley.

The room suddenly bloomed with ideas as each of the women tried to talk over the others to be the first to come up with a workable strategy.

Ceals: "Shoot the fuckers."

Jax: "Turn the volume up on your CD when the kids are sleeping and give them some of the same."

Fres: "Report the bastards to the RSPCA."

Bex: "Ask them to take the dogs to be properly trained."

Tiff: "Get an ASBO out on them."

Izza: "Teach the parrot to swear and hope the kids copy it."

And so it went on. An enjoyable, spirit series of What Ifs, Yes Buts, If Onlys and It's not my faults that lasted all evening and passed through the problems of the group, with the exception of Fresna for whom life was exactly how she wanted it to be, and yet none of their issues were resolved. Not Charley's bad neighbours, nor Jax's low self-esteem, nor Tiff's unsatisfactory love life, nor Izza's manipulative boyfriend, nor Bex's introversion, not even Celia's working life.

Because there was nothing any of them could do about any of it.

Was there?

BEX

I

Having folded the laundry neatly into the airing cupboard, Bex turned her attention to the vacuuming. Bex hoovered, dusted and polished her way through the entire first floor of her four bedroomed executive detached every Monday, Wednesday and Friday, following with the all the downstairs rooms on Tuesdays, Thursdays and Saturdays. With everything so regularly cleaned, it didn't take her long. On Sunday, she gave herself a day off. If one of her children was around, they might have lunch. If not, she might drop in at the Town Hall to listen to the Choral Society, perhaps visit some friends or take herself off for a long ramble in the country. She was sure to be home by six to put the finishing touches to the nourishing yet light supper she had prepared earlier so that it was ready to serve just as her husband returned from his club at 6.30pm sharp

It wasn't that Bex was naturally a person with an innate preference for routine. On the contrary, she would have preferred to spend her time plunging her neat, nimble fingers into the rich brown soil of the garden, embedding the dirt into her nails and showering herself in mulch and leaf debris. She would have liked to have been able to join the Rambler's Association, put on her wellies and tramp for miles through muddy fields, down winding lanes, whatever the weather, to some cosy little country pub where she could enjoy a hearty plate of sausage and mash in front of a roaring fire. She often imagined herself as a painter, throwing great splashes of colour haphazardly across a blank canvas, hopefully covering herself in a rainbow of acrylic in the process and earning a fortune as a contemporary artist. She had been known to fantasize about life as a traveller, dressing herself in tie dye cotton, espadrilles and an endless supply of clinking, jangling bracelets, surrendering her greying curls to the wind and earn her living reading palms or selling pegs.

It could definitely not be said that Bex was someone who enjoyed centering her life around the ticking of a clock. Rather, she was a restless spirit, a free thinker, a rebel, a changeling. How the hell she had ended up married for nearly thirty years to Mr. Stopwatch and embracing a life of neatly domesticated suburbia was beyond understanding. Why she stayed beggared belief.

II

In the early years, of course, Malcolm had been much more of a free spirit too. Back then, they would often drop everything, climb into his little Morris Minor and drive to wherever the mood took them, sometimes breaking into an empty beach hut for the night, eating fish and chips, wrapped in newspapers with their fingers, giggling together as they stuffed their faces full of the rich, hot taste of fat and salt. Back then, they had enjoyed making out in daring places – under a blanket amid festival crowds or amongst the dunes not too far away from sunbathing families, in an empty train carriage, wondering if anyone would pass by and see them or, on one very exciting occasion, in the ladies toilet at the local Roxy during a matinee performance of Grease.

Nowadays, Malcolm rarely went anywhere without his satnav, preferred the impersonal isolation of an executive hotel room and always used a knife and fork. These days they never giggled together. These days they never made love.

The children had come along and Malcolm eventually got himself regular work as Time and Motion Assistant at a local factory so that her carefree days had gradually turned into clockwatching days of four hour feeds and homework schedules, meal times and ballet classes, swimming lessons and nine to five. And, through it all, time had ticked inexorably by and somehow, seamlessly, second by tiny second, the leisurely ebb and flow that had been her early life had slowly petrified into the solid rock formation of conformity, monotony and routine.

And yet, it wasn't as if she hadn't been happy. She had adored watching and caring for her children over the years as they moved from plump, adorable babies through to wobbling, adventurous toddlers, to little people in their own right in over-sized uniforms on their first day at school and onto slightly awkward, mulish teenagers so that now she could stand back and take pride in them as fully achieving adults. She had relished being in their company, taking them here, fetching them from there, helping them with their homework and kissing their hurt knees. She had been more than content to stand by Malcolm's side too as his career flourished, as he rose from Assistant to Manager and upwards to Director; delighting in being able to ease his burden by offering him the warm, organised, uncluttered home he needed at the end of a stressful day at the office.

She had subsumed her former love of anarchy, her yearning for the different and disorderly to provide an anchor for her family, a haven from the storms outside, a place of peace, tranquillity and order.

But she hadn't expected this. No, she hadn't expected anything quite like this.

For as the years rolled by, somewhere between teenagers and young adults, somewhere between Manager and Director, Malcolm had changed beyond recognition. Her young, spirited, passionate boyfriend, her hardworking, affectionate, deskbound husband had turned into an obsessive, compulsive, authoritarian bully.

And her reaction to it was even more unexpected.

FRESNA

I

S he had her first and only child at sixteen.
Her lover, and the father of her unborn child, a man ten years her senior, had turned deathly pale on hearing the news and had hurriedly fled the scene, leaving Fresna alone and bewildered by his reaction. He had returned two hours later, wearing a sheepish grin, carrying a small mixed posy and a little carrier bag in which there nestled a tiny pair of lemon yellow, knitted bootees.

Following a difficult family conversation, Alex had proposed to her the following week, solemnly kneeling at her feet to proffer the tiny diamond ring. As Fresna smiled her acceptance, he dutifully slipped the simple solitaire onto her slender finger, effectively sealing their future. Fresna felt over the moon, delirious with happiness.

Since her mother had tragically died giving birth to her and her father, unable to cope with the depths of his grief and the demands of a new baby, had absconded for a new life in New Zealand, leaving his tiny daughter in the care of her maternal grandparents, it was only natural that Fresna should turn to them for support with the wedding preparations. Money was tight, but Granddad insisted that things would be done properly. Under the circumstances, he suggested a quick wedding followed by a short, low budget honeymoon. It was agreed that the newly married pair would live with her grandparents until more suitable accommodation could be found. The banns were duly posted.

Fresna and her best friend, Evie went shopping for the trousseau. Village custom dictated that she could not wear white and so she chose instead a fashionable, cream, lace mini-dress with matching jacket. Evie, who had agreed to act as bridesmaid, found some material at half price in a bargain bucket outside the haberdashery and made her own pale blue sateen, knee length creation. It was agreed that the handmade bouquets would consist of lilies and orange blossom with matching buttonholes for the men. When Fresna saw them, her heart soared. They were simply stunning. Granddad had arranged that he and Fresna would be taken to the church in the horse and cart owned by Johnny Pony, the baker.

Following the ceremony, a quiet chicken supper at the British Legion for relatives and close friends had been arranged. There was no money for an official photographer, but Uncle Earle had agreed to bring along his Instamatic so there would be a record of her perfect day. It was the best that could be done. It was more than Fresna had ever dreamed of.

On the morning of the wedding, her grandmother woke Fresna just before eight in the morning, quietly placing a cup of tea on her bedside cabinet, an act which both surprised and delighted her granddaughter, who had never before been allowed to eat or drink so much as a morsel in her bedroom. As Fresna lay back in the bed, relishing this unexpected treat, her grandma pulled back the curtains to let in the bright, early morning sunshine.

"Got a lovely day for it, sweetheart." she remarked and, smiling fondly at the lovely young girl still entangled in the cotton sheets, she crossed the room. "Happy is the bride on whom the sun shines," she added, softly dropping a kiss on her beloved granddaughter's cheek. "Take your time, my lovely. Breakfast will be ready when you are," she said and left the room as serenely as she had entered it, closing the door gently behind her.

Fresna found herself far too excited to eat more than a small piece of toast. Granddad, having mopped up the last of a loaded plate of eggs and bacon, smiled indulgently at the ecstatic child before him, scraped back his chair, put on his cap and announced that he was off to water his allotment and would be back when all the fuss and nonsense had died down. At ten o'clock, Mrs. Hobbs from No. 12 popped in to wash and set Fresna's hair. Having carefully put in far too many rollers, she left, promising to return at noon to do the backcombing and to weave some of the orange blossom into the bride's strawberry blonde hair. Just after lunch when Mrs. Hobbs had finished her most important duty of the day, Evie knocked on the door and the two excited young girls ran up to Fresna's bedroom to get dressed. Together, the two friends helped each other into their respective garments and applied simple make-up. Granddad would not allow either of them to look like painted trollops, no matter what the occasions, but despite his old fashioned attitude and disdain for frivolity, he had amazed the two young girls by insisting the family take the bus to the nearby town the previous weekend where, to everyone's surprise and to Fresna's utter delight, he had bought his granddaughter her very first pair of stiletto heels.

Thrilled, she had returned home to squirrel away her treasure in the depths of her wardrobe.

Almost reverently, Evie extracted the precious package and carefully removed the lid. The pair stared in awe at the cream, pointed bridal shoes nestling within the crisp lilac tissue. Kneeling beside her best friend, Evie took it upon herself to place one, and then the other, on Fresna's feet. The bride-to-be stood up carefully and then, without hesitation, walked purposefully across her bedroom, testing her balance against the unusual steepness of the daring heels. Turning, she broke into a delighted smile, causing tears to prick Evie's eyes at the sight of the stunning bride in front of her. The two friends just had time to hug each other before Evie had to leave for the church. Alone in her bedroom, Fresna looked around at the room in which she had spent many happy hours, gently touching her favourite childhood relics and contemplating the rosy future in front of her. How lucky she felt to have bagged such a prize as the gorgeous, gorgeous Alex.

Interrupted by a gentle cough from her ever prompt grandfather, Fresna made her careful way downstairs to the front room to where he was waiting to accompany her to the church; his back to the unlit fire as usual. As Fresna entered the room, the taciturn man looked up at her and smiled his slow, gentle smile, his eyes glowing with unshed tears.

"You look a picture, my lovely," he told her, his voice slightly trembling with the emotion of the occasion.

Despite the shock of the unplanned pregnancy and the dismay of having their only granddaughter in the family way before her time, her grandparents had steadfastly stood by Fresna, saying little and doing as much as they could to make this day wonderful for her.

At quarter to two on the dot, Johnny Pony reined his pony outside the little cottage. He had transformed his wooden cart, usually reserved for carrying less splendid cargo, so that it was now gaudily decked with cream organza, sprigs of honeysuckle and scarlet, plastic gardenia. Granddad helped Fresna into the back and, after spending a few moments chatting to Johnny about the cricket, he climbed in beside her and took her outstretched hand. They smiled at each other.

Grandma and Evie had already left in Uncle Earle's Morris Minor about fifteen minutes earlier so that the organist would know the bride would soon be on her way. The neighbours were out in force, smiling and waving at the pair, wishing Fresna well and secretly thankful it wasn't one of their kids starting married life on the wrong side of the blanket.

It was only a short ride up the hill to the church to where Fresna knew Alex would be impatiently waiting to take her as his wife. The beautiful bride could not contain her happiness and so, beaming and waving at the early summer shoppers in the small village high street, the little cortege made its way towards the church.

When the little group arrived at the gates of the little church, Fresna was surprised to see Evie still talking to the organist in the churchyard. The vicar and her grandmother both stood in front of the oak doors, talking animatedly together. The vicar was patting grandma's hand. Evie walked across to the bridal carriage and whispered something to Johnny Pony, who immediately clicked his teeth and stirred his old cob into action. To Fresna's dismay he took them for a slow amble back through the high street before, once again, climbing the hill towards the church. It was a beautiful afternoon for a carriage ride, but although Fresna was enjoying all the attention, she would have much preferred to be walking down the aisle towards Alex and her future. She couldn't help wishing he could have been on time for this, their most important day.

Back at the church, it seemed Alex was running very late so back around the circuit, the little bridal group rode. By this time, Fresna was becoming alarmed and, as they stopped in front of the church for the third time, she tried to get down from the cart, but granddad forbade her, announcing sternly that he would go and find out what was going on. She was to stay put. Johnny Pony would look after her. Granddad was firm and Fresna knew better than to protest. Still, she found it difficult to sit patiently in the cart whilst the butterflies of anxiety fluttered around the pit of her stomach.

She did not need to wait long before granddad was back at her side, followed by her unsmiling grandma and a rather anxious looking vicar. Evie was at the back of the little group, giving her arm to a wobbling, heavily pregnant stranger.

"The bugger ain't turned up sweetheart," granddad said flatly. "And here be the reason." He gestured towards the swollen stranger. "This be his wife and she's come across town to let you know he won't be coming, not now, not ever. That's the way of it, my lovely. There'll be no wedding today. Best we take you home and get you out of that getup."

Fresna froze. She felt light headed. She couldn't take it in. There must be some mistake. Alex? Not coming? No wedding? Impossible! And what on earth had this strange woman to do with it? His wife? Did granddad call her his wife? That can't be. Anyway she's pregnant too… pregnant TOO? Thoughts tumbled out of her like buttons from a box and she found she could barely grasp them. The world was spinning out of control. She tried to stand, but found she couldn't and somehow the bottom of the cart was rising to meet her.

When she woke up, it was dark. She was lying on her bed with a cold compress over her forehead and with her grandmother sitting beside her, quietly shelling peas. For a moment, Fresna had difficulty remembering the events of the day. Why was she lying in a darkened room with a wet flannel on her head? She lay back against the pillows staring at the ceiling, puzzled. Something was wrong, but she couldn't for the life of her think what it might be.

And then she remembered and she was immediately overcome with a deep sense of anguish and humiliation. The vision of the heavily pregnant stranger swam before her. Her heart lurched into her mouth and she felt sick. She was so ashamed. Her eyes filled with tears, her breathing began to heave and the sobs threatened to choke her. She struggled to sit up and, as she did so, her grandmother put aside her pot of peas and placed a comforting arm about her.

"Now don't take on so, my angel," she murmured, patting her back gently. "That bugger's a bad lot, but he'll get his. Don't waste your tears on him. You must put him out of your mind. The important thing now is that you concentrate on the bairn. Your granddad and I will do all that we can to help you. There now, don't take on so. Time and hard work will ease the pain. That's the way of it." And that was all she ever said on the subject. She simply pulled her devastated granddaughter into her gentle embrace and let her cry it out.

After that first evening, Fresna was never again allowed to wallow in self-pity. She was given work in the laundry at the local hospital. In the evenings, she knitted or sewed baby garments. On Saturdays, her grandparents gave her her spends and she was allowed to go to the cinema.

In late autumn, she gave birth to a baby girl.

Of Alex, there was no sign.

II

To her surprise, Fresna took to motherhood like a duck to water. Despite the fact that she had her heart broken every single morning as she bent over the cot and looked into the eyes of Alex in the face of the baby girl smiling up at her, she loved her daughter with every inch of her being.

When Verity was just six weeks old, Fresna resumed her job, working part-time, at the cottage hospital laundry. Great-grandma was delighted to take care of the child in her absence, rocking and crooning to the bairn for hours at a time. Great-granddad, despite his 'women in the kitchen' attitude and refusal to be a modern man, felt a great sense of pride as he pushed the enormous second-hand perambulator down the little high street on a Saturday morning to get the paper. The new little family was content.

Time passed and, all too soon, the time came for Verity to go to school. Through hard work and diligence, her mother had, by this time, risen to the dizzy heights of Laundry Manager at the hospital. Every spare penny she earned was spent on the child. Fresna was determined that Verity would never go without nor suffer from the stigma of her birth. She made sure that Verity's school uniform was immaculate, her shoes highly polished, her hair always off her face and neatly braided. In turn, Verity strove to be a credit to her mother and her grandparents. With careful budgeting on the part of the little family, Verity became the first child in the village to own both a Spirograph and a Cindy. The little family was blossoming.

Motherhood suited Fresna and, as she grew into her twenties, she was developing into a very beautiful woman; a natural strawberry blond with a lissom figure. Wherever she went heads turned and wolves whistled. Men noticed her and regularly asked her out on dates, but Fresna always refused, quietly but firmly. She simply wasn't interested, she told them. She was preoccupied with caring for her child and, in any case, her first taste of men had been undeniably disappointing. It was obvious to her that, despite how attractive it appeared she had become, how very fetching she was told she looked, how much every red blooded male seem to desire her, the reality was that few men would be willing to take on the upbringing of someone else's bastard.

Besides, for Fresna family came first. Her loyalty to her child and to her grandparents was absolute and, despite what had happened, she had worked hard to regain the respect of the village and she did not want to lose it. She was known to be a conscientious worker, careful to owe nothing to anyone, even refusing to let Mrs Baxter in the sweet shop give Verity a free lollipop when she went in to collect the newspaper for gramps when he began to experience the swollen and stiff joints that accompany increasing age.

Despite the adoration of both her great grandparents and her mother, Verity grew up unspoiled. An intelligent child, she passed her eleven plus with ease and settled quickly into the nearby Grammar School. For as long as she would allow them, granny accompanied her to the school bus stop every morning and gramps would be waiting there each afternoon to bring her back home. The little family was thriving.

To everyone's surprise, shortly after her thirtieth birthday, Fresna fell in love. He was a Charge Nurse at the cottage hospital on a two-year exchange programme from the Mercy Hospital, Atlanta, Georgia. He was single, over six feet tall and immaculately groomed. Furthermore, he had impeccable manners and was clearly well educated but, in the close knit community in which Fresna had lived all her life, George's African American ethnicity was something of a sensation. His culture, his unusual appearance and the colour of his skin became a source of endless speculation and gossip among the villagers.

For George and Fresna, however, it was love at first sight. They were soul mates. They were inseparable. They became everything to each other. He gave her bright, golden daffodils. She gave him homemade scones.

In their very quiet way, her grandparents were delighted for Fresna. The teenage Verity seemed outwardly unaffected by the love affair, but was secretly thrilled to see her mother so happy.

George sought a permanent nursing post and applied for UK residency. The happy couple looked for a way to be together and, after much discussion, George and Fresna moved into a little flat of their own close to the hospital where they both worked. Naturally Verity came with them, but the three of them made sure to pop in on Gramps and Granny several times a week. Thus began a very happy, very fulfilling chapter of Fresna's life. George continued to fill her life with sunshine and flowers; she filled his with warmth and beauty. Her only disappointment, and it really was such a tiny disappointment given all she already had, was that she never fell pregnant. How Fresna would have loved to have given George a son, to have given Verity a brother. But it was not to be.

During the summer that saw Fresna and George celebrate five years together, Gramps died suddenly. A heart attack took him quickly away after supper just as he sat down to watch the evening news and the football results. Just over a week later, he was buried in the graveyard of the village in which he had lived all his life; in the grounds of the church where Fresna was to have been married seemingly a lifetime ago. Without exception, the villagers turned out to say their goodbyes to this well respected yet taciturn man. His wife, stoical in grief, but unable to cope without her lifelong companion, succumbed to the flu that very winter and was lovingly buried, under an avalanche of flowers, beside the only man she had ever loved.

The rocks upon which Fresna had built her life had suddenly begun to crumble beneath her. She was inconsolable. She felt vulnerable and scared, but throughout it all, George stood steadfastly by her side, supporting her, comforting her, holding her. Whatever would she have done without George? He had become her salvation.

Six months to the day that they buried her grandmother in the little churchyard on the hill, driving back from a medical conference in Bristol, George's Cavalier was hit head on by a speeding lorry driver rushing to catch the afternoon ferry to Rosslare. George died instantly. Amongst the wreckage, on what should have been the seat beside him, they found a bunch of bright, golden daffodils.

III

There was not enough grief in the whole wide world to satisfy Fresna.

Almost overnight it seemed a bomb had been dropped onto her life, without warning, leaving in its wake denial, devastation and an enormous crater in the centre of Fresna's world. How Fresna hauled herself through the empty, hollow days immediately following the accident was remarkable. Her reason for doing so was, of course, Verity.

For Verity's sake, she had to cope with her all-consuming grief. For Verity's sake, she had to get out of bed each morning when she would really rather have turned to face the wall to stare at nothing. For Verity's sake, she had to leave the comfort of her little flat each morning and try to get through her working day. For Verity's sake, she had to go on living.

It was the last thing she wanted to do. It was the only thing she could do.

And, as the days turned to weeks and the weeks turned to months and the months turned to years, Fresna began to rally, to pick herself up from the debris of her shattered life, shakily at first, like a dazed survivor trapped within the rubble of a collapsed building staggers blinking towards the sunlight, confused, uncertain, not comprehending why this one had lived yet that one had died. Fresna was truly grateful for the support and assistance of her shocked and distressed neighbours and friends, who simply wanted to help her and yet puzzled by their ability to get on with the ordinariness of life, to go about their daily business and remain calm in the midst of such overwhelming tragedy.

Fresna tried hard to pull herself together; to bring herself back to the person she had been before the tragedy, but the wounds were deep and such injuries do not mend without trace. Something deep inside Fresna had died, something within had been altered irrevocably; something soft and giving had become hard and unyielding. Behind the facade of Fresna's warm smile and approachable manner, there now lay a cold, impenetrable core. Overwhelmed with grief and abandoned by her irreplaceable partner and much beloved grandparents, she wrapped up her heart and hid it deep within the fortified walls of her castle where she knew it could not be reached, then she raised the drawbridge, locked herself in the keep and threw away the key.

Fresna would never allow herself to be vulnerable again.

CELIA

I

Just as Celia's foot reached the second stair of the spiral staircase on the first floor, the phone in her office began to ring. Carefully, she reversed, deftly balancing the tray of cups and saucers in her hands, returned to her office and picked up the phone, tucking it neatly under her chin.

"Dumbleton's Toys, how may I help you?" she enquired politely. Putting the call through to Customer Services, she retraced her steps and this time managed to get the required crockery upstairs to the meeting room on the second floor. She had already brought up the sugar, milk and biscuits. All she needed to do now was bring up the flasks of tea and coffee from the ground floor kitchen. Later, of course, she would be required to bring them all down again and stack them neatly into the dishwasher. In the meantime, she had a luxury hour of sitting down and focussing all her attention on one single thing – recording the minutes of the meeting of the Management Team.

Not that she needed to focus all her attention on the meeting. Celia had enough experience of taking minutes to be able to fade in and out of the process and still capture its highlights. She only really concentrated when they began the number crunching since her boss would check that figures were recorded accurately. As for the rest, it was all jargon and she doubted anyone ever read her notes thoroughly anyway. She sometimes fantasised about adding a ridiculous extraneous sentence or two to the record to see if anyone noticed.

"It was agreed to paint the walls of the second floor meeting room bright pink the evening before the annual internal Company Event since it was agreed by everyone present that watching the paint dry would prove vastly more interesting than yet another round of death by PowerPoint." Action: "Carried."

"It was decided that the Management Team, in gratitude for all her sterling work, would donate the entirety of their combined annual bonuses to Celia's holiday fund." Action: "Agreed with immediate effect."

"A full and frank discussion took place on the reasons why the girls from Customer Services refused to even flirt with the members of the Sales Team. Several possible reasons were put forward but, in the end, the group agreed that it was most likely because all the sales staff were butt ugly, useless tossers." Action: "Agreed unanimously."

On the other hand, attending the meeting did give Celia a welcome break from the multi-tasking, fire-fighting circus act that was her job at Dumbleton's Toys. Although she grumbled constantly about her workload, Celia secretly adored her job. Every day brought new challenges. She had no time to be bored and she always felt she was being stretched, sometimes admittedly almost to the limits of her abilities, but above all that was the promise of promotion. At some future date when everyone was settled in the new building, Patrick, the Managing Director, had promised her the job of Office

Manager and she would have two administrative assistants working under her. Finally, she would achieve management status.

Celia's official title was PA to the MD and Finance Officer, but that did not describe even a quarter of what she actually did. She usually arrived well before normal office hours, stayed late most days and often went without a proper lunch break. Sometimes she even worked an occasional, unpaid Saturday. Since arriving at Dumbleton's two years previously, she had grown her job out of all proportion and her boss was delighted with her. Not that he ever particularly praised her efforts; more that he had stopped swearing at her and even brought her the occasional cup of tea.

She now worked as PA to the entire team of Directors, gave administrative support to the sales and marketing teams, undertook all the personnel administration, had become Health and Safety Lead, first point of contact and edited the monthly internal newsletter.

With the coming of the new distribution centre in the autumn, Celia's workload had increased even further. She was heavily involved in organising the move of two of the four main teams across to the new complex. The company would transfer from outsourcing warehousing to managing it internally and this meant the recruitment of a whole new team. The Warehouse Manager and his two assistants were already on board, planning the logistics of the new build and beginning the recruitment drive for the Department's forty or so new staff members. For the time being, Celia was required to support them on top of everything else.

Celia didn't know how she had kept so many plates spinning for so long, yet still they kept coming and still she kept spinning. She loved her job, she loved its pace but, over and above everything, she loved the thought of achieving the first rung of the management ladder. She couldn't wait.

In the meantime, the meeting was coming to a close and she would need to get a first draft of the minutes to Patrick by close of play. Before that, however, she had to parcel up several items of pristine merchandise for onward transit to the photographer for inclusion in the annual catalogue; organise travel and hotels for those members of the Marketing Team who were travelling to Germany for a conference; format Patrick's PowerPoint presentation for tomorrow's WebEx; meet and greet the delegation who were due to arrive shortly to talk to the Warehouse Manager about forklift trucks; nag those concerned to finish writing their articles for the newsletter; clear the upstairs meeting room; nip to the shop for milk and keep up with her emails.

As she came down the stairs, shorthand notebook in one hand, tray of used coffee cups in the other, Patrick was already back in his office, barking down the phone, signalling her to drop everything and give him her full attention ASAP. She could sense from the set of his shoulders that he was not a happy bunny. Out of the corner of her eye, Julia, the Marketing Director and Lydia, Head of Customer Services were hurrying across the floor in the direction of the MD's office, trying to keep the panic out of their faces. At times like these, Celia had learned to breathe slowly, think clearly and keep her wits about her. Something was about to hit the fan and she wanted none of its splash back.

"Two things," Patrick was barking at Julia as Celia entered his office and sat down, notebook poised.

"Dusseldorf is unhappy with the artwork sent over this week. Apparently, they have told you before that the logo is to be placed in the top left hand corner of the packaging. Why is it still on the right? Sort it."

"But Patrick," replied Julia, in the slow, soothing tones usually reserved for the slightly backward, "we have discussed this before and you agreed with me that if we put the logo on the left, we lose the space available for RAG. There is such a thing as compliance, you know, or is it different for the Germans?"

"I know, I know. Look, speak to Fredericke, see what you can sort. Karl is on the warpath," he retorted.

Dismissing Julia, he turned to his Customer Services Manager. "Lydia, what's with this month's returns?" he queried, pointing at the tiny rows of numbers on the sheets in front of him. "These have got to be inaccurate. We can't be reporting this many inactive lines. Get your lot to go over them again and tell them to get them right this time." Frowning, Lydia reached for the spreadsheets strewn across the desk, but before she could do so, Patrick, with one aggressive sweep of his hand, had knocked them onto the floor. Lydia's knees creaked as she bent to pick them up.

Turning suddenly in his black, leather, executive chair, Patrick looked pointedly at his secretary. "Celia, where are the warehouse plans?" he snapped. "I gave them to you late last Friday afternoon before I left. You were supposed to put them on my desk first thing. The surveyors will be here shortly and we need to study them before they arrive. I need them NOW," he roared. Celia blanched. She hadn't seen the warehouse plans since she'd given them to Patrick the previous Thursday morning and no one had told her the surveyors were on their way.

"And I need the file on Education pronto," he continued, without seeming to pause for breath. "Get Larry on the phone straight away. I want to talk to him. Have you done the bonus letters yet? Oh, and I need my slides sorting. I just emailed them to you. Do seven copies, double sided in colour and bound. On my desk before you leave tonight. I've decided to attend in person now. Cancel the WebEx and let Bill's secretary know I'll be there at ten. Tell her I need the large meeting room. I don't care who she has to throw out. Don't let me down on this one, Celia."

Having not yet opened her mouth, Celia stood up and began to leave. "Oh and fix me a pot of strong coffee. With all the stress you lot've put me under, I'm going to need a lethal injection of the stuff just to get me through the day. Shut the door behind you, there's a good girl," he finished, dismissively and again turned his attention to the remaining member of his management team. "Why are you still here Lydia? I need those figures pronto. Hop to it!"

II

When Celia closed down her office for the night, it was 6.30pm and she'd only been able to snatch a five minute break for a hastily eaten baguette from the sandwich van. She hadn't had time to go for milk, much to the annoyance of the Customer Services Team, who used it by the gallon, but felt it was beneath them to shop for it. Celia took her coffee black.

The bonus letters had been written, Patrick's presentation was sorted, bound and in his briefcase well before he'd left for the day. The warehouse plans had been found. Under close questioning from Celia, Patrick grudgingly remembered that he had not given them to her at all, rather he had taken them home to study over the weekend and had forgotten to bring them back to the office. Patrick gave no apology for his omission. Instead, he ordered someone to fetch them and had left Celia and one of the Sales Managers to entertain the surveyors until they turned up, at which point he smoothly joined the meeting and blamed his secretary for the lapse. Celia sighed. She was used to it. After that meeting, Celia had organised for a batch of samples to be couriered to the photographer, arranged travel plans for the Marketing Team and had progressed the in-house newsletter. She'd even found time to organise someone to come in and mend the mood prone photocopier as well as fielding innumerable phone calls, monitoring her emails and briefly discussing the recruitment campaign with the Warehouse Team in advance of a visit from the Manager of the local Job Centre. Patrick's monthly expenses had been reconciled, the bonus letters had been written and both had been handed over to the Finance Manager. Celia had been up and down the stairs at least a dozen times and had brewed several cups of coffee for people other than herself.

Through the half glass walls of her office, Celia had been able to observe several members of the Sales and Marketing Teams gossiping and laughing across the expanse of open plan floor. She knew she worked far harder than they ever did, ever could and yet they got a bonus whilst she did not. Still, as Office Manager, she reasoned all that would change. With two staff on board to share some of the load, maybe she too would have time to sit and gossip.

III

Unless travelling, Patrick arrived at the office at nine o'clock sharp each morning, fully expecting his Management Team to be already at their desks and fresh coffee to be on his. He always left promptly at five and frowned if anyone left before him. Although overtime payments were never offered, the Management Team were incentivised and the Sales Managers always worked from home on Fridays, so it was only the minions that grumbled at the long hours.

Lesley, the Finance Manager, a mild mannered woman, a little older than Celia had noticed how much overtime Celia put in and, by way of a treat, had invited her to London one evening to a West End show. She had bought them both dinner on expenses and had paid for all Celia's travel. For Celia, it was a surprising and much welcomed treat.

During the journey home, lulled by good entertainment, food and wine, Celia had decided to let down her guard and confide to Lesley how much she was looking forward to her forthcoming role as Office Manager at the new build and finally being able to manage some additional administrative support. Lesley had listened closely as Celia had outlined her aspirations for the future, agreeing with her that it had indeed been a long time coming and that no one person could be expected to take on the administration of an additional forty new members of staff.

Waiting at the station for them on their arrival home, was Bob, Lesley's husband. He had very kindly agreed to drive Celia home that evening, thus allowing her to completely indulge herself. By this time she put the latch on the door, Celia was somewhat tipsy and on a huge high, having thoroughly enjoyed her all expenses paid night out. It would be a long time before she experienced one of those again, she'd decided. Nevertheless, she climbed into bed contented. If nothing else, she had made a new ally at work and that was not to be sneezed at. She was still smiling as she fell asleep.

The following morning, Celia, feeling energised and alive after her fun evening out, was at her desk at eight, singing to herself in a contented way as she sorted through the post and prioritised her work for the day. She liked to spend her first hour preparing for the onslaught that was Patrick. At 8.45, she went down to the kitchen to brew his coffee. Returning upstairs with his fresh ground and her first instant of the day, she was surprised to find Patrick's door shut. Through the window, she could see him talking to Lesley. Unfazed, she went back to the kitchen for another cup, returned to the MD's office, tapped on the door and delivered her wares. As she entered the room she noticed that Lesley was looking distinctly uncomfortable and seemed not to be able to look her in the eye as she mumbled thanks to Celia for the unexpected beverage. Celia took it in her stride. These were stressful times at Dumbleton's what with the new build just a few months away, the summer catalogue to prepare for and the Germans always on the warpath to trim costs.

Still humming to herself, she returned to her desk and got on with her work. She had a pile of travel expenses to complete for the Sales Team, some orders to process on the unwieldy purchase order system. Furthermore, she needed to plan the recruitment drive for the next tier of warehousemen and she had a pile of well overdue performance reviews to type up. That would take most of the morning and this afternoon would be taken up by the Marketing Team's monthly meeting, followed by a visit to the nearby product store to collect the required list of toys to send down to photography.

She was halfway through the travel expenses when Patrick popped his head round the door and asked her, rather gruffly, to step into his office. Wondering what was amiss this time, she dutifully picked up her shorthand notepad, followed him smartly into his room and asked if she should make some coffee. Surprisingly, he declined.

"Come in and shut the door," he ordered.

He wasted no time, not even giving her a moment to sit down.

"What's all this I have been hearing about your being promoted to the job of Office Manager at the new build with a team of secretaries under you?" he threw at her angrily.

Celia's eyes opened wide in alarm and her heart immediately dropped towards her stomach. To steady herself, she took a deep breath and held on to Patrick's desk. There was no need to become defensive. Patrick and she had talked about this often. He knew that.

"You've told me several times that if I shape up now and work hard with the rest of the team to get us all smoothly settled into the new warehouse, you will promote me to the role of Office Manager and let me manage any new office staff that come on board," she replied with spirit.

"I have what?" he exploded, staring at her as though she was completely insane. "I most certainly have not. Wherever you picked that up from, it was definitely not me."

"You repeated it to me in my last performance review. I have it in writing that we agreed that my goal would be to work towards becoming Dumbleton's new Office Manager."

Patrick's face relaxed, increasing the levels of anxiety Celia was feeling. He smiled thinly. "Work towards, yes," he agreed, "but you are a long way from achieving it, my girl. There will be no immediate promotion for you once we move across town. There never was a role of Office Manager being offered and there never will be. There certainly won't be any new administrators coming on line, not now, not ever. The Germans won't countenance that; not with the meagre profits we are showing. They only just tolerate me having an assistant."

"But," Celia tried to interject. However, Patrick was in full flow and therefore unstoppable.

"Taking my words and making nonsense of them!" he spat at her disparagingly. "Get it into your head once and for all Celia. You are not going to be Office Manager at Dumbleton's not now, not in the near future, possibly not ever. There are not going to be any new secretaries and, if there were, you would most certainly not be managing them. You are the only full time administrator here and, as far as the foreseeable future is concerned, you will continue to be so. Got it?"

"But who is going to act as administrator for the new staff at the warehouse?" cried Celia in dismay.

Patrick only looked at her, his refusal to budge written all over his face.

"There are forty of them," reasoned Celia, emphasising the word 'forty'.

Patrick still said nothing. He sat there, impassively, waiting for her to work it out.

Realisation dawned and the shock spread across her face as she took it in. "B-but I can't take on the administration of a whole new team. I work at least ten hours unpaid overtime a week as it is." stuttered a stunned Celia.

Patrick sat back in his chair and looked down. He slowly smoothed out the invisible creases in his expensive trousers while Celia stood in front of him aghast. He paused a heartbeat more and then, raising his eyes to her face, he smiled coldly, reminding his reeling secretary powerfully of a snake.

"Celia," he said, gently, almost paternally, emphasising each word. "You know what your trouble is – you don't believe in yourself. Trust me, you can do this. You are a very capable woman. If it helps, I believe you can do it and the Management Team believe you can do it. Believe in yourself Celia and you will, in fact, do it."

He paused, turning to contemplate the bleak scenery outside his office window for a short while, allowing Celia to collapse into a nearby chair as she struggled to take in what Patrick had been saying.

Still staring out of the window, Patrick added mystifyingly "Ants and rubber tree plants, my girl. Ants and rubber tree plants." He rose from his chair and, crossing the desk to stand beside Celia, he patted her on the shoulder and beamed encouragingly at the horrified woman.

As Celia listened to the sound of her dream job being swallowed up in the bark that was proving every bit as painful as Patrick's bite, all she could think of was, "Ants and frigging rubber tree plants? What the hell have ants and bloody rubber tree plants got to do with anything?"

Still smiling winningly, Patrick opened the door to usher Celia out. The conversation was over and she was being dismissed. Crushed, Celia rose hesitantly from her chair and left the room. Humiliated didn't even come close to what she was feeling.

"Oh and Celia," called out Patrick, cheerfully, as the devastated secretary walked unsteadily towards the relative sanctuary of her office. "Pop the kettle on. I'd like that coffee now. There's a good girl."

TIFFANY

I

If only she'd kept her damn mouth shut. If only, she'd thought it through. If only, she hadn't acted so hastily. She wouldn't be where she was now. She'd be where she was then – where she still very much wanted to be. Not that she felt her new life was terrible. She wasn't bored or strapped for cash or out of work and her inconstant love life had continued inconstant throughout the entire debacle. No change there then.

It's just that she wished she'd had the good sense to stay calm, to rise above it, to bite her tongue. Instead, she'd lost her temper, stood her ground and bitten off more than she could chew, which was why she now found herself sweating inside a bulky flak jacket directing football traffic in the middle of the high street on a warm Saturday afternoon.

But then it's an ill wind.

Not that long ago, Tiffany had been very satisfied with her job as Training Advisor for the Joint Emergency Services. She spent some of her time organising and developing bespoke training courses for a discrete group of clients; she spent some of her time training the good, the bad and the downright useless in management skills and she spent some of her time coaching and mentoring the supposedly up and coming. Her particular skill lay in helping others to get the best out of themselves, which was ironic really given the outcome.

She had sat on the Development Committees of several groups, working alongside the Local Authority, the Police, the Health Service and the Fire Brigade. She had considered herself very fortunate to be able to spend quite a lot of her time out of the office, sourcing venues, delivering training or meeting clients, on top of which she was able to work from home writing course objectives, needs analyses and learning outcomes. She was particularly proud of her developmental work with the County Council around Risk Assessment and Disaster Management. She had developed a good working relationship with the different personalities within the group. She found that, on the whole, they were a good laugh – down to earth, friendly and professional. She felt it a privilege to be able to work alongside them. She had felt completely secure in her role so she had never quite been able to understand what had gone so disastrously wrong. She couldn't quite put her finger on it. She suspected it was her rejection of Fat Taff.

At a three day event at a hotel in Durham, he'd had one too many on the last night of the course and had made a pass at her. Tiffany, very aware of her glorious, good looks and tiny frame, was very used to more than her share of masculine attention and had thought nothing of giving him the brush off. It was something she did on a very regular basis. Besides, she felt it was highly unprofessional to mix business with pleasure. Worse, this particular guy was fat, Welsh and up his own arse and, whilst Tiffany was always partial to a little rarebit, she most definitely did not do fat or up the arse.

To Tiffany's surprise, Fat Taff seemed to take her rejection as some kind of personal affront to his masculinity and could not believe she'd had the temerity to give him the knock back. He seemed unable to accept she'd turned him down – a well set up Abergevenian with a four by four and no mortgage. What was she thinking of, the stupid cow? He'd show her. At that point, he'd pulled himself together and stormed off, leaving Tiffany slightly bemused and embarrassed by his onslaught. She decided it was best to shrug it off and leave the idiot to get over himself.

However, that confrontation signalled the beginning of the end for Tiffany. At each meeting of the Development Group, there would be an aside, a sneer, a put down or a contention. He found fault with her work, criticised her approach, laughed at her skill and mocked her enthusiasm. He refused to listen to her professional critique of his presentations and cancelled his coaching sessions. He stared out of the window, seemingly bored, whenever she began to speak. The gentle, flirtatious, admiring taffy was clearly showing the darker side of his nature, turning almost overnight, into a bombastic, belligerent, blinkered bastard. Yet no one else in the group cared, no one batted an eyelid, no one came to her defence. In fact, no one actually seemed to notice that anything was different.

Until it was too late.

II

It was just another course; just another overnighter with another gala dinner; just another excuse for a booze-up at an impersonal hotel. And yet, it was totally and completely different to any other training course she'd ever run before.

It had begun ordinarily enough. The average number of delegates were late, the average number of delegates were lost, the average number of delegates failed to show. There was the usual mix of the upwardly mobile and the downright reclusive. There was the usual melee of the know-it-all, done-it-all and seen-it-all mulched together with the don't know, don't care and don't ask brigade.

From Tiffany's perspective, the morning sessions seemed to go smoothly. There was the general rush for coffee and a crafty fag in the designated area during the first break. There was the usual complaint that there was no honey and lemongrass tea or gluten free, dairy free, taste free biscuits from the inevitable lacto-intolerant, hyperglycaemic, lipid averse, nut allergenic vegetarian, but nothing Tiffany wasn't able to handle.

The guest speaker in the afternoon had been late, but nevertheless had thankfully managed to cover all thirty of his power point slides, dismiss the company into break out rooms for a practical, gather feedback, sum up and disappear in record time, meaning that they only went slightly over schedule.

The Chair of the Faculty rounded off the day with a brief overview of the learning points so that the group was dismissed a mere thirty minutes over time, eager to head towards the bar for a quick drink before they trudged to their rooms to get themselves ready for the main event of the day, the Gala Dinner.

Tiffany breathed a sigh of relief as the door closed behind the final delegate. She wriggled out of her shoes and sat down for a few minutes, reflecting on how quickly the day had gone. She only had to pack up the data projector, tidy up the room in preparation for the following morning's closing session and lock up. Then she could sneak off to her room, avoiding the crowd at the bar and reward herself with a welcome soak in the tub before getting ready for the long evening ahead. Rubbing her aching feet, she congratulated herself on a job well done. She was beginning to believe that her particular star was in the ascendant so, of course, it was just at that moment that things took a spectacular nosedive.

Back in her room, just in her underwear, Tiffany spent a little time deciding what to wear. Over time, she had gathered a small collection of good quality evening wear, especially chosen for these occasions. Nothing too bright yet nothing too dull, nothing too revealing, yet nothing too severe, nothing too long, yet nothing too short, nothing too smart, yet nothing too casual. An outfit designed to get her noticed, but not so as to make her the centre of attention.

Satisfied with her reflection in the mirror, and with her shining, blonde bob straightened to perfection, Tiffany made her way to the dining room. It had become her custom to arrive there first since it gave her the opportunity to check that everything was ready, that the room was properly set out and looked welcoming. As the delegates began to assemble in the dining room, Tiffany made sure that she greeted each of her guests by name, working the room with practiced grace and charm, drawing the different individuals out of themselves, putting them at their ease, feeling herself to be the ultimate professional; so on top of her game.

The dinner itself was the standard melee of hotel food. There was the usual plate of unrecognisable haute cuisine, undercooked vegetables and questionable jus. There was the inevitable over creamy, over citrusy dessert. The barely drinkable coffee was, as ever, served lukewarm. The caterers had to be reminded to offer tea but, with the wine continuing to flow, everyone had begun to relax and enjoy themselves.

And then Fat Taff stood up.

He began by tapping his teaspoon against the rim of his brandy glass and calling the room to attention. He thanked everyone for coming, for their willing contribution to the event and for their avid attention to the speakers. He told a couple of rather risqué jokes to beddown his increasingly raucous audience. He followed that with a succinct overview of the developmental history of the course and its uniqueness within the public sector. Over the next fifteen minutes, he gave a somewhat rambling account of his own career; an over-exaggerated saga of his time in the marines, switching smoothly to a flamboyant tale of his time as fireman and moving on to his current, lofty position within its training section.

He then turned everyone's attention towards Tiffany.

"Of course, the person we most have to thank," he said, his lilting voice a caress, "is Tiffany here. Little Tiff. Lovely little Tiff. Beautiful little Tiff. Looks after us all a treat, she does. Nothing she wouldn't do for any of us. Bends over backwards for us, don't you pet? You only have to ask."

He paused and winked knowingly towards the men gathered around the cabaret style tables, who cheered back their complicity.

"Run the course single handed, she could, couldn't you my lovely? Doesn't need us, see. And always there first in the morning to hand out the bacon sandwiches, isn't it? No problem for her to stay behind to pack away the overhead projector and the pencils either. Do anything for any of us, she would. That's our Tiff. Lovely little Tiff.

He paused, dramatically, and looked directly at the somewhat alarmed, very upright, blonde centre of attention for the first time.

"Well there's something you can do for me, sweetheart," he continued. "Drop down to my room after dinner and give it the tidy up for me, would you? There's a girl. Left it in a right mess I have. Couldn't find your way round to giving it the quick hoover as well, could you? You don't mind do you, darling? And I've had a word with Chef. He says it's okay for you to nip into the kitchen after dinner and help with the washing up. You won't want to stay in the bar with the rest of us, will you? Not on your level, see. Best you stay behind with your own kind and help clear up, there's the girl."

And he paused.

There were a few seconds of uncomfortable, foot shuffling silence. There were a further few seconds of endless all-pervading stillness. No one knew quite what to say, quite where to look or quite what to do, but everyone knew something had just gone quite horribly wrong, but no one quite knew why.

Finally, there was a tiny sound as Tiffany stirred. Deep within her, the volcano had blown! Weeks of enduring subtle put downs, outright disrespect and flagrant sexism from the odious Welshman boiled inside her. Without pausing to consider her actions, she stood up, picked up her wineglass and walked purposefully along the length of the room to face her persecutor. In front of the shell-shocked onlookers, she raised her arm gracefully over the now silent Abergavenian and watched, as if from a distance, as the rich red contents of her glass streamed over Fat Taff's moist, balding skull. Heedless of the sudden explosion of noise in the room, she waited until the last remnants of her glass began to drip from his double chin and onto the distended bastard's dress shirt. Then in a clear, measured tone that reached right to the back of the room, she said, "Take that, you intolerable prick." Turning neatly on her four inch heels, she marched smartly away in the direction of the hall and, from there, fled to the sanctuary of her bedroom where, burning with rage and shame, she packed her bags and left. Gripping the steering wheel until her knuckles went white, she began the long drive home. "How dare he?" she stormed, jerking the gear stick into first. "How dare that overweight bombastic arsehole relegate me to the level of a skivvy? And in public! The fucking bastard." On and on she fumed, turning the event over and over in her mind, unable to let it go. What had she done to deserve such scorn? What had she done that was so wrong? And the fat turd had had the temerity to think she would date him. As if! She had never felt so humiliated nor so angry in all her life.

First thing the following morning, Tiffany phoned work, telling them she was sick. She couldn't face anyone so they would just have to get on without her. She felt mortified and couldn't quite believe what had happened. She struggled to come to terms with what Taff had said and what she had done. She catapulted between outright indignation towards the odious Welshman and simply wishing the floor would swallow her up so that she could die. Why had she so totally embarrassed herself? Why couldn't she turn the clock back?

At the end of the second day of her absence, her manager phoned her to ask how she was feeling and to enquire when she planned to come back to the office. Tiffany guessed it was because they were so very busy that month. Tough, they would just have to cope. She told him she had a bad cold and thought she would be back the following Monday. He wished her better, told her to take things easy and rang off.

On her first day back, she was surprised to find herself invited to step into the Director's office before she had even got her coat off. She was dismayed to see that a member of the Human Resources Team was already in the room and, sitting next to him, her Line Manager. Both of them looked grim. Obviously, the news was out. Still, she reassured herself, this was a serious situation and there would obviously need to be some kind of reparation and apology before things could be smoothed over. With a bit of luck, Fat Taff might get his lardy arse fired and she would never have to work with him again.

Nothing could have prepared her for the unbelievable news from the Director that, following a serious incident backed by several witness statements, she was now subject to a grievance procedure and from none other than the odious Welshman, as she had now begun to refer to him. The HR person gravely informed her that there was to be a full enquiry. Stunned and confused, Tiffany looked from one serious face to another. She was the cause of the grievance? What was he talking about? How did that work? Her Line Manager, behaving like a complete stranger, asked her, in a stiff, little voice if she would like a representative in the room. Outraged, she refused the offer. She was then invited by the Director to give her version of the events at the Gala Dinner a few days previously and watched as everything was written down. There followed a barrage of careful, persistent questioning, designed to check the consistency of her account. After quietly listening to her side of the story, the Director gently informed her that he had no choice, but to suspend her on full pay pending investigation. A charge of assault had been levied against her. She was hustled out of the building before she had a chance to greet any of her colleagues. Not that that would have been of any use – everyone had their heads down, no one wanted to look her in the face, let alone talk to her. To Tiffany, it seemed that she had already been judged and found wanting.

As the proceedings got under way, Tiffany rallied and found herself a decent solicitor. As they read through the witness statements together in preparation for her defence, Tiffany was appalled to learn that not one person present at the dinner on the night in question could remember anything untoward in the behaviour of Fat Taff yet everyone present distinctly remembered, with astonishing clarity, the sight of the furious Training Manager striding aggressively almost the full length of the dining room, to deposit the contents of a full glass of Merlot over her unfortunate colleague's head. And who could forget her now infamous words? In every state-ment given to the investigators, the words, "Take that, you intolerable prick," screamed up at her. To all intents and purposes, it was as if Tiffany had suffered from an isolated and very unfortunate incident of Tourette's. For some unknown reason, she had just got it into her head to get up and christen the innocent fireman with a full glass of wine and no one seemed to have the slightest idea why. So, instead of being seen as the very public victim of verbal abuse, she had been cast in the role of the unprovoked aggressor.

In vain, Tiffany tried to defend her position but she found she had few allies. The drawbridge had been raised, the gates barred and the enemy protected within its citadel whilst the unfortunate Tiffany had been left floundering in the moat.

Outflanked, isolated and with no heart for a prolonged siege, Tiffany decided she had no option, but to sheath her sword, cut her losses and resign her post with immediate effect.

If only she'd kept her damn mouth shut.

CHARLEY

I

Until a few short months ago, Charley had been more than content with her life. She earned enough money to maintain a decent standard of living yet leave her with enough free time to pursue higher interests. A legacy from an aunt had paid for an attractive semi in a quiet cul-de-sac in the best part of town and there was money left over to fund her sports car. She could afford to go to the beauty parlour several times a month and enjoyed the benefits of the best hairdresser in town, smoothing her locks into gleaming chestnut perfection.

She had never married, being easily bored and having no desire for motherhood. She told herself that snot and projectile vomiting were for lesser mortals. She was fortunate enough to enjoy her own company and she had more than enough acquaintances to enjoy the frequent conversation of interesting, accomplished adults, more especially on those occasions in which she was the absolute centre of attention. As a consequence, she cultivated a circle of very select friends and the regular ministrations of an extremely accomplished lover or four. It went without saying that everything Charley did was done with the utmost discretion and in the best possible taste.

Considering herself to be unashamedly bohemian, Charley was a regular patron of the arts, frequently travelling up to the 'smoke', as she laughingly referred to London, at weekends to enjoy the theatre or the ballet and to stay with an 'old friend' and, if that 'old friend', invited her to share his bed, so much the better. It was to be expected that Charley dressed well. She never wore anything other than Janet Reger beneath her sleek, designer exterior. Her frequent trips to London always included a trip to Harrods or Harvey Nicks. And if the 'old friend' with whom she had chosen to sleep also offered to buy her a little token of his affection, she always felt able to gracefully accept.

To her utter joy, her life was her own, supremely under control and hers to do with as she pleased, when she pleased and with whom she pleased.

At least it was until three months ago.

II

Gone were the days when Charley could sit quietly beneath her pergola, reading a good novel whilst sipping quality chardonnay or host the perfect dinner party for close friends or relax in her executive Jacuzzi, listening to classic fm. Dammit, she couldn't even partake of a soupcon of al fresco, late night intimacy with one of her accomplished lovers without one of those fiends from next door poking their sodding noses in.

If it wasn't one of that pair of demonised, scruffy infants yelling that they needed to pee pee or had lost their dummy or had fallen over (Charley had convinced herself that the twenty month old twins next door were incontinent, drooling cripples, who needed locking away in an institution to avoid offending decent society), then one of the dogs would begin barking for attention and inevitably the other three would join to form a chorus so that her tranquil afternoon in the garden would turn into a snapping, snarling, baying, yapping, growling, howling nightmare.

And if it wasn't the dogs, it was the cats. In the rare peace of a Sunday afternoon, when the Designer Gooneys next door had mercifully all gone out, she would lift her eyes serenely from the pages of her magazine to let them gently fall onto the sun-dappled, leaf fringed edge of her shrubbery to the delights of the ginger one haughtily shitting amongst her lupins as if it was doing her a favour. Failing that, she might step semi clad onto the shimmering dew of her lawn in the promising light of a spring morning to begin her day with ritualistic lungsful of fresh air only to feel her bare toes squish sickeningly into the regurgitated, unrecognisable, half eaten entrails of some unfortunate creature left behind after playtime. And, if Charley was spared either of those particular pleasures, then you could bet your sweet life that, just as she settled down to watch her favourite historical drama, it would no doubt be accompanied by the exquisite, ear-grating undertones of a parrot screeching, "Nothing for a pair in this game," followed by a prolonged cackle or an entire virtuoso of muffled, whirring, banging noises given out by an unidentifiable, teeth clenching, multi-functional drill.

Inspired, she had bought a cheap tape recorder and had spent a very unpleasant afternoon taping the Hounds of the Baskervilles over the fence. Every time she stepped onto the patio, the totally inharmonious barbershop quartet of the canine world would start and continue for at least twenty minutes. She spent the next evening taping the incessant squawk of the parrot through the wall of her lounge and part of the following day capturing the noise of the children in the garden, accompanied by the unpleasant whine of the mother nagging at them through the French windows. When she had finished her discordant recording, she took it next door and pressed play, but thugjeans turned it off after five minutes, declaring it was a set up and he didn't need to hear anymore. He then shut the door firmly in her face.

Charley then spent several fruitless hours researching noise pollution on the net. It seemed there was little she could do other than waste her valuable savings on an endless stream of solicitor's letters, which ultimately would prove useless, toothless and spineless and, since Charley simply refused to waste her precious money firing blanks, she decided to close down that avenue. She had then spoken at length to a very nice man from the Environmental Health Agency, who had advised her to keep a diary of the noise. He told her that someone from his department would visit the house in question to monitor the noise level after which they would get back to her. That had been weeks ago. No one had been in touch, nothing had changed and, when she had tried to follow it up, she was asked to quote her reference number and, as she didn't have one, she was told she would need to start again.

Undeterred, Charley turned her attention to drawing up a petition and canvassing her neighbours. She spoke to everyone in the cul-de-sac and also those in the immediate vicinity. She was relieved to find that, whilst she bore the brunt of the situation, everyone was suffering varying degrees of aggravation and delighted that someone was finally prepared to tackle the problem. One woman, whose garden backed on to theirs, told her that she had already been round several times to ask them to keep the noise down. The constant barking of the dogs in the afternoon was keeping her six-month old daughter awake and fretful. Uncharacteristically, Charley felt sorrier for her than she did for herself and reached out a tentative finger to stroke the grizzling child's wet cheek. The new mother, pale with exhaustion, managed a thin smile and said she hoped this would do the trick. When she felt she had collected enough signatures, she took the document next door. The DGs accepted the petition with good grace, refused her offer of a resolution meeting, closed the door politely and left Charley fuming with impotence in the porch.

The constant disturbance had already frayed her nerves and was now beginning to depress her. She had done everything she could think of to deal with the fuck-wits next door, barring harming anything and she had now begun regularly fantasizing about poisoned meat and slow strangulation. Talking to the airhead wife had been a waste of time; the husband had shown himself to be a chav in YSL.

Charlie felt exhausted, frustrated and, worst of all, she was beginning to feel defeated. Weeks of sleepless nights were beginning to show in the dark circles under her eyes and the pinched set to her mouth. Charlie loathed looking anything less than perfect. She had lost her appetite, her sex drive and she was struggling to maintain her composure. She felt that her normally high standards were dropping. It seemed to her that her life was spiralling alarmingly out of control. Worst of all, she was beginning to believe there was nothing she could do to change the situation. The ingrates next door rose effortlessly above her and, if anything, had seemed to increase their volume. Smug in the conviction that she was Hitler in a thong, that the entire neighbourhood were Fascists and there was nothing anybody could do to stop them, the DGs enjoyed being the clear winners.

Charley found her only relief was at the gym, taking her frustration out on her class, working herself and her group into a near stupor in the hope of relieving the itch of her irritation. Charley would have tried putting her house on the market, but with the recession in full swing, nothing was selling and anyway who would want to buy a house next door to Hell's Zoo?

III

Returning from class one night, feeling morose at the thought of another barrage of noise, Charley drove into the garage, switched off the engine, and exited the car, savagely slamming the garage doors behind her to give the ingrates next door a taste of their own medicine. She paused on the driveway, watching the pale moon flit between the scudding primrose tinted clouds and inhaled the welcome smell of the lavender that was just beginning to bloom in her front garden. She stood quite still for a few moments, simply enjoying the tranquillity of a late spring evening.

Charley stirred. She hesitated. Something was different but she couldn't work out what it was. Taking another lungful of air, she deliberately relaxed her breathing whilst outwardly probing the landscape with her internal antennae.

Something was different. It was quiet. Impossible and yet there it was again, the sound of silence – really quite deafening.

"My God," thought Charley. "They must have gone out." She turned to face her neighbour's house and saw that there were no cars on the driveway. For the first time since forever, the DG's were not at home. Her face relaxed into a delighted grin and she broke into a little samba on the flagstones as her mood changed from one of defensive apprehension at the thought of the noise inevitably waiting for her to one of sunlit goodwill and peace toward all men on earth. Immediately she decided to go for a late night skinny dip in the Jacuzzi whilst listening to her favourite CD before settling down to watch the news and then off to bed. She would break open the Prosecco and relax in the tub – bubbles on bubbles. Perfect.

Fifteen minutes later found Charley relaxing in the hot tub, naked under the foam with a glass of chilled wine by her side; her head comfortably resting against the padded edge of the Jacuzzi and her eyes closed as she listened to her favourite band, Il Divo. Lost in her own wet world and idly fantasising about what she would do if she ever got any of the Italian trio alone, Charley failed to hear the subtle squeak of a patio door opening and the swish of a tail against glass. Seconds later, the gates of Hades swung open.

As Charley's vivid imagination was enjoying unbuttoning the shirt of the darkly attractive Sebastièn, next door's three cats streaked soundlessly over the fence and into her shrubbery for a little late night defecation. As Charley imagined herself whispering something provocative in the Signorno's ear and anticipated his lips moving to meet hers, next door's dogs, free at last from the confinement of the house, began their frenzied barking. Moments later the drill began its whirring, toneless drone. Lights came on in the houses surrounding hers as neighbouring dogs, roused from their slumber, began a howling reprise and children, suddenly robbed of sleep, began to cry in protest. Amidst all the cacophony, the sensual vision that was the topless divo dissolved in an instant as Charley was cruelly catapulted back to reality. Startled from her reverie, she opened her eyes in time to see the curtains in next door's back bedroom twitch and, despite the furore around her, Charley swore she could hear the sound of suppressed giggling from above. From the corner of her eye, she noticed that the black and white one had perched itself on the edge of her patio table and was delicately licking its paws, confident of its absolute right to be in her garden.

The bastards. The absolute fucking bastards! They had set her up. They had set HER up and now they were laughing at her. Watching and laughing. How dare they? How fucking dare they? Who did they think they were? The arrogant, ignorant, sodding peasants.

Fuming, Charley hauled herself ferociously out of the Jacuzzi, barely managing to control the strong urge to unceremoniously shove the intruding cat off its precarious perch. Not bothering with her robe, she strode angrily towards the house, the water streaming down from her naked body to soak the tiles of the patio beneath her feet. She stepped into the house, slammed the garden door behind her, locking it with an angry twist of her wrist and leaving a puddle of frothy water in her wake.

"Enough already!" she fumed. This was too much. This was on purpose. This was untenable."

Charley was not easily provoked, but, once roused, she was a formidable opponent. It was time to change tactics. Not bothering to dress herself, and with aggressive, staccato movements, she brewed herself a pot of her favourite fresh ground Jamaican Blue, quickly grabbed a piece of paper and a pen from the bureau in the hall, scraped a chair back from the kitchen table and sat down. She began with six main headings:

Who? What? When? Why? Where? Which?

Late into the night, she sat and thought and wrote and planned, for once, oblivious to the assault on her ears coming through the walls. Amazingly, it faded into the background as her lists grew and her plans began to take shape.

Whilst she still had not come up with any concrete answers by morning, the first brush strokes of a few potential new strategies were beginning to colour up in her mind. Satisfied at last, she rose from her seat to stretch. Cramp hit first, sending shards of pain up and down her leg muscles. Carefully, she stretched out her stiff limbs, shivering with cold. She looked down at her naked, white flesh and cursed herself for not putting on her robe. Yawning, she meandered down to the bathroom where she took a long, hot shower, towelling herself down briskly. She stood for a moment to watch the sun rise, then crawled under the duvet and snuggled down to sleep, smiling to herself.

It was time to turn up the heat. It was time to fight fire with fire. It was time to take the battle to the enemy.

JAX

I

Well, she'd done it!! Okay not her exactly. To be precise, Izza had done it for her. After several months of angst ridden dithering and several tentative false starts, Jax had finally agreed to join an internet dating site. Well let's face it, she was too old to re-join the Youth Club and she felt it was somehow sad to sit alone in a pub reading a book in the hope that some erstwhile knight in shining armour might possibly ride by and offer to buy her a drink. She wasn't the least bit interested in attending evening classes in Italian cookery or creative writing and there was no way on the planet that she would go to a singles club. So how else was she going to find a man? Ruthlessly, Izza had summed up the situation. Slam dunk!

DesperDates was the very thing, her daughter had assured her, expertly writing her profile. Admittedly, she'd had a brilliant afternoon with several bottles of wine, and several of the girl pals, during which time she was encouraged to preen, parade and pose in a variety of outfits while Fresna clicked away with her new digital camera.

"Try to relax, you've a tendency to hunch those sexy shoulders," she'd advised from behind the lens.

"Suck your stomach in and stick your tits out," ordered Celia, leaning on the dressing table and draining the contents of yet another glass of wine. "Christ Jax, not like that, you look like an overstuffed bouncy castle!"

"Shut up, Ceals," growled Fresna. "You're not helping."

"Focus," commanded Charley, popping her head round from the behind the door to the en-suite where she had been grimacing at the stale contents of Jax's make-up bag. "Just imagine what you'd like to do with the man of your dreams and work from there, just work from there."

"Give me the dominatrix within, Jax, glare at the camera. You got to show the bastards who's in control," encouraged Fresna, moving the camera onto its end to try for a full length shot.

"Stop frowning, it makes you look ancient," mumbled Izza, sitting cross-legged on her mother's bed, head down, fixating on her mobile. Why hadn't he called?

By the time Fresna smiled the satisfaction that signalled the shoot was over, Jax felt exhausted, but the best was yet to come. For another sixty hilarious minutes, the girls joined in, helping themselves to the contents of Jax's wardrobes and pouting shamelessly at the camera until each one of them had at least one passable photograph to take home in memory of a fabulous afternoon. True, Jax had been left with the shambles of her bedroom where it seemed the entire contents of her closets had been spilled in crumpled polycotton ton profusion all over the floor. Jax grimaced. Did she really own that much beige?

Shutting the door firmly on the bombsite that was now her boudoir, the girls spent the evening and several more bottles of wine arguing, debating and giggling over the merits and demerits of the assorted photographs saved on Fresna's Nikon until consensus held sway and Izza quickly posted the best four images of Jax on the net before she could change her mind. She was out there.

There was a close up of head and shoulders to show off Jax's lovely green eyes; there was a saucy shot of her in Tiff's red basque top and what Jax considered to be a too short, short skirt. The third shot offered a full length picture of her in the garden, secateurs in hand, seeming to nonchalantly prune her roses and the fourth showed her walking Celia's dog in the local park. A variety of photographs for the discerning e-gentlemen at the other end of the ether to give them at least a remote e-idea of what they might be e-getting.

So there she was on the net in all her virtual glory, resembling some kind of surreal marketing campaign for the forlorn and dysfunctional. Jax seriously doubted she'd get a hit and that made her feel, at one and the same time, both reassured and anxious. As she lay back on the pillow in the haven of her double bed, contemplating the disorder of her bedroom, she could only keep repeating to herself, "Shit, what have I done?"

II

Incredible! Within twenty-four hours, twenty messages had dropped into her inbox. Jax was overwhelmed and somehow relieved by the attention she was getting from the male hopefuls on DesperDates. Over the next few weeks, it seemed like the whole single male population was interested in her and still the emails kept flowing in. Admittedly most of them weren't local. She had received emails from as far away as the USA, New Zealand and Hong Kong. The days when more than a short bus ride away was considered casting your net too wide were gone and, in the new age of instant communication, it appeared that a girl might be expected to cross the ocean in search of a date. Flushed with e-success, Jax set aside an hour each day to respond to her new far flung fan club. She figured that since they had bothered to contact her, the least she could do was respond.

Jax Log – Play Mate 14:
Jabba the Hut:

Hi there, read your profile and you seem so nice and look so lovely that I thought I would drop you a line. All the best Jabba.

Hi Jabba, thank you for your kind words. How are you getting on with this site? Have you been on here long?

Hi sassy lady, no I only recently joined and you are the first person I contacted. How lucky am I that your profile came up straight away? Love the photo of you in the red. What kind of top is that? Is it underwear? You look really sexy. Xx

Hi Jabba, again thank you for saying such nice things. I'm glad you liked the photo of me. Is there one of you? – It would be great if you could return the favour...?? I'd prefer to see who I'm writing to. Oh and just for info, I am not the kind of person who posts photographs of herself in her undies on the net!!

Hi gorgeous, not one to argue but it looks like a bra to me. Do you have webcam? If you do, I'd love to see you full length wearing that top. What size bra are you anyway? I only wish I could send you my photo but my pc and the dating site just don't seem to be compatible and I'm having difficulty uploading anything. Have you got any other photos of yourself? If so, why not upload them too? Xxx

Jabba, you seem very preoccupied with photos of me and what I look like and this from someone who is not so keen on showing me what he looks like. Anyway enough of this photo stuff – why don't you tell me more about yourself? I notice you are an IT Manager – what do you do exactly? Care to tell me about your hobbies? Maybe how you spend your free time, that kind of thing?

Hi J, my job is really boring. I manage servers offsite for clients. I spend alternate weekends with my kids and I love all sports – more of a spectator these days than a participant though. And I'm into the arts – well, artistic photography, which is why I am so interested in seeing more of you. You really are very photogenic – would you consider modelling for me sometime? I bet you have a drawer full of interesting lingerie for me to snap you in. xxx

Jabba, sorry, is it me? You don't seem to be listening. I said enough of the photo stuff. This is not working for me – you do not seem to want to KNOW anything about me or SAY anything very much about yourself. Good luck with your search. I hope you find what you are looking for.

Jax Log – Playmate 7
Slow boat to China

Hello there my name is Bobby and I work as a Director for a Publishing Company. I would like to get to know you better and will be on this site at 10pm tonight. Be there and let's talk. B

Hi Bobby, thank you for your message. I was unable to log on yesterday evening as I had a previous engagement. Unusual name. Why did you choose Slow Boat to China as a handle? Take care. Jax

Jax, well I did wait for you and was disappointed when you did not appear. I want to talk to you in person. When will you next be online and at what time? Can we cam as I would also like to see what you look like? I called myself that name because my friends tell me I am laid back and easy going – like a slow boat to China. Bobby

Bobby, I usually log on at about 7pm for an hour if I'm home. I should be online on Wednesday evening and can talk to you then. Jax

Wednesday is five-a-side night and I won't be in until 10pm. Can we make it later?

Bobby – sorry missed you again. J

I hope you are not just wasting my time. I waited for you for an hour on Wednesday night from 10pm until 11pm. I will be online on Friday evening at 7pm to talk to you then. Be there. I really want to get to know you better. Bobby xx

Bobby – I'm out Friday night

You are just like all the rest, playing with a man's feelings. I have given you every chance to talk to me and you just have not made the effort. I am now blocking you. Time waster!

Jax Log – Playmate 26
Stargazer125

Hi J, I think you and I would make a great match – pity about the distance. Love the idea of your crazy things.

The craziest thing I ever did was to jump out of a plane at 50,000 feet.

Hi Stargazer, I know just how you feel. I have also flown with that airline☺

J, omg, a sense of humour AND good looks. You are too much.

Stargazer – lol! So many compliments – you are making my head swell. What did you get up to this weekend?

Hi J, Sorry for the delay in replying. Well on Saturday I got up before dawn and went for a ride on the bike. The roads were empty. Everything was quiet and cold. There was a surprisingly heavy frost. I saw the sun come up. When I got home, I cooked myself a huge fry up. What did you do?

Stargazer – compared to that, my weekend was boring. Don't you just love the look of frosted cobwebs? You must have been famished when you got back – no wonder you needed a fry up. Maybe one day, I can join you on one of your dawn raids?????

Hi J, wow! Do you know how to ride pillion? Fantastic. I sometimes come your way for meetings. How about I look you up when I am next your way? Here's my mobile. Text me – weekday evenings are best. Sometimes my mobile is switched off when I am with clients, but keep trying xx

Stargazer, great to talk to you in person Thursday night. Missed you online this weekend. Maybe you were out on the bike????

Jax Log – Playmate 37
Soulm8

Hi there Jacqueline, I just felt I had to get in touch with you. I really enjoyed reading your profile. You seem like a woman after my own heart. You look beautiful in your photograph, but you sound like a real gentle and sweet lady. I am a construction engineer with an 8 year old daughter. My wife died four years ago of breast cancer and I have been through a tough time, but I feel I am now ready to reach out to find the woman of my dreams. I am looking for my soul mate, for someone I can share the rest of my life with; someone who is happy to be a homemaker and help me care for my daughter. Does that sound like something you would like to do? I do hope you get in touch. I am honest, reliable, hardworking and 100% genuine. Yours Desmond, Georgia, USA

Dear Desmond, thank you for getting in touch. I am sorry to hear about your wife. It must have been very difficult for your daughter to lose her mother when she was only four. I don't know whether I would call myself sweet and whether or not I am a woman after your own heart remains to be seen. My own children have grown and flown and I can't say that I am looking to be stepmother to anyone at this stage, but thank you for your compliments. The USA is too far for any kind of real relationship don't you think? Happy to be penfriends though. Tell me more about your life in the States. Regards Jacqueline

Dear Jacqueline, I knew I was right about you. Your honesty shines through and I am looking for a really honest woman to share my life with. Please do not put yourself down – I am certain you are a very sweet lady. I too am a very honest, very genuine man. Life has been hard for me but although I will never forget my wonderful wife, I am ready to move on and believe you are the woman of my dreams, the woman I can build a future

*with. Do not worry about being a mother again –
I am sure my daughter will love you. My email
address is des4certain@xxxxx.com. Please put my
addy into your contacts so we can IM each other.
Desmond xxx*

Dear Desmond, I have added you to my account. Not
sure about the practicalities of this given the time
difference – there are not going to be many windows
when we can talk directly to each other. Never mind, we
can still email each other. As I said, happy to be penfriends
and learn about your life in the States, but anything more
would be impractical. Take care. Jax

*Darling, do not worry about the details. We are
meant to be together. When I look at your beautiful face
and the light shining in your eyes, I feel so uplifted. You
have made an incredible impression on my life. I wake
up singing; I whistle throughout the day and go to work
happy. My friends have noticed a difference in me
and ask what is happening. I have told them all about
you and they rejoice at the joy within me. And
all because of you. When I take little Aimee to church,
I go down on my knees to thank God that I have
found you. I believe in the sanctity of marriage and hope
you do too. I cannot wait for us to be together. Aimee
sends her love. Goodnight my angel, your Desmond
xxxxx*

Desmond, whoa, slow down. We are barely off first
base – how can someone you hardly know give you such
joy? I think you are running before you can walk and
giving me all kinds of attributes that I simply do not
possess. Please stop. J

*My darling, you are worrying unnecessarily. The
Lord has set you aside for me. I know it and I thank him*

for you and all that you are from the bottom of my soul. I just know that we will be happy together. I understand that this is all new and strange for you, but I have great faith and belief in our future together. You will make me a wonderful wife and I will be a faithful, supportive husband. We will have a beautiful church wedding and a marvellous life together. Aimee is so excited for us both. All my friends are looking forward to meeting you.

Desmond, please stop this. It is ridiculous. I am NOT coming to America and furthermore since I am only just out of a relationship, I am not ready, nor do I want, to get married. And what makes you think I desire a church wedding? I am an atheist. Jax

Oh my love, please do not say that. My religion is very important to me. I would very much like to welcome you into my community and into my faith. The Lord walks with me every day and He has brought you to me. Do not worry, my angel, I will assist in bringing you to Him. He will be in our marriage and in our hearts forever. Trust in me as I trust in you and all will be well. I love you with all my heart. This weekend I took Aimee to our log cabin in the hills and we walked in the forest and spent quality time together. I cannot wait to share quality time with you. Your own Desmond xx

My angel, I have not heard from you in days. Are you sick? Are you hurt? I am worrying about you. Please stay in touch with me. Love Desmond xx

Jacqueline, where have you gone to? Please respond. I care about you. D x

Desmond, I have not been in touch because I find all these declarations of love and marriage flattering but unrealistic. We have not met. We don't know each other except for a few emails. How can you love someone you don't know? How can you want to marry me – you have not met me? You do not know anything about me or I about you. You have a responsibility to your daughter. You cannot just bring a stranger into your home and expect Aimee to treat her like a mother. Get it into your head. I am not coming to America and I am not marrying you. Jacqueline.

Darling, you just have cold feet that's all. People with little or no belief in the Lord find it difficult to understand the confidence that those of us in the Lord are able to show when we put our trust in him. I will slow down and try to understand that you are not yet of my faith, but you will understand and you will rejoice when we are together. I look at your beautiful face and know that our life together will be so happy. You do not see with the eyes of faith like I do so how can you know? I must understand that and make allowances for you. I have just brought Aimee home from school and am fixing her some supper but I am thinking of you. A friend is coming over to look after her for me tonight as I have to go back to work to complete some paperwork for the bridge my Company is building. I cannot wait for you to come over and count the days till you say I do. I know you will come to love me as I love you. Desmond xx

Dear Desmond, you are building a bridge – how fantastic. I would not know where to begin. What else have you built? Do you own the Construction Company? Do you work for it? I hope Aimee enjoyed her supper. Jax

My angel, I long for the day when you tell me you love me. I just know it will be soon but in the meantime, my

*love for you must be enough for both of us. I own my
Company and I have many employees. It is a big
responsibility. We have built many things here, but this
bridge is the biggest project so far. I enjoy the work that
I do and one day I hope to build you a house here in my
town. In the meantime, good night my angel. Your
Desmond xxx*

Jax Log – Playmate 46
Intellygent

*Hi Jax, thank you messaging me. What can I tell
you about myself? I run my own business. I suppose
you could call me a cross between a scientist and
an entrepreneur. I was born in Portugal, but brought
up and educated in the states. I am into heavy metal
music – particular favourite is Led Zeppelin, but I also
enjoy a wide range from jazz to Leonard Cohen. I am a
dedicated triathlete. I don't watch a lot of TV
except Frasier, which is a must. At weekends, I usually
have my kids over part of the time – I have two,
12yrs and 14yrs, both girls. I collect classic bikes
and am the proud owner of a 1930's Rudge, which
I am currently restoring. What about you? Any kids?
Any hobbies?*

Hi Intellygent, thank you for getting back to me.
I used to enjoy Leonard Cohen back in the day when
I was at college, but must admit that I haven't heard his
music for ages. I have three kids, but only the youngest
lives with me. My main hobby is amateur dramatics and
I am currently in the process of getting fit so I can be
found down the gym most evenings after work. I am
a partner in a holistic therapy business. No idea what a
Rudge is but it sounds fascinating. Have you restored it

yet? Do you compete in triathlons? Refresh my memory – is it running, cycling and swimming? J

Hi J, yep, that's right. I compete within my age group both regionally and nationally. The Rudge is a motorbike and it's currently in bits on the floor of my garage. My goal is to put it back together one day. The amateur dramatics sounds like fun – what sorts of things do you put on? By the way, everyone calls me PJ.

Well, PJ, I am a member of two groups. I prefer comedy parts to straight, but you have to take what you can get. I am not very good at singing, but I do love working an audience. One group concentrates mainly on serious dramas or musicals and the other does pantomimes, variety shows and comedies. We are currently rehearsing a Whodunnit – care to buy a ticket? J.

Well, J, maybe I will. Where are you playing? I am currently off work sick, having dropped part of the Rudge on my foot while working on the engine and can only get about on crutches at the moment. Bored as hell and spending my time watching repeats of Frasier. The woods at the back of my house are looking particularly tempting at this time of year and I am missing my runs. PJxx

PJ, Sorry to hear about your accident. How long will you be on crutches? The woods sound wonderful. Is that where you do your running? Maybe I should pop over to see you and bring a basket of goodies but then again is it safe or do I need to look out for the Big Bad Wolf? Jxx

Hey there Red Riding Hood. What goodies will you bring in your basket? Don't worry about the big bad wolf – that's me!! Xx

Oh my Mr Wolf, what big ears you have and what big teeth and oh Mr Wolf what a big er tail you have....lol... RRH xx

Jax's Log – Playmate 71
Looking for LoobyLoo

Hi Jax, my name is Andy. I am twenty four years of age and looking for a long term relationship with an older woman. I know you will say I am too young for you but I have never had a girlfriend of my own age. I have always been attracted to older women because they are so confident and so sexy. Please email me back. Andy xx

Hi Andy, well I must say I was very flattered to receive your email. Call me ageist, but I cannot possibly see why anyone as young and good looking as you are would be wasting your time with someone old enough to be his mother. But thanks for the boost and good luck in your search. Jax

Hi Jax, thank you for mailing me. I know you are old enough to be my mother, but believe me you do not look like my mother. You are incredible for your age. You have such a sexy face and a great figure. Mmmm nice curves. I would be proud to be your boyfriend. All the girls of my age are such airheads. Mature women like you are much more interesting in every way aside from which they are very experienced in bed. Andy xx

Omg, I cannot believe I am even keeping up correspondence with you. I have a son only slightly older than you and I can't help thinking this is all wrong. But I must say you are gorgeous. Jax x

Hi Jax, I am glad you think I am gorgeous. I am also young and fit with plenty of energy. I think we could be very good together and there is a lot you can teach me.

I would be very willing to be your slave, do whatever you tell me to do and if I am a bad boy you can spank me. When can I come over? Love Andy xxxx

III

It wasn't long before Jax wised up. She began by generally sifting through her messages, checking they contained both a clear image and a properly written profile before deciding whether or not to reply. New hits without photos, she ignored, presuming they must be terminally ugly, chronically overweight, frighteningly disfigured or married. She had heard every excuse under the sun for not uploading an image, ranging from "I don't want the girls at work to know I am on here" (aka I'm married) to "my IT system isn't compatible with the site, but I am happy to email you a private pic" (aka I'm married) passing through to "I have to use my works computer and am forbidden from uploading images" (aka I'm married). It was an interesting fact that the overwhelming number of men from whom she had heard described themselves as "IT Manager", but they apparently could not figure out the interface between the differing software.

The spring had proved a fast and incredibly fun learning curve for Jax. She had learnt to read the agendas behind the profiles, to spot the losers, the control freaks, the perverts and the players. In turn, she had learned to give as good as she got. Late at night in her office at home and with neat, ruthless efficiency, she flirted, lured and led on married men claiming single status, but only virtually available during office hours or in the wee small hours of the night and never at weekends. It was amazing how many single 40+ 'IT Managers' there were in the

UK. Most of them seemed to be on DesperDates and most of them had problems uploading a photo. More amazing was the fact that most of them had to work a 48 hour weekend because, of course, that's when the servers were quiet and no-one was in the office. Furthermore, it seemed that most of these offices seemed to be situated in some remote part of the planet, which swallowed up its IT workforce, rendering them largely invisible from Friday evening, but, come Monday morning, back they were online, large as life, and well up for that midweek date just as long as it ended up with coffee at your place with your knickers off. To Jax, the most amazing thing of all was that each one of the idiots believed they were the only one spinning the line.

Then there were the dates. Within six months, Jax had met about ten men. None of them pressed any buttons, but she loved the excitement of those first encounters – what to wear, what to say, what to do? Surprisingly, all of the men she met wanted a second meeting, which did wonders for her self-esteem, sadly battered by her failed relationship.

IV

Jax ought to have despised her ex. Despite having a reputation for being a good old boy, he was in reality, a cuckoo. He made his home in someone else's nest, contributing as little as possible and taking as much as he could get and, all the while, playing Mr. Nice Guy. Discovered, he moved on. Jax had loved him deeply and it had taken her a long time to wake up to him, but eventually, as with all his relationships, the lady worked it out and he moved on to the next mother hen.

From time to time, Jax bumped into him in town. At first, it hurt but then, as autumn gave way to winter, then spring and summer, whilst the ache was still present, it had diminished to a grey shadow somewhere to her right and behind her. It was no longer the all-consuming, ever hungry monster that it had been a few short months ago.

For the first time in her entire life, Jax was living without a partner. In the beginning, she had hated it. It scared her to be alone in the house; she felt she would not be able to cope without the company of a significant other, but it hadn't taken her long to realise that, not only was she wrong, she could actually do better on her own. Over the past few months, she had learned that there was an enormous difference between feeling lonely and being alone. She surprised herself by discovering that she actively enjoyed the latter and could strategise against the former.

The huge double bed in which she had forged many a happy memory with her ex was now totally hers. To begin with, she had felt able only to take up a tiny corner of it, unsure of her right to so much space. Later on, she relished sleeping slap bang in the middle and taking up as much room as she liked. Sometimes she threw off the duvet and lay naked on the top of the cover, spreading herself out like a star and luxuriating in owning every wonderful inch of its cocoon-like support. Furthermore, there was no one to grumble if she snored or took too much duvet or got up umpteen times to go to the toilet. There was no one else's kit in her bathroom, no nasty boxer shorts in the wash basket and two fitted, double wardrobes for her to fill all by herself. She did not need to think what to make for supper; hell, she didn't even eat supper if she didn't feel like it. Housework took minutes and could be done at any time or, better still, not at all. She found she could go where she liked, when she liked and with whom she liked. Even better, she could come home if she liked, when she liked and with whom she liked.

She had had to learn how to decorate and remembered clearly her first time with a paintbrush. Her ex had a penchant for bright colours and their house was a rainbow of rooms – deep azure blue bedroom, bright mustard cloakroom, and cerise pink lounge. Jax, herself, preferred more subtle shades or contrasts. Having been told for too many years that decorating was not for the ladies and that 'he would get round to it when he had the time, just stop the nagging', Jax was naturally a little apprehensive about the task ahead. She had taken herself to the local DIY store, spent ages reading the labels on the various cans of paints and had finally chosen a soft, dove grey to cover over the ghastly tangerine currently resident in her en-suite. She knew it would take more than one coat. Loading her car boot with a variety of brushes, rollers, masking tape and white spirit, she brought her parcels home. They stood on the kitchen dresser for over a week while she plucked up the nerve to use them. As she worked the paint into the wall, she wondered how on earth anyone could find this difficult. In her imagination, she had a vision of the house collapsing around her at the first lick of paint. She was even more astonished at how little time it took, even with three coats and how easily all the bathroom accessories had screwed back into the wall. She was rather proud of her ability with a screwdriver and had moved on to become an enthusiastic amateur with the electric drill. When she finally got round to decorating her bedroom (a light, warm coffee), she put up the new curtain rail all by herself without falling off the ladder or damaging any the walls. How gullible she had been; how vibrant and alive she now felt.

Admittedly, she missed the sex. Making love with her partner had been fantastic and she wondered if sex would ever be fantastic again. Her current situation was becoming increasingly 'not open for business' such was the paucity of talent in her vicinity! In an effort to pep up her love life, one Saturday morning, Fresna took her on a hush hush mission to a shopping centre three towns away where Jax hoped she would not be recognised. They were on the hunt for the latest in 'discreet battery products for ladies'. After a period of slightly confused browsing at the goods on offer and much poking and giggling, Jax had chosen something rather large in a nasty shade of pink that would send a real man off to the chemist for a large bottle of After Sun or some antibiotics! Fresna's choice had been a rather vulgar deep violet colour, which she promptly named Pervy Peter Purple. Fresna's open and self-deprecating approach to the whole venture had done wonders to offset the lurking feelings of shame fluttering away in a remote corner of Jax's stomach. She'd never needed to do anything like this before and she was surprised at how guilty it made her feel. Laughing, Fresna told her to get over herself and to stop behaving like she was still at convent school.

A few days later, Fresna, for whom, at least to Jax, everything seemed to come easily, phoned to ruefully let her know that she had discovered that she was allergic to Pervy Peter and so her assisted encounter with her intimate self had turned into a total non-starter. Ever practical, Fresna had insisted on debating the merits of selling the useless tosser on EBay, but Jax had managed to persuade her that, in this particular case, the phrase, 'one careful owner' might be seen as tasteless.

It had taken Jax several attempts to even get to first base with her machine. The girls fell about laughing at the hilarious account of her 'first time'! She had woken from a deep sleep, feeling horny but with no one to turn to. Remembering her recent purchase, she had leapt out of bed, and felt her way to the bureau opposite the bed where she fumbled around in the bottom drawer until she found her 'inflexible friend'. Returning to her bed, in the half dark, she took it out of its box and felt around for the on/off button. It took her a while to find the right switch, but no matter how she tried, she could not turn the damn thing on.

"Bugger me," interjected Celia, guffawing loudly. "You couldn't turn it on? What hope have you got with a proper bloke if you can't even arouse your vibrator?" she quipped. She was laughing so much at her own joke that she fell off her chair and landed in a heap on the floor where she curled into a ball and continued to giggle. "Oh Jax," she cried between bursts of laughter, "What are you like? You couldn't make this up." When Celia's fit of hysterics had quietened to a gentle series of hiccoughs, Jax continued with her story.

After several futile attempts, trying to switch on the unresponsive machine, it finally dawned on her that she had forgotten to put in any batteries. It had then taken her fifteen frustrating minutes in the gloom to finally get all three in the right way up, by which time she was bored and past caring. She lay back on her pillow exhausted. She smiled to herself as she recalled her actual first time when, at the age of seventeen, her teenage boyfriend, also a virgin, had spent so long fumbling with his condom, she had lost interest so they had sheepishly crawled out from under the hedgerow and gone to the chip shop instead, returning a few hours later for a second, and this time, successful attempt. "Woohoo," she thought and decided she should try frying herself some chips, but the cosiness of her bed was too appealing and the idea was swallowed up by sleep.

"Why ever didn't you switch the light on?" asked Fresna. Jax shrugged and couldn't answer. She turned to Celia, still giggling in the corner, and knew she was going to get teased relentlessly. It would take her a long time to live this one down.

V

Jax parked her car in the centre of her driveway and made her way indoors. Throwing her coat over the banister, she ran upstairs into the spare bedroom and switched on her laptop. While she waited for the sluggish machine to wake itself up, she brewed herself a cup of coffee. She had forty five minutes before she was due in class and she wanted to read her emails before she left.

Excellent! She had five messages and one new hit from Desper Dates. She checked the newcomer out first. No photo – no interest. She deleted that message without reading it.

Young Andy was back. She hadn't heard from him in weeks, but here he was again, begging her to let him take her out and then bring him home for some punishment. As if!

An IT Manager named John, who had taken her to dinner a couple of times, had emailed asking when they would be able to meet again, but the truth was she just didn't fancy him. She considered her options. She could accept and keep the poor guy dangling till he worked it out for himself, but then again, maybe it was better to let him go. In the end, she opted for leaving it a few days before answering.

The professor had been in touch again. At least, he started out by telling her he was a Professor of English, but further probing revealed that he was actually a village parson, trapped in a sexless marriage and looking for a pity fuck. She had spelt it out to him weeks ago that she was not prepared to go there, but they kept in touch because they shared a love of literature, in particular poetry, and she enjoyed their 'over the airwaves' conversations. He never failed to steer the topic towards sex and then would offer to come over to ease her lonely nights. She had to give him an A+ for trying; poor sod.

PJ had emailed. Jax really liked the guy, but he had proved to be very elusive in the meeting up stakes. She assumed he must be married. Under normal circumstances, she would have blocked him ages ago, but he had turned out to be both extremely intelligent and highly articulate. Jax was delighted. His message signalled the next instalment of a prolonged game of Sexy Jackanory involving vulnerable, yet horny damsels in distress, lascivious wolves and picnic baskets. Metaphor piled upon metaphor when PJ was online. Jax looked at the clock on the wall above her PC. Time was pressing. Reluctantly, she decided not to open PJ's message. It was sure to be filthy and get her juices flowing. She would keep it for later; something to relish just before bedtime – better than cocoa! She was glad she had remembered to buy spare batteries – she would be certain to need them tonight.

Her final message was from Clingy Desmond, no doubt declaring his undying love and asking her to give up her life, move to the States, become mother to his child and rattle a tambourine in church on Sundays. Not a chance. She opened his email and began reading.

My angel, I pray this email finds you healthy and happy. I have been thinking of you all day and look forward to the day when we can be together as God intends. Today has been a very difficult day for me. The IRS has been in touch and it seems I must find $50,000 in the next two weeks to keep my business afloat. As a single parent running my own company, you will understand how difficult it is for me to manage this. So today I went to Church and I got down on my knees and thanked God for you Jacqueline, for the fact that I have you to share this burden with me, to support me in my hour of need. I know that with you beside me, I can overcome this hurdle. It is very important that I pay on time otherwise I will not only lose my business, but also I will have to lay off the men, some of whom have been with me for a very long time. The problem is that I am unable to get my hands on that kind of money at such short notice. If I could get a loan of the money, even just part of the sum, just for a few short weeks, I would be able to keep my business running, my workers employed, finish building the bridge that has been at the centre of my life for these many months and pay for you to come over to see me. I trust in your help and advice at this time, my angel. We are in this thing together my darling so surely we can come up with a solution that will benefit *both of our long term futures. I know, I just know, my sweet angel, that you will help me. Trusting always in the Lord. Ever yours, Desmond.*

Jax read the email twice over, chewing her bottom lip as she did so. Was she reading what she thought she was reading? She needed to think this through very carefully.

IZZA

I

She was struggling into a pair of jeans in a dark corner of a Next changing room when it came through; ping, the text that changed their lives. She was to drop everything and come now, he needed her, where was she, he'd collect her, hurry up. And she did drop everything, throw on her clothes, run out of the changing room, race across the precinct to the car and into his waiting arms. And she mutely listened to all that he had to say and passively went with him to the garage and sat quietly while he explained the situation to the salesman, who duly filled out the forms and took his commission.

They had only bought a car together! A brand new car together!

She couldn't believe they'd done it. Sorted the finance, signed the paperwork, shaken hands with the Deputy Manager, picked up the keys and left the showroom in a blur of exhaust fumes and grinding gears, laughing hysterically all the way to his flat and straight into his bed for a quickie before he drove her home to her dad's place because there was live footy on at the Vic and his name was on the first round.

It didn't matter that she couldn't drive.
It didn't matter that it was her signature on the form.
It didn't matter that they had given her bank account details.

It didn't matter that the sex was over in minutes.
It didn't matter that she was home alone all night.
It didn't matter that it was a week before she next heard
from him.
Did it?

II

Izza had met Tony through a friend nine months
previously. She was seventeen and a half; he was
twenty-one. He was of medium height with brown hair,
hazel eyes and a wide smile. They flirted over Facebook
for several weeks before she finally agreed to date him.

He came to collect her in his car. That would be a first.

He took her out to dinner. No one had ever done that
before.

He behaved like the perfect gentleman. No one had
ever done that before either!

He showed an intense interest in her and her family.
Nor that!

He walked her home and gave her a chaste goodnight
kiss on the doorstep. Gulp!

He sent her a medium sized bouquet the following
afternoon. Double gulp!

He charmed both her mother and her father.
Unheard of!

He had a six pack. Yo!

He texted her morning, noon and night until she
finally agreed to be his girlfriend. They began seeing each
other regularly and were sleeping together by the end of
that month. He was adoring, attentive, fun, fit, sexy and
a bully, but she loved him.

And she couldn't see what was staring her in the face.
But then none of us do. Do we?

III

For six months, Tony played the part of the perfect boyfriend. He took her to the cinema, bowling, to the pub, shopping, to dinner. He bought her a silver necklace with a heart on it and, a month later, a matching bracelet. He took her for a weekend break at a Travelodge just outside Southend. He chewed the fat with her dad over a pint at the local. He charmed her mother by helping with the washing up after Sunday dinner. He played in the garden for hours with her brother's step daughter. Even her hard-to-please sister thought he was okay.

Everyone believed he was one of the good guys and he was warmly welcomed into the family. Izza had snared herself a keeper. She hugged herself. She knew this was IT!

The family discussed him openly. Wasn't it a shame about his own parents? His mother had turned her back on him, his brother had disowned him. His father had committed suicide and Tony, poor bugger, had been the one to find him, hanging, black tongued, from the rafters of his upstairs maisonette. Jax remembered seeing it in the papers and mentioned it to Izza's father, her first husband. What a dreadful business. Her sympathies went out to the young man. No wonder he sometimes seemed a bit odd, a bit reclusive, a bit needy. He was only twenty one after all. What he needed was a warm, friendly, family environment.

And then he hit Izza.

It wasn't his fault of course. It had been an accident. He hadn't meant to hurt her. She had provoked him. He apologised profusely. It would never happen again.

Tearfully, she forgave him and he made her a giant cup of hot chocolate with marshmallows. He even missed the first fifteen minutes of the game in order to go to the corner shop and bring back her favourite cream egg as a treat. He didn't want her getting fat, mind, but these were exceptional circumstances. After the game, he took her to bed and spent the next twenty minutes persuading her that coming too soon meant in fact that he loved her. He told her that he would have liked to take her to dinner to make it up to her, but, given the state of her face, he felt it best to borrow a score from her purse and ring up for take-out instead.

A couple of days later, he turned up on her father's doorstep. Her father, who wanted to land the little sod one of his own, was persuaded over a bevy at the Vic that it was a one off; an aberration. He hadn't meant to give his daughter a black eye. He would never do it again.

Tony took flowers round to her mother's place where, over a cup of tea and a ginger biscuit, he begged for forgiveness and, as the tears streamed down his cheeks, he looked so forlorn and pathetic that she almost believed him. Almost.

Because no one ever slams their fist into someone else's eye by mistake.

Do they?

IV

Over the next few months, Izza changed beyond recognition. She stopped spending time with her friends or with her family. She spent long periods alone, sometimes not bothering to get dressed. She spend days trudging around the house in the same shabby pair of pyjamas, curling up under the duvet and watching puerile drivel on TV. She became sullen, withdrawn and unkempt. She was on edge all the time, defensive about Tony. Whenever anyone tried to talk to her about him, she blew up in their faces. They just didn't understand him. They hated him. He had done nothing wrong. It had all been her fault. It was her family's stuff. They were the ones with the problem. Leave him alone. Leave us alone. Leave me alone.

Her life, and by consequence that of her family's, was dominated by her mobile phone. Its mere buzz could change the atmosphere in a millisecond from tranquil to ecstatic; from calm to despair. The rollercoaster ride of Izza's love life was beginning to grate on her family. They had all learned to be afraid of the Nokia; to be very afraid of the Nokia.

On good days, he texted her constantly, demanding proof of her love, her fidelity, her loyalty, her availability and her obedience, which usually ended with Izza taking a sneaky trip to the hole in the wall for a quick withdrawal. On bad days, he didn't text her at all.

Her mother tried to reason with her. Her sister suggested she talk to the doctor. Her father offered to pay for her to see a counsellor. They were rewarded with shrugs, cold shoulders and slamming doors.

They tried paying her more attention, encouraging her out of herself. Her mother took her shopping and they spent a wonderful hour choosing Izza a new outfit. While her mother queued at the checkout, Izza received a text. By the time, the clothes were paid for, Izza had disappeared. No explanation, no apology. Tony came first.

They tried ignoring her, leaving her to her own devices, struggling not to comment on the disgusting state of her jogging bottoms or her lack of hygiene. They left her to prepare her own food so she just raided the fridge and took whatever was there. Either that or she simply failed to eat at all.

Nothing worked. Izza was hooked and she simply couldn't care less about anything else. Whatever it was that Tony had and, for the life of them, no one in her immediate circle, could imagine what IT might be, he had it and she wanted it. Even if it meant being broke, being crushed, being manipulated, being ignored, being used or being hit.

Just when the family thought things couldn't get any worse, they did.

Shortly after her eighteenth birthday, Tony took her to a garage in a nearby town and persuaded her to buy him a new car. It was her name on the finance and his name on the logbook. The fact that she was only working part time at the time and could not afford the repayments was immaterial nor was it relevant that the paperwork was faulty and nothing had been dated. According to the powers that be, the debt was hers and she had to pay it.

Of course, Tony meant to contribute, but somehow he never had anything spare at the end of the month and so her father ended up paying the lion's share whilst Izza grudgingly gave what she could out of her minimum wage at the supermarket.

Three months later, the car was mysteriously torched on Tony's driveway. Nothing was ever proved and no arsonist brought to justice. Tony pocketed the money from the insurance pay out, bought a decent second hand car and dumped Izza till the heat died down. Everyone believed that Tony had set fire to the car himself – everyone that is except Izza, who blamed her father for the break up because he had gone to the Police to discuss what he considered to be a clear case of fraud. Nothing could be proved and so, with very little choice in the matter, Izza's father stoically continued to pay the instalments. Despite the petulance and the indifference, he never failed to support his daughter and continued to hope for a happy ending.

Surely, it couldn't get any worse. Oh, but it could!

One morning, to the horror of her family, Izza announced her decision to move in with Tony. She packed her clothes and what few possessions she had and left the house without a backward glance. As it turned out, it didn't last more than a month. Neither of them knew how to look after themselves let alone each other. Just when her mother had got used to her absence, she would hear the scratch of the key in the lock and the swish of an opening door. Jax would look up and there would stand Izza, make-up smudged, heartbroken, suitcase in hand, swearing it was over. She vowed she wanted no more to do with him. He was a filthy, two timing slime bag, he was a domineering, retarded weasel, he was a bastard waste of space. And she was never going back.

Two weeks later, she was stuffing her rucksack into the back of his car, made up, loved up and fucked up. Only he understood her completely; only he satisfied her needs unreservedly; only he knew how to love her. Her family were interfering, overbearing shitbags, old fashioned, psychotic control freaks, narrow minded, pig headed arseholes and she wanted nothing to do with them ever again. She was never coming back.

Until next time.

V

Izza had been persuaded out to a Candle Party with her sister on the evening her world fell apart. She was taking a short cut through the local park on her way home when it happened. She was surprised to recognise Tony's car in a deserted corner of the grounds. Astonishing, given that he told her he was working overtime that evening. His car should have been at least fifteen miles away at the back of the golf club. Izza immediately decided that he must have lent it to someone. How else could it have got there?

She moved a little closer to the vehicle, which seemed to be rocking from side to side. The windows were all steamed up and she thought she could hear muffled snorts and wheezes from the inside of the car. She pulled away, anxious. She leaned in closer, intrigued. Her heart was thumping in her chest. She knew. She didn't want to know.

Her sister, on the other hand, knew and did want to know. She marched straight up to the car, wrenched the passenger door open to find Tony and, what she later referred to as, 'that total slapper', making out on the front passenger seat.

Without thinking things through, Izza's sister firmly grabbed a hank of the topless girl's hair and yanked, thus uncoupling the hapless pair. Barely conscious of her own strength, she pulled the girl right out of the car and then suddenly let go, dropping her screaming to the ground. Without pausing for breath, she reached into the car and thumped Tony twice to the side of the head, shocking him with her viciousness. Despite the difference in size, she then hoiked the boy effortlessly out of the car and onto the grass beside his shocked lover. She slammed the door of the car shut, stepped neatly between the two stunned figures on the ground and moved round to the driver side where she deftly removed the keys from the ignition, locking the car with a double click of the fob and leaving the petrified half naked duo exposed to the elements. Walking briskly away from the car, without a backward glance, she threw the keys into the brook that rimmed the far edge of the park. She looked up. It was beginning to rain and the first fat drops were smacking her face. She felt as if she had just woken up.

It was then that she remembered Izza and turned back to comfort her, but Izza had disappeared. Whilst she herself felt delighted to have uncovered Tony's nasty little secret, her heart bled for her little sister. She began to search the park, calling her sister's name and ignoring the pleading and the shouting from the two semi-clad people huddled against the car, trying to shelter from the rain. Alarmed, she poked amongst the bushes and shrubs that fringed the edge of the green. In the end, she decided Izza must have run home and went to find her. She needed to know her sister was okay. To her dismay, Izza wasn't there. She had not gone round to her father's and increasingly frantic phone calls revealed that none of her friends had seen her either. Izza had disappeared.

She was gone for three days. Her family were beside themselves with worry and rang every one they could think of? Had they seen Izza? Had they heard from her? Did they know where she was? They visited their local police station and spoke to the Duty Sergeant, who calmly filled out a missing person's report, said he would be in touch and then politely showed them the door. Outmanoeuvred and not even slightly reassured, they stood outside the station talking over their options and watched in amazement as the officer concerned walked out of the door, got into his patrol car and, giving them a cheery wave, drove in the direction of the high street, returning ten minutes later with a carrier bag full of fish and chips. Muttering something about tax payer's money, Izza's father stomped mulishly home.

Just as her mother was sitting down to a quick microwave lasagne before making yet another pointless drive round the streets to look for her daughter, Jax heard the familiar sound of a key in the lock and the gentle swish of the door and there stood Izza – unwashed, unkempt and famished.

Jax's relief was palpable. She simply folded her face in her arms and wept. To her amazement, her daughter gave her a big hug and apologised for causing a fuss. Then she put the kettle on and made her mother a cup of tea. Jax dried her eyes and watched as Izza moved quietly around the kitchen. When her mother had calmed down, Izza borrowed her phone and called her father to let him know she was back. He came straight round. She assured her worried parents that she was perfectly okay and asked if she could make herself a sandwich. Her parents looked at each other puzzled. Who had stolen their daughter? Well, whoever it was, thank God for them because they vastly preferred this version of her to the one they had had to endure before. Then again, they told themselves, it might not last. Gently, they tried to get her to talk.

But no matter how many times they asked her, begged her and even tried to wheedle her, Izza simply refused to tell them where she had been, what she had done or how she had coped.

When he heard she was back, Tony sent a friend round to her place of work to let her know he was sorry. It was a one off. It would never happen again. He would meet her at the usual place at eight o'clock that night. Perhaps she would like to go for a curry. He would pay.

For once, Tony was on time. Izza stood him up.

SLY

I

Sylvester had always known he was different. He couldn't quite put his finger on the reasons why – he just knew. He had never shown the slightest interest in the Dinky cars his father had brought home each Friday payday, preferring instead to sit quietly beside his mother, feeling the fabric of whatever it was she was stitching as she sat in front of the old Singer sewing machine in the back room where the light was strongest.

Despite his sturdy frame and endless stamina, he refused to join the junior football team and showed not the slightest interest in either cricket or rugby. In vain did his father try to encourage his son's interest in sport. In the end, he gave up, pocketed his dream of ever walking down the street with his son on a Saturday afternoon to watch the local team beat the pants off the opposition and tried not to feel rejected. He struggled to understand why his only child preferred messing about with scraps of material.

The child had shown such an interest in his mother's work that she had finally given up and secretly bought him a doll. Sly spent hours cutting and gluing, stitching and sewing, turning the tiny scraps of stuff his mother could spare into fabulous creations for the tiny puppet. In fact, it absorbed him. If there were no bits and pieces to be found, then he would pore over his mother's enormous button box, sorting and sizing her fabulous collection. He loved the shiny ones best and squirreled them away into his bedroom where he began to build a small collection of his own, which he hid under the dresser out of sight. Late at night, when his parents were asleep, he would often open the box and run his fingers through the pile. He just loved the feel of them rippling under his fingers.

It didn't take his father long to decide that his son had to be a pansy. His mother scolded her husband gently and told him that Sly was just in touch with his feminine side and implored him to leave well alone. She was sure it would all work itself out.

As far as his father was concerned, his son's only saving grace was his passion for the sea. He loved anything to do with it and would happily abandon his sewing for a trip to the coast where he would immediately take off his socks and sandals, roll up his trousers and wade into the shallow, foaming waters at the edge of the sandy beach.

Satisfied, he would turn his attention to the boats sailing past because it wasn't just the sea that tugged at Sly's heart, boats did too – all kinds of boats – old fashioned, hand-made rowing boats with sleek oars and brass trimmings, dazzling white, multi-storied cruise liners, thronged with sightseers, brightly painted tin barges decorated with assorted pots of gardenias, enormous, ugly cargo boats stacked from end to end with containers – from riverboats to sailboats to motorboats – you name it Sly was fascinated by them.

When Sly had had his fill of watching the sea and the boats floating by, he would run back to his parents sitting in their stripy deckchairs, fall at their feet and turn his attention to the sand spread out before him. Yet here again, he had to be different. The lonely, single cast of an upturned bucket or the slightly more adventurous forts, trimmed with flags built by the other children were not enough for him. He designed amazing castles several storeys high, beautifully decorated with shells and bits and pieces of debris that he found scattered along the shore. To the astonishment of his parents and their neighbours on the beach, his creations showed great imagination and grew, as if by magic, before their very eyes. Sly was clearly talented. His father shrugged and tried not to wish that his only son preferred rugby.

Although Sly was often teased by his friends for his unusual hobbies, he was never ever bullied. Somehow, it was his openness about being different that seemed to protect him. He never showed the slightest sign of embarrassment for his love of dressmaking and design or for his attraction to the sea, but then again he never felt the need to talk about his hobbies either.

Sometimes his schoolmates would call round and suggest a game of soldiers in the nearby woods or an apple scrumping escapade and sometimes he would go with them, striving desperately to enjoy himself, but the truth was that he loathed the very physicality his friends seemed to stir up in one another – all the back thumping, arm wrestling and scuffling were simply not for him so he inevitably ended up shuffling along aimlessly at the back or simply looking after the coats.

II

When Sly was ten, to everyone's astonishment, his mother fell pregnant. The old pram was retrieved from the shed and Sly's cot was given a fresh coat of paint. His father, pipe jammed in his mouth, began decorating the spare room in anticipation of the happy event, secretly hoping for a more normal kind of child.

Although she was not old, Sly's mother was no longer a slip of a girl and found the pregnancy long and hard. Her ankles swelled and her blood pressure rose. She was forced to rest, but Sly found it no hardship to help care for her. He would bring in her breakfast before he left for school and ran straight home to make her a cup of tea and run errands. Under her patient tutelage, he even learned to cook and soon began to serve up tasty suppers for the little trio. His father, embarrassed to see his son doing women's work, tried not to wince.

He was sitting at the back of the geography class, drawing patterns on his exercise book when the headmistress popped her head round the door and asked him to come into the corridor. She took him to her room, sat him down and told him his mother had been taken into hospital. The baby was on its way. Sly felt ill. He didn't know a lot about babies, but he knew it was too soon. Miss Frith brought him a glass of water and told him not to worry. His father was on his way and they would go to the hospital together.

All his life, Sly would remember the eau de nil of the hospital waiting area he seemed to sit in for hours and the nauseating smell of over-boiled cabbage mingled with some kind of disinfectant that permeated every inch of the place. Now and then, a nurse would pass by; the starch of her apron rustling as she walked or he might see a doctor, in a long, white coat with a stethoscope around his neck, hurrying by. A kindly lady, wearing a wraparound apron, offered him a cup of tea but Sly didn't feel he could swallow anything. His father sat quietly by his side, fiddling with the edges of his cap, saying nothing.

Finally, when Sly felt he could endure no longer, a surgeon appeared in the corridor and approached them. His father looked up. There was something in the silent exchange between the two men that made Sly's heart almost stop beating.

Something was terribly wrong.

Leaving Sly by himself, the doctor took his father into a side room and sat him down. Sly watched through the window as the news was imparted. The doctor tried to look encouraging. His father just sat there, still twisting his cap in his hands, grimly staring at the floor. Finally, the two men stood up and shook hands. The surgeon gave his father a final pat on the shoulder and showed him the door. He walked back into the waiting area to where his son, anxiety written all over his face, was waiting.

"It's a boy," he said, flatly. "You've got a little brother, Sylvester."

"And mum?" asked the boy, holding his breath.

"Your mum's okay, son," replied his father. "Bit tired that's all. It's a big bit of work for a lady, bringing a baby into the world," and, finally, he smiled down at his son. "Now then," he continued in a brisk voice, "I'm going to fetch you a glass of squash and then pop in to see your mother. You're to stay where you are. You can visit tomorrow when she's feeling a bit better," and he turned and walked away.

Sly sat down and tried to stop his legs from shaking. Relief washed over him. Everything was going to be okay.

But it wasn't.

III

Down's syndrome is a genetic disease that affects about 1 in every 920 children in the UK. It is characterised by learning disabilities, reduced muscle tone and slightly altered facial features. Whilst it was true that the stigma of being born with a handicap was thankfully beginning to die in the bigger cities, that could not be said of the little backwater village in which Sly grew up.

Instead of the usual chattering cluster of women dropping in and out of the house, running errands and popping on the kettle, Sly's mother's return home was marked by silence and a turning away of heads. It was almost as if she had done something wrong. Only her best friend, Jane, came to visit and even she struggled to find something positive to say. The forced cheerfulness of the midwife and, later on, the Health Visitor, drove Sly's father to the allotment where he dug endless rows of potatoes until, worn out, he finally returned home for supper.

Instead of people cooing with delight at the sight of the beautiful bouncing baby and congratulating its mother, folk bending over the pram found themselves straightening up in something of a hurry upon seeing the flattened, moonlike face and slanted eyes of the little boy looking back at them so innocently. Sometimes there was a bit of a pat on the arm and a muttering of regret, but most people seemed to want to run away from the tiny monster in its padded, four-wheeled cage.

Sly simply couldn't understand them. He would walk happily beside his mother as she pushed the pram to and from the town, holding its handle in case the brakes should fail while his mother visited the butcher or the baker or the greengrocer. He did not know what to think as he watched their neighbours avoid his mother's eye or nip around a corner, pretending not to notice them. What on earth was wrong with everybody? Because from the moment his mother had put Alistair in his arms, Sly was enraptured. The tiny fingers, the long, dark lashes, the way his tiny tongue stuck out when he concentrated, even the epicanthal fold at the corner of his eyes fascinated him. He was fiercely proud of his little brother and never tired of helping his mother dress him or feed him, bathe him or change him.

When Ali woke in the night from a bad dream, Sly was always there first, soothing him and rocking him back to sleep. When he took his first, staggering steps, just short of his third birthday, it was to Sly that he reached out his short, fat fingers and it was Sly that caught him just before he fell, lifting him up and tickling him till they both collapsed in a fit of giggles. He never lost patience as Ali slowly developed the motor skills that other children never seemed to even think about. He instinctively understood his brother's slow, drawling speech and never once complained as he tirelessly constructed tower block after tower block only to watch his brother knock them all over and beg him to build them again.

As Ali grew into a sturdy toddler, the street began to recover from the shock of his birth. Indeed many came to regret their earlier prejudice and began to make allowances for the little family. The sight of the two siblings walking side by side, one trying to curb his long strides; the other struggling to keep up, brought many a tear to the eye. People could not help but smile as they watched Sylvester patiently push his brother up and down the pavement in the little red pedal car his father had bought him; Ali singing tunelessly, in his slightly sibilant voice, the song his brother had taught him, "That's my brother! Who? Thylvetht! Got a row a forty medals on his chetht. Big chetht! He gets no retht."

Sylvester still loved his dress design and sometimes found a little spare time to sketch or work with his mother's cut offs in the evenings after his homework and when he had finally read his brother to sleep. Trips to the coast were even better. He had someone to talk to about boats and to build sandcastles for. Alistair needed him. Perhaps it was the other way round.

When Sly turned eighteen, he unexpectedly turned down a scholarship at the Art College he had long ago planned to attend. It was a place where he could have finally unleashed his creative genius, but Ali was not yet eight and Sly found he simply could not leave his little brother behind in order to head for the big city, a long train journey away. His mother pleaded with him to go; his father begged the lad to fulfil his strange ambition, but Sly was adamant. He was not leaving. He looked around and finally settled for a place at the small Medical College in the next town. His patient handling of his little brother had awakened a new pull inside him and so he decided instead that he would become a nurse.

It has to be said that the itchy, starchy uniforms irritated him greatly during his student years because Sly's love for soft fabrics, glitter and glamour never left him. Instead, a few years previously, it had chosen a new and exciting way to express itself.

PART TWO

Cat's Chorus

Having worked their butts of at Charley's Thursday night step class, several of the girls agreed to meet up in the Whiskerly Room as was their custom. Sly arrived first and was quickly joined by Jax who, after briefly ordering herself a drink from Alex, the bartender, struck up a conversation with him, eager to glean a few more background details about the extraordinarily private man but, although he was pleasant enough, Sly gave little away other than to let her know that he owned a flat by the canal.

Jax was feeling great. She was not quite the little mouse she had been a few months previously and she was losing weight. Several classes a week and a balanced diet were doing wonders, not only for her figure, but more importantly, for her stamina and self-esteem.

Celia arrived next, unusually pale and with surprisingly little to say. Ignoring, the twosome at the bar, she crossed the room and slumped in a chair by the window, seemingly transfixed by the flock wallpaper. Jax brought her a drink, which she accepted without comment, running her finger in fixated circles across the top of the glass. To Jax, the normally outgoing, upbeat Celia looked closed and reflective so she decided to leave her be and re-joined the reticent Sly, secretly hoping that sooner or later someone more lively would turn up.

It turned out to be Bex, flushed and happy, eager to share with Jax the news that her oldest daughter was finally pregnant and that she was about to be a grandmother again. She could barely contain her excitement. Felicity and Michael had been trying for some time to have a baby and, just as they had begun to give up and turn towards science, Felicity had fallen pregnant. The two ladies took their drinks and sat happily with Celia discussing babies until Tiffany joined them and the conversation inevitably turned towards the subject of her current, turbulent relationship.

Izza followed in Tiffany's wake and easily struck up a lively conversation with Sly about the state of the Health Service. The change in the young woman over the last few weeks had been astonishing. The sullen, text-obsessive brat seemed to have vanished into thin air like an overstretched bubble. In her place, there now stood an outgoing, engaging, confident young woman, whose company the older woman actively enjoyed. For her part, Izza relished the companionship offered by her mother's friends and saw them as role models. Rising from the coffin of her dead end relationship, she had not only found herself a new job, she had made sure it came with the promise of a real career. She had cultivated a circle of friends of her own age and sometimes, incredibly, she even went out without her mobile.

Charley and Fresna arrived together. Whilst Charley was still looking slightly strained, there was something different about her – a steely glint in her eye perhaps, her back a tiny bit straighter maybe or possibly just an air of determination. Not one to pass up a golden opportunity, she headed straight for the bar and began to subtly flirt with the only male member of her class, ignoring the love-struck Alex and forcing him to retreat to a corner where he could only watch and wish.

Fresna took her drink and joined the table at which the others sat. Upbeat, relaxed and delighted to hear the news about the baby, she rained down questions upon the excited grandma-in-waiting – when was the baby due, did they know whether it would be a boy or a girl and did Bex have a preference, would it be a home or hospital birth? If Fresna's shoulders sagged a little and she seemed not to be fully concentrating on the answers, no one noticed. Fresna looked happy and appeared to be brimming with her usual self-confidence.

It was half way through the third round that the strangely silent Celia finally opened up and, surprisingly enough, at a prompt from Tiffany.

"Well, don't you have anything to say about that?" Tiffany had challenged her.

"About what?" replied Celia half-heartedly.

"About what?" replied the incredulous Tiffany, "haven't you been listening? He only wants me to move in with him."

"And will you, do you think?" answered Celia, staring out of the window.

"Der, he's only unattached and loaded, Ceals. What do you think I should do?"

"Do you love him?" asked Celia, turning to face her friend.

"Do I love him? Don't I always? What's wrong with you tonight, babes?" asked Tiffany, reaching forward to touch Celia's arm. "Aren't you going to tell me I'm delusional to believe I'm in love with a man I've only known five weeks? Aren't you going to tell me it's doomed to failure like all my other relationships and

I would do better to withdraw from normal society and become a nun? Or that I have more chance of forming a stable relationship with the invisible man?"

"It's your life, Tiff. It's not for me to tell you what to do. What do I know?" replied Celia with a dismissive shrug and turned once more to look out of the window.

As the sea pulls away from the shore before the onslaught of a big wave, the little group of women seemed as one to move away from the slumped figure in front of them. Their posture changed so that they suddenly seemed to rear up in their seats as if mirroring the emerging tsunami. Even the trio at the bar sensed the change and paused mid-conversation. For a few milliseconds, nothing moved as all chatter around the table stopped and several pairs of eyes fastened on the apparition in front of them. It looked like Ceals, it dressed like Ceals and it drank like Ceals, but who the hell was it? The tidal wave hit the shore as the impact of Celia's words crashed into them, pulling them forward in its wake, transforming the familiar and much loved landscape of the woman in front of them. Their normally, loud, opinionated friend wasn't actually admitting the possibility that Tiff could choose for herself, that others might know better than she did, that she might not know it all after all. Was she?

This was way off beam; something was very wrong.

"Beam me up, Scottie," muttered Fresna under her breath.

"What do you know? Since when did you care about what you knew? Shoots from the hip; let's us have it right between the eyes and takes no prisoners. Where are you at tonight, honey?" asked Tiffany in a stunned voice.

"And since when did you start letting understanding the facts get in the way of a little unsolicited advice?" added the equally astonished Fresna.

"Your way or the highway, Ceals," remarked Izza, who had picked up her drink and was making her way towards the table.

"Oh my god, the great and wonderful Celia has gone belly up. What's happened? Going soft in your old age? Hit the menopause or something. For Christ's sake Ceals, you're scaring us," said Tiffany.

"Whatever it is, you can tell us," encouraged Bex, gently.

"If you can't tell us, then who the hell can you tell Ceals?" asked Charley, now also approaching the table, having decided that whatever was going on across the room was infinitely more interesting than being professionally stonewalled by the gorgeous Sly, who was following in her wake. "We're your friends, you poor cow, for better or worse and besides, right now, we are all you've got," she concluded.

Celia turned from her reverie and looked into the concerned eyes of her friends and decided they were right. It was time to open up. She began quietly, embarrassed to reveal her mistaken assumption, but gaining in confidence as the faces of her friends echoed her outrage at the cavalier way in which she had been treated at work and, as her tale came to its close, as women do everywhere, her friends began the healing process with her, making her laugh by wading in with a brainstorm of off-the-wall suggestions about what to do with that bastard, Patrick and his arselick of a Management Team. Even Sly added a few madcap ideas of his own, delighting them with his ability to just be present and simply fit in.

When Celia's wound had been fully examined, appropriately soothed and properly bandaged, Tiffany decided to go next and told the group the sordid story of her humiliation at the hands of Fat Taff. Fresna's secret came out next and it seemed that each of the women had a story to tell; a story of injustice or victimisation, hurt or outrage, the inevitable baggage of misdirected choice. Only Bex and Sly stayed quiet, feeling no need to contribute, both choosing to remain slightly aloof, listening intently and revealing little about themselves as was their habit.

Still, something amazing was unfolding. As each woman began to open up and reveal a little about her situation, her past or her vulnerability, the bond between the little group who met in the bar after class began to blossom. The dynamics were changing even as they spoke so that the power of one became the power of eight and the possibilities were endless.

The Whiskerly Sisters had been born.

II

"Oh my god, it's happened to all of us. We've been shafted. Every one of us," declared Tiffany, although that was not quite true.

"You're right," replied Fresna.

"In a variety of different ways, mind you," added Tiffany, trying for clarity.

"Is it us do you think?" asked Izza. "Are we giving out something – you know – like negative vibes?"

"Don't be daft, Izza. Of course, we're not. It's just a coincidence," replied Charley.

"No such thing," retorted Jax, disagreeing.

"It's just that shit happens," added Celia.

"Mmm maybe so, but it seems to me that most of us get to be standing right under the bucket when it gets poured out and I for one am getting mightily fed up with it," said Charley.

"Me too," agreed Tiffany, "but what are we going to do about it?"

"What can we do?" asked Izza.

"Buy an enormous umbrella and crowd under it?" suggested Sly, making them all laugh.

"I know what I'd like to do to Patrick," remarked Celia with a sour look on her face. "Cut off his balls and feed them to the fish in the foyer."

"Ouch," said Sly, drawing his legs up under him and protecting his groin with both hands. "Bit harsh!"

"Sorry," offered Celia. "There are some decent men in the world – it's just that he isn't one of them."

"Damn right," declared Jax. "You're being way too soft on the bastard."

"Yeah, so take his dick off too," giggled Izza.

"And hang him out to dry on top of CenterPoint," added Fresna. At this point, the girls had to stop and laugh at Sly, who had got down from his chair and was trying to take cover under the table.

"I surrender," he cried, "and I'm claiming the Fifth Amendment."

"Not you, you goose," said Charley, grabbing his arm and trying to pull him back up into his chair. Any excuse for a little physical activity with the adorable man.

"I'd enjoy taking Fat Taff down a peg or two," mused Tiffany. "Not that I've seen hide nor hair of him since I left and, since I hope never to see the arsehole's ugly face again, I guess I'll just have to suck on it."

"Eew, that is not a good image," said Sly, who had been persuaded back into his seat.

"What isn't" asked Tiffany, confused.

"Sucking on the arsehole's ugly face, darling," came the languid reply.

"Oh shut up," she replied and hit Sly lightly on the arm, much to the annoyance of Charley, who believed he was her territory.

"I guess we all will," said Izza hopelessly.

"All will what?" asked her mother.

"Der! Have to suck on it. Like she said," replied Izza.

"There must be something we can do," said Celia. "I couldn't live with myself if I let Patrick get away with this. The bastard lied to me – straight faced lied to me and he damn well knows it."

"And I am not for one second going to let the gooneys next door get away with setting me up and laughing at me," Charley added fiercely.

"But what can we do?" asked Tiffany, frowning.

It was at this point that Bex, who had barely said a word all evening, sat up very straight in her chair, took a very deep breath and replied, "Subversion. It's the obvious answer."

"Subversion?" enquired Charley. "What are you talking about?"

"I'm talking about getting your own back. Going in under the wire. Guerrilla warfare if you like," replied Bex with spirit.

"Guerrilla warfare? Where are we – sodding Mozambique?" asked Celia.

"Joined the ANC have we?" mocked Tiffany.

"What? You mean combat trousers and blacking our faces with boot polish and crawling around on our stomachs with frigging machine guns?" suggested Celia. "Are you insane?"

"If that's what it takes," asserted Bex. The girls looked at each other in amazement. What had happened to their mild-mannered, serene friend?

"Oh goodie," interjected Sly, clapping his hands together and breaking the mood. "I know just where to get the uniforms."

"Cool," said Izza practically. "I'm game. When do we start?"

"And just what the Holy Mary do you know about guerrilla warfare, Bex?" asked Celia, her voice rising with incredulity.

"You'd be surprised," replied Bex and there was something in her voice that made everyone shut up. For the second time that evening, several pairs of surprised eyes were fixed on one single member of the group.

"You know about guerrilla warfare?" asked Jax. "What from a book or the Open University or something?" she added, doubting her friend.

"You are taking the piss," decided Celia, although not quite with her usual force, "aren't you?" and her voice wavered a little with uncertainty.

"Actually, I'm not," replied Bex firmly and sitting up even straighter. "If you must know, I am in fact something of an expert on the subject."

It was at this point that Bex opened up and allowed her friends a glimpse into the secret side of her nature and it transpired that she was right – when it came to guerrilla warfare, Bex was indeed something of a seasoned campaigner.

BEX

I

Like so many things, it had started out as a tiny, tiny nugget of an idea, a whisper of a notion, a fleeting thought, but it had blossomed. As the proverbial acorn grows into the study oak, branch by branch, stem by steam, leaf by leaf – just one hundredth of a millimetre at a time until, one day, Bex realised that this thing was enormous and had grown out of all proportion until it had become part of the fabric of her life. In some ways, whilst it was way beyond acceptable, it was, to her at least, really quite ordinary. Not worth thinking about really, just something she did routinely such as putting out the recycling or plumping up the cushions, which of course it wasn't. Anything but.

It had started almost insignificantly as these things do. Malcolm had had a particularly bad day at the office. Revolution was in the air and, although he was supposed to head up the small, yet dynamic Transformation Team and take responsibility for ensuring effective change within the business, Malcolm actually loathed change. As a creature of almost unalterable routine and habit, anything even slightly different unsettled him, made him feel upset, even agitated and Malcolm couldn't bear feeling that kind of discomfort. There was no way he could express this at work where he had to put his best foot forward, seize the day, embrace the challenge and all the rest of the rag, tag and bobtail bullshit rhetoric his boss enjoyed shoving down his throat. So Malcolm did the next best thing.

He kicked the cat. Not that Malcolm and Bex owned a cat. Jesus Christ no – think of all that unwanted fur on the back of the sofa or the unsightly vision of half eaten cat food strewn across the parquet flooring or, god forbid, the height of all things disgusting, a soiled litter tray. Mr A Place for Everything and Everything in its Place Tidy Shorts couldn't have dealt with that, shouldn't have to in fact. So the cat he kicked was Bex. He had done it many times before and it always worked. It made him feel better. He didn't enquire as to how it made Bex feel. He simply kicked. Job done.

On the evening in question, he found fault with the tidiness of the towels in the linen cupboard, complained about the consistency of the sauce Bex had spent hours slaving over and admonished her over her somewhat unkempt appearance. All this was done in a calm, patronising tone. He tisked and he tutted; he hummed and he hawed; he fussed and he whinged. He got under his wife's feet and up her nose. He behaved as though he was being perfectly reasonable, totally justified and completely objective when all the time he was being a perfect idiot, a total prat and a complete tosser.

After complaining mightily about dinner, but managing somehow to devour all of it, he dabbed his napkin over his moustache, requested a cup of ground coffee and retired self-satisfied to the lounge to watch the news, oblivious to the upset he had caused yet content to have transferred his anxiety onto another.

As Bex swallowed a sigh and rose to fill the kettle, it crossed her mind that it might be enormous fun to add some ex-lax to the brew to pay him back for his putdowns. Not a lot, of course, just enough to perhaps give him an eensy teensy tummy ache. She killed the thought almost as soon as it arose, horrified with herself. Acutely aware of her disloyalty to the marital breadwinner, she quickly ran upstairs to tidy herself up and to change into something a little less comfortable before nipping back to the kitchen to pour a perfectly perked cup of his favourite Columbian brand. Contrite, she served it to him alongside a couple of home-made macaroons, her specialty. Malcolm accepted her offering with a grunt of dismissal, failing to notice either her change of appearance or her culinary attentions to detail, being totally engrossed in a trailer about painting the Firth of Forth Bridge. Bex, still feeling guilty, returned to the dining room to clear the debris and then scurried mouse-like to the linen cupboard to give it a thorough sorting.

It was only in the quiet of her bedroom after midnight that her thoughts disturbingly meandered once again towards the subject of laxatives and, although she tried hard to dismiss them, to think other less alluring thoughts, time and time again, over successive pre-dawn awakenings, her imagination refused to be diverted, but stubbornly forced her to explore the delicious, far away horizons of payback time. She fantasised about adding a variety of substances to Malcolm's coffee – garden rubbish (too bulky), bleach (too smelly), shampoo (too frothy), something next door's cat had been playing with. Stop it! But she couldn't. Passive aggression will have its way. It was delightful, it was fun, it was simply irresistible and Bex was hooked.

III

Over the next few weeks, Bex began a little scientific experimentation. Naturally, the first thing she tried was her original idea – a little ex-lax in Malcolm's after dinner coffee. It failed to have any effect because Bex, feeling scared and anxious, could only bring herself to put the tip of a spoonful into an entire cafetiere. She spent the rest of the evening feeling so bad about what she'd done that she had to retire to bed early, complaining of a headache. Not a very good start.

Over time, however, she began to gain confidence and gradually grew bolder until, eventually, she got a result. Malcolm phoned her from the office just before lunch, complaining of a dickey tummy and asked her to drive round to the factory with some Milk of Magnesia. Covertly, mind you! She wasn't to be seen marching into the building with a bottle of medicine in her hand. She had to pretend she was just passing and had popped in to see if Malcolm was free to take her to lunch. As if! Bex could barely contain her excitement. Her tiny addition to the cornflakes had worked. Grabbing her coat and the required remedy, she hurried to catch the bus. And guess what she added to the milky white remedy before she left. Oh yes, she did.

And so it began. A sprinkle of hoover dust in the jalfrezi, a splash of washing up liquid in the steak and kidney pie, a trickle of glue in the syrup pudding.

And then it continued. A couple of squirts of carpet cleaner in the sauce au poivre, cat food and pickle sandwiches for lunch, a pair of sweaty socks included in a marinade.

And then she graduated. A teaspoon of spit in the coffee, a little bit of shit in the spaghetti bolognaise, a globule or two of snot in the gravy.

Bex became quite the little womble, gathering here, collecting there, judicious in her choices, eager to try out an alternative recipe or two, to pepper up the menu, to spice up her life and to give Malcolm a thorough taste of her spleen. Being a long time vegetarian, Bex was easily able to pass over her adulterated meals and, since she was always watching her weight, preferring to eat either yoghurt or fruit for dessert, it was no problem for her to add a little unexpected variety to Malcolm's puddings.

Growing increasingly daring, she turned her attention to Malcolm's laundry. A little dash of itching powder applied to the heel of his socks or the collar of his shirt or even to the crotch of his underpants and he was sure to be scratching himself surreptitiously.

IV

As time passed, Bex began to justify her actions. It wasn't as if she did this sort of thing every day. She never did anything when the children were around or she had company and, besides, she only did it when she felt Malcolm deserved it, when he took out his temper on her, when he unjustly berated her or simply left her feeling putdown or irritated. Furthermore, she was very, very careful. She read up on her products and knew just how much to add. She didn't want to alter the taste of the food; her goal was to enhance it with a little hidden revenge. She didn't want to cause a violent reaction; her aim was much more subtle so she thought it best not to over-egg the pudding. And it wasn't as if this could ever be classed as poisoning. God forbid! It was just a small nonsense, a delicate redressing of the balance, a little settling of the scores.

For his part, Malcolm, apart from beginning to worry that he might have the beginnings of irritable bowel syndrome and some anxiety-driven dermatitis, noticed nothing. Why would he? He hadn't looked at Bex properly for years so why would he spot what was going on under his nose. Quiet, gentle, boring little Bex, who never said boo to a goose, why on earth would he think she was up to something so spiteful?

It was wrong of course. Totally out of order. An offence probably, but Bex didn't care. The internal rebel, the subversive within, the radical core had been re-awakened from their slumber and, after such a long sleep, they were hungry for attention, eager for reaction, alert for opportunity. Bex had not had so much fun in ages and she intended to keep on enjoying herself for a very long time to come.

It didn't always work out as planned of course. There were a few hiccoughs along the way. There was the time that Malcolm sat back from a rather large second helping of apple crumble, replete and satiated, to congratulate her on the quality of her custard. It was probably the phlegm she thought to herself and, as the ridiculousness of the situation took hold, she dissolved into a fit of hysterical laughter, which she had to cover with an outbreak of exaggerated coughing. She ran to the upstairs bathroom where she collapsed over the basin in a fit of giggles, tears pouring down her face with the absurdity of it all. Malcolm had felt quite concerned, going so far as to bring her a glass of water and suggest that she might need a tonic.

A tonic? Hadn't she already got one?

Sometimes she forgot to keep a low profile. She was beginning to feel so full of exuberance inside that it occasionally spilled over onto the outside. Coming in from the garden one summer evening with a basketful of fresh linen and humming pleasantly to herself, Malcolm complimented her on how lovely she looked. How radiant and fresh. Alarmingly, he made a rather clumsy pass, a saucy little squeeze of her behind, a hint of a suggestion of resumed intimacy. She froze. Jesus Christ, she'd thought those days were over and a good job too. The passionate, erotic lover of yesteryear was dead and had been buried long ago. In its place, there stood an overbearing, overweight, unappealing fumbler with a tendency to roll over and fart within seconds of it being over. She had learned, over the years, to surrender to his embrace, make as little fuss as possible, say something nice and then slide to the far side of the bed as soon as the deed was done. In time, his advances had lessened and, eventually, praise the lord, had stopped altogether.

God, he couldn't possibly want to start all the nonsense again, could he? The alarm bells were ringing the Hallelujah Chorus in her head. She must remember to keep her down, to come across as somewhat bland, to play the vacant little wife.

Besides, she had a lover. She didn't need Malcom's odious, night time offerings. She had begun an affair with the man who ran the delicatessen on the other side of town. David was a widower, gentle, intelligent and understanding.

And he was a bloody good fuck!

So, whenever they could both manage it, they stole away to a distant hotel to get down and dirty.

It seemed the worm had turned!

Turned? It was doing bloody great cartwheels up and down the hall carpet.

V

Bex did not stop there. If ever there was one for biting the bullet, it was her and she wasn't so much biting the bullet as sucking out every last, rich drop of its marrow. Eventually, she turned her attention to the thing that mattered most in Malcolm's life. His car.

Malcolm's black classic BMW was his pride and joy. How he fussed over that machine. It was an affair with an alternator, passion with a piston, foreplay with a four stroke.

It was kept safely out of sight of the garage during the working week when Malcolm drove his company car to the office, but, without fail, every Saturday morning, he cleaned, polished and hoovered his 'precious' inside and out before driving it to the golf club for a little practice or a nine hole pair. Malcolm was never home on Sundays since he was either taking part in a golfing tournament or else spending the day with the boys from the Beamer Club, talking dirty about sparkplugs, lusting over a shapely camshaft or drooling over a V8.

Since they rarely went anywhere together these days, Bex hardly ever saw the inside of the damn thing. Besides, she herself had never learned to drive. In the early days, there was always a good bus service, latterly she could afford a taxi whenever she wanted one. If all else failed, a friend or neighbour would usually offer her a lift. She knew nothing whatsoever about cars and cared even less.

Or so Malcolm thought, for Bex – her victories accu-mulating, her confidence growing and her self-esteem on the up and up – had decided to learn to drive. It was David who taught her as their budding relationship grew into something far more than a shag or two on the sly. Together, they bought her a car, a little Honda Civic, which she kept on David's drive away from prying eyes. They used it to drive to out of the way places where they could make love unnoticed – amongst the corn, on a deserted beach and, on one very exciting occasion, under a picnic table during a performance of L'Elisir d'Amour at Glyndebourne.

Having passed her test on her first attempt and, discovering she was rather good at things technical, Bex decided to have a go at mechanical engineering. It was a huge risk of course. Being the only woman in the class and not a young thing, she was bound to be noticed, to accrue some unwanted attention, to be the talk of the college but, because she was able to sign up for a course at a school twenty miles away, she got away with it.

So whereas in the early days, she had only been able to inject the flesh wounds of retribution, she was now poised to go for the jugular and so she did. Again, she was very careful. There was a very real possibility of discovery and she didn't want any suspicion coming her way. She put a lot of thought into these vehicular assaults and used this avenue only very occasionally.

She began with almost insignificant things. One Saturday morning, she removed the canister of engine oil he kept in the garage so he had to go out for more, and, while he was gone, she put breadcrumbs on the bonnet of the car so that, upon his return, his beautifully cleaned BMW was covered in pigeon shit and he had to start again.

One evening, while Malcolm was watering the garden, Bex, feeling incredibly bold, stole into his briefcase, which he always left in the under stairs cupboard and removed his car keys. As soon as she could, she took herself into town and had a duplicate set made. The keys were gone for a blood chilling seventeen hours during which time Bex felt barely able to breathe. However Malcolm, always a creature of the most regular habit, would not need the keys until the weekend and therefore did not spot the loss. The following evening when he went out for his usual brisk walk to the paper shop, Bex sneaked into the garage, using the spare set of keys he kept secreted away at the back of the right hand drawer of his bedside table, unlocked the car and rubbed fish debris to the underside of the mats. Bex was delighted with the result. In the confined space of the garage, the smell of rotting haddock lingered for weeks. Malcolm had been beside himself and couldn't work out where the smell was coming from or how it had got there in the first place. How he fretted over that one.

She made the tiniest tears in the leather seats on the backseats. Malcolm had been so very puzzled. He couldn't imagine how they had got there. The car was always handled with the utmost care and, besides, it had been locked up all week. He decided that it must be mice and hurried off to by some traps.

Mice with quickunpicks, Bex supposed, supressing a grin.

She grew bolder. She punched a hole in the exhaust, loosened the jubilee clip, even going so far as to drain the battery one night when he was away at a conference in Belgium. The car began to spend more time in the repair shop than in his own garage. Malcolm was beside himself. He took such care of his pride and joy. How could these things have happened?

Throughout it all, Bex played the role of the confused wife. No, she hadn't been in the garage. No, she was certain no one else had been in there either. No, she had no idea how a car that hadn't been out of the garage all week had got damaged. She didn't drive, she knew nothing about cars and, in any case, she never had any need to go into the garage for anything. She didn't even have a set of keys herself.

It had absolutely nothing whatsoever to do with her. Had it?

VII

As the game went on, Malcolm became increasingly paranoid. He took to checking the car each morning before work and each evening as soon as he got home. On a couple of occasions, he even dropped by at lunchtime, once almost catching Bex red handed on the way to the garage to rub the remains of a trout over the back seat of his best beloved. Five minutes later and she would have been undone. Fortunately, she was able to back pedal towards the dustbins where she quickly got rid of the evidence. She made a mental note to be more careful in future.

As time passed, Bex decided to weave another spell. She began to make Malcolm believe he was getting absent minded, losing the plot, possibly becoming a little neurotic. As usual, she began gently and was easily able to convince Malcolm that these little incidents could well be symptomatic of the pressure he was currently experiencing at work.

She would move his glasses when he wasn't looking and when he protested that he could have sworn he had put them down on the table beside the sofa, like he always did, she assured him that he had taken them off in the dining room and left them beside his plate. She told them that she had tidied them away to the sideboard whilst clearing the table and she would get up and return the missing spectacles to the baffled Malcolm.

Papers would disappear from his briefcase and turn up in the most unexpected places. How could they have got down the side of the bed? Had he forgotten he had been reading through them in bed the previous evening, boning up on their contents in preparation for the following morning's meeting, Bex would remind him. Malcolm was beside himself. He could have sworn he had read nothing more exacting than the local newspaper. He decided that he must be getting forgetful in his old age. Bex demurred sympathetically.

Disturbingly, a variety of tools went missing from the potting shed only to turn up a few days later in the most absurd places. Malcolm, who believed in running a tidy ship, couldn't work out why he hadn't put them back where they belonged as was his custom. Why on earth would he leave the trowel down by the side of the freezer for goodness' sake? And what was he thinking about when he decided to store his collection of clay pots under the sink. Malcolm was mystified.

Malcolm's world finally came adrift at the annual President's Ball at his local Golf Club where it was the custom for each table to nominate a member to donate a spot prize. Competition was fierce amongst the golfing community to donate the best prizes. This year, it had been Malcolm's turn to represent his table and he had gone out of his way to purchase a presentation set of six expensive golf balls. He sat back in his chair confident that his donation would be well received but, when the lucky winner opened the beautifully wrapped gift to discover it contained six ordinary ping pong balls in a cardboard container, Malcolm was lost. He could not believe his eyes and the colour drained from his face. Instead of being congratulated on a choice well made, he was the laughing stock of the room. In vain, did he try to make excuses and bluster his way through the faux pax, but it was too late. Malcolm's 'booby prize' was born that evening and would henceforth remain a part of the proceedings of the President's Ball. He knew he would never live it down.

Malcolm felt that he had made a complete fool of himself and, unsurprisingly, it was at this very moment that he surrendered to the lie. He had to face up to the truth – not only had he been overworking and suffering from stress, he was also becoming absent-minded and couldn't even be trusted to put on his own trousers.

And throughout the whole sorry episode, by his side, sat the ever faithful Bex, smiling up at him sympathetically.

FRESNA

I

Fresna smiled lazily as she stretched her shapely, athletic body across the bed. The man beside her mumbled something in his sleep and rolled over. They had made love all afternoon and, of course, it had been incredible. She had come for England. She would not have been there if she had not been certain of a more than acceptable performance level from her lover, but now it was over and the sultry, golden afternoon was yielding to the first whispers of evening. The corners of the room were beginning to darken and ghosts of shadows had started to steal their gloomy progress across the bottom of the bed. It was time to go.

Not that Fresna needed to go; not that she had anyone or anything to go home to. Verity, now an accomplished actress, was on tour in Canada and would not be home for at least another three months. There was no class to be late for tonight either. She thought she might drop in on Tiffany for a coffee on her way home to catch up with the latest gossip and discuss the state of her friend's love life. Perhaps she would share a glass or two of red wine with Celia and be bombarded with all the latest goings on at Dumbleton's. She could suggest that she and Jax catch a film. The evening was young and full of possibilities. She had plenty of time to plan her evening. It was time to go.

Carefully, and with practiced stealth, she eased her way out of his bed. She retraced her way to the front door, dressing as she went; each discarded item a reminder of the tumultuous passion she had so recently enjoyed. She left silently and without a backward glance.

Quite by accident, she ended up spending the evening with Bex. She had pulled up beside her at a set of traffic lights, hooted with delight and invited her friend into the warmth of her car. Since Malcolm was away and Bex felt at a loose end, they decided to go into town to share a meal and a very long coffee. They talked animatedly together until the restaurant was empty and the staff made it clear that it was time to go.

Fresna was humming to herself as she parked her Tigra on the driveway. Content with her day, sure of her life, a tad smug even. As she switched off the ignition, she glanced across the road and saw him – a lone man, lurking in the shadows beneath the trees.

The man with Verity's eyes.

II

As Fresna got out of the car, the man edged forward toward the street lamp and spread his hands in a conciliatory gesture, palms open towards her. She tiptoed a little closer towards him, peering into the gloom at the man the night had sent her, making sure to keep well within the confines of her territory, making the best use of the scant rays thrown out from the night lights that marked the edge of her driveway.

Without warning, he took a step towards her, moving further into the light. She backed away at once. Shocked, she turned and, fumbling for her key, fled into the welcome security of her hallway, locking herself inside;

her back pressed against the door and her eyes tight shut against reality. Her heart pounded in her mouth and she felt unable to breathe or move. She stood frozen, pinned to the woodwork by fear, waiting for the rattle of the door knocker to frighten her into action.

It didn't come. After a while, her body damp with a cold patina of sweat and her stomach empty with dread, she moved cautiously up the stairs and into the front bedroom. Keeping the lights off, she sidled slowly towards the window and, oh so carefully, peeped out towards the edge of her garden and then further, across the street, to where the unexpected figure had stood.

He had gone. She looked up and down the street as best she could from her half crouched position by the window. She could see no one. Growing more daring, she straightened up and, moving the net aside, took a good look around the area. There was no one there; he had disappeared. Sweet relief flooded her veins, making her tremble so that she slumped shakily onto the edge of her double bed and rubbed the sweat from her palms off onto the duvet. Thank God – he had gone.

Or had he? Fear forced her upright, stabbing at her stomach with renewed energy. He could be on the driveway round the corner by the front door or, worse, in the back garden. Shit! What should she do? Almost reflexively, her hand stole towards the telephone at the side of the bed and, impulsively, she followed it. She was dialling 999; as she caught herself. Just exactly what was she going to say to the operator? Some old flame that had got her pregnant and then jilted her a thousand moons ago was back and might be hiding in the back garden. Could they please come and arrest him. Feeling stupid, she put the phone down.

In the end, she found the big torch she kept in the cupboard under the sink and courageously took a tour of her garden, front and back, checking in the shadows and under the bushes for a glimpse of a man she had not seen in over forty years. Satisfied he was not lurking anywhere, she returned to the house, bolted the doors and tried to relax in a hot bath.

II

He was back again the following evening on her return from work. Sitting across the road on the stump of an old elm tree that had come down in a storm a few years previously and which the council had turned into rather an attractive seat. This time, she didn't hesitate to walk over to him and, as she did so, he stood up.

"Hullo," he said, the whisper of a smile touching the corners of his mouth.

"Alex," she breathed in wonder.

Only his eyes had not changed. Gone was the glossy mane of black curls, the ruddy complexion, the lantern jaw and the darkly curved brows, framing those lovely eyes. Gone was the upright posture, the broad shoulders, the narrow waist and the athletic eyes. In their place stood an old man. Grey-white wispy tendrils surrounded a balding pate; his jaw was jowly and his complexion dull. He was stooped and thin yet with a slight beer belly; his legs seemed to be permanently bent at the knees. He looked like a man down on his luck and yet with a hopeful gleam in his eye. A man who thought he might have seen a tenner in the gutter but, on closer inspection, suspected he might well have discovered this week's winning lottery ticket.

"Back from the dead like a bad penny," he said, shrugging his shoulders to hide what Fresna took to be slight embarrassment.

"What are you doing here?" she asked incredulously, not wanting to hear the reply and yet hardly able to wait for it to announce itself.

"I was just passing," he began, his face creasing into a half apologetic smile and his eyes screwing up in concentration.

Just passing? thought Fresna to herself. *What, he was out taking a stroll in the early evening air and just happened to find himself in her area and thought it might be nice to look her up; maybe have a cup of tea and a cosy little catch up kind of just passing? Forty plus years down the road just passing?*

"I mean," he hesitated. This was hard. Just how do you approach these sorts of circumstances? Just what is the correct form of etiquette for such an occasion? Just what do you say to the person you dumped at the altar three months pregnant more than a generation ago?

"I mean I thought it was time," he asserted, straightening up and finally deciding on the line he was going to take with her. "I've been meaning to come and see you for a while since I've been back in the country but, you know, somehow time passes and before you know where you are..." he trailed off, possibly because he had seen the disbelieving look in Fresna's eyes.

Oh yes, she knew all about how time passed and she knew even more about before you know where you are – probably better than most.

"You're looking well," he offered, changing the subject and it was true because, unlike Alex, the years had been extremely kind to Fresna. She certainly did not look anywhere near her age. Her posture was upright; she was still reasonably flexible and lithe from her commitment to exercise. Admittedly, her glorious strawberry blonde hair owed more to a bottle than it did to nature these days, but her complexion still glowed and her blue eyes were bright and clear.

"What do you want?" she asked. She had decided to face it, whatever it was – the bottom line.

"Well," he began and she waited. She could hear it coming in the distance and she could see it in his face, in his smile, in the way that he stood and in the way he was dressed. Eventually, after messing about on the fringes for a few more minutes, out it came.

A sorry little monologue from that well known character, "poor me"!

III

His wife had sadly died of cancer, his children had grown and flown and he had retired from business and moved to the South of France to pass the rest of his days in warm, tranquil, comfortable retirement. He'd had a bit of bad luck with a couple of investments and somehow his warm, tranquil, comfortable retirement had come to a cold, brutal, painful end. The kids were busy with their lives, raising their children, working hard and with no time for pops. There was no spare cash to ease his distress. "You know how it is," he'd suggested, oblivious to her stunned yet undivided attention.

He'd come back to Britain with what little he had left of his savings and was living in a small flat on the outskirts of town, etching out a living at a variety of dead end jobs, washing up in a café here, temporary work at a factory there. He would do whatever it took to supplement his small state pension. He'd heard on the grapevine that she was only living a few miles from the village in which he had courted her and had decided it was time to look her up, he explained and their eyes met. He wanted to meet his child; he wasn't sure if it was a girl or a boy and he felt there was no time like the present so he had decided to come round to see how she was doing, to find out how the child had fared and, Fresna's head told her, to see if either of them were up for a bit of soft soaping.

Fresna, who somewhere between the wife dying and the retirement fund drying up found that she had invited him into the kitchen, was fascinated. Here he was after all these years sitting in her home, drinking coffee as if nothing had happened, asking about her health, asking about their daughter and wondering if maybe she had a little nip of brandy to add to his cup. She was in a whirl; her brain in over-drive. What was Verity going to say? What was she going to do? Here was her father back from the void after over forty years. How was she going to react? Was she going to welcome him back into the fold, grateful that he had finally come for her or tell him to sod off, that she didn't want a damn thing to do with him?

Yet throughout the whole sorry soliloquy, Fresna was able to keep her nerve. She sat composed, listening carefully, head tilted, managing to look concerned and giving nothing at all away. In fact, to the sad sack in front of her, she appeared quite soothing, sorry for him even, possibly even anxious to please.

But then appearances can be deceptive, can't they?

IV

After she had finally managed to prise Alex out of his chair and send him home, Fresna took a slow walk around her garden, deep in thought. She had a lot of reflection to do and some very serious decisions to make. This was not just about her; it concerned her daughter and family had always been very important to Fresna. She had to weigh this all up very carefully, taking her time and bringing into play her good judgement and keen instincts. It was essential she made the right decision for everyone. This was not something she could rush at like a bull at a gate. She sat down on the swing chair under the pergola, absent-mindedly watching the shadows play across her garden as the moon waned and the clouds trawled slowly by, turning things over and over in her mind. She stayed there for a long time, wrapped up in an old blanket, one foot trailing on the ground as she swung herself to and fro in the moonlight. She held tight to the cup of cold coffee laced between her fingers. She would not rush this; she would give herself plenty of time to think things through; she needed to be spot on.

In the end, she decided to tell Verity about her unexpected visitor. In the end, she was glad she did and she was grateful too that she chose to tell her friends, to inform the Whiskerly Sisters.

The very next evening, having put down the phone on Verity fully aware of her daughter's attitude to this unpredicted intrusion into her life, she called the Whiskerlies round for a council of war. She apprised them of her new circumstances and brought them up to date with the differing reactions to these uncharted waters.

Her daughter and her partner, Sam, were flying home, cutting short their time in Ontario. They would settle their affairs and get back as soon as they could. It had been agreed that they would not come directly to Fresna's, but they would lodge with Sam's brother a few miles away. That way their homecoming would hopefully remain unnoticed. After all, Alex had managed to track Fresna down after more than forty years; he might be able to do the same with Verity and she wanted no surprise visitors on her doorstep – at least not until she was ready to face them.

In the few short weeks since 'the awakening' as they like to call it amongst themselves, the solidity of the little group of friends had become second to none. Having shared their innermost secrets with one another, there was nothing any of them could say or do to each other that would breach the loyalty they shared.

After the mind blowing revelation of Bex's secret life, there had been a slight hiatus. There was general concern that Bex might have gone too far, might be out of control, might in fact be mentally ill. It was discussed in gentle, hushed tones, touched upon with delicate strokes and hinted at by the merest tip of the toe in the water.

Bex convinced them otherwise. She regaled them with tales of Malcolm's petty tyrannies. How she had to stand in front of him, on a quarterly basis, to explain the telephone bill; any call over six minutes needing an interrogation worthy of the Spanish Inquisition. Why she was not allowed to use more than two inches of hot water in the bath – did she not understand anything about the alarming rise in the cost of utilities these days? God forbid, Malcolm should find the dustbins out of alignment during his daily inspection of the back yard or dust on top of any of the picture frames that were displayed with symmetrical precision throughout the house. Sheets and towels were to be folded with hospital corners to a military standard in the linen cupboard. He would not tolerate out of date tins in the kitchen cupboards and heaven help her if any of the labels were not facing forward. There were to be no half empty, untidy packets on his shelves. Everything, right down to the washing powder, had to be unpacked into the requisite plastic container and stored hygienically. Even the pots and pans in the kitchen had to be stacked according to the Book of Malcolm.

In the end, the girls figured he was getting his just desserts and nothing further was said. On the other hand, wonder of wonders, it seemed they had a genius in their midst and, when it came to the planning of Fresna's particular Waterloo, she was delighted to have her very own Wellington on board.

The Whiskerlies took up positions in the lounge. Alcohol was deemed unsuitable since this was a serious situation, deserving of everyone's complete and sober attention. As a group, this would be their initial sortie into subversion, virgin territory you might say. It would take a great deal of thought, planning and discussion. There was a time and a place for alcohol, fits of feminine giggles and group hugs, but this was most definitely not it.

But it was. Of course it was and so Sly and Celia were despatched to the minimart around the corner in search of several bottles of wine and several packets of snacks. On their return, with full glasses to hand, everyone got down to a riotous game of how are we going to up Alex?

It was agreed to wait until Verity had been fully briefed since she had to agree to the plan. After all, this was her father, albeit, long time, absent father but, nevertheless, feelings were involved and, of these, Verity's were paramount. In the meantime, though, the girls agreed that a little research and some furtive sleuthing wouldn't hurt and might actually prove very entertaining.

Fresna was expecting a call from Alex the next day. They would take it from there.

V

It was agreed that Alex would be invited to dinner the following Friday evening. A meal in an impersonal restaurant simply wouldn't cut it. He needed to be off guard for them to lure him in. The order of the day would be a well prepared, home cooked meal. Fresna readily agreed to this consensus, grateful for it, since she felt strongly that she needed to be on home turn to carry out 'Phase One'. Since the buses were somewhat erratic, and to convey a false sense of security, it was agreed that Fresna would volunteer to drive over and collect him.

Everyone agreed that this was to be a regular meal; a little light poisoning a la Bex would be unsuitable at this juncture, although no one ruled out the possibility that it might be called into play further down the track. Given that Fresna was under orders to be seen tucking in with relish, she was relieved at the decision since she simply felt she was not up for a mild tummy upset the following morning.

Charley and Jax fretted over the menu. They agreed it could be nothing too up market or haute cuisine, but on the other hand, a quarter pounder and fries wouldn't cut the mustard either. In the end, it was Sly, who gently took Fresna back down Memory Lane and planned a classic meal which cleverly incorporated some of Alex's favourite tastes from way back when.

On the appointed day, the Whiskerlies turned up en masse to clean the house within an inch of its life and to set the table. Sly arrived with a home-made centrepiece of freesias and dwarf iris. Tiffany sighed at the sight. She felt he would make someone a wonderful wife one day. The meal had been cooked to Charley's incredibly high standards (not that she had lifted a carefully manicured finger to prepare it), carefully wrapped in layers of foil and placed in Fresna's American style fridge. All she needed to do when she got back home with Alex, was to sit him down with a glass of Frascati while she warmed the meal through and lit the candles, thereby offering a tiny hint at romance in a homely, inviting atmosphere for their first meal together in a very long time, and yet with a subtle whiff of maybe a whole lot more to follow. She was to offer Alex a place where he could unwind, a place where he felt at ease and where he might just try to put his feet under the table.

Although Fresna was nervous, she carried things off well enough. The prawn crostini went down well. Alex, with his Italian blood had always been partial to gamberini and fondly recalled the times when he and Fresna had driven down to the estuary in search of fresh shellfish. Alex, ever hungry, would polish off a huge plateful.

After a couple of glasses of his favourite, chilled white wine, Alex was beginning to relax. To Fresna, sitting opposite him, he seemed just like a perfectly ripe melon, eager to burst open and spill forth his juicy secrets.

He sighed at the sight of the main course, his favourite Osso Bucco. She had remembered. Together they shared a fond smile at the memory of happier times.

Fresna, seemingly relaxed and at ease, watched her former lover like a hawk. One of her greatest advantages lay in the fact that she had always been a great observer of men. She felt confident in their company and she knew how to listen to them, how to converse with them and how to be interesting without ever giving away the slightest detail about herself. Tonight, she was captivating. Leaning forward, radiating maturity and interest in his tales, she listened to him. At one and the same time, Alex appeared to be full of humble gratitude for his warm welcome back into her life and unbearably arrogant, taking it for granted that he would still be wanted after all this time. During the first part of the evening, he took the opportunity to embroider the tale of his current, woeful situation, sure in the knowledge that Fresna was falling for it, which, of course, is exactly what she wanted him to believe.

It was over the cheese and biscuits that she made her move. After listening attentively to his pitiful story for the last hour and barely uttering a sentence other than the odd consoling phrase, she expressed her sympathy that Alex's two sons had felt unable to help him out of his current situation. She expressed surprise at their ingratitude after all he had done for them and she shook her head at the wonder of modern family life.

Alex swallowed the bait. Despite being a dedicated parent, both his sons had abandoned him shortly after the death of their mother. He put it down to grief. He was still in touch with them both, but only by a thread. In fact, his oldest son, John, the one his wife had been carrying at the time of their short engagement (and here Alex paused, looked down at the floor, spread his hands out in a gesture of apology, and shrugged) was unaware that his own father was living within three miles of him.

Bingo! John was local.

Alex's younger son, Ben, on the other hand, lived in the very north of Scotland and worked for an oil company on the rigs in the North Sea. Quite what he did up there was a mystery. Alex grew vague, but he was able to tell her that both boys were married; John to Katie and Ben to Lucie and that both were family men. He didn't see much of his five grandchildren, but that was not because he himself was unwilling. It was unfortunate that both boys had chosen to marry stuck-up bitches, who didn't seem to want anything to do with their father-in-law once the money had run out.

With dinner over, Fresna was eager to get Alex out of the house. She felt she needed time to reflect on all that had been said. Although, she had been assiduous to glean every small fact she could from Alex and had listened closely, she felt worried that if she didn't write it all down quickly, she might forget.

Alex, on the other hand, well fed and cosier than he had been for several months, was in no hurry to move. He suggested to her that, after all the trouble she had gone to that evening, collecting him and cooking him such a wonderful meal, it would be wrong of him to expect her to drive him all the way home. Fresna was thrilled and rewarded the delighted Alex with an appreciative smile. *What a brilliant idea*, she thought to herself. She only had to drive him to the taxi rank and he would be out of her face, but she was wrong. Encouraged by the response he had received from his casual suggestion, he pressed home his advantage. Rising from the table, he moved to her side and took her hand in his. He pressed it to his mouth and then squeezed it tenderly. He told her that he would like to reward her for such a lovely evening by offering her a little something in return. During his life, he told her, he had often reflected on their short time together and, undoubtedly, they had been fantastic together in the sack. He asked if it would be wrong of him to suggest that they turn back the clock. Of course, if she wasn't into all that these days, he was quite happy to stay in her spare room. She could drive him home in the morning.

Fresna listened to his proposal in astonishment, barely able to disguise her anger. Unbelievable! After all the trouble she'd gone to, he wasn't intending to shift his arse, call a cab and sod off to his grotty, little flat under his own steam. Outrageous! Not only was he suggesting, and on only his second sighting of her in over forty years, that they take up where they had left off, but that she might also not actually have had much more than the sexual leavings from the table since he had buggered off. Did he really believe that she, who hadn't slept with a man less than five years her junior in the last ten years and who had lovers coming out of her ears, might actually be in need of a pity fuck from the crumpled old man, ten years her senior and dressed like Hillory Hocker's fucking tramp, smiling down at her warmly.

Luckily Fresna was quick to rally. Leaning back in her chair, she forced herself to look directly into his eyes and smiled an apology. It sounded like a wonderful idea, but she had a wickedly early start. She had booked a workshop in the West End the following morning so she needed to be up early. Could she possible take a rain check? Besides, at her age, he would understand that she needed all the beauty sleep she could get and, in any case, he was right. She had given up any thought of sexual activity a long time ago, never having found any man comparable to him in the bedroom. Reluctantly, she had surrendered herself to the life of the lonely celibate. It was surprising what you could get used to she told him. Mustering up every single one of her life skills, she smiled thinly at the man in front of her, forced herself to relax her jaw and slowly removed her fingers from the grasp of his waxy, veiny, old hand. Inwardly, she shivered with disgust as a boiling hot stream of anger surged through her blood.

If Alex noticed her undisguised hurry to get him out of her home and into her car, he didn't mention it nor did he seem to think that her maniacal style of driving was out of the ordinary either. He appeared unaware of the almost militaristic manner in which Fresna drove him home, back ramrod straight, shoulders by her earlobes, knuckles white against the steering wheel and foot to the floor almost the whole journey through. Mercifully, he fell asleep in the passenger seat almost immediately, lulled no doubt by the myriad glasses of wine he had drunk at her expense, and so Fresna found she did not have to keep up the accepting little woman charade for too long. Alex was surprised at how quickly the return journey took and apologised for napping. They agreed that traffic was light at this time of night. Getting out of the car, he thanked her for a very pleasant evening and told her that he was so glad he had got in touch. He was very much looking forward to meeting Verity at some point in the future, but would leave it with Fresna to work out the details. He reached over to peck her on the cheek and left the car. Fresna watched as he walked up the path towards the utilitarian block of flats in which he lived. From his jaunty air, she deduced that he looked mighty satisfied with himself, secure in the knowledge that everything was going to plan.

But whose plan exactly?

VI

It was long after midnight when Fresna arrived home. To dissipate her rage, she had taken herself for a very long, very fast drive and it had worked. The flood of anger she had been experiencing had abated and she now felt an icy calm glowing within her. It was just as well she hadn't met any traffic cops, she reflected, and if she had been caught by the speed cameras, she felt it would have been a small price to pay. Still, the audacity of the man! He truly believed he was about to be welcomed back into her open arms; that the bad luck which had been dogging him was about to change and that his generation long absence in the lives of both Fresna and Verity was a mere blip in the scheme of things.

After the exertions of the evening, Fresna allowed herself the luxury of a long lie-in the following morning. When she finally dragged herself out of bed, around lunchtime, she felt decidedly unwell, which was unusual for her since she always asserted that she had the constitution of an ox. She decided she must be getting old or not dealing properly with stress, but keeping up the façade the evening before had definitely left her feeling wiped out. She hoped the payoff would be worth the effort. Taking the duvet with her, she made her way to the lounge, sat down in its warm embrace and dialled a number on her mobile phone.

"Thank Christ," roared Celia. "We thought it must have gone tits up." There was a muffled exclamation next to her. "Hang on, I'm putting you on speaker phone," she said. Seconds later, she heard the voice of Jax.

"How did it go?" she enquired eagerly. Fresna gave her two friends the highlights and it was agreed they call a meeting of the Whiskerlies after class the following Tuesday. Putting down the phone, she hauled herself back to bed. She felt exhausted, in need of sleep, but her brain was whirling and she couldn't settle.

Foregoing their regular trip to the bar, the girls opted for green tea at Jax's as the venue for the general update. They gathered in the lounge with Celia and Sly sprawled on the floor and listened carefully to what Fresna had to report. Despite the stress, the clever woman had managed to skilfully extract a massive amount of information from the clueless Alex.

After Fresna had brought the group up to speed, Bex took the floor as unacknowledged leader of the pack. It might have seemed odd to choose the quietest of them all to take charge but, when all was said and done, she was the agreed expert. Phase Two would begin the following morning she told them, with Charley and Tiffany taking the lead for this part of the operation. The girls crowded together as Bex outlined her plan. After a little discussion, and a few small adjustments, the team reached consensus and the meeting broke up.

VII

There were thirty-two people listed in the phone book with the same surname as Alex and with the initial 'J'. One of them had to be John unless, god forbid, he had opted to be ex-directory in which case Tiffany would need to discreetly exercise her constabulary powers. Meeting together mid-morning at Tiffany's, she and Charley agreed their approach. They were an independent market research organisation, undertaking a telephone survey on behalf of the council about the amenities offered in the town. At the end of the spoof interview, they were to casually ask for a few personal details – first name, age range, children – all routine stuff and nothing that wouldn't normally be recorded by the Local Authority.

They got off to a shaky start when the first few calls went to voice mail. Charley agreed to try those again later. The old lady who answered call number eight was so deaf that Charley had to shout at the top of her voice just to get a response. She crossed her off the list in front of her. Wrong sex, wrong age. She then spent an anxious couple of minutes explaining to call thirteen why he had never heard of their organisation and why it didn't have a website so that he could check their validity. She kept her nerve and eventually he hung up.

Call fourteen was answered by a lady named Katie, who was in the right age group and told them freely that she had two children. Tiffany circled her entry on the page. Call twenty-one was picked up by a child who told Charley that her mother was in the garden. Charley gently asked if she could go and get mummy and the child went off to find her but never came back. Distracted no doubt, thought Charley and marked it down for a second call. Call twenty-two was answered by a posh sounding lady with a broad Scottish accent. No, she didn't need double glazing, a time share or car insurance, thank you and good afternoon. Another question mark. Call twenty-seven was picked up by a bloke on nights, who was not at all happy to be disturbed for such a trivial reason. He slammed the phone down. Tiffany made a note against his number to call him back again and make sure it was late afternoon or early evening.

By the end of the third day, the two women had managed to contact every one of the thirty-two names and had sifted them down to six possibles. Satisfied with themselves, they phoned Bex to report in. She congratulated them and told them she would update the others. She would be in touch when she had decided how to take the next phase forward.

In the meantime, it was time for a spot of sleuthing.

VIII

"I can't believe I'm doing this," announced Jax to Izza, as they sat in her parked car at six am the following Monday morning, a few yards from the home of the first possible on the list and with a very clear view of the front door.

"Can we get some bagels when the bakery opens, mum?" asked Izza.

"No, we cannot get some bagels when the baker opens missy. We sit tight until someone opens that door and then we watch. If needs be, we follow them," Jax replied tartly. "There's some coffee in a flask on the back seat and I've brought some fruit. If you're lucky, there might be some mints in the dashboard, but Christ knows how long they've been there."

Together they sat and waited while Izza fiddled with her hair and drank all the coffee. They waited a full hour and a half before the front door opened and a blonde woman, wearing a dressing gown, briefly put out some rubbish before shutting the door again.

"Well, at least someone's home," said Izza. "I was beginning to think they might be doing a bunk or something."

"Doing a bunk? Why would they need to do that then?" asked Jax, more because she was bored than because she needed an answer. Her backside was beginning to ache and she needed to stretch her legs. She knew she would need to pee shortly too and felt a little distraction might ease her torment.

"I don't know. Maybe they know we're onto them."

"Onto them?"

"Yeah, you know, they could have defaulted on the mortgage or something and be planning a moonlight flit."

"Or they could be spies and think we're MI5 and that they've been rumbled. Phone Q Miss Moneypenny and ask for some of that special chewing gum that explodes on contact with wood." Jax had decided to join in the game.

"I'd rather Q brought bagels," replied Izza, gloomily.

"Shut up," replied her mother.

"Wilco M. Do you think they might have a huge pair of binoculars in the front bedroom and they're watching us watching them."

"No, I think she's an early morning burglar, who broke in through the back a couple of hours ago, ransacked the place and now she fancies a quick cuppa before she nips off over the garden wall to sell the loot to her fence."

"You think the loot is in the rubbish she put out?"

"Of course."

"Let's hope it's not bin day then," replied Izza, laughing.

They were both having so much fun trying to outsmart each other that they almost missed the suited gentleman with the briefcase, who came out of the front door and walked down the path. Closing the gate behind him, he turned towards the car and headed straight for them. Holy shit!

As one, Jax and Izza straightened up and then slumped back down again, trying to look nonchalant and failing miserably. Trying to appear as if they had every reason to be in the road at this time of day, that there was nothing out of the ordinary going on at all, that the last thing on their minds was staking out his property proved very difficult because, let's face it, that's easier said than done when you have never done it before and can't help but wonder what might be about to happen next. Was the guy in the suit going to march up to the car, wrench open the door, poke his head through the gap and insist on knowing what the fuck they thought they were doing?

Jax was panicking – why the hell had she agreed to this? She forced herself to keep breathing and to try to remain calm. Both of them waited with bated breath; their hearts thumping so loudly in their chests that surely to god someone was going to complain about the bloody noise any second now. That's if their hearts kept beating at all. The atmosphere in the car was so tense that there was a real possibility of a double cardiac arrest.

As it turned out, the suit walked straight past their car without seeming to notice them. He was simply on his way to work. "Who says there's anything wrong with an anti-climax," thought Jax, sagging with relief. Izza, wiping the sweat from her upper lip, watched the man's retreating back from her passenger wing mirror. When she thought he had gone sufficiently far down the road, she glanced at her mother, who nodded. Izza got out of the car and began to follow the man at a distance. Jax remained where she was and continued to watch the house. About forty five minutes later, the front door opened and the blonde lady re-emerged, fully dressed now and with two young boys in tow. Jax tailed them to the local Junior School, then phoned Izza, who had followed the suit all the way into town on the bus. Jax reversed the car and drove off to collect her.

Across town, Charley and Sly were sitting outside a garage, having tailed another one of the possibles to his place of work. They had agreed to park up nearby and wait another half an hour before Sly exited the car, leaving Charley to drive into the workshop to enquire about the price of a service. Striking lucky, she found their quarry sitting behind the information desk. Deftly flirting with him, it didn't take her long to know for certain that this was a seasoned divorcee, hoping for a chance pick up with an attractive woman. Mentally, she crossed him of the list. The man they were looking for was definitely married.

Tiffany and Celia drew a blank from the house they had under observation. They waited three hours, gave up and took themselves off for a calorifically high breakfast.

By close of play that evening, the girls had information on four of the people on their list with only two left to go, but it was more than a painstaking week later that they felt certain they had narrowed it down to one of two possibles and, by that time, Verity had arrived back in the country.

It was time for Phase Three.

IX

"Am I doing the right thing, Samantha?" asked Verity for the umpteenth time that morning. "I could be opening up a whole can of worms."

"That's what I love about you, kitten," came the reply and then Sam began to sing, "Always look on the bright side of life, te tum, te tum, te tum, te tum."

"Shut up. This is serious," whispered Verity. "I'm scared."

"Look, we've been over this before. I have a ream of paper at home with a list of things that could go wrong scrawled all over it, but we're still here. Now, get out of the car, walk up the drive and knock on the flaming door," instructed Sam sharply.

Verity stood outside the door of number fifty-seven and paused to reflect. Just how should she approach this? What was the right thing to say? "Erm, excuse me, but I think you might be my step-brother. How about I come in and we bridge the forty-five year gap? And, yes please, I'd love a chocolate hobnob."

Which strangely enough was almost exactly what happened, but not because Verity found any of the right words, but because the man standing in front of her on his own doorstep was able to look into her eyes and see his own father. After that first meeting, John quickly organised a second and, only a couple of weeks later, Verity, along with her mother and a highly intrigued Sam, were invited to sit down with their brand new step family and hear a very different version of events.

Well, there are always two sides to every story, aren't there?

Neither John nor Ben knew anything at all about a long lost step sister, but they were unsurprised to find that they had one. It seemed that the affair had been glossed over before they were both born and had never been mentioned again. John and his parents had settled into cosy domesticity and, a little while later, Ben had come along. However, it wasn't long before Alex began his philandering again. To the best of their knowledge and belief, there were no more itinerant siblings littering the planet, but John told them that, as far as he and his brother were concerned, their lives had been marred by the constant arguing of their parents. They were never without a marital storm on the horizon, usually followed by a short summer and then the skies would darken once again as the thunder began to rumble; sometimes in the distance, sometimes directly overhead. Still, the couple stayed together for the sake of their boys. Whether that was a good thing or a bad thing, Ben felt unable to say.

There seemed to be a period of peace as the boys entered their late teens and, in turn, left home, but that might have been because they had found their independence and were moving on. John had followed his father into the insurance business, but worked for a different outfit. Ben went to University. Both boys developed interesting lives outside the family and seldom felt the need to return home. They both remained close to their mother, telephoning her weekly and dropping by to take her out to lunch every now and then. However, there was a definite gulf between father and sons, which time only widened.

It was about seven years ago that it had happened. There were some discrepancies in Alex's accounting. Money had gone missing from the firm. During the inevitable investigation into alleged theft, it transpired that Alex had been less than honest with his figures and, as it turned out, had been defrauding the company for several years. Although the Police had been involved, it was agreed, after a prolonged and somewhat heated debate, not to press charges on the condition that Alex left quietly. He was to clear his desk immediately, leave the building and never return. He would forgo his pension.

The shame was more than their mother could bear. Despite everything happening behind closed doors, Alex was suddenly and inexplicably out of a job. Tongues had begun to wag and rumours were flying up and down the street. Humiliated once more by her treacherous husband, their mother took things very badly and withdrew into their home, feeling unable to face former friends and neighbours. She even refused to open the door to the window cleaner and, in a very short space of time, went from an outgoing, gregarious woman to a thin, fragile recluse. An emergency family meeting was held at which both brothers agreed that the only option was for their parents to start afresh somewhere far away. Twelve difficult months later, the house was finally sold and, with what little savings they had left, husband and wife retired to Northern France. Far away from the gossip of the neighbourhood, the two boys hoped their mother would slowly recover from the shock.

It was not to be. Within a year, she was informed by a kindly doctor in a French hospital that she had developed ovarian cancer. Despite the benefits of a good health system, she failed to rally and, over time, the cancer spread. It was almost as if the trauma she had endured on the outside had finally begun to eat away at her on the inside. Disgraced by her dishonest husband, she found she had little fight left. Just before the end, she chose to return home alone to die in the local hospice with her children and grandchildren around her.

Besides themselves with grief at the loss of their much loved mother, the boys blamed Alex. They were cold with fury and, as one, refused to let him put so much as a foot over their thresholds. They wanted nothing to do with him. As far as they were concerned, he was an utter turd; an adulterous, thieving, manipulative turd and he had murdered their mother. True, he might not have put the knife to her throat and sliced, but he had killed her all the same with his disgusting behaviour. They would have none of him.

And, they told Verity, that if she knew what was good for her, she would have none of him too.

CELIA

I

Patrick was panicking. A delegation from Head Office in Dusseldorf was due to arrive shortly and the pack he had promised would be ready for discussion on their arrival still needed photocopying, but the bloody machine was jammed. Patrick was no use whatsoever with technical things. Lydia had tried her best to clear it and several members of her customer services team were crowding round it, scratching their heads and trying to work out what to do next. No one seemed to know where the handbook was kept. No one seemed to know how to contact the repair man.

Damn Celia! The one day he needed her to pull her flaming finger out and she'd let him down. She'd phoned in first thing full of apology. Her car was refusing to even start. It was still on the drive and she was waiting for the man with the van to turn up and sort it out. No, she had no idea what was wrong with it. Yes, she knew Karl and Fredericke were arriving today. Yes, she knew it was bloody awful timing, but it was just one of those things. She promised to be there as soon as she could. In the meantime, the Dusseldorf folders were on her desk, partially stuffed, only needing the papers Patrick had still been working on when she left promptly at four. Yes, it was unfortunate that she had been unable to stay back to finish them off. Yes, that would've saved all this unnecessary, last minute pandemonium, but she had a doctor's appointment. She'd given Patrick plenty of notice. She'd had to leave.

By mid-morning, Patrick was pacing his office, his mobile stuck to his ear, trying desperately to reach Celia. She would know how to fix the blasted machine. He'd decided to send someone to collect her; either that or she could take a taxi to the office and he would reimburse her, but the landline kept going to voice mail and she wasn't answering her mobile. A glimmer of hope settled over his shoulders. Perhaps she was on her way at last! He hoped she would hurry up. Just at that moment, his colleague, Dan walked into the room, smiling broadly. "Forget the photocopier," he announced. "We can just print the stuff off and then bind it. It shouldn't take long."

Finally, someone with the sense they were born with. Patrick relaxed for the first time that morning and, without realising he was talking to his Sales Director, ordered him to make him some coffee. He just managed to prevent himself from calling a member of his top team a good girl. "God, man, pull yourself together," he thought to himself as he watched Dan march angrily in the direction of the kitchen.

II

From the cosy warmth of her bed, Celia idly wondered if anyone would work out what was wrong with the Xerox. She knew it would play up; it always did when asked to do double siding. The trick was to remove the paper in the upper tray thus forcing it to use the lower one. It had taken Celia ages to work that out so she very much doubted if anyone at Dumbleton's would know what to do. Still, there were other options. They could copy the presentation single sided; they could send the document straight to print. If they thought hard enough, they could probably sort themselves out a Plan B and, if they did, there would just be the binding to do. It was possible that one or two of the girls in the customer services team might know how to use the binder and, given time, any member of staff should be able to work it out. Hell, it wasn't rocket science, but then they would face obstacle number two because, although the binder was sitting in its normal perch just outside her office, Celia doubted if anyone would be able to find any binding rings and that would be because she'd hidden them in her shopping bag just before she'd left for her spurious doctor's appointment. Right now, they were sitting on her hall table. With no binding rings, the presentation would have to be stapled, which would not go down at all well with the German perfectionists who, according to the clock on the bedside table, should be driving through the gates of Dumbleton's just about now.

Oops!

Celia's landline rung again and she ignored it. No doubt, her mobile would sing too any second now. She would ignore that too. She stretched lazily in the bed, made herself more comfortable and settled down to watch a little morning TV, secure in the knowledge that the car on her driveway had recently been serviced and would therefore start first time. There was no need for a mechanic at all. She would leave for work in about an hour or so, she decided, thereby giving Patrick's boss plenty of time to enjoy the fun.

Celia grinned to herself. She wondered if anyone knew where the data projector was kept. If they did, they would have difficulty locating the spare bulb since that too was sitting on her hall table.

III

Celia had rehearsed her story thoroughly. As luck would have it, she explained to the frustrated Patrick when she finally got to the office, all her car needed was a little love and attention. Wasn't if fortunate that the guy who turned up knew just what to do? So, in no time at all, her car was purring gently and ready to take her to work. It could have been so much worse, she explained to her seething boss, who hoped to god that things could never get any worse than the humiliation of this morning's meeting with Fredericke. Celia explained that she had considered taking a taxi, but hadn't wanted to cause the company unnecessary expense and, besides, the man with the van told her he was on his way. It wasn't her fault she hadn't been properly prioritised. She was sorry she had missed his calls, but she had spent most of the morning outside trying vainly to start the car and, somehow, her mobile had been switched to silent. She agreed that it was also a pity that she had not been able to get into the office until after lunch, but then she had been forced to wait for the recovery man and, since she was on her own driveway, she was apparently not considered important and so no one had rushed to her rescue. Still, she had got there as soon as she could and she was sorry she had missed meeting Fredericke, who had apparently left in something of a hurry.

Patrick's tirade was awesome. The meeting had been a total balls up from start to finish, the photocopier had jammed and no one had been able to locate the manual. Why the fuck did no one but Celia know the number of the repair man for Christ's sake? Why hadn't she written it down somewhere? And why hadn't she had the foresight to train someone, anyone how to use the binder? On and on he stormed. In the end, he informed her icily, Patrick's bulky presentation had had to be separated into sections and stapled together. If that hadn't been bad enough, when they had finally managed to locate the flaming data projector, no one knew how to make it work. With Fredericke watching in stony silence, they had managed to set it up with some assistance from a member of the visiting team, but the bulb had failed and no one knew if there was a spare. In the end, they had been forced to go through the slides using the hastily stapled documents in the presentation folder. And Jesus, Mary and Joseph, would you effing well believe it; the retards upstairs had managed to staple some of it upside down. What a fucking cock up! The Germans had not been impressed. Karl had said nothing; he didn't need to since his face said everything. Why oh why for god's sake had her car had to go and break down today of all days; the one day in the year when he needed her most.

Celia shrugged. She couldn't for the life of her imagine.

IV

The next few weeks proved even more of a trial for Patrick. So many things seemed to suddenly be going wrong. When he urgently needed to email across to Head Office the contracts relating to the new build, it turned out that the scanner had broken down and that the contractor was unavailable to repair it until the following week. In the end, the paperwork had to be couriered across to Germany and, sadly, did not arrive in time for Fredericke's meeting with Karl, the top man. Celia might have suggested they get the solicitors to email their copy direct, but she felt it prudent to keep quiet.

The huge A1 printer in the main office went on the blink, meaning that the posters for a forthcoming showcase had to be outsourced at exorbitant cost given the short notice. The final proofs for the Christmas catalogue went walkabout from the Marketing Department, meaning several days' worth of work had to be re-done. German deadlines were missed and production time cut.

Patrick left some vital documents on the desk in his office and so lost an important sale. He could've sworn he'd put them in his briefcase alongside the client file that Celia had meticulously prepared for him.

In the old days, Celia would have been by his side, nurturing him through his working day and ensuring he never forgot anything, but these weren't the old days and Celia was no longer available to work the unpaid overtime she'd once undertaken without a murmur. It was regretful, she agreed, but her mother had become ill and needed her support. Celia was now only able to work the agreed hours stated in her contract. No, she couldn't work through her lunch hour; that was when she had to pop to the shops or the chemist or the post office for her mother. It was a slow business, she demurred, but she felt sure her mother was making progress and that it wouldn't be long before she was back on her feet and managing her own affairs.

Patrick fervently wished that the damn woman would bloody well hurry up. Things were going from bad to worse and, over the past few weeks, he had come to realise how much he depended on his secretary. He was even thinking of giving her a small pay rise, but it was not to be.

Out of the blue, Celia handed in her notice.

V

Patrick was devastated. He'd had no idea she was unhappy at Dumbleton's. He'd had no clue she'd even been thinking of leaving. What was the problem? Was it the hours? He could be more flexible while her mother was sick. Was it the money? He would give her a rise. How much did she want? What about a bonus? A bigger office? A promotion? And so it went on, but Celia would not be swayed. It was none of those things, she assured him. It was simply that an opportunity had arisen that she could not afford to miss. Regrettably, she was unable to work her full four weeks' notice because she was owed two week's leave. She would be leaving at the end of the following week.

Patrick protested. He couldn't possibly allow her to do that. There would be no time in which to recruit a half decent replacement. It would be impossible to organise an effective handover. Given all the knowledge that Celia had about the administrative side of the business, all that she undertook single-handedly, all the gaps she bridged, there was no one who could possibly cover all that she did at such short notice. Please don't force them into getting a temp, he begged. Celia sat patiently through it all. He cajoled and pleaded, blustered and stuttered, tried every strategy he could think of and offered all manner of incentive, but Celia was adamant. There was nothing he could do to encourage her to stay.

There would be no last minute reprieve. She was leaving and the sooner he accepted that, the better.

As a conciliatory gesture, she did however, offer to put together a little 'How to' manual for any would be successor, but only on condition she was given enough time and space to develop it because, given all that Celia covered off and with most of it on automatic pilot, it would take a great deal of thought. She smiled into Patrick's eyes as she told him that sometimes even she didn't quite know how she did what she did. Patrick gratefully agreed to her one compromise.

VI

She had reached her final week at Dumbleton's and was supposed to be working on the promised handover manual while the girls from customer services held the phones, but Celia couldn't concentrate. She kept glancing up at the clock on the wall. Was it her or was it actually going backwards today? She thrummed her nails on the side of the desk impatiently. "Come on five o'clock," she begged it, but the dials stubbornly remained where they were. Sighing, she went to make herself another cup of coffee in an effort to pass another long fifteen minutes. She comforted herself with the thought that she knew she would get away on time. She needed to. She had a very unusual evening ahead.

Despite being in her notice period and therefore supposedly able to ease up a little, the previous few days had been fraught. Timing was crucial and she was terrified of the consequences of getting caught if she got it wrong. Thank god for the Whiskerlies; they had buoyed her up and had helped her to believe in herself.

They were behind her every step of the way and convinced her she could pull this off.

To pass the time, she recalled how the first part of her plan, implemented the previous week, had gone. She had had to wait until Patrick had left for his meeting with the architects at the building site. Most of the marketing staff had gone up to the big show in London or else they were working from home. The Sales Managers only ever came in for meetings so their desks were empty. At the chosen hour, and with Patrick and Lydia out of the office, she knew the customer services crew would be in mid-afternoon slump mode or else gossiping.

Swallowing hard and trying not to think of the enormity of the job in front of her and worse the outcome if any single part of it went wrong, Celia had risen, picked up a batch of post and had forced herself to walk normally towards Patrick's office. Entering the room, she had approached the desk and had then casually let herself drop the letters to the floor with a little flick of her wrist. As intended, they had scattered around the floor, thus enabling her to kneel down in order to pick up the little trail of envelopes now littering the carpet. She had remembered not to look round and had tried not to look furtive. Raising herself up slightly, she had lifted one arm and grabbed hold of the small badminton cup that Patrick kept on the bureau to the left of his desk. She had tipped it towards her and had been rewarded by receiving, from its depths, a tiny key. She had quickly pocketed it and then replaced the cup. Rising, she had placed the hastily gathered letters into the in-tray and had left the room, trying not to hurry. In the relative safety of her office, she had put on her jacket, grabbed a bunch of keys from her own top drawer and had rushed downstairs, letting old Vince in Finance know that she was just popping to the store room for some samples.

Once in the storeroom, Celia had delved into her jacket pocket and had pulled out a pair of leather gloves. Drawing them on, she had made her way towards the back wall of the room where stood an ancient, rickety three drawer chest; the sort of thing no one would like at twice except to wonder why it hadn't been dumped ages ago. The chest was locked and so she had pulled the tiny key from her trouser pocket and unlocked it. So far, so good. Stooping down, she had opened the bottom drawer and had extracted an unsealed, white envelope. Turning it over in her hand, she had looked down at it with reverence. This little thing was going to change her life. Swiftly closing the drawer and re-locking the chest, she had grabbed a few of the nearest toys stacked neatly on the shelves behind her and had made her way towards the exit, remembering to lock the door behind her.

As she turned towards the main building, her luck ran out. Shit! Standing on the other side of the tarmac were two members of the customer services team, taking five for a crafty fag out back. They had acknowledged her as she made her way across the concourse towards them, heading for the back stairs.

"Nice day for it," remarked Sandra, drawing on her cigarette and looking up at the weather.

"Beautiful," muttered Celia, trying to act normally and feeling as though the stolen envelope, perched on top of the factory samples, would suddenly turn from white to scarlet and begin self-rotating. She half thought it might begin to beep or pulsate alarmingly to alert the two smokers that it was stolen property.

"Depends what IT is," remarked Graham, who winked knowingly at Celia, whom he had long fancied, but unfortunately had never made it past first base with.

"You saucy bugger," Sandra said to Graham. "I never knew you had it in you." Pausing, she had then turned to Celia and had begged her not to rush off. "You're always in such a bloody hurry these days. Where's the fire? No one will notice if you slow down for five minutes. We're all desperate to know what made you hand in your notice. Could've knocked me down with a feather – I thought you were here for life. And what's all this about an amazing new job?"

"Yeah, Celia, how can you up sticks and leave me behind?" asked Graham ruefully. "I'm gonna miss you."

"Sorry folks, you know what it's like round here – busy, busy, busy. Tell you what, I'm planning farewell drinks at the Crown next Friday and I'll tell everyone all about it then," replied Celia, thinking on her feet and trying to sidle past her two colleagues, but only succeeding in barging into Graham, who was in no hurry to see her leave.

"Sorry," she had muttered, stepping away from the man and then hot footing it back into the building. Graham had called after her, but she had taken no notice of him. There was no way she was going back. Breathing a sigh of relief at not having roused their suspicions, Celia had hurriedly made her way up the back stairs and into the rear of the building.

"Just one more load to get," she had called down to Vince as she tried to walk normally back to her office. Vince wouldn't bat an eyelid; he was close to retirement and just wanted an easy life these days. Sending out samples was part of Celia's job so she was often seen popping in and out of the storeroom. Back in her office, she had dropped the toys onto the spare chair in her office. Placing her hands on the desk, she had then taken a series of deep breaths in an effort to calm herself down. It took some time as she felt her heart pounding and her temples beginning to throb. Slowly, she had regained her composure and, when she finally felt steady, she had turned back to the office chair and began rummaging through the medley of samples in search of the envelope.

It wasn't there. It had to be! She had tried again and still couldn't find it. Her heart began to sink and she felt herself growing colder. Taking a very deep breath, she had searched again, a third time, this time lifting each toy in turn and placing it on the floor. Now she was sure; the envelope was most definitely missing. Fuck no! Oh Christ, please no! How could it be missing? It had definitely been on top of the pile when she had left the storeroom and crossed the road. She could remember seeing it when she was speaking to Sandra. Oh no, oh holy Christ and all the saints, no! Realisation struck her full in the stomach. She must have dropped it when she had knocked into Graham. Oh shit! Oh holy, sodding shit! What the fuck should she do now?

Forcing herself to stay calm, Celia again left the office and had begun to retrace her steps when the stair doors opened and Graham walked in with Sandra, back from their fag break. Celia looked at them and there, in Graham's hand, was the missing envelope. Celia's heart turned to ice. Had he looked inside it? Did he know what it was? Jesus, it didn't bear thinking about.

"Celia, you twerp" called Graham, cheerfully, "You dropped this on your way in," and, mercifully unaware, he had passed over the little envelope. "I called after you, like, but you were in too much of a bloody hurry. You ought to pay more attention to what you're doing and stop rushing from job to job. You'll give yourself a bloody heart attack if you don't watch out."

That's the fucking understatement of the year, thought Celia, who had merely smiled and taken back her property.

Returning to the office once more, Celia had sat down, put her head in her hands and had taken several more, slow deep breaths. What the hell was she doing? That had just been too bloody close for comfort! As soon as she had felt calm enough, she had grabbed a sheaf of papers and had made her way directly to the photocopier. Amongst the documents she had hurriedly copied was the single sheet of paper from the envelope. Back at her desk, she had separated it from the rest, had tucked it carefully into her handbag and had then locked that away in her bottom desk drawer. She had then made her way back downstairs to the store room and had returned the envelope to its rightful place, thankfully remembering to collect a few more samples for her return journey to the main building.

Once back upstairs, she had taken some files from the cabinet and had taken them into Patrick's office and put them on his desk. On her way out, she had simply dropped the tiny key back into its resting place. The whole exercise had taken less than twenty minutes, but she had been left trembling with exhaustion. She had then gone into the kitchen to make herself a very strong cup of black coffee. Her heart pounded, her head ached and she felt sick, but she had completed the first stage.

The next stage would be considerably more difficult.

VII

Just after midnight, Charley dropped Celia a few hundred yards from the back of the Dumbleton's buildings and then drove her car round to the front door, parking just short of the entrance. She took out her mobile and dialled Celia's cell phone. Excellent, she was in position. She keyed in a short message, returning the device to her pocket without pressing send.

Driving her car to the very centre of the forecourt and leaving it there, Charley entered through the front door, walking confidently towards the front desk. The night watchman stood up and looked at her in surprise. He was rarely disturbed at this time of night and never by so glamorous a visitor. He looked at her questioningly, the admiration beginning to reach his eyes. All Charley had to do was hold his attention for the next few minutes. This was going to be a piece of cake.

With a flash of her beautiful smile, Charley explained that she was having trouble with her car. She seemed to have lost her breakdown card otherwise she would have called the rescue agency for advice. She shrugged and looked up at the night watchman guilelessly from beneath her long lashes. She was hopeless at technical things she told him. Could he possible take a look? With a shrug of his shoulders at the incompetence of women and the gallantry of men, the captivated man followed the lovely lady outside. It was at this point that Charley, who'd kept her left hand inside her pocket, fingers clasped around her mobile, pressed the send button.

Celia, dressed all in black and pressed flat against the back wall of Dumbleton's just a few steps from the back gate, had been wondering what the hell Charley was doing. Get on with it Charley, she silently begged. This wasn't Ocean's fucking Eleven; this was real life. If she was caught, she could be prosecuted, might even end up in prison. Was it worth it? At the sudden buzz of her mobile, Celia nearly jumped out of her skin. Her hands were damp with sweat inside the latex gloves Sly had supplied from the hospital. This was it; she had minutes. It was now or never.

While Charley and the night watchman looked under the bonnet of the car for clues, Celia crept into the back of the office, easing her way through the foyer and up the stairs to Patrick's office, stopping in front of the safe. Once there, she took out a single sheet of paper from inside her jacket. It was the same one that she'd hidden in her bag only a week before on the day of her first robbery. She had memorised the numbers on it, but, as a way of reassuring herself, she checked them again by the light of her pencil torch. She keyed in the combination, opened the safe and removed a large manilla folder. Checking that the information it contained was what she wanted, she placed it carefully inside her jacket, closed the safe and tiptoed back downstairs, past the security cameras and back towards the most vulnerable part of her journey. Celia was untroubled by the cameras since she knew they were empty; back in the day, they might have caused her a problem, but a cost saving exercise a while back had taken that particular burden off her shoulders. Tiptoeing towards the foyer, Celia crossed her fingers and hoped that Charley was still holding the night watchman's attention. Butterflies crawled through her stomach at the thought of meeting him face to face in the foyer.

As she sneaked through the empty hallway, she could see that Charley was doing a brilliant job outside on the forecourt. She had positioned her rescuer so that he was standing with his back to the front door and she was making damn sure she had all his attention. From the short distance between them, Celia could've sworn her friend was flirting with the man. Silently, she sent a prayer of thanks towards the heavens for the nerve of the woman. Still, if that's what it took to get the job done, she would do it too. Charley's full attention seemed to be focused on her prey but, out of the corner of her eye, she had been watching for Celia and the moment she saw her, she almost jammed the poor guy's nose into the car engine. Taking advantage of the situation, Celia sped down the hallway, through the foyer and made her way towards the back door and out of the gate. From the safety of the quiet lane that backed the property, she sent her own text message to Charley, giving her the all clear.

She had done it!

VII

When Celia met the Whiskerlies after class the following day, she had a lot to report. So far, although there had been several stressful moments, everything had gone according to plan. Head Office had become aware of the increasing inefficiencies in the UK Branch and Patrick had been summoned to Dusseldorf. Unfortunately, he had been unable to catch his flight as he had somehow lost his passport. Celia grinned as she told her friends that it might have been because at the time he was supposed to leave for the airport, the document had been locked in Fresna's top drawer. Fredericke had flown in the following morning and had met Patrick at a hotel a few miles from the office. A warning had been given; there could be no further incidents.

Despite nearly pulling out at the last minute, Celia's raid had gone very smoothly. Patrick had no need to access the safe for a couple more months so the crime should remain undetected for the foreseeable future, giving the burglar plenty of time to use the theft to its best advantage.

Sly, who had taken a small, yet significant role behind the scenes, was able to add that his meeting with the buyer had gone better than expected. A price had been negotiated and an exchange date agreed.

Jax finished off with the news that her meeting had also proved very successful. The contact Charley had given her had proved very knowledgeable and was able to provide just what they needed. There was a price of course, but Celia was only too happy to pay it.

All in all, the Whiskerlies had to agree that it had been a productive, if nerve-racking few weeks. With a bit of luck and a fair wind, the sting should hit its target. As Celia popped open the champagne, she felt amazed at how things had turned out. Who'd have thought that Charley would have such an unusual contact?

TIFFANY

I

Oh my god! She blinked; she couldn't believe her eyes. It couldn't be – not after all this time. It was! Tiffany had imagined all kinds of situations over the past eighteen months, but she had never envisaged this one. She had pulled the car over as part of a regular stop check; just a random car in a stream of passing traffic and yet why had she picked this car of all cars? Sheer coincidence? The luck of the draw? Or just one of those things? Who knew?

The man, smiling up at her from behind the open window, was trying to tell her how good it was to see her again, trying to remember how long it had been, commenting on how well she was looking. Feeling like the worst professional in the world, she stuttered her way through the request for his driving licence and waited, heart fluttering, for its deposit into her waiting hand. The polished smoothness of its leather casing in her palm seemed to steady her. She moved onto the next stage, going through the motions, hardly aware of what she was doing. In the comfort of routine, she hoped to regain her composure.

She examined the document, asking the standard questions and listening intently to the answers. He was on his way to a training course in a village just outside town. He was running a bit late since traffic on the bypass was heavy at this time of day. He wasn't sure of the location so could she be a pet and hurry up? He didn't want to keep his audience waiting. There's a love. Lovely. Lovely little Tiff. Who'd have thought after all this time…?

For a split second, all was still and, in the same instant, time grabbed her by the shoulders, shunted her backwards and dumped her where she did not want to go. Back to an oak-panelled dining room, a table littered with half empty wine glasses and cups of stale coffee, a roomful of silent, shadowy faces and those patronising, humiliating, demoralising words, "Lovely little Tiff."

Her stomach dropped into her hips and lay heavy like granite against her pelvis. She felt a cold flush slowly creep into her armpits and the beginnings of a blush began to warm her face. She struggled to take in air. She was lost in an old nightmare. Her saviour came in the form of metal butting against her thigh. In a flash, Tiffany was back, fast forwarded to the present as the door of the black Porsche in front of her began to open. She became aware of the feel of the sun on the back of her neck and the smell of leather in her hand. He was trying to get out of the car. Pulling herself together, she rallied. She was not a helpless, put down Training Manager now. She was a member of the Police Force at work on the beat with a job to do. He was reaching out towards her, repeating his earlier plea. He needed to get going, could she speed through the formalities; he had a job to do. There's a pet. There's lovely. Lovely little Tiff. There it was again. No need to consider what to do next; he was making the decision for her.

Straightening herself up, Tiffany forced herself to look the overweight Welshman in the eye and then frowned, shaking her head from side to side as she did so. Keeping a tight hold on his driving licence, she began a slow, a very, very slow tour of his vehicle. She took a good look in the boot and poked around its space. She checked each of his tyres and took her time inspecting the general condition of the Porsche. Her partner, astonished at her diligence for what would almost certainly yield diddley squat, went back to the police car and began working through some forms. In the end, Tiffany made certain she did a thorough roadside check, deliberately keeping him standing by the roadside a full thirty minutes.

After the first five minutes, he stopped trying to sweet talk her and instead began following her, trying to convince her that she was wasting her time. She wasn't going to find anything. It was a brand new car for pity's sake. After about fifteen minutes, his frustration was beginning to reach boiling point and she had to warn him about his language. By the end of the exercise, he had shut up altogether, returned to his car and was slumped in the driving seat, eyes closed and foot tapping. The message had sunk in; there was absolutely nothing he could do, but wait so Tiffany gave him plenty of time in which to do just that.

Throughout the entire check, Tiffany ensured that she exuded an air of relaxed, polite indifference. She made no apology for her actions, nor for holding him up. When she was quite finished, she ended the driver's torture by wishing him a good evening and enjoyed the unexpected pleasure of watching him pull away from kerb kangaroo-style, thus evidencing his feelings.

Tiffany checked her watch. It was time to return to the station for her rest break and a soothing cup of Earl

Grey Tea. Whenever she recalled the incident, and she chose to remember it frequently, she always remembered it as one of the highlights of her career.

The day she gave some back to Fat Taff.

II

Tiffany sat curled in one of Celia's big armchairs, toying with her glass of Merlot and pondering on the state of her love life. Across from her, sitting on a pouffe, Jax was entertaining the Whiskerlies with a funny tales about the fire safety lecture she had attended a few evenings previously. The trainer had arrived late and full of apology. In his haste to make up for lost time, he had tripped over himself, trying to reach the small stage and had ended up sprawled across it. He had followed that by dropping all his brochures on the floor. During his presentation, he was so stressed that he stumbled over his words and kept repeating himself. As if that wasn't enough, when it came to the short video, he couldn't get the projector to work. After faffing around for a few minutes, a member of the audience had stepped in to rescue him by simply plugging the damn thing in.

For the joy of it, Jax again went over the delicious moment when the bumptious, overweight fireman had fallen over his great big feet onto his great fat arse. Jax thought that, as a training office, he made a great comedian, especially given his strong Welsh accent.

Deep in thought, Tiffany was only half listening, but somehow the essence of the story percolated some remote part of her brain and made the connection. She sat up, tilting her head towards Jax and listened more closely. She felt sure she was hearing something important, but was struggling to catch the thread. It couldn't be – surely it was too much of a coincidence.

Fully concentrating now, Tiffany asked Jax a few pertinent questions and suddenly everything clicked into place. The lecture had taken place the very evening she had been on traffic duty and doing roadside checks. It had taken place in a village hall on the right side of town and the lecturer was an overweight Welshman but, and at this point Tiffany balked, eighteen months previously, if her assumptions were correct, that same trainer had been at the top of his game, lecturing on catastrophe management to gold level command at comfortable hotels up and down the country. To Tiffany, it now seemed that her former tormentor was reduced to delivery routine fire awareness training in unheated halls in backwater villages to the lowly homeowner.

What a come down!

III

The Whiskerlies were eager to know why Tiffany had suddenly shown such an interest in Jax's story and so she told her friends all about her recent, unwelcome reunion with the Welsh bully from a previous career and explained that, if she wasn't much mistaken, the bumbling, stumbling lecturer, who had so entertained Jax a few nights ago for all the wrong reasons, were one and the same.

"How could that have happened?" mused Tiffany, almost to herself. "He was one of our shooting stars, one of a small, elite group of experienced officers with a remit to deliver top level training in a very specific field."

"A shooting star, who shot you down without a second thought," Celia reminded her.

"It must be a one off," decided Tiffany. "Perhaps they all have to take turns doing the shit jobs."

"Must it?" asked Sly. "Maybe he didn't get away scot free after all. You don't know what happened after you quit your job. You may have left before they could convene the tribunal, but that doesn't mean they didn't complete the investigation and maybe, just maybe, some of the mud stuck. Perhaps some of the questions that were asked didn't quite get answered in the way Fat Taff would've liked."

"You never know, someone might have come forward after you left and supported your side of the story or perhaps, they reasoned that there's no smoke without fire and, given your exemplary record up to then, they might have decided it was unlikely that you just had one too many, decided to tip the contents of your glass over your respected colleague's head and call him a prick for the hell of it," suggested Jax.

"An intolerable prick, actually," replied Tiffany, smiling at the memory.

"From the sound of it, I'd say you were pretty damn spot on," remarked Fresna. "I'd give a hundred to one that he is very definitely the owner of one intolerable prick."

At that offensive remark, the entire group crumbled into snorting fits of laughter and only managed to restore order by drinking several more glasses of wine.

"I want to know what happened to him after I left," said Tiffany, resuming the conversation.

"Of course you do," replied Bex.

"Okay, so what do we know?" asked Izza, getting straight to the point.

"More to the point, who do we know?" replied Charley, sagely.

"More to the point, who do YOU know?" remarked Sly because it was astonishing just how many contacts the fitness instructor had.

After a brief discussion and a little online investigation, it transpired that the County Fire Service was indeed hosting a series of early evening safety awareness lectures around the area. The very next one was taking place the following week in a village nearby. It was agreed that Sly should go and check it out. For the hell of it, their chosen sleuth decided to go in disguise. At the very least, it might make a potentially boring evening much more fun. In any case, taking on another character might make the whole thing far more believable and it would give him a chance to legitimately go out in public as his alter ego and, in the unlikely event of Fat Taff meeting him at any future point in the company of Tiffany, he most definitely would not be recognised.

If Fat Taff was surprised to see a flamboyant, scarlet haired hippy marching towards him at the end of his next lecture, he didn't show it. After all, there was always someone ready to hold him back with a question or two, usually about fire alarm testing or escape plans, normally the elderly or lonely and, almost always, a woman. It often amused him that people behaved in this way. There was always ample time for questions from the floor at the end of his lectures but, no matter how much time he offered his audience, there would always be one or two introverted individuals hanging back at the end of the evening, waiting to ask him a question in private. Unfortunately for Taff, most of them were either plain, homely-looking ladies or white haired old women, but every now and again he got lucky and something much more attractive would seek him out. If the climate was right, he was never averse to a little light hearted banter but, given his previous experience, he was always very careful not to let matters get out of hand.

This particular evening, his luck was out. The lady striding towards him from the back of the hall was just not his type. Overly tall for a woman, somewhat muscular and clearly struggling to walk in her killer heels, she hurried towards him. In a low, throating and somewhat unpleasant voice, she began by praising him for what she called his inspiring workshop and then launched into a series of rapid fire questions about his lecture tour. He informed her that he was the lead for this particular series and that he had been touring for about twelve months now, following a continuous circuit around the county. Somehow he found himself telling this strange woman all about his previous careers. After twenty five years as a fire fighter, he had gone on to become a successful trainer. In fact, only a short while ago, he told her that he had been at the peak of his career, but had been forced to give it up on account of a prolonged period of poor health. He had had to take six months off, having discovered that the constant travel up and down the country, was proving too much of a strain. When prompted, he offered her a leaflet on fire safety and a poster detailing the rest of his courses. She told him she would come again and bring some of her friends with her; she had found the whole evening most interesting. She then offered to help Taff load his car, thanked him again for an inspiring night, turned on her deadly heels, tossing her brightly coloured poncho over her broad shoulders and strode off towards her car.

V

The following evening, the Whiskerlies couldn't wait to meet to find out how Sly had got on. Bex sat back in her chair, watching them and smiling to herself. When she first told them her secret, she had not envisaged that this would be the outcome. Here she was, acknowledged leader of the pack, assisting her team to what they all hoped would be another successful sting.

"So, it seems your man didn't get away unscathed after all?" remarked Fresna, sitting at their usual table in the upstairs room of the Lord Nelson pub.

"Possibly not," agreed Tiffany, sitting opposite her, "but he most certainly is not MY man," she added pointedly, her blue eyes flashing.

"Calm down, Tiff," said Bex, "you know Fres didn't mean it like that. Besides, I have some information that will knock your socks off. I wasn't going to say anything, but, well, now it seems relevant."

The band of friends turned to look at Bex expectantly, so she wasted no time letting them know that Fat Taff was a keen golfer, a member of a rival club and that Malcolm had played against him many a time. Under careful probing from Bex, Malcolm had revealed to her that Taffie, as he was known to his friends, had been the unfortunate victim of a vengeful vixen at work, who had taken it upon herself to accuse him of inappropriate conduct and all because he had refused to respond to her advances. To top it off, the bitch had publicly humiliated him in front of his peers at a top notch dinner. Of course, she had been outrageously drunk or she wouldn't have got away with it. In the end, common sense had prevailed and she found herself hung by her petard, left out to dry by her managers and had resigned like the coward she was. Despite the fact that she had slunk away to lick her wounds in another job, he had been left with a question mark over his head for the rest of his career because some fool of a director had chosen to believe that there was no smoke without fire. A whispering campaign had begun in the office and he had found himself the target of smart remarks, sidelong glances and increasing isolation. In the end, Taffie had decided he could no longer cope with what he considered to be poisonous gossip and continued victimisation. His doctor had agreed to sign him off sick with stress. He had returned to work several months later and had been given something significantly less taxing. Malcolm had informed his wife that he felt sorry for the poor bugger and had insinuated that some women were born teasers and, as such, deserved all that was coming to them.

So now the team new Fat Taff's side of the story at the end of which, Tiffany sat pinched and white with rage. The Whiskerlies had to work hard to calm her down.

"That is not what happened," she insisted over and over again. "Wanker!"

"Reading between the lines, it sounds like Fat Taff didn't get everything his own way," soothed Charley. "What we do know is that he is now the county lead for fire safety and that is one spectacular come down."

"He took six months off work with stress," added Sly now wearing a more masculine style of dress.

"And he wasn't entirely believed," remarked Jax, "so it seems he might not have got away with it scot free."

"Which is probably why he complained about the gossip and why he got removed from the course by the powers that be. The likelihood is that he probably went off sick from the effort of having to swallow his pride and take on a lesser role in the dizzy depths of public awareness training," added Celia.

"Is that enough?" Izza asked Tiffany quietly.

"Enough?" What do you mean – is it enough?" stormed Tiffany, still pretty cross and now confused.

"Enough of a come down for you? Enough revenge?" replied Izza calmly, her mobile forgotten as she concentrated on the drama of the friend in front of her. These days she paid more attention to the people in the room with her than to the ping of her phone.

"No, it sodding well isn't," Tiffany spat back. "After what Bex just told me, I feel angrier than ever. The bastard!"

"Okay, so what do you want us to do to him then?" asked Izza, cutting to the chase.

"I don't know, but it had better hurt," replied Tiffany savagely.

So, after ordering another round, the Whiskerlies discussed their options and, by closing time, they had a pretty good idea of what they were going to do.

CHARLEY

I

It wasn't what you knew, it was who you knew and, fortunately for Charley, she knew all the right people. She was also intelligent enough to know how to use them to her advantage. In the end, it was a friend of a friend who offered a way out of her particular dilemma.

The Whiskerlies had debated at length the right way to go about settling their friend's noisy neighbours issue. Over the past few months, Charley had invested in various strategies of her own. A frontal attack had failed, several subtle sorties had similarly proved fruitless, and ignoring the problem had not made it go away.

Surprisingly, it was Izza, who came up with the best idea of all. Why not invite some of Charley's posh friends to a summer 'at home' and expose them all to the untuneful 'orchestral manoeuvres of the bark' from the retards next door? Surely one of them could pull the right strings. The girls carried the idea forward, embellishing Izza's original strategy until, finally, Charley herself began to believe it just might work. As they began to work out the details, Charley told them that she felt she didn't really need help from every member of the team and singled out Fresna, for her sophistication, Bex, for her listening skills and Sly, just because she fancied him, to come along as guests, but the others simply refused to be side-lined and suggested they come as waitresses instead. Celia swore she wouldn't swear and promised faithfully to keep her mouth closed and her strong opinions to herself. Charley told them she would think about it. In the end, Bex stepped in and persuaded her that she might actually need all the help she could get and told her to thank her lucky stars that she had so many loyal friends instead of picking and choosing among them like a duchess! Charley, rarely so completely put in her place, demurred and the game was on. Tiffany, consulting her diary, proffered her apologies. She would be on duty on the agreed date.

Tasteful, elegant invitations were posted out to all the right people. A few neighbours were also included. Bex, with Sly as sous chef took charge of the catering and, for the two weekends before the event, she encouraged everyone to cook up a storm. Individual gourmet desserts, sorbets, home-made mini quiches, vol au vents, canapés, dips and crudités were all beautifully prepared and stored in various freezers. The right wines were chosen. On the morning of the soiree, Bex prepared two whole fresh baked salmon whilst Sly roasted a side of beef. Several trays were delivered from Harrods' and there was also a visit from a local florist.

The garden was looking particularly lovely at that time of year and Charley had organised for it to be trimmed to perfection by hired hands. The house, never less than perfect by anyone's standards, had also been treated to the services of professional cleaners. All Charley needed now was for the sun to shine and for her neighbours next door to behave normally. Charley, never one to trust to luck, crossed her fingers and prayed to the gods of good weather.

II

The glorious weather Charley had ordered obediently arrived and the sun continued to shine all day as caterers, florists, delivery men and friends came and went. As the late summer afternoon began to give itself over to a russet evening sky, Charley began to welcome her guests. As always, she had dressed well; smart, yet casual, subtly expensive. Adorned with the right accessories and flawlessly made up, she moved with practiced grace through the select group of people, putting them at their ease and introducing them to potential new associates. Relaxed, yet attentive, sociable, yet slightly aloof, laughing in all the right places, Charley was the perfect hostess. However, not everything was going according to plan. It was just bad luck that the chavs next door had chosen the one day of the year that Charley needed them to behave outrageously to bugger off out the door. Charley was furious. "The sodding bastards," she thought. What a fucking waste of time and money her party was going to be.

Still, assumptions can be so wrong, can't they?

It was Celia, proffering a tray of canapés to a group of long time business acquaintances, who picked up the first clue. The overbearing, overweight lady in the vivid red suit talking to the Chief Superintendent, in a frightfully, frightfully voice, was fairly certain that a family member owned the house next door. Celia stiffened on hearing the news and gently edged forward. She listened more closely and discovered that the woman, whom she instantly nicknamed 'Scarlett O'Hara' had a brother who was a property developer and rented several properties in the local area. Scarlett couldn't be certain, but she was sure that next door was owned by his company.

Celia could barely contain her excitement and, ignoring the fingers of several guests wishing to taste the culinary delights on her tray, she rushed inside to tell Jax, who was washing glasses in the kitchen. Izza, entering mid-conversation to refill her tray, was sent to find Fresna and pass on the news.

Fresna, who had been flirting effortlessly with the Head of the Local Chamber of Commerce, listened carefully to the news. Returning to her conversation, she quickly made her excuses and began a slow circumnavigation of the party, finally bringing herself into the group next to the one with whom Charley was conversing. She positioned herself in front of Charley and signalled with her eyes. Five minutes later, the pair were upstairs. It turned out that Scarlett was the new partner of Jeremy, Chairman of the Round Table. Charley did not know her; in fact, she had only met her for the first time that evening. Returning to the party, she casually made her way towards Jeremy and began an easy conversation with him. It wasn't long before Scarlett returned to his side, uncomfortable that the glorious Charley seemed to be monopolising his attention. Inwardly despising herself for her hypocrisy, Charley turned her attention to the badly dressed woman and complimented her on her suit. Flattered, Scarlett opened up and it wasn't long before Charley had the woman eating out of her hand. Within a short time, she had memorised the names of Scarlett's brother and his company.

Fresna and Bex had deliberately spent a considerable amount of their time talking to Charley's neighbours. Eventually the subject of noise was raised and neither woman was surprised to discover how the other families in the cul-de-sac felt about the gooneys next door. In fact, it proved very valuable to hear, not only what they had heard, but more significantly, what they had observed.

Thank god for nosy neighbours.

III

From the point of view of the guests, the evening had been a great success, but Charley felt frustrated. She had not been able to expose her upmarket visitors to the intolerable abuses of her next door neighbours and the only information she had gleaned was the possibility that the house next door might be rented rather than owned. There might be some mileage in that, but Charley doubted it would be very much.

However, she had underestimated the eavesdropping abilities of her friends. Over hot chocolate in the lounge, after the last of the guests had left, she was less than fascinated to learn from Sly that the man of the house next door apparently worked as a window cleaner and had a round a few villages away. He couldn't be sure, but one of the ladies present was fairly certain that the white van on the shared driveway was often seen in her neighbourhood. Charley was unsure how she might put that information to use, but there was more to follow. Hot on the heels of that little nugget came the interesting news from Fresna that 'our man' had also been spotted by several disgusted neighbours signing on at the Job Centre. Charley's frustration melted like ice cream on a hot hob. She had just been handed enough information to take things to the next stage. It seemed that Mr DG was doing a spot of moonlighting. The Whiskerlies agreed to meet after Tuesday's class to discuss how to use what they now knew to its best advantage. Whatever they decided, a little research and a spot of stalking would definitely be on the agenda. Fresna rubbed her hands with glee and volunteered immediately. She was getting to enjoy all the sneaking around.

IV

Dressed all in black and with heavy eye makeup and darkened lips, for the second time in a week, Izza found herself trying to lean casually against a set of railings surrounding a boringly functional building while she waited for a signal Celia sitting, with a book on her lap, across the road on a park bench. Parked directly across the road from Izza, and with her driver's window down, Fresna was listening to Radio Two while she waited impatiently for the phone call from Charley that would let her know that her neighbour had left the house. Last week, it hadn't happened and Fresna had spent a tedious two hours waiting for an action that had failed to materialise. The plan had finally been aborted and the team were now back in place. Fresna very much hoped that their prey would show up. She tapped her fingertips against the steering wheel in irritation. If he didn't show this time, she might very well decide to pay an unscheduled visit on Mr. Fuckwit himself to tell him to get his finger out and stop wasting her valuable time.

Fresna's mobile buzzed, signalling that the show was on the road. Fresna opened the driver's door and exited her car, removing the equipment she needed from the boot before locking her car and moving to a spot in the small park area almost opposite the Job Centre. She chose the shade of a small willow tree and began to assemble her kit. For Izza and Celia watching from across the road, her actions indicated green for go.

Within ten minutes, Izza spotted him in the distance striding towards her. She straightened up and moved to the top of the Job Centre steps and sat down just in time to watch Celia walk into the building itself. As her prey reached the top of the steps, Izza asked him if he could spare the price of a meal. He ignored her and tried to move past, but she grabbed hold of his leg and began to plead. Turning back, he tried to shake her off, but she began to crawl up his leg in a seemingly shaky effort to stand up, asking instead for the blag of a cigarette. He refused her and roughly shook her off, swearing about young people these days, and entered the building not long after Celia.

Izza got up and bounced lightly down the steps to the pavement below and left the scene. Her job was done and, from the look on the face of Fresna, as she crossed in front of her, she could tell she had done a good enough job. Hopefully, Celia would finish what she had started and that Fresna had got what she needed.

Whilst Izza was acting her butt off at the Job Centre, Charley was sitting in the offices of Michael Gates, Property Developer, talking to its very attractive owner. Charley rarely felt non-plussed, but the man in front of her was exactly her type – broad, dark, suited and booted. His eyes were amazing; the same deep blue as her lupins, she realised. Mentally pulling herself together, she sat up straighter in her chair and opened what, after all, was supposed to be a business meeting. She had brought with her a signed copy of the petition she had previously secured from all the residents in the cul-de-sac, together with several letters alleging a series of noise offences against the occupants of No. 10. Accepting coffee from Michael's beautifully manicured hands, Charley felt a flush of heat run through her and settle deep in her hips. She paused, briefly allowing herself to imagine how those elegant hands might feel caressing her bare skin. It was rare for a man to have such an effect on her; it was usually the other way round. Disturbed, she cleared her throat to give herself a few seconds to pull herself back to the job in hand. Succinctly, she gave a potted history of the lows and even lowers of living next door to his very self-centred tenants. She cited examples of their total disregard and lack of respect for others in the area. She understood, she told him, that children made noise but, what with the wife screaming at her offspring from the patio doors, the dogs barking at all hours and the regular DIY, she felt she had come to her wit's end. Whilst Michael was sympathetic, he remained objective, possibly even a little unconcerned. Nevertheless, he was intrigued to hear about the handiwork going on in the house, especially as there were strict rules about what could and could not be done to the inside of one of his properties. He remarked that, whilst he personally had no problem with pets, he was surprised to learn that the household had a lot more animals than had been agreed pre-contract. Michael promised Charley that he would investigate the matter and do what he could to monitor the noise levels. Politely, he told her he would be in touch as soon as he had any news. Standing, he indicated that the meeting was over and gently led her towards the door. Charley was not going to be dismissed so easily. Before she left, she invited the property magnate to her home to give him a chance to witness the abuse first hand. Charley was disappointed with his response. Whilst Michael did not refuse her offer, he did not exactly bite her hand off either but, as Charley later admitted to herself, he was a very busy man.

First Sly and now Michael! Charley was beginning to believe that she must be losing her touch.

V

Tiffany yawned with fatigue as she sat in her car slightly left of the entrance to Charley's cul-de-sac. She had decided to look upon this as just another early shift, but she hoped he would hurry up and give her something to do. In reality, observation was not nearly as exciting nor as interesting as it was often portrayed in films or on television. On the contrary, it was mainly tedious, often lonely and usually cold. More often than not, it left her with stiff joints and an ache in her lower back but, this morning, she refused to complain. Her ordeal was for a very good cause.

To pass the time, she began reflecting on the state of her love life. For six months now, she had been in a steady relationship. For Tiffany, this was almost unheard of. She went through men the way other women went through tights, but this time it was different. This time, he had made all the right moves, said all the right things and taken her to all the right places. They had had several enjoyable weekends away and he had told her that he was falling in love with her. They had even discussed setting up home together; not marriage of course – nothing so permanent, but living together was definitely on the cards. Unlike the rest of Tiffany's previous relationships, this guy kept turning up. He was personable, sociable and apparently solvent. He seemed ideal but, recently, cracks had begun to appear in the shape of little white lies, insignificant slips, nothing to worry about really but, nevertheless, he was lying to her. It had begun really quite innocently when he told her that he would be unable to see her one weekend as he had to go to Birmingham on business. She was very surprised then to spot his car in the Leisure Centre. She had even driven into the car park to check that it really was his car. Why had he said he was away when he was clearly in the area? That evening, she took a trip to his home and, sure enough, lights were on in the house, indicating he was at home. When she next saw him, she asked him about his trip and, amazingly, he told her it had gone well and had gone on to colour in the details with a few humorous anecdotes. He even gave her the name of the hotel in which he had stayed. She began to wonder if he had taken the train and lent his car to one of his kids but, on further questioning, he let her know that he had driven there himself. Did he perhaps have more than one car and, if so, who had been using the other one? Back at home, she had rung the hotel to check his story and found out that no one of his name had checked in that weekend. Then there were the times when he said he was in when he was actually out. Tiffany had begun to check out his driveway so often that she was beginning to feel like a stalker. Was it another woman, she'd wondered or perhaps he just enjoyed telling porkies. Whatever was going on, she believed his behaviour was odd and she was unable to shake off the notion that she had actually stopped trusting him.

She was roused out her reverie by the sight of a white van coming to a stop at the white lines in front of her. It was him.

"Here we go," thought Tiffany. Although a fully trained CSPO, she had not been taught the finer arts of trailing. Still, he wouldn't be expecting anyone to follow him and he was probably the type who didn't look in his mirror enough. Pulling away from the kerb, she began to follow him, careful to keep two cars between them. He drove south towards the bypass, heading, no doubt, for one of the little villages that surrounded the town.

After about ten minutes, he drove into one such village and turned right onto a fairly modern housing estate where he parked his van. Tiffany drove straight past the van and took the next left. She parked her car, waited ten minutes and then got out. She had put on a green waxed jacket, floral headscarf and a pair of wellington boots. She grabbed a large canvas back from the front seat and walked back in the direction of the parked van. With her head down and the scarf covering her hair, she turned the corner and saw, further down the road, Charley's pain of a neighbour perched on top of his ladder, humming tunelessly whilst cleaning the windows of the first of the houses in the road. She looked around her and saw that there were no vantage points. There was nowhere to hide and nothing to hide behind. There was just a row of detached houses lining a quiet street. Bugger! Turning back into the road in which she had parked her car, she began to explore the estate. It took her some time to find what she wanted but, eventually, she found a close that exactly suited her purposes. She could still see the main road from behind a large forsythia bush. Watching the window cleaner, she estimated that it would take him about thirty minutes to get to where she needed him to be and then, in order not to bring unwanted attention to herself, she left the close and took a long, slow walk around the estate, careful to keep out of sight of her quarry. When she felt she had wasted enough time, she doubled back on herself and got into position behind the bush. She had only to wait a short ten minutes before the window cleaner came into view and began to work on the house directly opposite the little close in which she was hiding. She wasted no time taking her camera out of the large canvas bag she was carrying. She neatly fitted on its telescopic lens and waited until she had a clear view of the moonlighter. She took several frames of him cleaning both the ground and first floor windows of the house opposite, but had to wait until he made his way to the next house to get a clear shot of his face. For good measure, she went on to take several photos of his van.

Satisfied with her morning's work, Tiffany returned the camera to her bag and made her way to her car where she took off her scarf, coat and boots and stowed them in the boot of her car, along with the camera. She looked up at the sky. It looked like it was going to be a beautiful day. She then got into her car, called Charley and told her that the deed had been done. Between them all, she told her, she was sure they had him nailed.

JAX

I

The cursor in the password box was flashing its impatience. Taking a deep breath, Jax flexed her fingers and glanced across at Fresna, who smiled back reassuringly and nodded. The email from Des had been discussed at length among the girls and next steps had been agreed. Jax sighed and, once again, wondered if she was doing the right thing. Trying to deceive the deceiver was not going to be easy; she only hoped she had the skill to pull it off.

A prod from the impatient Fresna pulled her out of her reverie and away from the brink of self-doubt. Leaning forward, she placed both hands on the keyboard and tapped in her unique signature, thus accessing her account at DesperDates. It had been three days since she had last been on the site so she was unsurprised to find several messages awaiting her attention. They would have to keep. She had only one email on her mind and she searched back through the list to find it.

Hitting the reply button, she paused briefly and then typed.

"Hey Des, so sorry to hear about your financial problems. Naturally, I am happy to give you all the support I can but, from this distance, I'm not quite sure how I can help other than to say that you are in my thoughts and prayers. It must be very distressing for you to be facing the loss of your business especially given that you have a young daughter to support. Did you not plan for the day when the IRS would come calling for their tax? Let me know what I can do to help? Love Jacqueline xx

Beside her, Fresna smiled. "More than enough for now," she said and then, leaning over her friend, she pressed the send button.

For the next couple of hours, Fresna and Jax played internet cat and mouse with an array of players from the dating site. Sometimes they took the role of cat; sometimes the role of mouse, but always behind the e. flirting there lurked the incredulity of the farce that was internet dating. It never ceased to amaze Jax how the boundaries of good manners were heavily trampled upon over the ether. Somehow, the remoteness and lack of real intimacy that existed over the airwaves seemed to allow people to cross the line of good taste but, then again, sometimes Jax thought she might just be getting old. Still, she couldn't help feeling that any man she met in real life and who asked her bra size within five minutes would be lucky to get away with just a glass of Chianti over his shirt. Fresna found it hilarious the way men waved their dicks around online in the hope of bagging a half decent prize. She felt it was better than the telly! For herself, Jax found the whole internet dating charade equally fascinating. Still, she was looking for someone with his brains in his head, not in his Tighty Whities! Fresna laughed at her friend and told her she might as well start looking for a needle in a haystack!

Then there was the issue of 'cam fun'. Jax felt that the term, 'fun' was questionable, since the reality was a proposed videoed act of mutual masturbation. She shuddered at the thought and wondered how anyone could possibly consider this remote act intimate, loving or even sexy. Fresna was much more relaxed about it all, believing it took all sorts. Besides, she relished the opportunity of winding up some of the worst tossers who came her way, pretending to be their very own free sex hotline, letting them believe they were pressing all her buttons while she sat next to Jax, drinking green tea and laughing at the absurdity of it all.

After an hour or so, Jax received a message from Intellygent. She was delighted to hear from him. Here was a man, who knew where to draw the line. His emails were sexy, yet tasteful; stimulating, yet subtle, exciting, yet respectful. He used metaphor to tease her and turn her on. Never once had he used explicit language and yet his messages were clear. Jax found their storytelling session very edgy with their essence of underplayed eroticism. How often she had wished she could meet this man in the flesh, but he never came forward with a mobile number or personal email address or, shooting for the moon, a date.

This afternoon's theme was Sleeping Beauty in which she played the role of the beautiful princess dozing in pliant innocence in the tower whilst the determined prince climbed mountains, waded thigh deep through swollen streams, battled hosts of demons and hacked his way through half a forest in order to reach the side of his fantasy woman. After all that effort, her prince was hardly going to be satisfied with a chaste kiss of her cheek. No, here was a man who had earned the right to wield his weapon, had shown his skill in the use of a sword and knew exactly where he would like to plunge it. This was a fairy tale with a difference; it had the bite of innuendo and an undertone of good old fashioned raunch. Even Fresna, sitting quietly next to Jax, felt the sap rise at the cleverly turned phrases of the aptly named Intellygent.

Jax, more used to this wonderfully tense game of Sizzle, had considerably upped her repertoire over the past few weeks and was able to match him phrase for phrase in the sexual euphemism stakes. Eventually, the game was over and he had to go; the girls were coming over for supper, he explained. She sighed. If only, he would ask her out!

The pair were just about to log off when the next message from Des popped into her inbox.

My own angel,

Somehow I knew you would be there for me. The Lord told me and I had faith in him. It has been such a difficult few days awaiting your reply. I do not want you to think that I cannot be a good provider for you in the future. On the contrary, I have always prided myself on my ability to look after my family and I will do the same for you. You need not worry about that. It is just that right now I am over-stretched, what with all the overheads and building materials, so I find myself with something of a cash flow problem right now. I hesitate to ask for your assistance with what is, after all, my problem but our future together is on the line and it really would only be in the short term. I rejoice in the Lord that you care so much for us and for our future life together. All my love, sweetheart, your Des xxx

Jax and Fresna read through the message and then logged off. It seemed the bait had been swallowed.

II

The following evening after work, Jax fired off a response.

My Des, I will do what I can – of course I will. Please let me know what it is you feel I can do to help you. I am so far away and am at a loss what to do. Love, your Jacqueline xx

She didn't have to wait long for a reply:

My darling, how my heart leapt when I read your email. I knew right from the start that the Lord had sent me my very own guardian angel in you. Our future life together will be so good. With you by my side, there is nothing I cannot do. I just need a short term loan to get me over my present difficulties and so keep my men in full time employment. If it wasn't for them, I wouldn't feel so worried, but they have wives and children to feed and so, my love, if you could just loan me the money I need, I can then forward it to the IRS. I am expecting payment for completion of a project in a neighbouring town and can pay you back the loan with interest in a few weeks. Oh my darling, let me know what you can do to help. I am in your hands. Your Desmond xxx

Since Jax elected not to respond to his message, another, shorter reply soon followed.

The IRS have given me only two weeks to pay the bill. Hurry my love. I need your help so very much. Des xx

Des, $50,000 is a lot of money and I don't know if I can get my hands on it in such a short time. I will see what can be done. Love J xx

My angel, any help would be welcome right now – $15,000 or $20,000 would keep the taxman off my back. Please wire what you can as soon as possible. I am about to begin laying off some of my workers. I would

like to write more, but I am just off to collect Aimee from school. Let me know what you can loan me. All my love always, your Desmond xxx

Under instructions for her friends, Jax did not access her account for the next ninety six hours. When she did so, she found four messages from an increasingly desperate Des.

My angel, I went to church today and prayed for you. I am so blessed to know someone as wonderful as you, who believes in our future together as much as I do and who has no hesitation in offering her unstinting support to me. Oh my darling, how I love you and all that you are. Des xxx

My own Jacqueline, today I was forced to lay off some of my workers. It was hell, a black day for me. I have employed some of these men for twenty years. If you had seen the looks on their faces, you would understand how important your support is to me right now. I know you will not fail me. Send what you can. Let me know when you have the money and I will tell you where to wire it. Be assured of my love. I think of you every day and always last thing at night when I lay my head on my pillow. I only hope we are not too late to save our business, angel. Your Des xxx

My love, I have not heard from you. Is everything alright with you? Are you sick? I am worried about you. All my concerns here pale into insignificance in the knowledge that you might be hurt or unwell somewhere and that I cannot reach you to help you as you would do – will do – for me. Please talk to me angel. I am beside myself with worry for you. More workers were laid off today. It has caused me such grief. These people rely on me. What am I to do? Tell me, my Jacqueline, my own.

Help me. I love you. Your loving future husband, Des xxx

Jacqueline, where are you? Please talk to me. Des x

My dearest Des, I am so sorry to have caused you such concern and worry by not getting in touch sooner. I understand your situation and really do want to do all I can to assist you. I too hate to think of all those workers and their families without an income or food on their table when there is something I can do to help. However, things are happening here for me too in the UK. I have such amazing news and I only wish I could share it with you, but I cannot. Please believe me when I say that I have so much hope for us right now and that it will only be a short while before I can offer you all that you deserve. Please, please you must promise not to ask. I truly cannot say – only that I am so excited. I wish, wish, wish I could say more. Trust me, my love. All will be settled. Your Jacqueline xxx

My own true love, how my heart soared to receive your message. To know that all is well with you is enough. I cannot help but wonder at your news – I am human, after all, but I will not ask; only trust in the Lord and your loving support. I had another letter from the IRS yesterday. Time is running out for me, angel, but I must not think of myself only. You are always at the centre of my thoughts and all that I have is yours – only for the loan of a few thousand dollars and we can be together so that I can provide for you. Hurry my love. Time is short. Your loving Des xxx

My darling Des, fend them off. Say anything, but stall them. I am confident that, in the next few days, I will be able to surpass even your expectations and show you what kind of woman you are in love with. Only do not ask – you are a business man – you know how these things are and I must not risk disclosure at this time even to the man I trust most in the whole world. Oh darling, cross your fingers and pray for good news. I wish I could send you some of the money right this minute to keep those bloodsucking sharks at bay, but my money is tied up for just a short while and I cannot release it. Believe me, I so want to. I wish I could say more. All my love, your Jacqueline xxx

Darling Jacqueline, of course I trust and believe in you – my future wife, my loving spouse for eternity. Oh how wonderful life will be for us. I will hold the IRS back and do all I can to keep my business running while you do whatever it is that you must do to support our future. I eagerly await your good news. All my love, Des xxxxxxx

After reading Des's last message, Jax felt satisfied that things were going according to plan. Logging off, she went downstairs to fix herself something to eat. She had quite a bit of research and background reading to undertake after which she would report in to the Whiskerlies to confirm the final phase.

IZZA

I

Sitting alone at the formica table, sipping coke while the world came and went around her, Izza reflected on the changes in her life over the past few startling months. Could it really have been less than nine months ago since her sister had uncovered Tony in the front seat of his car shagging some faceless bimbo? Did the relaxed, contented, fulfilled young woman of today have any connection to the cowed, defensive, needy girl of yesteryear?

The clumsy, awkward caterpillar, crawling along on the ground, hiding under leaves and grubbing out its life in the dirt was gone. In its place, a glorious, golden butterfly had emerged from its chrysalis intent on fully enjoying its time in the sun, flexing its wings, feeling its inert power and sipping nectar from the choicest fruits. Izza grinned to herself at the thought. This bedazzling, bewitching butterfly was definitely planning a lot more than one brilliant summer.

It had begun on the fateful evening in the town park when she had unexpectedly come across Tony's car, but had she not met up with Darren and his gang, she probably would not be where she was now. She might have been dead in a ditch. She could have been whoring for drugs. She might even have gone back to Tony. She shivered inwardly at the thought of what might have been.

Having watched passively as her sister had ousted the unfaithful Tony and his lady friend from the passenger seat of his car and felt the horrifying force of yet another betrayal, Izza had simply bolted. Fleeing more from her feelings than from Tony, she had just run off with no destination in mind and she had carried on running mindlessly, possibly even in circles, until she found herself lost in the middle of a sink estate on the edge of town. She had finally slumped to the ground against the partly collapsed fence of a terraced house, crying bitterly into her folded arms, protesting heartbreakingly against what life had brought her thus far.

Nothing stirred while the girl poured out her heart into her hands. Eventually, the torrent began to subside and she looked up to examine her surroundings more closely. She surveyed her feet, which she realised were actually throbbing. Unlacing her trainers, she took one foot carefully out of her Nikes. It was red and pulsating, hot with the shock of such a long, unplanned sprint. She found she had several blisters. Her other foot was much the same. She looked down at herself. She was dirty and sweaty. Her mouth felt dry and she realised she was thirsty. How she would have loved to throw herself into a hot bath and have her father fix her something to eat. She needed to get home. Rising to her feet, she held the fence for support. She had no idea where she was. She decided she would just have to knock at one of the doors and ask for help.

II

It was just as she had made her decision that Darren came into her line of sight, swaggering towards her, water bottle in one hand and with a small gang of mates following in his wake. He stood swaying in front of her. To Izza, he seemed clearly high on something, but he didn't appear threatening.

"What-oh!" he said. "What have we here?" A pretty lady in distress – what do you think, lads?" he continued.

Clearly as leader of the group, his question was rhetorical and his friends just muttered under their breath, sniggered or looked curiously at the shoeless girl in front of them.

"Aw look, she's been crying. Had a bad day at the office? Daddy forgotten to give you any pocket money? Poor little lamb," he jeered. "Bit posh for round here, ain't ya?"

"Er ya, actually I'm lost," the girl volunteered. "Do you think you could point me in the direction of the main road?" she asked.

"Er ya, actually I'm lost. Do you think you could point me in the direction of the main road," mimicked Darren over-pronouncing his vowels in his attempt at an upmarket accent, clearly enjoying the opportunity for a little easy bravado in front of his mates. His friends immediately hooted with laughter at his mockery of the girl and began slapping their thighs in approval.

"Okay darlin', you can come with us. We'll see yer right, won't we boys?" said Darren, giving an exaggerated wink.

"No please, it's alright. I'll just phone my dad on the mobile and he can come and pick me up." Izza was now beginning to feel a little uneasy.

"Gotta mobile have we? Fabulous. 'And it over," ordered Darren, holding out his hand.

"Yeah, what else you got, darling?" added one of his underlings, stepping forward.

"Come one inch closer and I will knock your fucking head off," replied Izza with all the authority she could muster, shocking herself as much as the others.

"Ooh, got some spirit, have we? I like a girl with a bit o'fight in her. Listen, it's okay love, we're only playing with you. We didn't mean to frighten you but, seriously, you are a bit posh to be walking around here at this time of night. Come with us – we'll see you right."

In an instant, Darren had turned from slightly threatening to warm and friendly, but Izza wasn't buying it. She stood her ground, trying to look as aggressive as possible, but with her insides turning to jelly.

"Listen," continued Darren. "We're off to the common – that's where we live, but we go right past the bypass on the way through and we can point you in the right direction for the town centre. If you like, you can just follow us. We won't touch you."

Turning, he walked away with his friends following, leaving the frightened girl behind. Izza hesitated, unsure what to do. Should she follow them, she wondered or should she stay put? Perhaps she should stick with her original plan and knock on a nearby door to ask for help. Whatever instinct it was that told her to follow Darren turned out to be a life saver. Hesitating for only a few moments, watching the boys disappear into the darkness, she cautiously began to follow them, making sure she kept her distance. After a short while, Izza was forced to slow down. Her feet were too sore for her trainers, but she was struggling to walk bare foot along the path. Slowly, she drew further and further behind the gang of boys.

Eventually, she was force to stop altogether and that was when Darren turned and came back to her.

"What's up?" he asked and the girl indicated her feet. "I can't walk very well," she replied. "Blisters."

Darren edged closer towards her and stooped down. He took one of her feet in his surprisingly gentle hands and examined it.

Straightening up, he looked at Izza and said, "Only one thing for it," and, without further ado, he leant forward and swiftly lifted the surprised girl into a fireman's lift. Immediately she began to struggle but, after a few seconds, realised that it was futile. Whatever was about to happen next, she had brought it on herself. She guessed she could scream, but they were in an isolated spot and there were too many of them and only one of her.

After a while, one of Darren's mates took his turn and carried her piggy back style through a small housing estate, past a business park and on towards the common. Johnny, the tall, silent one took the final leg. Izza couldn't believe her eyes when the group finally broke through a small screen of hedges, bordering the common, and into what looked to her like a communal camp with several tents surrounding a central open fire. Johnny placed her gently on the ground in front of some girls, who were sitting around the fire, smoking and talking. They looked with interest at the newcomer, sizing up the situation quickly. Someone stood up and stirred a pot, which was bubbling gently over the campfire; someone else went into one of the tents and returned with a First Aid box. It wasn't long before Izza was sitting nursing a cup of tea whilst the worst excesses of her panicked flight were being sponged and antiseptic cream applied. Very little was said and no questions asked. A little later, she was given something to eat and offered a sleeping bag. As she gratefully eased her aching body into its comforting folds, she heard the sound of an acoustic guitar being played outside her tent and she drifted to sleep to its rhythm.

She was woken the following morning to the chink of pottery and stone as a cup of tea was placed next to her. She opened her eyes to find Darren grinning down at her.

"Feeling better?" he asked.

III

Izza spent three days with the group. In that brief period, she learned a lot about life, about herself and about survival. Darren and his gang were not the evil thugs she had supposed. True, they were thieves, they did drugs and they looked menacing, but they had hearts of gold and meant her no harm. They eked out their existence on a mixture of casual work, benefits and charity. Some of them were lazy and some hard working, but all of them had issues with what they saw as the fascist, capitalistic society in which they found themselves. Their camp was a reflection of their individual decisions to opt out of the system that they felt had failed them.

Despite appearances to the contrary, they were actually on the side of the good guys, defenders of the poor and downtrodden, grubby knights in shabby armour and were happy to support whoever seemed in distress. They had no problem sharing what little they had with the poor little rich kid, who had suddenly rocked up in their world and, if she needed a listening ear, she would get that too. If not, no dramas.

Over the next couple of days, Izza watched, listened and learned. She learned fast. Of the dozen or so young men and young women living rough amongst the hedgerows, she heard not one word of complaint. Oh yes, they had strong opinions on current affairs, politics in particular, but they did not moan about their individual circumstances. Instead they were, in the main, cheerful, resourceful and communal. They didn't give a toss about tidiness and yet kept themselves and their campsite reasonably clean. They had some kind of unspoken agreement with the local Police, who regularly moved them on without rancour and they lived from hand to mouth, moving around the fringes of the town and its surrounding villages like gypsies without caravans. They had little faith in the system and wanted as little truck as possible with, what they considered to be, the interfering morons from Social Services. They worked where they could, accepted charity and openly admitted to scrounging or stealing for the rest. As a group, they were down-to-earth, practical, realistic, tolerant and unswervingly loyal.

Each of them had a story to tell and none of those tales involved the good fairies, generous genies or heroic tales of daring-do. On the contrary, all of their accounts involved some form of abuse or misery, pain or abandonment. Darren, unquestioned leader of the gang, was the childhood victim of a brutal father and a drunken mother. He became caretaker of his family from the age of seven, was poorly educated and yet as bright as a button. Despite having endured several broken limbs and severe beatings from his dad, the intolerable job of cleaning up after his incoherent, vomiting mother and trying to find food for his younger siblings, he showed no anger towards the world and he refused to act like a victim. He was outgoing, personable, kind and yet tough. He came across as uncompromising and was no-one's fool. Given a different set of circumstances, he might have been climbing the corporate ladder. Instead, he lived the life of an itinerant and, as leader, he led from the front, expecting no one else to do what he himself would not do.

His girlfriend, Sophie, was a victim of child sex abuse. No one in the family had believed her story or, if they did, they had chosen to turn a blind eye. In desperation, she had run away from home at age thirteen, got in with a bad lot and had turned to prostitution to feed her emerging drug addiction. If it hadn't been for Darren, God knows where she would've ended up. She was a kind, motherly soul and had bathed Izza's feet on her first night in camp, applying ointment and sticking plasters to the worst areas. She asked no questions, spoke from the heart and refused to be cowed by her earlier circumstances.

For Izza, watching from the outside, these youngsters were a revelation. Her former ideas of social depriva-tion, hoodie menace, bad manners and thugism were swept away on a tide of friendliness, warmth and accep-tance. They listened closely to her woeful tale, but couldn't quite get what they were supposed to be sympathising with. They simply couldn't understand her problem. To them, the situation was clear cut. Here she was, pathetic little rich kid, the world at her feet, clean home, hot food, comfy bed and half decent parents yet she chose to be put down, abused and spat on by a needy, desperate retard of a boyfriend, who she allowed to steal from her, cheat on her and diss her. They shook their heads in disbelief and asked her, over and over, why she kept going back to him but, somehow, every time she tried to answer the question, she found she had no words. As she looked into their troubled, puzzled faces, realisation shot through her. Finally, the rubber hammer of sense hit home, the fog lifted from her eyes and she saw, really saw, for the first time, and with startling clarity, what had been staring everyone else in the face.

Nothing anybody had ever said to her before had made a different yet these kids, poorly educated, badly dressed, childhood trauma victims had been able to make her see that she had a choice. She didn't need to be a victim; she was choosing to be a victim. The message went home and, in that moment, Izza finally began to grow up.

When she felt ready, Izza informed them of her decision to return home. There were no hugs or kisses, nothing sentimental. Darren and Sophie simply walked with her to the edge of her estate, wished her luck and left without a backward glance. The only thing they asked of her was that she never disclose anything about the group or talk about what she had seen. They asked her to respect their circumstances as they had respected hers.

Izza was only too delighted to agree and so, no matter what the provocation, she never breathed a word about her 'time out' as she began to call it. However, she made sure to keep in touch with Darren and, occasionally, whenever she could afford it, she placed some money under a marked stone along the path over which they had carried her. No one thanked her. No one needed to.

IV

A shadow fell across her, interrupting her reverie. She glanced up. Smiling down at her, adoration etched across his face, was Callum. She'd met him a few months previously at a village hall meeting where he had been working as caretaker to pay his college fees. It had been love at first sight for Callum; love had taken a little longer for Izza, but it was blooming now. They were planning on moving in together when he had finished his studies and could afford the rent. In the meantime, they spent as much time as they could together; work and study permitting.

Jax and her first husband, Martyn, were delighted for her. After watching their daughter suffer, and suffering greatly themselves, for too many years at the hands of the awful Tony, they were more than happy to welcome normal, ordinary Callum into their lives. Of course, he had his faults. He often missed the point, he was untidy and he picked his teeth, but he didn't tell lies, throw punches or steal. Moreover, he worshipped Izza with every ounce of his being and was not afraid to let it show. His intentions towards her were clear and Martyn and Jax were in no doubt that he would look after her future.

As for Tony, his situation seemed to be in something of a meltdown. He had lost his job, his savings, possibly even his home and had recently been arrested by the Police. As Callum sat down beside Izza, she reached into her tote bag and silently handed him a letter.

She waited calmly while he read it.

SLY

I

It started innocently enough with a pair of tights, carelessly draped over the dressing table chair in his mother's bedroom. Ali had insisted on yet another game of hide and seek so Sly was pretending to search the house from the top to bottom to find his elusive brother. Sly always made a huge thing out of not being able to find him. He would search everywhere, calling out all the time to Ali to let him know exactly where he was looking. This made his brother giggle and so give himself away; not that Sly needed much help. He had a fairly good idea where he would probably be hiding since Ali rarely deviated from his top five hidey holes. Sometimes, their mother would join in and hide her youngest son somewhere different. It made the game more interesting for Sly.

"Not under the rug in the living room," he would yell. "Not behind the curtains either. I wonder if he has squeezed himself into the desk drawer... mmmm, where can he be? Where can my little monster be? Doesn't matter, I'm going to find you and when I do..." and here he would pause to listen for any tell-tale rustles or scrapes that told Sly where not to look just yet.

"Okay, so are you in the bathroom, hiding in the shower?" he would call out, scrambling upstairs to yank back the shower curtain. "Nope, not there. Hey, clever clogs, give me a clue." Another pause while Sly pretended to scratch his head and Ali tried desperately not to make a sound.

"Playing hard to get today, are you? Best I put my thinking cap on... got it, you must be in the fridge," and he would run back down the stairs into the kitchen to check, making the bottles of milk rattle against the metal barriers that held them in place.

"I know where you ah-are," he would sing out. "Under mum's bed," and off he would run again in the direction of the stairs, pretending not to notice the muffled sounds of giggling coming from the hall cupboard.

Sly never hid from Alistair. Ali was just not very good at the hunting side of their game. For a start, he never really looked anywhere. He would simply wander round each room of the house as if he expected to find his brother out in the open. He never thought to look behind the sofa or in the cupboard. Worse, he tended to get very frustrated when he couldn't find Sly almost immediately. Without saying anything, both boys had agreed that Ali always hid and Sly always sought.

On this particular occasion, Sly had run upstairs to look once again under his mother's bed where Ali was not hiding and, as he paused to think where to look next, he had let his hand rest on the back of the dressing table chair, thus discovering the tights. Sly had always had a love of fabric, but something about the silky softness of this particular material under his hands made him draw in his breath. He looked down at them and allowed his fingers to brush across their filmy surface. He had seen tights before of course; in the washing basket, over the clothes drier or on the line but, this time, it felt like the first time. Tentatively, he picked them up and ran his hand up and down their whole length, luxuriating in their feel. It made him shiver. He put his hand inside one of the legs and drew it up his arm. It felt wonderful.

At that moment, an indignant Ali cried out in his husky, sibilant tone, "Are you looking for me or not Thylvethst. I'm behind the thofa." Startled, Sly sprang into action once again and shouted back, equally indignantly, "Who locked me in the wardrobe? Was it you Ali? It had better not have been you, you little monster or you know what's going to happen. I'm coming to find yooooooooooouuuuu," and he threw himself back into the game, but not before, for some reason he was scarcely aware of himself, he jammed the tights deep into his trouser pocket. He had never taken anything without permission before and he couldn't for the life of him understand why he did it now; he just knew he needed to; that it was important.

The game of hide and seek always ended the same way. Sly would swoop down on Ali, throw him down onto the floor, bend over him and tickle him relentlessly until the pair could barely see for tears of laughter. Ali always begged his brother to stop, but both of them knew he didn't really want him to. Sometimes, Sly would go too far and Ali, whose chest was never strong, would start to struggle with his breathing. At this point, their mother would come in from the back room where she had been sewing to stop the game, scolding her oldest son and rushing to her baby boy to see if he was okay. Feeling his forehead, she would make him sit down and breathe slowly. Sly would be sent to fetch his medicine.

Ali was a robust looking little boy, slightly overweight, but with bags of energy. He didn't get sick very often, but his condition caused him a whole range of minor health problems that worried the life out of his mother and were the reason she tended to be over-protective of him. Ali understood her concern, but it also irritated him. He wanted to be out and about with the other boys in the street, who never treated him as though he were any different from the rest of them and always let him join, albeit clumsily, in their street games. All too often his mother frustrated him by keeping him indoors with his books and his jigsaw puzzles because she felt it was too hot or too cold or too wet for him to be outside. Thank god for Sly then, who could always charm his mother into letting Ali get a breath of fresh air on the promise that he would be there to look out for him and make sure he didn't catch sunstroke or pneumonia or fall in the pond.

II

That evening, after he had read his brother to sleep, knowing that his parents were downstairs watching the television, Sly stole up to his room and lay on his bed. From out of his pocket, he extracted his silky-soft, stolen goods and began to stroke them. As he did so, he felt his mind go blank and surrendered to the gauzy feel of the almost transparent material between his fingers. He almost drifted off to sleep but then, to his enormous surprise, he felt himself becoming sexually aroused.

Now, at sixteen, this had happened several times before, but always very unsatisfactorily. He had had the usual wet dreams but, although he felt he needed to, he could never properly masturbate and so often ended up feeling restless and cross with everyone. He had solved his own problem by taking up running and would get up early, before school, to run through the town, returning home for breakfast in a much better mood. This time things were happening of their own accord; really actually happening all by themselves and, this time, it turned out to be highly satisfying. In fact, it felt so downright delicious that he ended up doing it again twice more during the night and, although he often still went running, he found he no longer had the same desperate urge to escape from the rampant teenage hormones coursing through his blood.

That night proved to be a watershed for Sly. As a teenager, he was already testing his boundaries and trying to break down the barriers of his family life, but he was pinned in place by the overwhelming love he felt for his brother. An attractive boy, with regular features and auburn hair to die for, girls had been batting their eyelashes at him for years but, somehow, they didn't seem to be able to give him whatever it was that he was looking for. Consequently, to the utter dismay of most of the female half of the school, he was still a virgin.

For several weeks after the revelation of the tights, Sly felt content enough to leave things as they were – just stroking the nice fabric in the privacy of his bedroom felt enough. However, as his newly unleashed sexuality began to grown, often leaps and bounds ahead of his imagination, he began to experiment. His first idea embarrassed the hell out of him and yet he still knew he had to give it a go. Putting the chair up against the door in case anyone came in, he removed all his clothing and put on the pair of tights. They felt incredible against the rough skin of his adolescent legs. Hesitantly, he approached the full length mirror in his room and took a peek at himself.

He had always known he was different, but this was altogether something else. Never before in his life had he felt like this. Staring at the reflection of the awkward, almost naked boy in the mirror, he felt as if he had just stumbled across himself. Another idea rocked him. He dressed quickly, removed the chair and tiptoed across the hall to his parents' bedroom, returning with a couple of his mother's satin petticoats. He desperately wanted to take a pair of her knickers too, but felt that would be too disrespectful and so restrained himself. Back in the safety of his room, he tried on one of the garments, smoothing the gorgeous fabric against his thighs. He crept once more to the mirror and looked at himself. A tall, slender boy, with overly long auburn hair wearing a petal pink petticoat and a pair of fawn tights, gazed solemnly back at him. He felt an overwhelming sense of peace, quickly followed by a wave of emotion so strong that he felt the need to sit down on the edge of the bed. He began to sob, quietly at first, but growing louder until he thought he would choke. He smothered his face in his pillow in an effort to reduce the noise. Afterwards, he masturbated and fell asleep on top of the covers still wearing the stolen garments. When he awoke the following morning, he felt refreshed.

Sly had discovered sex.

III

Thus began a mercifully short, criminal phase in Sly's life. Having finally found a way in which to express his sexuality, he became obsessed with it. He yearned for new and different fabrics to place against his skin to turn him on. The thrill of his mother's satin petticoats and soft wool dresses soon began to fade and he increasingly found himself rifling through her underwear drawer. He could never bring himself to take anything, but he strongly felt the need to do something.

He began by stealing washing. He was careful not to do any pilfering in the local streets, choosing instead to cycle the long way home on the look-out for the bright, tell-tale signs of lingerie, fluttering on the breeze. He discovered that he adored lace and he would whoop with joy when he snagged such a prize, pedalling home furiously to squirrel it away in the locked suitcase he had bought at a boot sale and which he had hidden under his artwork at the back of his wardrobe. His mother had questioned his need to buy such an ugly, old thing so he told her it was an antique and might have value in a few years. She might have fainted if he had told her the truth.

By the time Sly was seventeen, he had a wide collection of underwear – stockings and tights, French knickers and tango briefs, even the odd push up bra or two and these he savoured late at night in the sanctity of his bedroom, alone in front of the mirror. By this time, he had begun to borrow the lipsticks and mascaras he found in his mother's vanity case. He was always careful to replace them the following morning when he went upstairs on the pretext of brushing his teeth. He would have died if he thought his mother had discovered his secret. He justified his acts by reasoning that he could hardly walk into Woolworth's and buy some of his own.

When he spotted a red and black boned corset adorned with tiny red ribbons in the lingerie section of his mother's spring catalogue, Sly nearly wet himself on the spot. He felt a rush of blood to his groin and, catalogue in hand, rushed to the toilet where he spent the next few minutes fantasising about how it might feel to wear something so beautiful. After he came, he cleaned himself up and returned downstairs to watch The Two Ronnies with his parents. He felt exquisitely languid, thoroughly guilty and very aware that he would have to find a way of buying something similar.

For a teenage boy, that was to prove incredibly difficult and it was to be over two years before he found a way to do it. In the meantime, he continued to satisfy himself with stealing knickers from other peoples' lines.

IV

After upsetting his mother by turning down Art School and choosing to go to Medical College instead, Sly never looked back. He thoroughly enjoyed his nursing training. The majority of the others on the course were women, but Sly had always enjoyed female company in an asexual way and he had long ago worked out how to avert their subtle advances. He never left anyone feeling rejected; he somehow instinctively knew how to let a girl down romantically and yet leave her feeling delighted to have found herself a new friend with whom she never felt the need to suck in her stomach. As a result, Sly thrived during his college years, easily understanding the theory and demonstrating real skill with the practical. When he finally found himself on the wards, the only thing he hated was the nasty material they made him wear under the guise of a uniform, but he solved that problem by wearing a pair of tights underneath his starched, white trousers and a silk chemise under his stiff, high collared tunic. Since he always made sure to change in the privacy of a cubicle, he felt his secret was safe.

In his final year, Sly moved into student accommodation. It was a requirement of the course that, at this stage, he live on hospital grounds. Whilst he was ready to leave, it was still a wrench to move away from his brother, albeit only a short bus ride away. Throughout his nursing career, he returned home as often as duty and lifestyle allowed. His mother was still to be found humming away at her electric sewing machine. Having developed her skill over the years, she had begun making wedding outfits. From miles around, young girls came to her to get something original and hand-made to make them feel even more special on their big day. His father was nearly always at the allotment, still digging away. Although, in his own way, he loved both his sons, he could never quite forgive himself for not being able to sire something more ordinary. He avoided his feelings by strenuously working the soil, ultimately producing more vegetables than his family could use.

By the time Sly graduated, Ali had begun attending a special school a few miles away where he could mix with his peers. He was thrilled with the bright yellow coach that collected him from the end of the street and returned him there every school day. Ali adored his new life. There were lots of activities for him to do at the centre as well as giving him a decent education. His favourite hobby was clay modelling. In pride of place on his brother's desk was a brightly painted, slightly tipsy pencil holder given to him by his little monster as a twentieth birthday present. In the kitchen, he had a selection of cheerfully coloured, hand painted mugs from which he always drank his coffee. He never allowed any of his fellow student nurses to use them; he gave them their coffee in more ordinary cups.

With Ali more settled than he had been in his earlier years Sly, at last, felt free to spend more of his time doing as he pleased. The other nurses were a lively crowd, who regularly invited him out with them. They had got to know him and he had somehow become one of them; one of the girls. He felt very comfortable in the role. They begged him to go with them when they went dancing. From their perspective, there was a man around to protect them if they needed it and to accompany them home, arguing happily amongst themselves as to whose turn it was for a piggyback from the only man in the group. Sly enjoyed these nights out too, but it was the shopping expeditions that thrilled him to the core. Safe at last in the company of women, he was offered the golden opportunity of following them into every boutique, every lingerie shop, and every accessory store the town had to offer. Furthermore, he often went with them into the city where he was able to discreetly indulge in his passion for lady's clothing. Even better, he found he had a new group of people from whom he could steal.

Sly never thought of it as stealing; he termed it borrowing because he always intended to put the items back. Sometimes he did; other times he could not bring himself to part with the material object of his desire. He never took anything brand new, figuring it would be easily missed and because he felt instinctively that it would be wrong. However, he liberally allowed himself to borrow whatever he wanted from the nurses with whom he lived and worked – belts and handbags, jewellery and scarves; sometimes even their perfume and make-up, but mostly it was their lingerie. He borrowed lots of their amazing, silky, lacy lingerie. He felt no guilt whatsoever wearing his colleagues' bras or panties, their lace top stockings and their flimsy nightdresses, enjoying the exquisite feel of these pretties against his skin and fantasising how it might feel to rightfully be able to wear such gorgeous things.

When one of the nurses decided to throw a hen party the week before her wedding, Sly finally got to buy for himself the kind of garments he could only previously have dreamt about. As one of the girls, he was naturally invited to the party, but was sternly informed by the bride-to-be that he could only come if he was prepared to dress like the rest of the gang in the chosen theme for the evening – as a tart! Sly could barely believe his luck and spent his next day off shopping with one of the nurses for his outfit. He nearly blew it with his enthusiasm for an enormous feather boa but, fortunately, his companion decided he was going over the top to make them all laugh and to impress the bride. No one quite knew what to do about Sly's footwear but, finally, someone remembered the outsize outlet in the new shopping centre where he eventually found something sparkly with a three inch heel that would just about fit. He found them immensely uncomfortable and it seemed to take him forever to learn how to walk in the damn things but, to Sly, it was worth all the potential future bunions in the world. As he gazed at his reflection in the mirror, he felt his Dorothy shoes made his legs, already clad in black, fishnet stockings, look amazing. He felt like a goddess.

V

By the time Sly reached his fortieth birthday, he had been a fully-fledged cross dresser for over twenty years, but always in secret. He had yet to come out fully but, so far, had never felt the need to, having always been slightly reserved in nature. He knew that there were clubs to which he could go and others with whom he could mix if he wanted to develop his lifestyle further, but he refrained. His love for his family and, most of all, his brother, held him back from openly going out in public dressed as a woman. He felt it would shame them. Only on those occasions when he had a justified reason to dress up – a hen night, a fancy dress party, the Rocky Horror Show – did he give full reign to his obsession, secure in the knowledge that his friends believed he was sending himself up to make them laugh.

If anyone wondered why Sly had never settled down, no one commented. His father had always though it was because he was a pansy; his mother never questioned his decision and it probably never crossed his brother's mind. His friends sometimes teased him about being the last man standing and women still came onto him, but he had learned long ago how to divert attention away from himself. The bottom line was that Sly didn't really need anyone to have an affair with. He had himself and, by this time, a secret lock up of all things feminine with which to give full reign to his sexuality, his fantasies and his desires. With the coming of the internet, he was able to fully indulge his passion and spent vast amounts of time and money, browsing and shopping on line for whatever he wanted and a place to store them that he could access whenever he felt the urge.

V

People with an awareness of Down's syndrome will tell you what incredibly loving people those touched with this disability can be and Ali was no exception. He was always extraordinarily happy, generous and thoughtful. Despite suffering the occasional fevers and chest infections to which he was prone, he never let them get him down. He always noticed when people seemed depressed and was always the first to offer comfort to anyone he thought might be lonely or sad. He also had a temper and was not afraid to let it show, but his outstanding quality was an overarching serenity with the world and everyone in it and this never left him.

At the age of thirty, Ali chose to leave home of his own volition and move into a hostel where he felt he could lead a more independent life out of sight of his still over-protective mother. The hostel was only a few miles away from Sly, newly promoted to Head of Nursing and thus the two were able to meet more frequently. The close bond between them was still strong and, in fact, Sly probably loved the adult Ali more than he had loved the child. Their parents had both retired and old age was biting at their heels. His father suffered chronic lumbago, probably from all the digging and his mother's hands were stiff and swollen with arthritis, probably from all the sewing. Sly and Ali still saw both of them at least once or twice a week.

It is a sad, but unfortunate, fact that people with Down's syndrome have a shorter than average lifespan and here too Ali was no exception. As he grew into his thirties, the chest infections and fevers, that had started to improve in his teens, began to make a comeback. His breathing became ragged, he began to suffer from palpitations and he found himself trekking backwards and forwards to the local surgery, returning home with various forms of medication and increasingly frequent hospital appointments in an effort to improve his health. Throughout it all, his spirit never flagged and, despite his steady decline, he remained steadfastly cheerful and unstintingly unselfish towards the people who crossed his path.

Sly was sitting in his office, working at yet another set of figures, trying to work out how to reduce staff costs whilst improving ward efficiencies when the hostel rang him on his mobile to tell him that his brother had stopped breathing and was on his way to the hospital. After years as a nurse, Sly had schooled himself to stay calm, even in the face of the worst kind of emergencies. It was this inner strength that kept him going over the next few hours. He immediately stopped what he was doing and ran down to the Emergency Admissions Department where he stood outside its large double doors by the wide parking bay to wait for the ambulance that would bring his brother to him.

It was too late. Despite all the advances of medical science, Ali had died on the way to hospital. All the adrenaline, cardiac massage and electric shocks in the world had not been able to save him. Still, the emergency team tried their best to bring him back, working at it until the Team Leader agreed there was no more they could do. The Ward Sister gently removed Sly into a side room where she kept him company until his parents arrived. He refused her offer of tea.

When his family at last gathered together in the little room, Sly insisted on giving them the news himself. Afterwards, he gently took his mother in his arms, allowing her to cry loudly into his chest as he stood beside his father and watched him twiddle his cap between his fingers just as he'd watched him through the ward window on that far away day when Ali had been born.

He instructed the nursing staff not to prepare the body, telling them he wanted to do that himself. At first, they protested, arguing that it was not his job, that he was too senior to undertake that duty. He was too numb to understand that his colleagues simply wanted to protect him or to, at least, take away some of his pain but, in the end, they were forced to leave him to it. As Head of Nursing, he outranked them all.

A while later, having convinced his parents there was nothing they could do, he put them in a taxi and sent them home with a promise to call round later. Alone now, Sly was finally able to turn his attention back to Ali. As he entered the shaded room in which his brother lay unmoving beneath a blue, cotton sheet, he found that all the materials he needed were to hand. The junior nurse, sitting beside the body, offered him a wan smile, rose and softly tip-toed out of the room. There was nothing to be said.

As Sly slowly and carefully washed every inch of his brother's body, the staff outside on the concourse could only wonder at the choice of song he was heard brokenly singing to himself, "That's my brother! Who? Thylvetht! Got a row of forty medals on his chetht. Big chetht! He getth no retht."

No one could have loved or been more than Ali, his little monster.

PART III

Cat and Mouse

The weekly meeting of the Whiskerlies was in full swing, evidenced by friendly banter, the occasional raised voice, peals of laughter and several empty bottles of wine. Bex sat quietly in a corner chair and watched the proceedings with an almost maternal air. The girls were feeling highly delighted with themselves, congratulating one another on their inspirational solutions and, despite a few bumpy patches, the continuing success of each mission. Bex, however, was aware that things were moving swiftly towards the final, crucial stages and the team would need every ounce of nerve to soar over the last few hurdles. If anything was going to go wrong, it would be now and the stakes, for some more than others, were high. She comforted herself with the promising news of progress on each front. Where there were obstacles, these were debated until there was a range of solutions on the table, any one of which might be used depending on the final circumstances. It was up to each team member to decide how she wanted to play out her own end game but, as leader, Bex was there to assist with the final decision making.

She felt immensely proud of her girls. They had shown themselves to be strategic, ingenious even and, best of all, they refused to accept failure. Bex sighed.

They would need to keep that thought in their sights in the days to come.

She turned her attention to Izza, sitting cross-legged on the floor, pouring over a set of photographs and in the midst of an argument with her mother and Celia. The noise level was beginning to soar as the women passionately debated whatever issue it was. Bex reflected on how far the girl had come in such a short amount of time. It was as if she had had a personality make over. She looked relaxed, focussed and determined to get her point across. Gone was the sulky, disinterested teenager of a few months ago. She was vibrating with health and glowing with happiness. Bex was delighted for her.

She looked across the room and caught the eye of Tiffany, who smiled at her. Despite still being overly self-focussed and dating losers, she had become integral to the success of the group in many ways. She had done an amazing job trailing Charley's moonlighting neighbour. It had to be admitted that without her working knowledge and ability to source the right information at the right time, some of the stings would have been very difficult to pull off. She was heavily and enthusiastically involved in most of the projects despite the evident risk to her career. She had turned out to be a selfless team player.

Fresna had absented herself from the meeting. She had chosen to spend some quality time with Verity. Sam and Sly were heads together preparing for the sting on Alex and so mother and daughter had decided on a girlie twosome, complete with onesies, depilatory cream, mudpacks and nail varnish. Bex was certain that there would be at least a couple of bottles of 'grape juice' to wash down all the fun. It had taken Fresna some time to come to terms with the bitterness and rage she felt towards the guy who had jilted her so long ago and who now seemed to expect a bit of a leg up (not to mention over) from the family he had ignored for years. With Verity back in the country, Fresna seemed to have reclaimed her inner joy and was focussing her attention on her family and her future.

Jax was glowing, sitting contentedly on the floor, back against the sofa, arguing happily with her daughter. Under the patient tutelage of Fresna, she had mastered the internet and was confident she would breeze through her own final stage. Bex let her gaze linger over her friend and sent up a little prayer that she would find what she was looking for on one of the dating sites but, from what she understood about them, Bex didn't hold out much hope.

To everyone's surprise, Celia had drastically cut down on the alcohol. Whilst she was not tee total, she no longer seemed to need it in the way she once had. The strain had left her face, the little lines around her eyes had eased away and she was looking fresher than she had for years. Given that she had a pretty tough day ahead of her, she was looking mighty confident. In a few short hours, she would be walking out of that damned factory forever with the promise of a new career on the horizon. She had come so far and had been so brave. "Go Ceals," encouraged Bex silently and raised her glass in the direction of her friend.

Nothing much had happened for Charley since she had held her afternoon soiree. The DGs were still in residence and, even though the property developer had visited them, the noise was still almost as bad. Whilst it was true that the evening drilling had stopped and the parrot seemed to have shut up, Bex felt that improving Charley's situation might well turn out to be their only dud since they had little control over the outcome. They were going to have to hand that one over to others and pray for the right result. Bex sincerely hoped that Charley could remain patient long enough for things to turn out well.

Turning inwards, Bex reflected on her own personal situation. Things at home had turned sour. Her petty malices towards Malcolm had lost their bite and no longer offered her the satisfaction they once had. She had begun to feel quite uncomfortable with herself and her lifestyle. She had decided something had to give and, after turning it over in her mind for many weeks, she had at last made her mind up what that something was going to be. Still, she did not need to do anything in a hurry. There was no need to rush. For the time being at least, she would continue to lead and support her friends as they each worked through the final stages of their stings.

Leaning quietly back in her chair, she took a sip of wine and sat quietly, serene as ever, watching over her friends and giving nothing of her plans away. No one needed to be told anything yet so her secret was safe. Still, she wondered how her friends would react when they finally got to learn of her decision.

BEX

I

Bex had been feeling restless and unhappy for weeks. Her former easy serenity seemed to have deserted her and gone walkabout on its own. She was finding it increasingly difficult to glide through the days, content in the knowledge that if Malcolm kicked off, she could hand out a small, devious retribution. Somehow her ulterior justice had lost its shine, its bite, its flavour. She pulled her gaze from contemplation of the rhododendrons, just beginning to lose the best of their soft pink bloom, and forced herself to concentrate on lining up the dustbins before Malcom's return home.

Since the gala dinner at the golf club, things had taken a serious downhill turn. Malcolm had become insular, watchful and afraid of his own shadow. The worst of it was that he had increasingly begun to become overly dependent on her, seeking reassurance at every turn, constantly asking for her opinion and second guessing both of them. His surrender to her game had caused him to turn from an obsessive-compulsive, arrogant, blustering bully into a lily-livered, weak-kneed, delusional neurotic.

They were watching him! They were following him! They were out to get him! Christ alone knew who 'they' were!

He had resigned from the golf club. The utter humiliation he had experienced in front of his cronies and their wives had seen to that. He found no joy in playing with his Beemer and he had taken extended sick leave from work due to stress. His fussing had increased alarmingly and he rarely left the house. As a direct consequence, Bex found she was spending more and more of her time tending to him. She had no time for herself, no time for the gym and, worst of all, no time for her little assignations with David. Her only respite came when he took himself out for yet another unproductive visit to the doctor.

No wonder Bex was beginning to feel depressed. Sweet revenge had turned against her. The little paybacks for Malcolm's errant behaviour had all fallen flat. The former pleasant taste of her poisonous paybacks had turned inward and now lay heavy and sour in her stomach. There was little pleasure to be had in that direction. In fact, if she was honest, there was none at all. She had become wet nurse to the paranoid hypochondriac Malcolm had become. Life had become tedious and her days, which had previously seemed to fly by, were turning out to be endless. She was fed up to the back teeth of sitting at home all day with nothing much to do but clean the already spotless house or sit by her husband's side while he watched yet another of his terminally boring documentaries about transport, bridges or the history of war.

She sighed. The situation was hopeless and so there was no choice. It was time for a change of direction.

II

Sitting in the kitchen of the house that had been her home for longer than she cared to remember, nursing a cup of rooibos tea, Bex looked around and felt a deep sadness envelope her. This was not a home, it was a museum; a place where you looked but saw nothing; where you touched, but felt nothing; where everything was kept in little plastic boxes behind oak fronted cabinets.

She remembered how happy she had been here many moons ago in the early years when Malcolm had been young and relatively carefree; when she could immerse herself in caring for her children, all of whom had long since flown the coop and now had lives and families of their own. She loved them all dearly and saw them regularly. With the coming of the internet, she had learned to communicate with them over the ether. It wasn't quite the same as seeing them in person, but with webcam, Skype and all the other modern applications available, it was possible to keep in touch with anyone anywhere in real time.

The house had become too big for the two of them – too quiet, too neat, and too lifeless. She would have preferred to have moved into a smaller house – something cosy where she could relax and be herself, but she knew that Malcolm would never move. He had never been able to abide change. For herself, she didn't need much in the way of material things. They had never been important to her. Her craving had always been for personal freedom and fulfilment and, whilst she could appreciate that there would be those who would consider her selfish and cruel, she truly believed that she had taken into consideration the welfare of both of them whilst coming to the difficult decision about their future.

It had been great fun getting back at the infuriating Malcolm, growing and learning in the process, but the taste of revenge was now bitter in her mouth. The joke had worn itself as thin as a bubble and it now seemed like it was on her. She was ready now to burst that bubble and let it evaporate away into frothy nothingness because that's how her life felt right now – as empty as a soap bubble.

But not for much longer!

She checked her watch. Slowly she rose from the chair and, more out of habit than a desire for orderliness, she pushed it back to its proper place under the kitchen table. She took her cup to the sink, rinsed it and popped it into the dishwasher. She fitted a tablet into its dispenser and switched on the machine.

She took another good, long look around the room. Everything was where it should be. Satisfied, she wandered through into the hall and, from there, into the lounge, touching and stroking well-remembered, well-loved memorabilia – the little porcelain clock that her children had bought them for a significant wedding anniversary, the crystal vase inlaid with playful otters that she had bought on a trip to Lake Como, the silver photograph frame on the mantelpiece, reminiscent of a happy family trip to London. How young they had all looked; how dated their clothes now seemed. She moved slowly through the room and finally found herself looking out of the French windows at the neat shrubberies and well-manicured lawn in front of her.

The house was pristine. She had done the laundry and had tidied it away, hospital style in the airing cupboard, giving Malcolm no reason to fret. She had put fresh sheets on the bed, stocked the larder and filled the freezer. She had placed a casserole in the oven. She could do no more.

Coming out of her reverie, she realised there was actually one more thing she needed to do. Purposefully, she walked out of the magazine-style neatness of her lounge and back into the kitchen. She reached into her handbag and took out a small cream and gold business card. She turned it over in her hand, smiling at the memories it brought back to her. What a glorious year it had been. What fun she had had. Carefully, she placed the little card on the kitchen table next to Malcolm's glasses where he would be sure to find it.

III

At a toot of the horn from outside, Bex gathered the little collection of bags she had earlier stored under the hall table. Standing before the mirror, she shook her hair free of its combs and let it hang loose around her neck the way he liked it. She picked up her jacket and left through the front door. She turned and swiftly locked the door on her previous life. She popped the little key through the letter box. She wouldn't need it again.

With a light step and a happy heart, she walked up the path for the very last time without a backward glance and climbed into the camper van parked in the lay-by opposite the house, smiling up at the man in the driver's seat as she did so.

It was time to explore new horizons, to spread her wings and to experience a different sunrise. She gently tapped the pocket of her jacket to check that her passport really was there, threw her hands in the air and whooped with joy. It was time to go travelling.

David watched her indulgently then leaned forward to kiss her. Putting the van into gear, he reached for her hand, then pulled away from the kerb.

The next adventure was about to begin.

FRESNA

I

Alex couldn't wait and had consequently arrived early at the restaurant. Dressed well for the occasion, he passed the time reflecting on how his luck had changed for the better over the past weeks. He had been overwhelmed by the warmth of the welcome he had received from Fresna. He hadn't expected that. He had known she was a soft touch, but he had thought she might put up some resistance. On the contrary, she seemed delighted to have him back in her life. She had grown quieter over the years; no longer the excited, chattering teenager he had once known. Still, he appreciated that in a woman and found the silences between them quite restful. He checked his watch and smiled. Anytime soon he would be meeting his daughter for the first time and who knew what improvements that would bring to his life.

He was startled out of his daydreaming by the discordant ringing of a mobile. He looked up and saw a dishevelled blonde in the booth opposite rummaging about in her bag. He shook his head in disbelief at the way young people dressed these days. She was all in black, wearing workman's boots over laddered tights and had decorated herself with an abundance of silver bangles and belts. He could just about glimpse white skin beneath an enormous pair of sunglasses. He felt shocked. Sunglasses in a restaurant for pity's sake! Whatever next?

Finally, 'blondie' found her cell phone and began to listen. Whatever it was, Alex felt sure it was bad news. He could tell from the sudden downturn of her black-lipsticked mouth. Suddenly she stood up, still listening, told whoever it was on the other end that she was coming and went to put her phone away. In her hurry to be gone, she mistimed the manoeuvre and knocked her handbag across the table, spilling its contents in a wide arc across the bistro floor; a small collection of feminine essentials rolling and skimming along the ceramic tiles and coming to rest finally under a table here or a chair there. The woman cursed under her breath and looked impatiently at her scattered belongings. She clearly did not have time for this. She was impatient to leave.

Gallantly, Alex stood up and, forcing his arthritic knees to bend, stooped down and began to retrieve some of the forlorn girl's possessions. He found her purse under his chair, a lipstick by the door and a packet of tissues in the space between the booths. He collected all he could find and returned them to their owner who, by this time, had begun to scoop up the things closest to her. Hurriedly she took the proffered goods, grabbed her coat and ran out of the door, ignoring his efforts. The drama over, Alex returned to his chair and sat down, wondering what the world was coming to. The young hussy hadn't seemed the slightest bit grateful. Turning his thoughts to the future, he again checked his watch. A pair of hands reached over his shoulders and drew him into a brief hug. Blondie was back and murmuring her thanks in his ear. She left as quickly as she came; a nameless, faceless woman, one of many seen in any town on any day of the week. Alex thought no more about her and again began to reflect on his recent good luck.

Things had certainly changed for the better since he had caught up with Fresna. Look at the way he was dressed for a start. Only a couple of weeks previously, he had begun receiving a series of unexpected parcels through the post. Opening them, he was stunned to find a variety of garments – suit, shirt, tie, shoes, even underwear – all good quality if the receipts were anything to go by. How thoughtful Fresna had been. She had wanted him to look his best when he met his daughter. Alex sighed. She was still an incredibly attractive woman for her age. What a pity she had no appetite for the occasional romp on the old two-backed beast! He would have enjoyed climbing into bed with her again. Still, he was a lucky man to even be here and perhaps in time, she would change her mind.

Alex sat back in his chair eager for the evening to begin and for all that was to come.

II

Verity threw off her sunglasses and smiled brilliantly at Samantha as she climbed into the back of Fresna's waiting car. It had all gone like clockwork. She had successfully planted Izza's credit card in the jacket pocket of the unsuspecting Alex when she had briefly returned to the restaurant to thank him. Izza would wait until tomorrow before reporting its loss and cancelling the card. She would then telephone the restaurant to see if anyone remembered the handbag incident and if they had any details on the elderly gentleman sitting in booth number sixteen, who had so graciously risen to help her gather her belongings. Fortunately, the restaurant would be able to oblige since Verity had made the booking in Alex's name, giving his details. In the meantime, Izza would buy a few masculine items over the net and arrange for them to be sent to his address.

After reporting the incident to the Police, Izza would leave it to Tiffany to pick up the trail. Interestingly, her investigation would raise some doubts about the honesty of the so-called hero in the bistro, which would ultimately cause her to turn up on his doorstep with a few questions. Being thorough, she would be sure to check Alex's pockets where the card would hopefully still reside. Regardless of the outcome and working on a hunch, Tiff would decide to conduct a more thorough search of the flat and return with a search warrant. The search would reveal a second stolen credit card, some jewellery and a quantity of cash tucked away in a small shoe box at the back of his wardrobe. A little more digging would reveal the owner of that property to be none other than Fresna herself. She had reported the card missing some time ago and would feign surprise when shown her missing jewellery. She would pretend she had no idea it had been stolen, but reveal that the suspect was an old acquaintance from way back when who had suddenly turned up on her doorstep. She would admit that he had visited her home several times over the past few months and pretend to be outraged by his thievery.

In reality, it had not been difficult for Verity to plant Fresna's property in Alex's wardrobe because Celia had come up with the bright idea of lifting his front door key from his pocket whilst he was having one of his regular home-cooked meals with Fresna. All Fresna had had to do was pass it out of the toilet window into the hands of the waiting Jax. It had been a piece of cake for Jax to run round to the local supermarket and get a replica cut on the spot. The original was back in its usual place in less than thirty minutes – stolen right under its owner's unsuspecting nose.

No one could predict how Alex would feel when questioned about his alleged use of Fresna's card. He would obviously protest his innocence, but the facts would show that the card had recently been used to buy men's clothing at a nearby internet café and, whilst the owner of the café could not be certain of the face, his records would reveal Alex as having booked the sessions.

Working in the theatre, Sam had made short work of ageing Sly into the seedy, old man the café owner agreed he had seen in his shop several times, shopping on the internet. Alex might well protest his innocence and rant against the injustice on the system, but it would be in vain since Tiffany's thoroughness had turned up some earlier information on the suspect involving a possible case of fraud against his previous employers, which had eventually been dealt with by the Company themselves but which had nevertheless been recorded by a diligent clerk.

III

Fresna waited for her satnav to warm up and then tapped in the required postcode. While she waited for the little machine to plan a route, she turned round and grinned at the two women cuddled up together in the back, sharing a bar of chocolate. Humming a little tune of contentment to herself, she drove sedately down the busy street, passing the restaurant in which the expectant Alex was sitting. The three women debated how long he would wait before he realised no one was coming. They also wondered what he would make of the little cream calling card, inscribed in gold with a cryptic message, that Verity had left in his coat pocket as he'd chivalrously sprung from his seat to chase after the scattered contents of her handbag. Since he was down on the floor with his back towards her, she had had plenty of time to plant it.

Whilst they could not be certain of the outcome of any police investigation, the three car passengers were confident in the knowledge that Alex would not be bothering them again and that, for them at least, justice had been done.

It would be several hours before they reached their destination in the very north of the country – Aberdeen, home of Alex's second son Ben where both brothers would be waiting for them, completely ignorant of what had just taken place.

For Fresna, who adored anything to do with family, it felt like coming home.

CELIA

I

For the third time that afternoon, Celia found herself lugging yet another flask of coffee up the stairs to the second floor meeting room where the Top Team were gathered, and where an atmosphere of deadly seriousness, absolute concentration and complete bafflement had even silenced the normally belligerent Patrick.

Below them, the rest of the Dumbleton's workforce was in uproar. It was unbelievable, it was dreadful, and it was hysterical. It really rather depended on the stance the different employees chose to take. At any rate, no one was doing any work as people gathered, in small groups, around the now silent banks of computers. From Celia's panoramic view, there was a load of head shaking, head nodding and frowning, interspersed with occasional bursts of laughter. All in all, it was a very fitting end to her last day. Over the past fortnight, there had been a burst of intensity in her workload – so much to do, to finish, to hand over before she left. It was unsurprising that she had not progressed far with the agreed hand over manual. She had met with Patrick that morning to discuss next steps. He was very anxious about how the office would cope without her, given the move to the warehouse creeping steadily nearer and Germany breathing down their necks over every minor incident. No replacement had yet been found so Patrick had reluctantly agreed to hire a temp for Celia to instruct on office procedure. The poor girl had left after two days, citing too much donkey work for her taste. Whilst her replacement was definitely more robust, she was proving totally incompetent. Once again Patrick had begged Celia to stay on a few more weeks and had even offered her a generous wage, but the lady refused to budge.

In the end, she and Patrick had agreed a compromise in which she would work on the handover notes during her forthcoming holiday. Dumbleton's would pay heavily for the work and Patrick had had to agree to Celia's terms of half immediately and half on completion. The cheque was in her bag waiting to be cashed.

Just after lunch, the proverbial had well and truly hit the fan. No one quite knew how it had happened, but there was a phone call from Germany in which Patrick was informed that he had somehow attached a short, pornographic video to an email. At the same time, long-time customers began to ring in to complain about the same attachment. By the time the server had been shut down, several members of staff and some of Dumbleton's best customers had been hit. No one could figure out how to stop the video from being attached. The incident was proving far beyond the capabilities of their normally capable technician. Patrick's laptop had been quarantined and the Executive Team had retired upstairs to discuss the incident and plan their damage limitation strategy.

With the office more or less shut down, the staff had gathered to speculate on the incident. The question on everyone's lips was which staff member had had the audacity to post a clip of the film on the noticeboard overstuck with an image of Patrick's head. Patrick was seething; he had no clue who had done it, but he knew that whoever it was would be for the chop.

Someone declared it had to be a worm, another said it was sure to be a virus, but no one could work out how it had got into Dumbleton's in the first place given the strength of their firewalls. The message had leaked downstairs that Karl was flying over immediately with his own technical crew and he was not at all pleased.

It seemed that Karl was spending quite a bit of his time being not at all pleased.

II

Celia carefully set the coffee flask down on the table in front of her and quietly began refilling the empty cups littering the table. Locked in a heated discussion, the Directors barely noticed her presence. Given the furore around her, she guessed that the planned presentation and farewell present were probably no longer on the agenda, but she couldn't have cared less. In fact, she was delighted since it meant she could sneak out unseen using the backstairs and that played directly into her plans for the afternoon. Placing a cup of coffee in front of her boss, she stood back and watched him take a gulp.

They had used her and abused her. They had offered her empty promised and had treated her like dirt, but hers was the last laugh. Leaning in her own little bubble against the back wall of the office, she watched as several people in the room, paused mid thought shower and took an automatic sip of their coffee. Smiling maliciously to herself, she thought, *Serves you right, you bastards!* Gathering herself together, she left the room, struggling with her mirth. As she reached the first floor, she glanced back up at the office, gave a two-fingered salute and walked down the corridor in the direction of her office.

Back in the safety of her room, she marvelled at her audacity. Taking a leaf out of her friend, Bex's book, she had added a jugful of her own warm urine to the last batch of refreshments. "*That'll teach you lot to piss on me*," she thought savagely as she delved into the holdall on the spare seat to close down the small device hidden at the bottom beneath the weight of her personal belongings. She took a few minutes more to finish clearing her desk, placing more memorabilia into the bag and then called in her wide-eyed replacement for a few final instructions. Leaving her with more than enough to do, Celia gathered her things together. Amidst all the fuss, no one noticed her enter Patrick's office one final time to drop a mysterious communication on his desk. Carefully, she placed the top quality cream business card in a corner of his untidy blotter. In the flurry of events unfolding, he would probably not waste much time wondering who the hell had left it there, but he might just stop to puzzle out its cryptic message, "Job Well Done!" Knowing Patrick, the message would most likely go right over his head and he would toss it in the bin.

She left unnoticed. There were far more serious things to discuss than Celia's departure. Staff were beginning to think about their jobs and wonder if they would have them for much longer. Given her good understanding of office politics, Celia could have reassured them. She knew there would be an investigation and someone would have to take the blame. She felt certain who that one person would be and would enjoy hearing from her former colleagues how his head had rolled.

Making her way across the car park, her head held high and her step light, she glanced up towards the second floor where the Top Team were again trying to stop Patrick from swearing. She guessed they would be there well into the evening, possibly even until Karl and his team arrived to fix things. They would never get to the bottom of the incident. Charley's contact had programmed the virus remotely using the device in her bag to bypass the server. He had arranged for it to wipe itself out within an hour of her shutting it down. All Celia had had to do was follow his very precise instructions. It had been easy peasy and well worth the outrageous expense.

As Celia left Dumbleton's forever and turned left towards the airport and a well-deserved break in the sun, Celia couldn't help wondering how Patrick would react when he found they had been robbed. Her daring raid of a week ago had proved outstandingly successful, not to mention lucrative. What would Karl say to her former boss when he flicked through the product catalogue of a close business rival and noticed it was full of their designs? How long would they take to work out that the blue prints of their future products, thought to be safely stored in the safe in the office of the UK MD, had been copied and sold? Who could have done such a thing? It was a no brainer. Patrick was the only one who knew where the combination to the safe was hidden.

Wasn't he?

TIFFANY

I

Commander Munro frowned as he read through the letter. Hitting a button on his phone, he asked his secretary to bring in the personnel file of Bryn Jones. This was the fifth complaint in as many months and he now felt he had to act fast. At first, he had thought it best to play things down. It was a matter of one person's word against another and so he had sent a solicitous reply to each complainant, informing them that he was dealing with the matter and would be in touch in due course. This time, however, there was an independent witness plus the girl's mother had seen it all. This time something had to be done.

With a curt nod, he took the proffered file out of his assistant's hand and thumbed through it. He had a distant memory that there had been something similar not too long ago. He located the page and read it through swiftly. An incident almost two years previously when things had got out of hand at a training course that Jones had headed up at which a very aggrieved woman had poured a glass of wine over his head, claiming he had acted in an offensive and unprofessional manner. Jones had fought back by raising a grievance against his colleague, proclaiming he was innocent and that she was 'off her rocker'. There had been an enquiry where it had been decided that the woman concerned had been drunk and had been heard to use offensive language against the man. Since no one present claimed to have witnessed anything provocative in Jones' behaviour, the woman concerned had resigned and the matter was closed, but that had not been the end of it. Rumours began to circulate that Jones had had a crush on the woman and had been seen to flirt openly with her, that he had been turned down flat on more than one occasion and, in fact, had directed some unfortunate remarks to her at the event dinner. Since no one had bothered to come forward at the time, the remarks had been considered either spurious or malicious, but a note had been placed in Jones' file.

Sighing heavily, Munro concluded that something similar was beginning to raise its ugly head. He reached for the phone and made two calls.

If Bryn was surprised to be called at home on his rest day by the Commanding Officer and asked to report to Headquarters first thing, he gave no sign. Switching off his mobile, he took another swig of his favourite, Speckled Hen, and carried on arranging his bedding plants. He took great pride in his garden, boasting the largest number of hanging baskets in the avenue. In fact, his garden came a very close second to his other great love – golf.

Bryn found himself wrong-footed when he stepped into Commander Munro's office to find a member of the HR Team already there. Nonplussed, he sat down opposite the two senior officers. He was told not to worry and assured that the meeting was merely a necessary formality. He was informed that he could have his own representation and that, if he chose to do so, they could defer the meeting to a future, mutually convenient date. With icy fingers of anxiety plucking at his stomach, Bryn forced himself to sit up squarely in his chair and placed his hands on his knees. In a steady voice, he informed the pair that he would exercise his options when he had heard what they had to say to him.

II

Back in the HQ car park, Bryn leaned back in his car and closed his eyes. His face was ashen, his breathing was shallow and his palms were damp. He felt physically ill. He wondered how it had come to this. He had believed he was doing a decent bit of work, establishing rapport with his mainly female audience, possibly doing a little bit of subtle flirting and telling a few humorous anecdotes to relax everyone. He had been happy to stay behind at the end to answer the questions of those who were too shy to put their hands up at the end of his lecture and all the time the she devil bitches were only too happy to put the flaming boot in.

Five of them! Five of the stupid bloody cows and all of them during this round of courses apparently! He could not work out what he was doing differently. He had a vague recollection of talking to the last one, the young one who had turned up with her mother. How could he forget her with her big anxious eyes and fluttering little hands, but she had been mistaken. He had even felt sorry for the poor wee thing. However, he could have dropped dead when he learned that four others were also claiming he had behaved inappropriately towards them too. He had sworn on all things holy and unholy that he had never laid a finger on any of them. He cursed loudly as he recalled the moment when the HR bastard had informed him in a small, cold tone that each of the ladies concerned had written in personally to complain about him. He wiped his forehead with his sleeve and tried to breathe slowly. He couldn't understand it.

In fairness, Blisters Munro had done his best to remain impartial through the proceedings. He had been informed that there would have to be an enquiry and that he would have the opportunity to defend himself but, in the interim, Blisters had told him that he had no choice but to suspend him on full pay pending investigation and possible future tribunal. He had then had to suffer the added humiliation of being escorted to his cubicle and asked to remove his personal belongings. Blisters himself had escorted him to his car where he had told him not to return without written permission. It was suggested that he might like to have Union representation, but he would be left to organise that for himself.

Bryn covered his face with his hands and groaned inwardly. With considerable effort, he pulled himself together and started the car. "*What the hell,*" he decided suddenly. He would look upon the whole thing as a few weeks' unexpected paid leave. He drove out of the car park in the direction of the golf course. *May as well enjoy my bloody self*, he thought sagely.

Try as he might to remain positive, the worry stayed with him. Like an invisible piece of chewing gum stuck to his shoe, it seemed to follow him wherever he went, causing him to lose his normal jaunty step and walk carefully as if there were danger everywhere. He felt he was being treated very unfairly. He couldn't believe that anyone with half a brain would waste their valuable time on such a load of crap. However, it seemed that sexual misconduct was being taken very seriously in the Fire Brigade these days and, unfortunately for Bryn, Commander Jones had decided to focus his very considerable and sharp brain on the matter.

Over the next few weeks, one question continued to haunt him. What the hell had he done to deserve this?

III

Meanwhile the Whiskerlies were beside themselves. Everything had come together with magical precision. Over the previous few months, each of the girls had attended one of Fat Taff's lectures. At the end, they had made a point of waiting behind for him to finish packing up and then asking an incidental question about his presentation or about fire precaution in general. They had been careful to keep to the back of any queue so that the hall had usually emptied by the time their turn came. If he even showed the slightest interest in them, they flirted with him coquettishly and then hurried home to write a different version of events.

The final coup had been to coax the young janitor at one of the local village halls to make a statement saying he had seen Fat Taff touch Izza inappropriately. It had been fortunate that Jax and Izza had turned up early enough to witness the fireman giving the youth a piece of his mind about the state of the hall. It had not been difficult for the very lovely Izza to leave her seat at the back to go into the kitchen and begin a conversation with the lad whilst Fat Taff droned on about combustibles. The pair had hit it off immediately so that when the not-as-shy-as-he-looks caretaker asked for her number, Izza didn't hesitate.

At the end of the evening, Izza waited until the very last minute before shyly approaching the trainer with a question about fire blankets. Making certain that Fat Taff was facing the front of the hall, she was able to pick the exact moment to make her move. As Jax appeared from the side room at the back of the hall with the unwitting witness a few paces behind, Izza suddenly slapped the Welshman very hard across the side of his face, pushed him away from her and fled down the aisle into the arms of her mother. She even managed to throw the word 'pervert' over her shoulder at the confused man as she legged it down the hall.

There followed a mumbled apology from the very puzzled trainer, a little awkward laughter and a smoothing over of the whole incident. It was agreed that there might have been a bit of a misunderstanding. Bryn had been at a loss to know what he had done wrong, but the young girl had looked so distressed that even he came to believe that he must have unwittingly alarmed her somehow. He apologised as best he could, but then made the mistake of trying to pat her hand consolingly. Jax had snatched it away and told him fiercely to leave her daughter alone. Chagrined, he had grabbed his stuff and left as fast as his rotund body would let him. The whole sorry incident had been watched with a great deal of interest and no small measure of spite by young Callum, the hall caretaker, still steaming from his earlier dressing down. It had not been hard to convince the boy to make a statement about something he had not actually seen. One look into Izza's enormously sad, melting dark brown eyes and he was more than happy to kick the fat bastard's arse into another universe. In fact, to his surprise, he found that he was ready to do anything at all for her so Izza graciously let him. From her point of view, it was a double whammy. Not only had she helped deal with Tiff's tormentor, she had pulled, for Christ's sake. It was high fives all round at the next meeting of the Whiskerlies.

Even so, the girls had not finished with Fat Taff.

IV

Everyone agreed that the second part of Operation Swansea would take a considerable bit of planning and a certain amount of careful interrogation of the increasingly malleable Malcolm. There would need to be a dry run, together with the competent use of stopwatches and mobile phones. With a bit of luck, they might even be able to attack on one front while teeing up another. The girls congratulated themselves on their ability to multi-task and opened another bottle of wine in celebration.

It was agreed that Tiff would borrow the right gear from Charley and, because she was the only other member of the group with the appropriate outfit, it was decided that Jax would accompany her to the killing ground.

"Scratching post might be a better turn of phrase," Bex suggested wittily to the amusement of everyone present.

Fresna would park in a convenient spot outside the perimeter fence and act as a link to Charley, who would park in a lay-by a few hundred yards to the south. It was agreed not to involve either Bex or Izza in this sting since both had a high chance of being recognised. Izza was delighted since it meant another date with the handsome Callum. For her part, Bex promised to try to think positive thoughts throughout the day, but the chances of that were slim since, amazingly, Malcolm had agreed to go out with the Boys from the Beemer Club that very same day so naturally she would be taking advantage of his absence to spend the day with David.

Towards the close of the meeting, Charley asked if anyone had seen or heard from Sly. He had not been to class for over a month and he was not answering his mobile. The group shook their heads and spent several minutes wondering if anything was wrong. In the end, they decided he was an adult and would be in touch when he was good and ready. Charley frowned, feeling the decision was wrong. He was a close friend and she felt instinctively that something was very amiss. She decided to take it upon herself to seek him out, but right now, there was work to do.

At ten o'clock on the appointed Sunday morning, the girls swung into action. Despite the fact that the dummy run had gone well, it had thrown up a couple of glitches that would need to be dealt with on the spot. Tiff's hands were clammy and shaking slightly as she waited for Jax to pick her up. If things went wrong, she had a lot to lose. Given her position, if she was caught, they would no doubt throw the book at her, rip of her regalia and kick her out of the force. Still, she had faced disaster before so she was prepared to face it again. However, this time, she was buoyed up by her friends, who had no intention of letting her fail.

For the third time in as many minutes, she checked that the corkscrew was in its rightful place in her back pocket and tried to breathe steadily. She jumped at a sudden noise and then realised it was her friend sounding the horn. Grabbing hold of her bag, she took a gulp of air and ran out of the door. It was time to face her nemesis.

Well nearly!

V

The first part of the operation was easy. All they had to do was follow the herd and try not to lag too far behind. They did not want to attract any unwanted attention so, until they got where they wanted to be, they played as quiet a game as their inexperience would allow. The fun would start once they reached hole number seven, which bordered the car park. As they approached the tee, they would be in full view of Fresna, who would alert Charley to get into position. They would have fifteen minutes in which to strike.

Four hundred yards to the south, Charley was listening to Classic FM whilst leafing through the current edition of Cosmopolitan. She felt relaxed and comfortable about her part in the proceedings. Over the past few months, she had become something of an expert at this and had no misgivings about what she was about to do. She had dressed carefully, managing to look both classically elegant yet slightly sluttish at one and the same time. Her clothes were expensive, her heels high and her skirt short. Her mobile rang three times, signalling the off. It was time to rev up her car and get on with it.

Smoothly, she put the car into gear and drove towards the golf club, bringing her car neatly to a stop across the entrance to the car park, immediately gaining the attention of the young guard on duty. Getting out of the car, she took care to show more than a glimpse of sleek, silk clad thigh. She straightened up, flicking her long chestnut hair carelessly over her neat, lightly muscled shoulders, thus creating a look of subtle abandon. Knowing she was being watched by the astonished young man in the booth in front of her, she smiled winningly and walked almost casually towards him and yet with all the cunning of a cat stalking a mouse. Fixing her eyes on her prey, she shrugged helplessly. She was lost, she explained, her seductive looks continuing to engage his interest. The young man followed her willingly to her car where together they discussed the failed technology of her satnav, hunted for the right page on the roadmap she kept in the net behind the front passenger seat and debated the potential routes she might take. In all, she kept the poor boy talking for just over fifteen minutes, all of the time acutely aware of her body language and his and making sure to show him just enough cleavage, just enough curve and just enough leg to keep him totally engrossed. At no time did she look into the car park spread before her. At no time did she allow the attendant's attention on her to wander. Her goal was to keep his eyes glued on her and she did it with sickening ease. Just as she had come to the decision that she had given her partners in crime more than enough time to carry out their part of the plan, there was a noise behind her as some punter tried to access the car park. The man concerned gave two short blasts of his horn. She turned, frowning, swiftly assessing the situation. Deciding her next move almost immediately, she acknowledged the driver with a helpless gesture, thanked the lust-struck young car park attendant, got quickly into her car, reversed carefully and drove away. Almost in a world of his own, and believing himself half in love, the smitten young man returned to his booth where he sat fantasising about the possibility of repeatedly screwing the fabulous older woman that had been sent by the Gods to brighten his miserable day. As a consequence, he was completely oblivious to all that had been happening behind his back.

For their part, Tiffany and Jax had reached the car park slightly later than planned due to some idiot in front of them landing in a bunker and spending too much time trying to decide which club he wanted to use to chip himself out.

"I'll give him a flaming club in a minute," fumed the impatient Tiff, waiting to tee off. "Right over the top of his damn skull. Bloody get on with it, man," she muttered.

When they finally reached the seventh hole, matters improved. Jax mistimed her swing to perfection, causing it to drop into the rough just short of the north end of a row of cars lining the car park. Tiff fared no better. As the seemingly hopeless pair of golfers headed off in search of their balls, they took a little time to scan the course. The foursome ahead had almost reached the next green several hundred yards away. They were too intent on their game to look back. There was a gap behind them since no one had yet reached the sixth hole. The two women walked causally towards the cars, swinging their clubs as if looking for Tiff's lost ball. They dropped down into the car park and spotted the right vehicle almost at once.

There was no time to be lost. Tiff crossed the car park quickly and dropped out of sight behind a magnificent black Porsche. As she did so, she heard a car horn blast impatiently from the other end of the car park. It was swiftly followed by another blast. Tiff looked back towards Jax crouching in the rough at the edge of the car park. She signalled frantically at her friend to get out of sight and then backed away. Cautiously, Tiff peered over the boot of the Porsche towards the front of the car park where Charley was taking her time reversing across its entrance to make way for the impatient driver of a white BMW.

"Shit," she thought, trying to stamp out the panic that was flaring in her chest. She looked frantically around her for an escape but there was none. Of all the rotten timing! What was she supposed to do now?

With the white car beginning to make its way into the car park, Tiff took the only course of action available to her. She simply dived beneath the body of the Porsche and froze. She hardly dared breathe as the car pulled up beside her. She watched as a pair of brogues got out of the driver's side and made its way to the back of the car. She heard the boot open. Presumably, whoever it was, was removing his clubs. There was a slamming sound and then the retreating crunch of gravel underfoot as the golfer strode off in the direction of the clubhouse. Tiff waited another long five minutes before carefully poking her face out from beneath the car. She checked around her. She saw Jax giving her the thumbs up and assumed the all clear. She hauled herself from under the car and squatted beside the driver's door. For a few seconds, she hung her head in relief and brought her breathing back to normal.

Taking the corkscrew from her back pocket, she scratched a large heart across the entire width of the driver's door. What Fat Taff would think of the strange message, and the tiny drawing of cat's whiskers inscribed within the heart and sent to him on behalf of the Whiskerly Sisters, she would never know and she didn't care.

Tiffany had just defaced her nemesis!

CHARLEY

I

Snuggling deeper into the hot froth of the Jacuzzi, Charley was enjoying the feel of the warm, scented water massaging her naked body. Languidly, she reached out a lazy hand and took a sip of chilled Moet. She opened her eyes to look beyond the lighted candles surrounding her haven, peering into the gloom of the garden hiding in the darkness. Nothing stirred. Nothing moved. Best of all, there was no sound from next door, nothing to interrupt the muted tones of Il Divo crooning softly in the background. This was the life. This was more like it. This was what she deserved. Her lips curled round in a smile of obvious satisfaction as she closed her eyes once more, sinking further beneath the bubbles, luxuriating in their sensuous feel and relishing the peace that heralded victory.

In the end, Charley had not needed the property magnate to turn up and evict his delinquent tenants on her behalf. She found she had no need for a knight in shining armour. She found she had secured victory for herself by making best use of the photographs taken by Tiff and Fresna. Large, full colour snaps of Mr. DG entering the Job Centre and signing on, together with images of his under the wire occupation as a window cleaner, sent by recorded delivery to the appropriate Government departments, had eventually produced the result she had worked for. Ever impatient, she had been forced to cool her heels while the wheels of justice turned slowly in her favour. When it finally came, Charley took all the time she needed to relish every sweet second of it.

She was lucky enough to witness the endgame first hand. Early one morning, just as she was about to leave for her regular appointment with the nail technician, she stood on her driveway and watched while a gentleman in a suit knocked at her neighbour's front door. The ensuing conversation had not been pleasant and had ended with the DGs cursing and slamming the door. She quickly dialled a number on her mobile phone, changed the time of her appointment and went back inside to wait for the next instalment.

It was not long in coming. The guy in the suit returned a short while later with two uniformed Police Officers. When the conversation again began to get heated, one of the officers stepped in, but Mr. DG had completely lost his rag and Charley enjoyed watching his arrest. Other than Mrs. DG leaving the home a short while later with the twins, nothing much happened until the evening when the family finally returned home.

Charley felt that the whole incident had ended up as a bit of a damp squib. She had relished the bit where Fuckwit had been arrested, but here he was back home and nothing much had seemed to change.

She couldn't have been more mistaken. Charley was awoken just before dawn by the sound of a slamming door. Puzzled, she had gone to the window and looked out at the scene unfolding on the driveway below her. She had stood for over an hour, thoroughly entertained by the scene before her as the DGs moved purposefully between house and van, transferring their belongings from one to another. Holy shit! They were leaving.

Feeling incredibly brave, Charley had slipped into her robe and had sneaked out onto the driveway. Hiding against the wall, she waited for the ousted pair to step back into the house and had then tiptoed to the open passenger door of the van where she had placed a single item on the untidy dashboard before darting back into the safety of her house, heart pounding in her chest, amazed at her daring. Amongst the clutter of the van, she could not be certain that her little business card would be found, but she knew that she had to follow in the wake of the rest of the Whiskerlies. She would not let them down.

Back upstairs, she watched from the safety of her bedroom window as her persecutor finally left the driveway, swiftly followed by Mrs. DG driving the children and hell's zoo, safely tucked up in the back of their estate car. The moonlighters had decided to do a moonlit flit. Perfect! Charley waited until she could see them no more before returning to the warmth of her duvet. As she drifted off to sleep, she wondered if her former neighbours would work out how the little cream card, neatly inscribed in gold with the words "Job Done!" had got into the van. Perhaps they would never find it; perhaps they would not care, but she had done what she needed to do and that was all that mattered to Charley. Yawning, she turned onto her side and, for the first time in a long while, she slept soundly. Order and peace had returned to the cul de sac, not before time, and all was well with the world.

Disturbed by a movement in the swirl of water around her, Charley opened her eyes, the glow of triumph lighting her eyes, the disordered loveliness of her hair framing her oval face. Her lips curled into a seductive smile as she relished her hard earned victory to the full. There were no dogs to disturb her activities now, no cats to destroy her garden and no drills to wreck her tranquillity. Beautiful in success, Charley settled her head more snugly against the padded headboard of the Jacuzzi and tuned into the harmony that was her favourite Italian quartet. She would have enjoyed fantasising about the sensual possibilities of a meeting with Sebastien, but circumstances dictated otherwise.

As she relaxed into the churning water, a small sigh escaped her lips. A large, warm hand was snaking up her leg, moving leisurely but insistently towards the softness of her inner thigh. She arched her back slightly, enjoying the moment and, with it, the promise of all that was to follow. She opened her eyes and found herself looking directly into a pair of lupin blue, velvet eyes, liquid with lust. Slowly, oh so slowly, the rest of him floated towards her seductively poised body and his lips met hers.

It seemed Charley had not lost her touch after all!

JAX

I

Jax leaned back in her chair and re-read her message to reassure herself that the detail was correct. The previous two weeks had sometimes seemed overly stressful, but she was surprised to find there had also been some amazingly good fun too. However, it was time for her to grasp the nettle, take the bull by the horns and go for broke in an attempt to swindle the swindler. With a bit of luck, Des might actually fall straight into her trap and, in doing so, she might even kill two birds with one stone.

Swallowing her anxiety, she reached for the cursor and pressed, sending her insincere little message winging across the wires and straight into the inbox of her intended victim.

My own true love, I hardly know where to begin. I haven't been completely honest with you about myself because I have had to find out the hard way that there are some unscrupulous people in the world – men who are only interested in a woman for her money or her property. I rejoice that this is something I will never have to worry about as long as I am with you. Forgive me, my angel, for deceiving you. My business partner and I run our own PR Company here in the UK and we are fortunate enough to have some European A-Listers on our books. We have recently been approached by a major player in the States with a view to buying us out. If all goes well, we will sell our business very soon and, from my share of the profits, it may be that I need never work again. I will easily have enough to loan you the money to pay off the IRS. It would be wonderful for me to know that you need not worry about the debt anymore, that you would be free to focus your thoughts on little Aimee and sleep well at night. I would rush to wire you the money, but you must be patient my darling. My business is currently being audited on the US side and so my money is temporarily tied up. I am confident the process will not take much longer. Go to church, my angel, get on your knees and pray this deal comes off. I may not get to mail you regularly over the next few days, but I will be thinking of you every step of the way. Love always J xxx

Jax wasn't surprised to receive a very speedy reply.

My darling, what wonderful news. Not only is my own angel a beautiful woman, but now it seems she is also a talented one. I was unaware of your successful business and I wish you luck with the sale. That we are both in business is just something else we have in common. Material possessions are of little interest to me (except that with your help I could settle my accounts and return my men to work). What is in the heart is far more important to me and our hearts are full of one another. I have been to church every day since we first began corresponding and thank the Lord for your love and constancy. If you are able to wire me the full amount, I promise to return it with interest within a month. I rejoice at your news and will wait patiently for your next message. All my love always, your Des xxx

Des, I can't believe it. We did it! We sold! I have been offered the post of Director in the new Company, heading the European field but, with my share of the sale, I can afford to begin a new life anywhere in the world and I would just love it to be with the man I love. I will be flying to America at the end of the next week – to Austin – only a two hour flight from my own sweet man. I have taken the liberty of adding a week to the end of my trip so that I can fly across over to finally be with you and meet little Aimee. We can plan our future together and I can meet your friends. Isn't that just the most wonderful news? Finally we can meet. I am so excited and so happy. All my love, your own J xxx

My darling Jacqueline, I rejoice in your news despite my own troubles. I had a final demand this morning from the IRS and consequently am facing the imminent loss of my own business. However, what is that compared to the abilities of my own beautiful love? I wish, I so wish I could meet with you when you fly to America, but I must fly to Kenya to discuss another building project. We will meet, my darling, and soon. Hurry and wire me the loan – it hurts to see so many men out of work and all because of me. I promise to pay you back and will love you forever for your support. I must work all the harder in order to keep up with my own clever girl. Your very own Des xxx

Oh my darling Des, what disappointing news. I was so looking forward to meeting you at long last and planning our future together. Still, what can I expect from such an experienced entrepreneur? Of course you must fly to Africa and I hope you get the business because that would make missing you worthwhile. I have put a deposit of £5,000 in an account for you.

Below are the access details. We can work out the repayments later. I promise there is more to follow but for now – take care and I hope you get all you deserve. By the way, what do you think of my new company business cards (attached)? Neat, aren't they? Your very own Jacqueline xxx

Smiling to herself, Jacqueline logged off the internet. She sincerely hoped that Des would access the bank account details she had sent him. It was the return serve, the payback, the sting she had been diligently planning over the previous few weeks – ever since she had received Des's cunning invitation to be deceived.

She tossed her head with impatience and smiled grimly to herself. Who did Des think she was? Did she come across as so green and so gullible as to actually fall for such an obvious scam? Of course, she reflected sadly, there were endless numbers of women out there, so desperate for love and attention, that they fell into the traps of these leeches, but she was not going to be one of them – not anymore she wasn't. Been there, done that, got educated.

So, with the help of her compatriots, Jax had planned a counter move of her very own. Convinced of his ability to deceive her, she had let Des think that she had fallen for his lies and was head over heels in love with a man, thousands of miles away and whom she had never met. In a short time, she had convinced him into believing that she was a rich business woman, that she had sold her company for a fortune and, most importantly, that she would be willing to part with several thousand pounds of her hard earned cash to some faceless, anonymous criminal, who had probably never set foot in America, let alone been widowed and fathered a daughter.

When she felt she had him exactly where she wanted him, when she had lured him with some bait of her own, she had casually given him the details of someone else's bank account; someone she personally would be delighted to see robbed blind.

She prayed Des would fall into her trap.

II

As the email traffic passed back and forth between them, she had printed off a copy of each of their messages, thus owning the entire transcript of their internet history. She planned to post a copy to the Fraud Squad when the time was right and to advise DesperDates of her suspicions. She didn't think it would take Des long to withdraw some of the cash she knew was sitting in the account waiting for him, but she had decided that patience was indeed a virtue at this stage of the game and would give Des all the time he needed to enter further into her web.

Switching off her computer, she left her office, flipping off the light and closing the door. Tripping breezily down the stairs, she entered her living room where Celia was in the process of opening up a bottle of champagne to toast another potentially successful venture. With her friend's help, she had even managed to attach a pdf copy of the cream and gold business card that signalled the work of the Whiskerly Sisters.

Accepting a glass of bubbly from Celia and a round of applause from her friends, Jax settled herself down in her favourite armchair. Idly, she wondered how the ignorant owner of the bank account she had mailed to Des would feel when he discovered the loss of his savings. What the hell – the bastard had it coming! She didn't reflect on the hoped for outcome for very long.

She had much more important things on her mind. To her complete surprise and utter delight, Intellygent had finally stepped up to the plate and asked her out to dinner the following Saturday. Full of mischief, she brought up the next crucial item on the Whiskerly agenda. What did the girls think she should wear when she met her man – the Red Riding Hood outfit or the Snow White suit?

Woohoo! The burden of choice.

IZZA

I

As she sat and waited for Callum to read the letter she had handed to him, Izza watched the world buzz around her. Business people in smart suits, carrying briefcases or laptop bags, and with the inevitable mobile phone pressed to their ears, moved purposefully by; excited young children with bright, eager faces scampered past often followed by harassed, anxious looking parents, overloaded with cases but intent on shepherding their flocks safely to their end destination; love-struck couples, arm in arm and eye to eye, floated by lost in a world of their own; other couples, past the first flush of romance, ambled past; some hand in hand in close conversation, others worlds apart and with nothing to say to each other – so many different people coming together with the same purpose in mind. Izza watched and wondered about their stories. All these people with so many different places to go and things to do, but she knew none of them.

She glanced down at the crumpled paper in Callum's hands. Cheap, lined paper littered with the scrawl of worthless, trite words. A letter from Tony.

He needed to see her, it began. He had tried to call. Why was she blocking him? Could she unblock him cos he needed to talk to her? He had changed. He hadn't meant to hurt her. Christ, how many times did he have to repeat it? The stupid bitch in the front seat of his car had meant nothing to him. It was a one off. He thought they were on a break so it wasn't as if he had been unfaithful or anything. Could she please just talk to him? At least be friends. That's all he wanted. He would wait for her at the usual place every night this week. Please come. It was important to him. He wouldn't touch her. He just needed someone to talk to. That's all. Why was she avoiding him? Why was she doing this to him? What was with the agg?

Had she heard he'd lost his job? Not his fault of course. He'd only been helping out some woman with a failed satnav who had got herself lost. Was it his fault that, for the five minutes his back had been turned, someone had done some criminal damage on one of the posh cars in the car park? It wasn't true that he'd been flirting with the old cow as his manager tried to make out. He'd simply tried to help her. They'd worked out how to get to her destination using the map in her car. It had been a bit of PR for fuck's sake. She was a classy mare so she might join the golf club any day. What was he supposed to have done? Ignored her, told her to bugger off 'cos he had a car park to watch? Yeah right. Of course, he hadn't meant to go for his boss and threaten to punch his lights out. The bastard had provoked him. It wasn't fair. He'd done nothing wrong and now he was out of work and broke.

Yeah broke. Had she heard? Someone had got into his private savings account and stolen over £5K! A legacy from an aunt. He had been meaning to tell her about it, but she'd blocked him? He was going to use it to pay her back for the car, but that was fucked now. Some arsehole had got wind of his account and cleaned him right out.

How the fuck they had got into his account he didn't know. Done online apparently. It was being looked into of course, but he had no protection and the manager had said the right access details had been used. How the fuck had anyone got hold of his password and log in details? The bastards at the building society were trying to make out that it was some kind of fraud on his part. WTF was that all about?

So now he was right up against it. He'd do anything to get her back. He realised he'd been a bit of a tosser before and he was sorry, right. Could she please just meet him tonight at the usual place? Please! He was begging, right! He'd changed. Honest! He would never hit her again. He'd never meant to hit her in the first place; it was just that she pressed all his buttons. And he would never ever ask her for money again only just this once if she could bring a pony with her, he swore he'd never ask again. Never ever, just this one time. He was desperate.

Besides, he wouldn't be where he was right now if she hadn't dumped him. He'd found he couldn't live without her and his life had just gone from bad to worse since they'd split up so please, please could they just meet up again tonight at the usual place. Just as friends if that's all she wanted. Just please come.

Had she heard that some fucking blonde police bitch had been round to his flat on a tip off? They'd found some stuff at the back of his wardrobe. How the fuck had that got there? She knew he wasn't into drugs; she knew he didn't deal. Anyway, they'd shoved him in a cell and questioned him for ages and now he was on a charge. Could she come to court with him and tell them that he didn't deal? Ok, he used a bit, but nothing heavy. She knew that. For fuck's sake, he was scared. He needed her to stand by him. Please would she meet him? He had no one else. She was his world. He loved her. This time it would be different.

Please don't let me down.

II

Callum finished reading the letter and passed it back to her in silence, but she shook her head. Smiling, he reached out for her hand and squeezed it across the top of the table. He got up to buy them both a coke. With Izza watching, Callum crumpled up the letter and dropped it into the closest bin. Alone at the table, Izza reflected on Tony's current situation. At the back of her mind, she wondered if she had let things go too far. She had not intended for him to lose his job, but the Whiskerlies had been delighted to discover that Tony worked as the car park attendant at the golf club where Fat Taff's sting had taken place. It meant that they could try for a double whammy and hit him at the same time. They had hoped he would get a ticking off for spending too much time flirting with Charley, but his temper had intervened and he had ended up being sacked. Izza was fully aware of the theft from his Building Society since her mother had given his account details to the internet fraudster she had been baiting. During the course of their relationship, Tony had been careless enough to give Izza his access details. He must have forgotten since, after their break-up, he'd never bothered to change them but, even then, her mother hadn't finished with her abusive ex-boyfriend.

It had not been difficult to plant drugs in his flat since Izza still had her own key. She had to admit that, when her mother proposed the idea, she had been stunned to find that Charley knew just who to contact to get the stuff. It cost Jax a pretty penny, but she considered it money well spent. Tiff gladly followed through by tipping one of her colleagues the wink. A visit had been paid and enough drugs found to convince the lead officer that Tony could be a dealer. It was only then that mother and daughter finally agreed enough was enough.

III

She was brought back to the present by a touch on her shoulder. Callum was back with their drinks. They began to discuss happier things; future things and then, all too soon, her boyfriend checked his watch. He smiled at her as he stood up, lifting her bag onto his shoulder effortlessly. Izza grinned. She could watch him do that forever! It was time to go. They walked together towards the queue. That was as far as he was allowed to go. He took her into his arms, kissed her, whispered that he would miss her and walked away quickly, but not before she saw the moisture in his eyes. Soppy sod!

Out of the corner of her eye, she saw Tiffany and Charley walking towards her, talking animatedly. She grinned at her friends, who nodded despairingly in the direction of the far wall of the crowded room to where an enamoured couple were kissing as if their lives depended on it. Izza's eyes flicked towards them. The enmeshed eight-limbed creature began to unfold itself and reshape into two distinct human forms. She smiled at the smaller of the two, the female, caught her eye and signalled the time. The woman glanced at the screen in front of her, smoothing her hair as she did so. The man beside her moved in for another fervent embrace.

Who'd have believed it? A few short months ago, Izza would have been horrified; disgraced even at the sight of her own mother snogging in public, but now she simply felt delighted for her, glad that she had found someone who loved her. Her mother's affair with Peter had begun several months ago over the internet. After a wealth of e.traffic, they had finally screwed up the courage to meet. Neither of them had looked back. The encounter had soon turned to romance and, from there, had quickly flourished into a sizzling affair, fulfilling yet surprising both of them.

Who knew what her mother's future held? Who could say what her own future held, wondered Izza, watching Jax? Whatever, they were both happier than they had been in ages. Even better, they had a fortnight's holiday in front of them. Fourteen days of togetherness, giggles, over indulgence and insobriety. Not to mention travel, culture, sun and uniforms.

Well, they would, she mused, if only her mother could tear herself away from Peter, or Intellygent, as he had been known on DesperDates, and get her flaming arse into the departure lounge.

SLY

I

When he thought back about it afterwards, it seemed to Sly that he spent the first two weeks after Ali's death on automatic pilot. He could barely remember the funeral other than that the church had been filled with both people and flowers. He knew he'd stood up and read something, but couldn't remember what; he knew he'd stood for a long time shaking hands outside the church, but he couldn't remember who with. He must have guided himself and his parents through the whole terrible business, but he couldn't remember how.

What he could remember was the huge feeling of relief when it was over; when the last sandwich had been thrown in the bin, the last left-over drink had been thrown down the sink and the last guest – well – he hadn't exactly thrown anyone out of the door. It was simply that he couldn't have cared less if people stayed or left even though all of them were Ali's friends and in such huge numbers, crowding the tiny house in which his parents lived. He doubted that more than a handful of folk would have turned up if it had been his funeral, but it hadn't been. *More's the pity,* he thought to himself morosely.

Instead, it had to have been Ali's. Generous, thoughtful, loving Ali, who had never harmed anyone in his entire life and had been such a force for good in the world. If there was a God, then Sly felt that He needed shaking all the way down to his sodding heavenly sandals. Of all the people in the world, why did He have to pick on his little monster?

After the funeral, Sly's memory seemed to desert him altogether; everything had dropped into a black hole. He knew he had been given indefinite leave from the hospital. He knew that he had spent hours of that leave lying on his bed staring at nothing. When he could be bothered to get up, he remembered sitting in the lounge staring out of the window, but he had no clue what he'd been looking at. He had no clue what he had eaten and he couldn't remember whether or not he had showered or got dressed. It simply ceased to matter.

It was only when there was a knock on the door that he rallied slightly. He chose to ignore the knock at the time and only opened the door when a neighbour shouted through the letterbox that there was a large crate causing a blockage in the shared passageway and could he please deal with it. Reluctantly, he crept down the hallway and cautiously opened the front door to find the damned thing on his doorstep. A note on the top simply read, "No wish to disturb". Half intrigued, despite himself, he dragged the crate inside and left it undisturbed in the hall for a few days more. When Sly finally found some energy and decided to open it, he found, to his dismay, that it was full of Ali's stuff so he quickly sealed it back down again. Feeling like all kinds of coward, and wanting only to feel nothing, he fled to his bedroom and barricaded himself in for the rest of the day. He just wasn't ready. He didn't believe he would ever be ready.

His parents dropped round several times to try to chivvy him up or to bring him some shopping or a cooked meal in the hope of convincing him to eat. He found he could barely look at either of them, let alone talk to them and so, eventually, they left him in peace, trying instead to get through to him on the phone. He responded by turning off his mobile. In the end, having run out of patience and fearing for her only son's welfare, his mother turned up unexpectedly and hammered on the door until he was forced to open it. Unlike the normally serene person he was used to, this time, she stormed through the door, yelling at him. He couldn't remember much about the tirade, but he did remember the bit, after she had calmed down, when she icily informed him that he wasn't the only one who was grieving; that she had in fact lost one of her two boys and so had his dad. That one piece of information at least permeated through the mush of his brain and hit home. After she had gone, he stared for a while at the back of the front door. All he could think was that he still wasn't ready and he knew he was never going to be ready so, in a strange way, he was in fact as ready as he was ever going to be so he might as well get on with it.

With living. With the business of living. If only he could find the energy.

For three more days, he stared at the box on the floor, now dragged into the lounge where it sat sulking, accusing him silently of neglect. Every time he went to open it, he found himself exhausted and had to walk away, choosing to retreat to the other end of the flat behind his bedroom door.

And then Charley turned up.

II

It was unusual for Charley to worry overly about anyone. She believed every adult had the right to make their own way and their own choices through life. It had nothing to do with the fact that Sly had not shown up in class for quite a while and she missed the money. It was normal for people to drift in and out of the gym; something she saw all the time. It had nothing to do with the fact that she fancied the man either. She was astute enough to know when she was being given the knock back even when it was liberally laced with roguish charm. She knew Sly wasn't interested in her in that way and shrugged it off. It didn't happen often. She would cope. It was just that there was an indefinable something about the guy that pricked at her conscious like a nettle sting and nibbled away at her infallible instincts until she felt she had no choice but to go and find out for herself why Sly had dropped out of her life.

When Sly opened the door to her, she was shocked. He looked as though he hadn't slept for days, nor eaten for that matter. He was pale with dark circles under his eyes and quite a growth of what might eventually prove to be an awesome beard. He had aged and seemed way to thin for his baggy, grubby sweats. Worst of all, he quite clearly needed a shower. Morning breath – nightmare!

If Charley was shocked, Sly was more so. He thought it was his mother on the rampage again. The last person he had expected to see on his doorstep was Charley or any of the rest of the gang. He couldn't imagine why they would be interested in him and he had no idea of the impact his sudden disappearance had had on the little group of friends. He knew a lot about what was happening in their worlds and about their secret stings, but he had always been able to make friends with the girls that crossed his path and they regularly offloaded their hopes and dreams onto him, swearing him to secrecy in the process. He had supported them in some of their operations. It had been great fun and he felt glad to have been able to help. Even so, he felt this unwelcome intrusion into his private life was way over the top.

"Aren't you going to let me in then?" Charley asked after they had both stood there for a while staring at each other in disbelief.

"Uh! Oh! Oh, yes, yes of course," replied Sly, standing to one side to let her in, adding, "It's a bit messy."

It actually wasn't too bad. The large, square lounge with its big picture window overlooking the canal was reasonably tidy except for the rather messy duvet scrunched up in one corner of the sofa and the sealed storage container in the middle of the room. The kitchen was the worst, but only because there were several plated-up dinners on the counter that looked like they had seen better days, together with an endless amount of stale cups of something or other. Charley was not invited to inspect the rest of the flat.

"We've missed you," admitted Charley, turning back towards him as she entered the lounge.

"Yeah, not been up to it recently," came the terse reply.

Charley placed her bag carefully on the wooden floor and perched on the very edge of the black leather sofa and peered up at her friend.

"What's up?" she asked shortly.

"Nothing. Look, I'm okay. It's just that, well, I've been working a bit hard lately," he told her.

"Rubbish," countered Charley scornfully. "Sorry to be blunt, but look at the state of you. Something's happened."

There was a pause while the pair stared at each other.

"Right," said Charley firmly. "I'm going into your kitchen now to make us both a cup of coffee. You can sit there and think about telling me the truth. I won't accept anything less," and she stalked out, leaving Sly staring after her, feeling awed at her directness and a tiny bit afraid.

It took Charley a little more time to persuade Sly to open up and tell her about his brother's recent death. She proved to have a very sympathetic ear and, by the time he had finished, she knew more about him than anyone outside his family, but she didn't know everything. Sly still held his closest secret back.

"So, that's his stuff," she said when his story came to its end, and nodded towards the box in the centre of the room.

"Yep," replied Sly briefly.

"Do you want to open it alone or do you fancy some company?" Charley asked, looking at him. "Whatever you want."

"Dunno, I keep looking at it. I'm not sure. Can you do it?" replied Sly, a lump beginning to form in his throat at the thought of what might be to come.

With Sly sitting in the far corner of the sofa, with his arms crossed over his belly as if to protect himself, Charley knelt in front of the box and, almost reverently, unsealed and removed its lid. There was a short pause and then the memories, so long trapped in their wooden cage, released themselves and gently began to pervade the room.

On the very top of the pile of bits and pieces, lay the little green comfort blanket Ali had had as a child, still dog-eared and frayed from previous use. "Okay, I can deal with that," thought Sly as Charley handed it to him and he found his heart was still beating. He even managed to stroke its scruffy pile and the world amazingly kept turning.

There were a few photograph albums, which Charley took out and laid on the parquet floor. She knew instinctively that they might be a step too far for the very vulnerable Sly. Underneath the albums, they found Benson, the stuffed Dalmatian, which had always been Ali's favourite childhood toy. As a toddler, he had refused to put him down. Sly smiled wanly as he took the little dog from Charley's proffered hand. He gave it a little squeeze as tears welled into his eyes. He held them in check.

"Seen a few places, haven't you boy?" he whispered gruffly as he placed Benson on the arm of the sofa. "His favourite," he explained. "Never went anywhere without him." Charley merely nodded. Into the box, she dipped again, pulling out several items wrapped in newspaper, which turned out to be bits and bobs of Ali's homemade pottery.

"Prolific little chap," said Charley, as she unwrapped each one and carefully placed each item on the floor.

"Loved his pottery," remarked Sly proudly. "I have loads more in the cupboards."

There were a couple of swimming certificates, together with a framed picture of a beaming Ali receiving a medal from some far off Sports Day. Sly remembered the photo, which had held pride of place on the cabinet in Ali's room at the Hostel. In a little black box, they found the little tin medal itself. Sly fingered its cold, metal edges, clearly recalling the day he had cheered his brother home as he won his first sack race.

Filling up a large section of the crate were several long storage tubes. "Shall we see what's in here?" asked Charley, picking up one of them.

"Probably his chalk drawings," replied Sly. "How he loved playing with chalk." Again Sly found he could smile at the recollection.

To Sly's great astonishment, he found that the tube contained several of his own original, hand drawn designs, worked on at the dining room table or on the lounge floor under his parents' feet throughout his childhood. Clipped neatly around the edges were scraps of fabric, bits of ribbon or shiny buttons, indicating exactly how Sly imagined each design should look as a finished outfit. At the bottom of each one was his own careful signature and the date.

Charley sat back on her heels and examined each drawing carefully and drew in her breath.

"My God, Sly," she gasped, having spread out the contents of the first tube across the floor. "These are amazing."

Sly was stunned. He hadn't seen his designs for years and this batch pre-dated Ali's birth. His mother must have begun collecting them and then, somehow, his brother must have taken over. He thought they must have been thrown away, but instead they had been carefully collated and stored away safely. A lump began to form at the bottom of his throat as he found himself moving from the sofa to kneel on the floor beside Charley. Tentatively, he stretched out a finger and gently stroked a tiny piece of lace clipped to the corner of the nearest drawing. For a few seconds, he remained completely still, save for the trembling finger held against the scratchy fabric, and then he crumpled over, drew both his hands over his face and began to sob in huge, heaving waves of noise, which threatened to swallow him up. Charley waited. She made no attempt to touch or comfort the man. Instead, she sat quietly on the floor beside him, her hands resting lightly on her knees and watched as he cried it out. Finally, when the sobs began to recede and his breathing slowly returned to normal, she leaned over and gently put an arm around his shoulders, drawing him into her, letting him nestle into her side and draw comfort from her presence.

When Sly finally stirred and drew apart from her, she reached into the box and drew out another of the tubes and then another. Together, they opened them all and examined the contents of each. Charley began to question him about the different images, gently encouraging him to talk about his passion.

Slowly, Sly began to open up to her, eventually beginning to enjoy himself as he told her about his love of design and fabric. He went on to tell Charley about his mother and her work as a seamstress and how, for as long as he could remember, he had sat beside her, playing with little remnants of material and making patterns out of the different buttons. He explained how he had first begun to design for the little doll she had bought him and discussed with her his ideas for each of the designs. He could not get over the wonder of his past, come together again and spread out before him; his artwork from way back when.

As he thought of his little brother secretly squirrelling away his work, his voice quavered and he began to shake. Briskly, Charley turned his attention away from his memories by instructing him to put on the kettle. As he left the room, she carefully began to pack away the drawings into the empty tubes. Charley was staggered by the quality of the artwork and the designs. She felt that what she really needed was a stiff drink, but she reasoned that alcohol, on empty stomachs, would do neither of them any good.

"Come on, spit spot," she called to Sly from her place on the floor. "I am dying of dehydration here."

"Coming right up," he replied cheerfully.

"Get those cups washed while you are at it," she ordered. "I want that kitchen cleaned up by the time I'm finished here."

"Bitch," replied Sly mildly and with more than a trace of his former self in his tone.

"Better believe it, Designer Boy," she retorted smartly, continuing to pack up the box. When Charley walked into the kitchen to collect her coffee, she found Sly washing up. She grabbed a tea towel and lent a hand. Together, they made short work of the untidy kitchen.

"How long since you had a proper meal?" she asked.

"Dunno," came the reply.

"Hungry?" she ventured as they finally took their coffee into the lounge. Sly shook his head. He bent down to pick up a photo album, perched on the top of the unopened box and placed it on his knee. Charley gently retrieved it and returned it to its place.

"Tomorrow," she said. "Enough already for today." Sly looked at her gratefully. "I don't know about you, but I could murder a pizza," she continued and, without waiting for a reply, took out her iPhone and made the call, ordering her favourite vegetarian without asking his opinion. With supper en route, Charley manoeuvred Sly in the general direction of the shower.

"And don't come out until you are presentable either," she called after his retreating back. When he returned some time later, freshly shaved and smelling better than he had in weeks, Charley had laid the table and had taken the liberty of opening one of the bottles of wine from the rack in the corner of the kitchen. She had drawn the curtains and switched on the uplighters. The pizza box was lying on the centre of the table.

"Dinner is served," she told the astonished Sly and, with a flourish, directed him to a seat at his own table. Throughout the simple meal, Charley peppered Sly with questions about his brother, encouraging him to talk and filling in the gaps whenever he fell silent. She left him better than she had found him, promising to return the following afternoon for to go through the photo albums with him. She made him swear he would not touch them until then.

He would hardly have dared.

Over the next couple of weeks, Charley spent quite a lot of her spare time with Sly, coaxing him through the painfully sharp twists and turns of Memory Lane. He nearly lost it when they opened the second album and stared down at a small black and white photo of him pushing his brother up the street in a smart pedal car. Ali, hands on the steering wheel, was grinning broadly at the camera whilst Sly looked hot, bothered and grumpy. He wondered how many hours he had spent behind that car. He could not remember who had taken the picture; in fact, he had been unaware of its existence.

There were dozens of photos of the pair of them. Several at the seaside, standing side by side in front of amazingly complicated sandcastles, gaily decorated with all kinds of seaside debris, bits of seaweed and tiny black stones; others of them standing in front of various English landmarks, often with their mother by their side. There were a series of snaps of Ali on his own – at school, modelling clay or cooking or blowing out candles from a birthday cake. There was one of him at the Hostel, holding a huge bunch of blue balloons and a lovely one of him smiling mischievously with a pint of ale raised in a toast.

"I took that one," said Sly fondly, recalling the occasion on which he had bought his younger brother his first pint. He turned over the page and examined another raft of photographs in which his brother beamed out at him. Laughing, curious, loving Ali, living his life his way with the people he loved. Tears threatened Sly's eyes at the joy that was his own little monster.

As the days slowly passed, Charley continued to offer her unstinting support to Sly. They had become quite close and yet Charley knew there would be no romance. She wasn't worried since she had recently begun frying other fish. Nevertheless, Sly continued to intrigue her; instinctively, she knew there was something else. She didn't know what that something was, but her gut told her that it centred on his drawings.

In time, Sly came back to class and, as a fully paid up member of the Whiskerly Sisters, he was welcomed back with open arms. A lot had happened during his absence and the girls wasted no time bringing him up to speed. He had to laugh at Tiff's near miss in the car park. He couldn't imagine the smartly dressed blonde squeezed underneath a car with her face pressed into the floor and her heart in her mouth. He laughed loudly when Celia told him what she had put into her boss's coffee, but agreed it served him right. When Fresna butted in with her update, he admitted that he did feel quite sorry for Alex left waiting in the restaurant just as he thought his family life was improving. Fresna almost snarled at the remark and told him that he was a lightweight, but she said it lightly and without rancour.

In reality, the Whiskerlies were relieved to see him back even if he did seem a little drawn, a little thinner and not quite as well groomed. They showered him with tokens of their affection, taking round homemade pies and cakes, bits of shopping and bottles of wine. Several of them offered to do his laundry, but he waved them away laughing and told them he could manage. Charley encouraged him to show them his artwork and he was amazed when they responded with the same awe that she had shown. They couldn't understand why he wasn't a rich and famous couturier with a suite of rooms in the West End, flitting between Europe and America in a haze of fashion shows, but they nodded empathetically when he explained his reasons.

Three months after the funeral, Sly finally felt ready to return to work. The hospital had been more than generous with him. He felt that his life was beginning to return to normal, but not once since Ali's death had Sly felt the need to visit his lock-up.

III

It was Izza, who inadvertently winkled out his deepest secret. She and Callum had bumped into him in the city and, while she elected to carry on browsing around the precinct, Callum begged him to go for a pint. When she finally joined them in the pub, Sly was keen to see what she had bought. At first, she didn't think much about it, but there was something about the hunger behind his eyes when he fastened them on the soft pink boa she had bought to go with the prom dress she had tucked away for a special occasion. He had seemed like a starving man at a cake sale and she felt a little shiver caress her spine as she observed the way he had, almost unconsciously, reached out his hand to stroke the tiny petal pink feathers. At that moment, she realised he had to be gay. As he looked up into her face, Sly read her thoughts and, reacting as though he had been scalded, he snatched back his hand, gathered up his few parcels and made haste to leave. He hadn't realised the time, he explained hurriedly and damn near ran out of the pub.

Izza shared her thoughts with Callum, who merely shrugged. Maybe he was; maybe he wasn't. Callum felt it didn't matter all that much as long as the guy didn't come on to him. Together, they laughed at the doubtful prospect and began to talk of other things. Nevertheless, the feelings lingered so Izza brought it up again later the same week when she found herself alone with her mother. It was a rare event for them both since her mother was spending more and more of her time with Peter and she herself almost always had Callum in tow. Her mother listened to her daughter's theory carefully and took her much more seriously than the dismissive Callum. Jax certainly thought the notion had legs and it certainly ticked a lot of boxes for her around the aloof Sly – the absence of a girlfriend, the impeccable grooming, his reluctance to talk about himself and just how damned comfortable they all felt in his company. He really was just one of the girls. The clincher had to be how outrageously good looking he was. Every woman's lament – how come all the gorgeous ones are gay? Such a bloody waste and the two women laughed at themselves. Jax stored the conversation away; she knew she would be coming back to it.

She repeated it to Fresna and Charley over morning coffee a few days later. Both women agreed that they were not trying to square a circle. Fresna remarked that it felt like they had just completed a decent part of the jigsaw puzzle that was Sly. Charley secretly felt relieved since, although she had accepted the man's lack of interest in her, the rejection still rankled somewhere deep inside her. This would certainly explain everything. She was simply the wrong bloody sex. She wondered out loud how none of them had worked it out since, when you fitted it all together, it was obvious. They finally agreed that sometimes it is impossible to see the wood for the trees and concluded that the direction of his sexual tendencies was unimportant. He was one of the girls and they loved him.

They began to discuss how they were going to get him to 'fess up.

IV

They needn't have worried. As soon as Ceals heard the gossip, she bullied the truth out of the poor guy. She did it nicely, of course, but she would not relent until she got what she wanted. They had all told him their secrets, she had reasoned, so now it was his turn. They wouldn't think any the worse of him whatever he told them and, in any case, what the fuck did it matter which way he swung. On and on she ranted, pinning him to the back of his chair, refusing to let him refuse until he had no choice but to cave in and come out.

He wasn't gay, he told them. At least, he didn't think he was. He certainly didn't fancy girls, but then he didn't fancy blokes either. Instead, he had his own way of dealing with his sexuality, alone, in comfort and with his precious things around him. As the girls listened, sometimes incredulously; sometimes with pity, but always with their mouths shut, he cautiously revealed his secret and when he had finished telling them all about it, he found that he had the confidence to show them all about it. Hardly able to believe what he was doing, having never taken anyone else there since he had signed the lease, he invited the seven fascinated women to his lock-up. Tucked away in a quiet corner of town, it didn't look anything special from the outside, but from the inside, at least to him, it was very special indeed; a place, far away from prying eyes, where he could completely embrace himself and all that he was.

Or she was, depending on your point of view.

He didn't take them there immediately. It took him a few weeks to muster up the courage, during which time the girls came to terms with the enormous curve ball he had tossed at them. As they drove to the venue, the girls found they could hardly contain their excitement. They had no real idea what was coming, but they could hardly wait.

Sly was there ahead of them, leaning casually on the metal skin of the container next to the unlocked door, padlock in hand. He swung back the door with a flourish and allowed his friends to walk in ahead of him.

Nothing in their lives had prepared them for this.

V

It was somewhere between the inside of a celebrity-at-home special and a tart's boudoir. The floor was covered in a pale grey, deep pile carpet, which offset the lilac stud walls, each sporting at least one full length, ornate mirror. Between each mirror, and held in place by clips, were a glorious profusion of fans – delicate feather fans with intricate handles, traditional Spanish fans in bold colours, Chinese hand painted fans in muted shades. Amongst them, or draped over the mirrors were necklaces, bracelets and combs of every sort, shape, colour imaginable. Dominating the room were two deep purple, velvet covered chaise longue, which faced towards each other and between which stood a low, lacquered table set with a silver tea set. Standing opposite each other against two of the walls were what looked to Charley like Victorian chiffoniers; on each of which stood a collection of inlaid jewellery boxes. At the far end of the room was a door on which hung several expensive-looking oriental silk dressing gowns, together with several enormous feather boas. Next to that, stood a large rack of boned, netted cocktail dresses; the kind usually worn in films by can-can dancers and to which Fresna and Jax were immediately drawn. Finishing the room, to great effect, was a large crystal chandelier, which swayed gently from the central point of the ceiling and gave off a soft, lemon light so that the very space around it seemed to shimmer. The girls, normally highly vocal, meandered around the room in almost total silence, trying to take everything in whilst Sly leaned against the closed door, arms folded, almost amused by their reaction.

"Wow," breathed Celia finally.

"May I?" asked Bex, indicating one of the jewellery boxes. Sly nodded and watched as Bex cautiously opened a black veneer lid close to hand and stared down at the startling collection of costume jewellery within. A dazzling array of rings, necklaces and earrings sparkled and twinkled up at her. Catching her breath, she tentatively reached out to try on one of the rings. It was way too big. Meanwhile, Izza had draped herself in a long yellow and black boa and was admiring her reflection in one of the mirrors. Pulling open the bottom cupboard of one of the chiffoniers, Charley found herself face to face with an impressive collection of footwear. She reached inside and drew out a single, red leather thigh boot; its heel long and spiked and inlaid with diamante.

"Jesus Christ, will you look at this?," she said and began stroking the soft material almost reverently.

Other drawers revealed a profusion of silk and satin underwear; the kind most girls only dream of. Basques, corsets, stockings, hold-ups, thongs and French knickers, trimmed with ribbons and lace, spilled out of the drawer Tiff had opened. She found a whole festoon of elbow length satin gloves in the drawer beneath.

"Open Sesame," she declared at last because for each of them it did seem like the most spectacular Aladdin's Cave they had ever seen and quite beyond their wildest speculations in the days leading up to the event when they had sat together and wondered about the secret world of Sly.

What woman could resist such temptations? Their incredulity soon gave way to utter abandon and it wasn't long before they were trying on the net dresses, draping themselves in the costume jewellery and gloves or buttoning each other up in the frothy bustiers. It mattered not that most of the garments were way too big, having been designed for larger frames and different muscles. They were intent on pretending to be models, impressing an imaginary audience on the catwalk or staring solemnly at their images in the huge mirrors like a clutch of children trying on their mother's cast offs.

With an enormous sense of relief, Sly watched them, feeling almost physically lighter for having shared his burden and with no sense at all of the crushing shame he thought he would feel at being outed. Instead, his friends seemed delighted with him and with themselves, calling attention to one another and laughing at their appearance in the outsize dresses. After a while, Sly crossed to the far end of the room, almost ignored in the melee of strewn underwear and scarves, and disappeared through an end door behind which was a tiny kitchen, returning a little later with a tray of fresh coffee and macaroons.

"Time out, ladies," he announced, carefully carrying his load towards the low table in the centre of the room. "Shove over," he ordered Celia, resplendent in a blue can can dress and who had draped herself along one of the chaise longue. Sulkily, she hitched up her knees and batted her eyelashes at him coquettishly from over the top of a large silk Spanish fan, decorated with frills and flounces

"Shove over, your Ladyship if you don't mind," she replied, emphasising the word, ladyship.

Together, the pair squashed up on the sofa with Izza whilst the rest sprawled carelessly on the floor or shared the remaining sofa in a profusion of over-excited ribbons, net, jewellery and femininity.

"How often do you come here?" demanded Charley, mid-nibble.

"I haven't been here for a while; not since – well, not since..." began Sly.

"Before that then? How often did you used to come here?" butted in Izza quickly.

"All the time," replied Sly. "Several times a week. After my shift, after class, when I couldn't sleep, when I... well... you know," and he shrugged, suddenly shy.

"We should've guessed," said Charley. "I noticed you were shaving your legs, but I decided it was because you were a cyclist or something."

"And your eyebrows are always so neat," added Jax.

"What's cyclists got to do with?" asked Celia, trying not to spill any of the delicious coffee over her gorgeous, gorgeous dress.

Sly felt deeply grateful and mightily impressed with the easy way in which his friends seemed to have accepted his nether world. It felt as if they had always known about it; as if they had been dropping in for years and not at all as if they had never experienced anything quite like it before.

"Can we borrow stuff if we need to?" asked Izza, pleased with the idea.

"Izabelle!" her mother reprimanded her.

"Just asking," came the mumbled reply. "Sorry."

"It depends on what you want to borrow," said Sly. "Some of this stuff is quite expensive and most of it has never seen the light of day. We'll have to see," he told the embarrassed girl.

"Not seen the light of day?" queried Celia, baffled. "Then it's about bloody time it did. I would die to go out in some of this stuff."

"Me too," added Tiff.

With coffee over, the girls began a further investigation of the room, delving deeper into the cupboards. They concluded that Sly had expensive taste in cosmetics and perfume, but a rotten collection of handbags. Towards the end, Fresna pulled an oddly lumpy, flesh coloured garment from deep inside a drawer. It resembled a body, but it was made of some kind of spandex. It was padded at the bra and over the hips.

"What on earth is this ugly thing?" she asked Sly.

"Oh," he shrugged at his embarrassment. "That's my girl suit."

"You're what?" shrieked Celia.

"In for a penny, in for a pound," replied Sly mysteriously and then said, "Watch and learn." Without preamble, he stripped down to his shorts. The girls sighed collectively at the sight of his naked back. What a bloody waste! He stretched out to take the girl suit from Fresna's hand and wiggled himself into it. Reaching out towards the clothes rail, he selected one of the dresses at random and threw it over his head. One step ahead, Bex tossed him a pair of shoes and he climbed into them. As a finale, he reached into another drawer, pulled out a long, blonde wig and clumsily put it on. He then turned to face them.

"Ta da," he announced. "What do you think?" he added shyly. With baited breath, he waited for their reaction. "It gives me my girl shape," he finished and bizarrely, it did actually give him something of the natural curve of a woman, although he still very much looked like a man. The girls just stared. No one spoke.

Sly began to wish he had not been so bold. He coughed to cover up his shame and then said,

"Of course, you'd need to see me in my make up too. You know, full costume and bling to get the full effect," he said, feeling somehow suddenly completely naked under the unwavering stare of his friends.

It was Charley who rescued him by announcing, "Bloody hell, you brush up better than the rest of us put together," which was not at all true, but it did break the spell. The girls found it difficult to believe that Sly rarely ventured out as his alter ego and it was then that the deal was struck. They agreed on a night on the tiles with their fully made up, fully kitted out newest Sister and, if anyone dared to look askance at the overly tall, rather ungainly blonde with the Adam's apple, then Celia declared loudly that she would thump that individual very hard somewhere very painful with the enormous leather handbag she intended to borrow from Sly's collection especially for the occasion.

It turned out to be the first of many enjoyable nights out with Imelda, the name chosen by the girls for Sly's alter ego because of his fabulous collection of shoes.

After its maiden voyage, Sly's ship headed for deeper waters.

Part IV

Cat out of the Bag

The Boeing 757 landed safely slightly ahead of schedule amid glorious sunshine and azure blue skies, eager to discharge a group of particularly high spirited passengers. As they headed towards passport control and the interminable wait for luggage, Charley hung on to the slightly weaving figure of Tiffany in an effort to prevent her going astray and crashing into anyone.

"If you barf, you are on your own," she informed her friend with mock disgust. "In these jimmy's, I don't think so."

"Lighten up for God's sake, you anal cow. We're supposed to be on holiday. Chillax, I've only had a couple," came the indignant and somewhat slurred reply.

"Don't you anal cow me! We'd only just got off the sodding ground when you started. I don't think we'd crossed the channel before you were slaughtered," Charley replied theatrically and wagged a finger in the direction of her friend.

"Shut up grumbling the pair of you," ordered a very confident Jax, "or we'll send you both packing where you came from and bloody good riddance."

Suitable chagrined, the pair continued to stumble their way forward, following the herd in front of them.

Behind them, Jax had already switched on her mobile and was endeavouring to send a text to Peter, informing him of her safe landing and her undying devotion. By the time they arrived at the baggage carousel, the ping pong of emails was beginning to irritate Tiff.

"Put the man down for Christ's sake," she told Jax, getting right into her face. "Give him a chance to miss you, you numpty."

Izza repressed a grin. Now whose life was being dominated by the Nokia?

Charley's designer luggage was easily identifiable and obligingly early, but they had to wait an irritating twenty minutes for Tiffany's to arrive. Whilst the four of them felt inconvenienced by the hold up, they were equally glad that Celia had not travelled with them. Patience had never been her strong suit and the air would have been purple by the time the tardy bags had turned up, on top of which, they would have had to waste time while she complained, in no uncertain terms, to the nearest customer service operator that was unfortunate enough to catch her eye.

Mercifully, she wasn't with them and neither was Fresna so thanking God and all that's holy for their infinite wisdom, and not a small amount of pre-planning, Charley hurried her friends through the barricades into the arrivals lounge, finally exiting the terminal building itself and walking into the dazzling sun, which almost blotted out the scenery around them, such was its searing strength.

Reacting strongly to the glare, they blinked in the unfamiliar surroundings for a few seconds until Charley had the presence of mind to put on her sunnies, which meant that she was the first to spot the slight figure, waving energetically at them from the other side of the car park. They had not seen each other for months; not since their friend had absconded the country with her lover in a campervan, intent on a trip around the world. The girls had been furious with her at the time for not letting them into her plans but, following an individual postcard to each of them explaining her reasons, they had long since forgiven her.

How different she looked! Gone were the tidy, respectable hairstyles and neat black combs; gone were the prim, drab outfits. In their place stood a Bohemian princess with glowing russet, shoulder length curls, which suited her more than the former grey and offset a tan, which was the envy of them all. She ran towards them unselfconsciously wearing a brightly coloured tie dye vest over a long cotton skirt. There were bracelets around both wrists and a silver anklet chain so that she tinkled musically as she came towards them. The girls were amused. She had finally turned herself into the gypsy she had always imagined she would be and none of them would have been surprised had she tried to sell them pegs or tell their fortunes. She simply glowed with health and had even put on a little weight, giving her previously gaunt features a pleasing roundness. Delighted to be reunited with their absent friend, the girls embraced her warmly one by one and then in an enormous group hug, which blocked the road to the annoyance of the hooting taxi drivers. Ignoring the commotion, they took their time greeting Bex properly and then, picking up their luggage, they followed noisily in her wake, peppering her with questions as she led them across the car park towards the ever patient, David, who was waiting in the camper van to ferry them across to the next stage of their journey.

II

From the airport and out onto the motorway, David expertly drove his precious cargo through the heavy traffic, confident in his ability to drive on what would always be, to him, the wrong side of the road. Relaxing in the back, the little group of travellers chattered with Bex as if it were yesterday, as if no water had passed under each of their individual bridges. Modern technology meant that they were able to keep up with her news despite the distance between them. As the noisy flow of conversation bounced around the back of the van, time began to fly by and it was no time at all before Bex glanced out of the window and checked her watch.

"Here we are," she announced and nodded at the view from out of the van's tiny windows down towards the vast island harbour, which fairly bustled with activity. Vehicles were coming and going, people in uniform strode purposefully around, strings of people queued in the sunshine, talking animatedly to one another or simply enjoying the view.

Bringing his vehicle to a gentle stop, David deposited his partner and her friends onto the pavement in front of the embarkation booth. Handing each woman her luggage, he wrapped them up in a bear hug and wished them well. Finally taking Bex into his arms, he kissed her a shameless farewell and promised to be waiting for them all on their return. A swift, final kiss for Bex and he was gone. The girls collected themselves together and hurried to join the end of a growing throng of people in front of them. With so much to see and comment on, it was hardly surprising that the paperwork seemed to take no time at all. A few forms and several questions later, they were climbing the steps of a tiny passageway and back out into the brilliant sunshine. Drinking it all in had made them dizzy with excitement and yet they paused in awe as they appreciated the sight of the tall, sleek, shimmering white liner that towered above them, making them feel like Lilliputians in the face of the mighty Gulliver.

At quay level, in the very centre of the boat, was a canopied awning, signalling the entrance to their floating monolith. Standing to one side of the entrance, stood a blond, muscular Adonis in full dress uniform. Tiffany, suddenly very sober, raised her eyebrows at Charley and a message was passed. In perfect synchronicity, the bold as brass pair sashayed flirtatiously towards the smiling stranger. Bex, watching them, simply shrugged and smiled resignedly at Jax.

Hand in hand, the two women followed in the wake of their purring, predatory compatriots when suddenly they were stopped by the sound of familiar voices. From the top of the boat, two tiny figures hollered down towards them, waving their arms frantically in an effort to be noticed.

"Put him down. You don't know where he's been," squealed Celia. "Besides, he's a flaming pouffter. Ask Fres. She's been stalking him all sodding week."

"S'right," yelled Fresna. "Not so much as a sniff. Gay as Christmas if you ask me."

"Get a bloody wriggle on," roared Celia. "The cocktails are getting sodding warm."

"Besides which, we'll be on our second bottle if you don't bloody well hurry up," added Fresna, smiling and blowing kisses to her friends way below on the quayside.

"Tell you what; we're coming down to meet you. Wrench you from the arms of the pouf in the uniform," screamed Celia, heedless as usual of any political sensitivity that might have been offended. The two women disappeared from view. Several minutes later, the group of women met in a flurry of hugs and kisses on the embarkation deck of the holiday cruiser, blocking the hallway for a considerable amount of time and causing the purser to purse his lips in disapproval and encourage them to hurry along.

Some hope! With the exception of Bex, whom no one had seen in ages, the others hadn't seen each other in over a week. The purser and his entourage could sod off. They would embrace each other for as long as they wanted to and, if he didn't back off, they would hug him too. If that didn't work, then Celia would probably stick his clipboard where the sun didn't shine!

Eventually, when they were good and ready, the new arrivals made their way to their cabins to stow their bags, squeaking with delight at the miniature perfection of the bedrooms, cleverly designed to make the most of the tiny space given to each of the guests. Freshening up hastily, they each made their way to the top deck where Fresna and Celia waited impatiently for them; drinks at the ready, together with a few plates of nibbles taken from one of the innumerable eateries that littered the ship. Not a good place for a diet, a cruise liner!

Since the vessel would not be sailing until midnight, the girls settled themselves down to a little light sunbathing and a huge amount of light hearted banter. Several months had passed since their little paybacks had come to an end and the winter had seemed flat and endless after all the fun they had been having. As a reward for their hard won revenge, they had decided to treat themselves to a Mediterranean cruise. Away from home, relaxing in the sun, they decided it would be a fun to reminisce on their twelve months of mischief. An embarkation party had been planned by the cruise ship, under a twinkling canopy of fairy lights, when the booze would flow and plenty of hair let down.

Over the course of the next few days, the plan was to relax and enjoy. They had been downtrodden, they had been used and they had been hurt, but they had turned the tables on their tormentors and, incredibly, they had won!

Bex had rediscovered her youth and, with it, her freedom and peace. She was living with her soul mate and, as a consequence, she found she had no desire to rebel against anything. Her children were only a phone call away and, modern travel being what it was, distance was nothing. She was still their beloved mother and she regularly visited her children. Finally, she was living the life she had only previously dreamed of. Once again, she was wild and free.

Fresna had lain to rest the ghost of her youth and had been blessed with a new family. Since family had always been a source of great joy to Fresna, she felt she had enriched her life with her bravery and intuition. Fresna, always the teeniest bit smug, was glorious in contentment.

Celia had decided that she wasn't actually suited to administration and had decided instead, in her usual all guns blazing approach, to start her own business, caring for pets. Celia loved animals so her new venture suited her perfectly. She was her own boss and she was able to use her well-honed organisational skills to the full. Instead of the barking of other people's orders, her days were filled with the barks of other people's dogs. She walked them, groomed them and fed them while their owners relaxed on holiday, content in the knowledge that Celia would care for their little treasures as if they were her own. Despite less money, and less opportunity for travel, she had finally found fulfilment. As an added bonus, her furry charges were happy to listen to her strident voice and strong opinions, without comment, wagging their tails and cocking their ears in total agreement with all that she found to rattle on about. They adored her for her playful nature and ability to live in a house full of rubber bones, half-chewed slippers and lost balls.

Tiffany had decided to give up on men entirely for a while so that she could concentrate on loving herself. She had begun to realise that it was her own desperation, her own neediness that, despite her loveliness, had ultimately repelled the moths that came to her flame. She had been her own worst enemy, ruthlessly sabotaging herself at every turn. She now wanted to become her own best friend. As a consequence, whilst she was happy to 'flirt and skirt', she put herself and her interests above everything and everyone. Strangely, she still never lacked male attention.

Charley had regained control of her world and, with it, another rich lover. Perhaps hers was the tiniest of changes, the least significant of victories, but for the perfectionist within, it was vital to her nature that her life float carefree on a tranquil sea. Whilst Charley relished each and every one of the adventures she had experienced alongside her friends, deep inside, she felt that the whole thing had been just a tiny bit demeaning. With her life back under control, she felt she could once again rise above the flotsam and jetsam of the ordinary and regain her place at the helm of her life, confident of the breeze in her favour and her mastery of the waves beneath.

Despite her initial misgivings, Jax was delighted to have met a man she both liked and respected, and on an internet dating site! She reflected back to her earlier misconceptions about the e-meat market and how green she had been only a short while ago. She had climbed a very steep learning curve to learn a lot about life and love and men, but most of all she had learned about herself. She had not always enjoyed every lesson, but she was grateful for the benefits they had brought to her.

Izza had reclaimed her self-esteem, taken back her life and, with it, her joy and her youth. She had found the love of a good man; a man, who adored and respected her. Furthermore, right now, that man was back home, waiting for her return and planning a future for them both. She had learned about the nature of choice and she no longer chose the path of the victim. Her career was moving forward and she had her whole life ahead of her. From where she was standing, things looked pretty damn good. The butterfly was out of its chrysalis and enjoying its time in the sun.

III

Having danced their feet off until dawn, the girls would have loved nothing better than to have slept in late, but

Health and Safety dictated otherwise and so the four new arrivals were given no choice but to don unglamorous safety vests and make their way to their pre-appointed muster stations to listen to an over-long lecture on emergency procedures. Tiff found that she was barely able to stand, let alone pay attention and leaned on an increasingly irritable Charley until it was over. Whilst Tiff went straight back to bed, the remaining trio decided on strong coffee and croissants. They were joined by Celia and Fresna, who suggested a tour of the boat. They pointed out the well-equipped gym, the quiet, comfortable library, the sleek beauty parlour with its tiny spa, the glitzy casino on the seventh floor where punters were already gathered, eager to post their coins into the greedy mouths of the banks of slot machines. The three girls followed meekly in the wake of their two experienced friends who, after a week, seemed to have seen it all and done most of it. Up and down the passageways, they trooped, discovering the overwhelming variety of cafes, restaurants and bars. There seemed to be an overwhelming number of waiters, cleaners, porters, sailors and bar staff eager to help folk enjoy whatever time they had set aside to be with them on the cruise ship.

Jax, with her passion for amateur dramatics, was over the moon when she found herself in the beautifully furnished theatre. Despite the closed mustard velvet curtains with their scarlet fringing, she couldn't help but take a peek at the stage behind. She was impressed by the quality of the large posters either side of the stage, promising an amazing display of talent and virtuosity over the coming week.

"You wait. You haven't seen anything yet," Fresna told her with a knowing look at Celia.

"Damn right, Fres. Are you lot in for a surprise," her friend replied, smiling wickedly.

"What?" asked Charley, not wanting to be left out in the cold. Someone knew something she didn't and that didn't suit her style at all. She stared pointedly at both her friends, waiting for them to tell everything, but Celia turned her back on her whilst Fresna merely told her to wait and see.

"Come on," cried Celia suddenly. "Who's for a dip in the pool? Last one in fetches the drinks," she yelled as she ran out of the room and up the stairs in the direction of the top deck and its fabulous seawater pool. The bait was swallowed and the others scrambled in her wake, Charley tried to prevent Fresna from leaving, intent on getting some answers, but her friend shrugged her off smiling. Reluctantly, she followed the others, seething that she had been stonewalled. Whatever it was, she would winkle it out of them, but for now she would go for a swim. She had all the time in the world.

"Wouldn't Sly have loved this?" breathed Izza, an hour or so later. Leaning over the rail, sipping on her Sundowner, she gazed out across the wide expanse of sapphire blue sea.

"Wouldn't he just?" replied Jax, following her gaze. "Isn't it heaven?"

"Where did he disappear to this time, do you think?" Izza asked her mother. "I miss him, don't you?"

"And our outings," Celia joined the conversation.

"Happy days," said Fresna, draining her glass.

She was right. They had been happy days right up to the last time when the Sisters, with the ever immaculately clad Imelda, took themselves off to the Rocky Horror Show, taking the place and the audience by storm with their outrageous costumes. Shortly after, Sly disappeared once more into a puff of smoke but, this time, no matter how hard they searched, neither sight nor sound could be found of their gorgeous friend. It was as if the earth had swallowed him whole and was holding him captive in some dark corner of its depths. They had tried his flat several times, but the neighbours told them they hadn't seen much of him in the first place so they never knew if he was in or out. Izza and Callum wasted a few hours hanging out in the vicinity of the lock-up and Charley had visited the hostel where his brother had lived in search of news. She and Fresna had then driven round to his parents' house where his mother told them the startling news that Sly had suddenly handed in his notice at the hospital, begging to leave at once and before a suitable replacement could be found. A few days later his parents received a picture postcard, letting them know he was in Europe and that he was alright. Reluctantly, the girls had been forced to let the matter rest at that, but that had not prevented them from endlessly speculating about his whereabouts and, more importantly, why the hell he had not had the decency to let them know he was dropping off the flaming planet!

For their first on board dinner, the girls made sure they dressed to impress. To a woman, they were immaculately made up, well groomed and wearing their finest gowns. As the little group of women swanned gracefully into the dining room towards their allocated table, the atmosphere in the restaurant suddenly came to life as heads turned in acknowledgement of the beautiful procession. There was something of the goddess in each of them and they knew it and they were making damned sure everyone else did too!

The only drinks allowed at their table that evening were sparkling water and the best champagne. After the excitement of the previous day, everyone ate heartily. Charley and Fresna embarked on a flirting competition, vying for the attention of their two very attractive waiters, but it was done in good spirits. They agreed between them that they would definitely have one each before the week was out. If neither woman had a particular favourite, they would toss for it.

The rest of the conversation gravitated around their fabulous adventures and they regaled each other with memories of a year well spent.

A hilarious wine fuelled photo shoot, Sly dressed as a flame haired hippie, a furious drive through the countryside with Hillory Hocker's tramp snoring in the passenger seat, an unforgettable evening in the tub with Il Divo and a certain property magnate, several spiteful recipes, a soupcon of criminal damage and a downtrodden girl reborn.

It had been a wild time, a heady adventure, an oasis from the storm. It was something to be savoured between them for years to come. The women grinned at each other, relishing the secret they shared and a bond of sisterhood that could never be broken.

It was Celia who broke the mood by standing, somewhat shakily, to her feet and expertly popping the cork of yet another bottle of champagne. She gently poured its golden bubbles into her friend's proffered glasses.

"A toast," she announced. "To us."

As the girls rose from their seats to take up the call, one of the women stayed firmly in her place and with her hand over her glass.

"No," said Charley fiercely. "One of us is missing. We do this together or not at all."

"You're right," replied Fresna, sitting down again. "We can't do this without Sly."

"Agreed," demurred Tiffany, "but we don't know where the hell he's disappeared to this time and if he'll ever be back, so I say on with the toast," and she raised her glass.

"Charley's right," said Bex firmly and sat back down. "Not without Sly."

"He is one of the girls," said Izza.

"Isn't he just?" replied Celia and began to laugh, causing the rest of the girls to giggle alongside her.

One by one, the girls sat back down until Tiff was the only one left standing. She scowled at her friends.

"Suit your flaming selves, but if he doesn't turn up soon, you need to know that I will be proposing a toast to myself and all who sail in me!" With a smirk at her own joke, she dropped back into her seat.

"Oh I am sure he'll be back when he's good and ready. Maybe sooner than you think," replied Fresna mysteriously and there was something in her voice that made Charley look at her sharply.

"Out with it," she said.

"Not on your life," replied her friend.

IV

A couple of days later, Celia proposed a trip to the on board theatre. It was Gala Night she told them and the show was outstanding. Fresna was fairly buzzing with excitement at the idea even though she had seen it all before. Charley's antennae were on red alert; her instincts telling her something was going on. How she hated not knowing what it was. Celia rushed the group through dinner, insisting that they bag their seats early. She felt certain it would be crowded and she intended to be right at the front along with her friends.

"Where's the fire?" muttered Jax, reluctant to be dragged away from dessert.

"You'll be sorry for the rest of your life if you don't move your arse right now and drag it all the way to the theatre," replied Fresna, removing her dish and grabbing the arm of her friend.

"Your choice though," added Celia from over her shoulder. Swallowing a sigh, Jax followed her friends across the corridor and into the almost empty theatre with its plush velvet curtains and comfortable, padded seats. Despite the silence, an atmosphere of hushed anticipation hung in the air. Flinging her bag onto one of the seats, Celia staked her claim. The others followed suit. Fresna was sent to the bar to get in the first round.

"Way too early," muttered Tiff to Jax. "Our backsides will be stiff before the damn show even starts."

"Your backside will be kicked if you don't flaming well shut up bitching," replied Celia with a glare.

There was nothing to do but sit and wait. They spent their time sipping cocktails and watching the room slowly fill up. Celia had been right. It wasn't long before there was nowhere to sit. Fresna ramped up the excitement by telling everyone about the fabulous show they had seen the week before. Celia nodded enthusiastically.

Suddenly, the lights were dimmed and an expectant hush filled the air. There was a momentary pause followed by a burst of piped music while the audience settled into their seats. Since cruise ships are renowned for their first class entertainment, everyone was certain of a good evening ahead. The star of the show, the beautiful, willowy Giselle, was eagerly awaited. As hostess for the evening, she would be opening the show. There was a swish as the curtains were pulled back to reveal an empty stage. A spotlight appeared and into walked a tall, fabulously clad blonde. As she walked to centre stage, the diamante in her lavender, thigh-slashed gown shimmered and sparkled under the lights. She wore wickedly high grey suede shoes with matching arm length gloves. Diamante sparkled from her ears and her neck. She was stunning.

Something in Charley stirred. She sat up, leaned forward and looked more closely at the woman directly in front of her on stage. The woman looked straight back and then, astonishingly, gave Charley a saucy wink.

It all came together in a blinding flash. She gasped and her mouth fell open. She turned to her friends and found them staring too. It couldn't be! No fucking way! It couldn't be, but it was.

Sly.

As the girls turned in their seats to stare at one another, she found Fresna grinning at her broadly. She knew! This was what she had been keeping up her flaming sleeve. Celia, on her immediate left, nudged her elbow and whispered, "Bet you weren't expecting this?"

"Bitches!" Charley whispered back. While the women on the front row caught their breath and settled down, Giselle towered above them, standing serenely on the stage, waiting for the little furore to die down. When everything was quiet and she had the room's full attention, she approached the mike.

"Ladies and Gentlemen, welcome," she began in a low, throaty voice. "Tonight is such a special night for me since I have some very special friends in the audience. Such dear, dear friends of mine and I hope you will allow me to introduce them to you." The audience stirred and Giselle waited.

"Well?" she asked eventually, putting one hand on her hip and yawning sexily. "Talk about making a girl wait." She waggled her hips at the audience, who roared their approval.

"Thank you," she demurred coquettishly.

Turning her attention to her friends on the front seats, and with great confidence, she made them stand and turn to face the audience. Even Bex, who tended to be shy, was given no choice.

"Darlings," she trilled to her audience. "I give you my friends, my companions, my ladies in waiting. I give you the Whiskerly Sisters," and, regardless of the fact that no one in the audience had a clue what she was talking about, they nevertheless applauded.

The rest of the evening passed in a blur. The girls were mesmerised by the transformation in front of them. Giselle, still obviously a man, had all the charm and elegance of a woman. Furthermore, she was funny and witty; she knew how to work an audience and get them to do exactly what she pleased. Charley couldn't help wondering where the hell Sly had found his theatrical skills. When she left the stage to other actors, she was missed and the whole room welcomed her back. The show was excellent, but its centrepiece was magnificent – the incomparable, the superb, Giselle.

All too soon the show came to its finale and the stars took their bows. The curtains closed, the lights were turned up and the room was filled with the sounds of subdued piped music and muted conversation.

"Fucking pinch me," said Izza to no one in particular.

"Exactly," replied her mother. "I wasn't expecting that."

"See, I told you he would turn up when he was ready," said Celia smiling widely.

"I'm speechless," said Tiffany. "Amazing!"

"That'd be a first," retorted Celia, full of herself now and bursting with pride and excitement. It had been a tough few days for the normally outspoken women, but she had not let the cat out of the bag. Fresna had threatened her several times with hell and damnation if she had dared.

"You cows," said Charley, quietly. "Why the hell didn't you give us a heads up?"

"Yes," agreed Bex. "You could've let us know."

"And spoil the surprise. Not on your flaming nelly," replied Fresna. "You should've seen your faces."

"Cow," repeated Charley without malice.

"You should've been here this time last week when we saw him. You could've knocked me down with a feather and I wouldn't have got up for a week," Celia told them.

"Eyes front ladies, here she comes," announced Jax and, as one, the girls turned back towards the stage to find Sly, shrouded from head to foot in a magnificent fur trimmed, silk dressing gown, walked towards them.

"Can I get anyone a drink?" he asked as the girls crowded round him. "You look as if you need one," he added laughing and bending his head to receive their hugs and kisses.

"Where the hell have you been?" demanded Charley.

"And how the hell did you end up here?" asked Jax.

The girls crowded round him eagerly, admiring his gown, peppering him with questions. They wanted to know everything. How come he had disappeared again? Why hadn't he been in touch? And how, in the name of all things holy, had he ended up here, top of the bill on the floating theatre of a flaming cruise ship?

Never in a million years!

"Out with it," insisted Izza as soon as they had all sat down. A waiter had been dispatched to fetch more cocktails and the girls were frantic to hear his story.

"Don't leaving anything out," Charley warned, looking Sly straight in the eye.

V

Following on from his night time rites of passage into the outside world in the company of the Whiskerlies and, finding his confidence growing, Sly, or Imelda as he had begun to call himself, began experimenting with solo trips. He began slowly, taking short excursions to neighbouring towns, testing the water as he went. Finding nothing much to worry about, he explored further afield, trying a day's shopping followed by a trip to the theatre or the cinema. As he began to take on more and more of the personality of Imelda, to his surprise, he found that he began to crave what he had previously shunned; the company of others in similar boats. Eventually, he found his way to a club on the outskirts of Milton Keynes where a weekly Drag Night was held. Suddenly feeling like a very small fish in an enormous pond, he retreated into his aloof self, took himself off to a corner of the bar and stood drinking alone until a kindly tranny by the name of Cynthia took him under her wing and introduced him to her crowd. They greeted him warmly, but like no one out of the ordinary, which made Sly, who had always believed he was different, feel completely normal for the first time into his life. He began to delve deeper and deeper into this much misunderstood, cross-over, cross-dressing world, revelling in the knowledge that he was not alone.

It was on a trip to the West End for the Alternative Lifestyle Ball that he met up with Fjordors, a slender, flaxen haired Latvian in his late thirties. Fjordors, or Fee as his friends called him, was not a cross dresser, he wasn't a tranny. He was gay and he was quite simply the most stunning individual that Sly had ever met and so it was that, at the age of forty seven, Sly, at last, fell head over heels in love.

They began a passionate affair, crossing the distance between them as often as work would allow. Having lived alone for most of his life, and never really needing anyone, Sly found himself consumed. Together, they explored the depths of Sly's increasingly demanding sexuality, lying together naked, tangled and breathless amidst the satin of Fee's king-size bed.

Fee told him little of his life in a tiny, tucked away village in Northern Europe, merely remarking that he had found it difficult to express his artistic nature in such a corner. As soon as he could manage it, he fled to London and apprenticed himself to a self-employed seamstress, working alongside her in the glamorous world of high fashion. In the evenings, he attended college where he practiced his English and, when he felt he was ready, signed up to a beauty course and discovered the world of cosmetics. Using his new found skill, he developed his career by working freelance as a make-up artist and costumier. His talent for both was such that he was never short of work and often sought after for special period dramas or fantasy films where his creativity was given free reign. After several years of hard work and long hours, living in shabby, rented accommodation in seedier parts of London, he had finally saved up enough money to put down a deposit on a little flat in the suburbs.

He told Sly that he hadn't really wanted to go to the Ball that night, but had been dragged there by the crowd he was currently working alongside. They had flatly refused to let him stay home when there was a party going on and had organised a taxi to fetch him. He shuddered inwardly at what might have happened if his friends had not been so insistent.

The affair could have gone on as it had, without much change, if Fee had not been woken up in the night by persistent knocking at his door. Sleepily, he had climbed out of bed and picked up the intercom. He was shocked to hear the voice of his brother at the other end, ordering him to open the door and let him in. Their father was very sick and he was needed at home in the family business. Slamming the phone down and refusing to answer the door, Fee stumbled back to bed and lay awake shaking for the rest of the night, remembering his childhood. His brother had not gone away and followed him to work the next morning, shouting angrily at him in their native tongue about family loyalty and Fee's disgusting self-centredness. All this was accompanied by dramatic gestures and thumps. When Fee refused to respond, his brother tried to grab his arm and pull him along. Fee wriggled out his grasp, ran across the crowded road and leapt into a passing taxi, disappearing quickly into the bustle of the London traffic. Later that evening, he turned up unexpectedly on Sly's doorstep with a heart full of love and a tale full of hate.

They had to get away he told the astonished Sly; his family would never let him go. They would track him down relentlessly and force him back to his homeland. They had found him once, they would do it again. In vain did Sly try to calm down his lover, even warily suggesting that a short trip home to visit his ailing father might be a good idea. Fee was frantic, yelling at Sly that he could never understand what it had been like. Sly was wasting his time if he thought for one second that he would ever go back. He would rather die! On and on he stormed, pacing up and down, gesticulating wildly to emphasise his distress and working himself up into a frenzy.

It took Sly the rest of the night to calm his lover down, after which, they spent the next three days talking and planning. An agreement was reached. They could not bear to be apart, but Fee felt he had no choice but to leave the country. He could never be free in England again.

Fee never returned to London. Sly resigned from his post as Head of Nursing, convincing his bosses of an emergency so strong that he was forced not to work out his notice, thus leaving his colleagues bewildered and very much in the lurch. Together, they crossed to the continent and worked a series of low paid jobs. It was Fee who came up with the idea of applying to a cruise line and they were both successful. Fee worked behind stage supporting the cast and happily resumed his life, content to be among the paints and powders, wigs and costumes he so loved. For Sly, the transition proved much more difficult. Whilst he enjoyed his role as a nurse in the tiny Medical Centre, caring for the wide variety of minor injuries and illnesses that came his way – sunstroke, nausea, the occasional bout of diarrhoea, strain and stress injuries from overdoing it at the gym or falling off a donkey – he suffered terribly from seasickness. For eight long weeks he endured until he finally found his sea legs and began to enjoy his new life on the ocean wave.

It was quite by accident that he took on the role of Giselle. The ship's multi-national, fast turnover crew were very used to the unusual and found nothing strange in the passionate love affair between two of their shipmates. Shipboard romances were common, usually short-lived and so no one turned a hair. Given their very different working schedules, Sly found himself increasingly behind stage, assisting Fee with the costumes, a button here, a stitch there and, in between times, he renewed his interest in costume design.

During a sudden outbreak of Delhi Belly amongst the crew, the theatre company found itself several stars down and with an audience expecting to be entertained. When the Director decided that the show must go on, the programme was re-jigged and a hasty rehearsal scheduled with whoever was available. It was all hands on deck that afternoon and Sly launched himself into the frantic venture with gay abandon. To everyone's amazement, he blossomed. The Director watched him with amusement, then interest and then wonder as Sly's long hidden alter ego took to the stage like a natural. Her timing was perfect, she found she could hold a tune, she found she had an innate sense of comic timing.

And a star was born!

In reality, it wasn't that easy. There were other stars to consider, other flamboyant artistes with signed contracts and quick tempers and, in any case, Sly still had a job, yet somehow the Theatre Director waived away all the obstacles to insist that Sly join the Company as soon as the paperwork could be signed. In the meantime, he took him under his wing and taught him as much about stagecraft as he could.

A compromise was reached with the shipping line. Sly would work out his time as a nurse but, two evenings a week, he would join the rest of the cast on stage in the shape of the sultry, sexy, fabulous Giselle. He delighted his audiences so much that his fame spread like wild fire; even members of the crew crept into the back of the theatre to watch him on their nights off.

The girls listened avidly to their friend's story and somewhere in the middle, somewhere between the Drag Nights and Fee's brother, a slender, blonde figure eased his way through the curtains, down the front of the stage to take Sly's hand and listen quietly as his lover continued his amazing tale.

VI

The Whiskerlies fell in love with Fee almost as quickly as Sly had done. For one thing, he returned Sly's love with such wholeheartedness that the girls could only imagine, and secretly envy, the depth of their relationship. Furthermore, he was a good looking man with neat features and deep blue eyes. His long bright hair fell past his shoulders and he had a slender, almost girlish, frame. As for his voice, they found that they couldn't get enough of his harsh, slightly hissing accent with its long drawn out vowels and barked consonants. They sat fascinated watching his quick, nimble fingers stitch and mend the fabulous costumes the actors wore on stage or easily turn blotchy, florid skins into creamy, lush complexions with deft, soft strokes of his brushes. He turned the agony of being a woman, with its endless round of eyebrow plucking, hair straightening and leg waxing, almost into a pleasure such was his skill.

As the cruise flowed seamlessly on through the calm seas of the Mediterranean, the sun a perfect yellow orb lighting the azure blue sky, the girls spent as much time with Sly and Fee as they could. They approached the Captain to ask permission for them to sit with them at dinner but, although he listened to their case sympathetically, rules were rules and the crew ate their meals out of sight and out of mind of the paying passengers. To no avail did Fresna storm, Tiffany sulk, Celia swear, Izza shrug and Jax reason. The Captain was adamant.

Until Charley changed his mind.

How she did it remained a secret, but Izza later told Callum that she must have promised him the mother of all blow jobs to pull off that particular stunt. Whether or not she delivered was never disclosed but, on their last day, the Captain himself came down to the departure lobby to kiss her hand romantically and whisper in her ear. To the rest of the girls watching, there seemed to be a glint of shared pleasure in his eye, but that could just have been the sunlight.

The Whiskerlies were ecstatic that Charley had pulled off the seeming impossible. Under Fee's critical eye, the girls outshone themselves on the night of the planned dinner so that, once again, it was a head turning event when the girls finally entered the dining room and approached their table where Sly and Fee stood, resplendent in tie and tails. As the buzz in the large, oak-panelled room subsided, the girls settled into their seats. A fabulous dinner was served and the conversation ebbed and flowed easily amongst the group, centring on their holiday and the fleeting wonders of the Italian landmarks they had visited along the way – the famous, drunken campanile, torre di Pisa with its 294 steps, Michelangelo's Florence with its profusion of sculptures and the famous Bobili Gardens, the choking bite of sulphur on the steady climb to the top of Mount Etna, the crowded dash through the ancient streets of Pompeii with its open pizza ovens and remarkable Luperina.

With dinner over and coffee served, the dining room began to empty as guests took themselves off in different directions, eager for entertainment. Lulled by the good food and ample amounts of alcohol, the Whiskerlies grew quiet. Celia again broke the spell, pushing her chair back noisily to stand up, champagne flute in hand.

"A toast," she said simply, looking around the table and into the faces of each of her friends. Solemn now, each girl pushed back her chair and stood up to join Celia. The waiters watched from the edges of the room, slightly curious, but having seen almost everything before as the little band reached out to hold hands, heads bowed for a few seconds. Bex, breaking the contact, thrust one flat hand out towards the centre of the table and placed the other over her heart. The others followed in turn. Finally Bex removed the hand covering her heart and reached for her glass. She raised it and made the toast.

"To us," she said quietly. "To the Whiskerly Sisters."

"And a fucking fabulous adventure," added Celia, raising her own glass.

"Yeah, don't mess with us," said Izza, smiling at her mother.

"Or you'll be sorry," added Sly with a grin.

The girls each drained the contents of their glasses. Tiffany turned to hug Fresna, which began a long round of group hugs, a few tears, a lot of laughter and fondly remembered adventures. Finally, the girls seemed satisfied and sat down. They were replete, almost drunk. They had taken on their persecutors and had kicked them to the kerb.

What else was there to do?

It was Sly who pointed them towards their next destination. He did it unintentionally towards the end of the cruise late one night in the emptiness of the theatre after his show when the little band of friends had gathered for a nightcap. Motivated by the ease of his disclosure to these compassionate women, he simply encouraged Fee to tell his story. Once begun, the girls would not let him leave until he had told them everything; once begun, Fee found himself quite unable to stop. The room grew quiet as the Whiskerlies drank in his every word, horrified by the brutality of his early years and impressed by his remarkable courage.

VII

Fee could never actually remember a time when he wasn't harassed or belittled by his brothers. The fact that he was built like his mother, slight and slender, did not help. Why he could not have been blessed with his father's giant, bear-like frame as his brothers had been, he could not say, but for some reason, it irritated the other men in the household, who believed him to be cross-born.

The fact that he did not enjoy the physical pursuits of their outdoor lifestyle irked them even more. He trudged along half-heartedly when the men went fishing or hunting. To make things worse, he loathed the taste of beer and vodka. He much preferred curling up in front of the fire with whatever books he could find to interest him in the tiny, village library, or better still, online when Wi-Fi finally came to town. He also loved to paint and would often escape, for long hours, into the countryside to sketch the flora and fauna. He never brought his work home, choosing to destroy his art rather than risk making a difficult situation worse. He instinctively knew that his artistic nature would infuriate his brothers so kept it secret.

His father, proud and vast, made no secret of the fact that he regularly roared his indignation to the bleak, grey skies that his woman had given birth to a girl in a boy's body. He refused to hide the fact that, in his grandfather's day, this changeling, this offence to nature, would have been put out for the wolves before his mother could put him to her breast.

Fee had refused to join the thriving family business which, under the guise of a removals company, successfully smuggled illegal goods across the border, accompanied by a heavy blend of deceit and ill will. For this, he was often beaten and told he must not disgrace his family. His father held an important place in the village so honour was at stake. Grudgingly, Fee was forced to agree. Even so, he declined to carry arms and instead, at the age of thirteen, had become their watcher, blending effortlessly among the trees or standing, almost invisible, behind some rotting outhouse on the look-out for nosy neighbours or other unwelcome pests that might disturb the hurried exchanges between vehicles. He took on whatever paperwork came his way, carefully counting the crisp piles of currency they threw on the table, checking and re-checking in case they had somehow been defrauded, in which case a visit would be paid and blood spilled. When Fee was certain that everything was in order, he would hand the books and the money over to his father, who would dole it out to his family; sometimes sparingly, sometimes generously depending on his prevailing mood.

Fee hated it. He hated them. He hated the deceit, the lies and the greed. He hated the loud laughter and the heavy thumps on the back in front of the roaring log fire as they toasted their success along with their toes. Most of all, he hated his parents. His mother, tiny, cowed and withered, who had never fought for him or defended him, who let him be put down and beaten when it took his brothers' fancy. His father, loud, moody and offensive, who treated him like dirt and would not allow his youngest son to be himself. He knew, from an early age, that he had to escape. He knew he would need to be very careful; he knew he would have to watch and wait for his opportunity to present itself.

It came unexpectedly just short of his nineteenth birthday when the driver of the van, in which the current stock of drugs was due to be transferred, became ill with a violent migraine and had to be hastily shoved into the back seat of his brother's land rover to recover. They had travelled light, expecting no trouble on that dark and gloomy September evening. Madars, the middle brother, chewed his lip and stroked the trigger of his Ceska Phantom while he thought the matter through.

Finally, he came to a decision. There was no choice. He whistled softly towards the trees to call his brother to him. He told Fee to help him unload the van. When that was done, Madars instructed him to drive the van back to the city and return it to the Vilkssons, who would be waiting for their cut. Fee must pay them and then find somewhere to hole up for the night. His brother would organise for him to be picked up and returned home in the morning. Madars would phone him with the details. He gathered his brother into a big hug and wished him a gruff good luck. He told him to keep his wits about him and to keep himself as invisible as the 'spoks', which were rumoured to haunt the woods. Above all things, Fee must not get himself noticed.

Releasing him, Madars gave his brother a rough shake and told him fiercely not to let the family down. Turning his heel, he climbed into his vehicle and drove off into the night without a backward glance. Fee watched the tail-lights of the land rover disappear into the gloom, feeling sick at the huge responsibility that had just been placed onto his shoulders. Climbing into the large van, Fee took a deep breath before switching the engine on. He shakily steered it along the wet track and finally onto the main road, turning in the direction of the city. Concentrating hard on the task in hand, cursing the dubious honour of his family, Fee eventually pulled up outside an isolated shed on the fringes of the city and stopped the car. Two men immediately stepped out of the shadows and approached the driver's window. Nervously, he opened the door and explained the situation to the doubting pair. A call was made and his story finally verified. Handing over the keys to one of the two dark strangers, he beat a hasty retreat. He kept walking until he eventually found himself in front of the Liepaja docks, staring at the ships anchored in the harbour.

Alone on the quayside, Fee realised that his time had come at last. He had safely delivered his cargo back to its point of origin and no one expected him to be anywhere until morning. Still unsure, he thought a while longer and then, at last, he came to his decision. Moving swiftly, and keeping in the shadows, he edged noiselessly towards the nearest vessel and stared up at it, contemplating the huge iron chains that held it moored against the dock. Buttoning his jacket, and discarding his mobile phone into the murky waters of the harbour, he flung himself at the nearest chain, catching it easily and allowing himself to swing to its rhythm as it gently bucked against his weight. As lithe as a cat, he hitched his way up its metal length, finally easing himself over the edge of the boat. He scanned the deck in front of him, relieved to find it deserted. Creeping along the railing, he eventually came to the relative safety of a lifeboat and crawled under its canopy. Lying as still as he could, he waited until, finally, he heard footsteps ringing the stairs to the deck, the muted exchange of conversation and the noise of routine. The big engines suddenly throbbed into life and, not much later, the ship began to slowly move away from the quayside and into deeper waters, bringing its stowaway a long twenty four hours later to Kapeliskar where he waited until after midnight to leave the ship the way he had entered it. He then stowed aboard a freight ferry bound for Rotterdam, finally arriving in Felixstowe on a container ship. He was dirty, hungry and thirsty, but, so far, he had survived.

He wandered around the North Suffolk town slowly, managing to clean himself up a little in the public toilets. He found a large supermarket from where he stole some bread and cheese, which he took to a park bench and ate ravenously. He slept rough for the next few days, eventually finding shelter in a broken down shed on a neglected allotment. He turned this into his temporary headquarters and, over time, managed to make it into a passable dwelling. Fortunately, the autumn weather remained unseasonably warm and dry. He was able to find occasional work in the local cafes and bars, washing up, fetching or carrying – whatever it took to earn a little cash with which to keep himself going.

After several weeks, and with winter beginning to bite, he found a way to bed down for the night in the warmth of the kitchen of one of the cafes in which he worked, always leaving well before dawn so that he was never discovered. He managed to survive like this throughout the dull, wet British winter until, one day, he decided he needed to move on. He never thought about the family he had left behind; he took things one day at a time and concentrated solely on his immediate future.

One day, in the middle of the following spring, he packed his meagre belongings and hitched a lift to London where he worked for several years as a machinist to an Indian clothes manufacturer in Ilford. It was through this kindly man that he finally met the seamstress with the brains to recognise the creative genius behind the humility of the young Eastern European and who offered him more lucrative employment, together with the promise of a real career. Once she had persuaded him to join her, she went on to support Fee's UK Citizenship and to help him to improve his English. In what little spare time he had left, he enrolled at College and began to study the world of cosmetics. In the arty world in which he moved, it was not difficulty to befriend others of his sexual persuasion and he soon found himself at the heart of a group of men and boys with a passion for fashion and the theatre. The wheels of life had begun to turn in Fee's favour and he began to find himself content with his world.

And then, on a reluctant night out to the Alternative Lifestyle Ball, he met Sly.

By the time, Fee had finished his story, a pale lemon smudge was beginning to lighten the horizon and the ship that never slept had grown quiet. The theatre in which the little group sat enthralled, had been deserted long ago by its staff, save for one night owl slumped in a corner dozing.

Sly explained that Fee had felt so strongly that he could never go back to the UK nor return to his native Latvia, that the pair had decided to simply disappear. Here in the Mediterranean, far out to sea, they felt safe. Fee could not imagine that his family would ever think to search for him here and, if they did, he could easily hide in the womb of the vast ship with its bustling, below decks village where everything was noticed and nothing ever mentioned. In the underground world of his ruthless family, his lifestyle would be despised and crushed. Nothing would ever convince Fee to return home where he felt his only choice was to submit or bleed.

The girls were silent in the face of this appalling story, churning the tale over in their individual minds as they digested the details. They looked at one another and a silent message passed between them. Sly read it and began to protest – it was too dangerous he told them, out of their league, monstrously stupid, but the dye was cast. Fee begged them to leave well alone, berating himself for his loose mouth and his lover for his powers of persuasion. He left the room in a storm of hysterical tears, swiftly followed by an anxious Sly.

Alone in the theatre, the Whiskerlies sat for a while in silence, staring glumly out of the porthole windows at the slowly rising sun and the beginning of what looked like a perfect day to explore the beautiful Emerald Coast of Sardinia, their final cruise destination.

"It has to be done," said Celia finally.

"Don't be ridiculous," countered Jax, "you heard Fee. We wouldn't be dealing with noisy neighbours or dodgy exes this time. These people sound like serious thugs to me."

"So what?" argued Charley, furious at the cruelty that had been inflicted on her friend's lover.

"I'm game," said Izza, earning herself an exasperated look from her mother.

"Me too," agreed Bex, "although not a word to David."

"What do you think we should do?" asked Tiffany practically.

"Suggestions?" asked Bex, taking the lead as usual, but the group was tired and, in the end, it was agreed that the best plan would be to head off in search of breakfast and hot showers before meeting later to take the coach to the historic town of Tempio Pausania.

The glorious scenery was lost on the girls, who found it difficult to rally much enthusiasm for anything but discussing Fee's incredible story and the options facing them because of it. When the travellers finally got back to the ship, Charley wasted no time finding a disconsolate

Sly and told him that she thought he was right. The group had discussed it over and over, but had finally decided to leave well alone. It was too big a step for them to take on a band of Latvian thugs. Sly's relief was palpable. Bending to give his friend a swift kiss, he ran to find Fee and tell him the news. Watching his departing back, Charley sighed to herself and, not for the first time, wished her best male friend was not gay.

Back in her cabin and preparing for their final dinner aboard, Charley informed her cabin mate that Sly had swallowed the lie. Using all her innate skill, she had convinced him that the Whiskerlies had agreed to rest in peace in the payback stakes, but the truth was that they were hooked. They had no clue how they would pull off a European sting. They knew it would be dangerous and far harder than anything they had done before, but they felt they owed it to themselves and to Fee to at least try to settle the scores.

The two conspirators looked at each other and smiled. Charley was looking forward to a new adventure and a serious dollop of fun. Bex was a little more prudent as she sketched out the first few steps in her head. No one could predict the future and it may well transpire that they were about to bite off far more than they could chew. Still, a little internet research and some crafty sleuthing couldn't possibly do any harm.

Could it?

A note about the author

BB Occleshaw is a pen name for the author, who lives in Suffolk and runs an Holistic Therapy business as well as continuing her writing. She writes what she terms "pantomimes for the 21st Century" for Amateur Dramatic groups. If you would like to know more about her writing, she can be contacted at occleshaws19@gmail.com

The Whiskerly Sisters is her first novel and the first book of a trilogy on the theme of revenge.